# NEVER ENOUGH

A Novel

By

Alexandra Y. Caluen

# NEVER ENOUGH

*The playlist:*

A Million Dreams – P!nk

Never My Love – The Association

Every Time We Say Goodbye – Annie Lennox

Come Rain or Come Shine – Ray Charles

Never Enough – Loren Allred

I'll Fight Hell to Hold You - Kiss

Bridge Over Troubled Water – Simon & Garfunkel

Always Remember Us This Way – Lady Gaga

Never Gonna Give You Up – Rick Astley

*NEVER ENOUGH*

Chapter 1

January 2019

"Mother *fucker*."

Victor Garcia turned his head toward the voice in the bathroom. "Everything okay, baby?" His husband didn't answer, only stepped into the doorway and pointed at his crotch. That word, 'husband.' It was a year old now but Victor wasn't anywhere near over it. Wasn't anywhere near bored with that body, either. He gave the whole naked assembly a good long look. "Been there, done that."

Andy Martin turned his pointing hand up, changing fingers, pretending to be irritated when Victor laughed. "Another gray hair. Shouldn't you have noticed that?"

"I had other things to think about." Victor propped himself up on an elbow and took another look. "You know every hair on your body could be gray and I'd still think you're the hottest. The sexiest. Jesus, look at you. Every fifty-one-year-old in the land should look like you."

"Almost fifty-two."

"Like I care." Victor put a hand on his cock, throwing the sheet off so his husband could see. Stroked himself, eyes locked with Andy's. "Does this look like I care?"

Andy shifted a little, posing. Watched Victor play with his dick. "For someone who's been there and done that, you're looking kind of eager." Victor was giving Andy the hot-eyed stare that had sent them straight to bed before they even really knew each other, a little over six years ago now. Six years since Andy stopped looking at anyone else. "Is this what you want? Let me give you a better look." Now

1

he turned his back to the door frame so Victor could see his body in profile. He didn't really even need to touch himself, only needed to watch his husband. God he loved that word, in any language. "Quieres esto, mi esposo?"

"Quiero todo. Jesus, Andy. Get over here." That profile, almost a silhouette, was killing him.

"Oh, I don't know. I like watching you." They could both get off like this. Would, most likely. It wouldn't take long at all. Andy let his gaze travel down Victor's body, those tawny legs, those wicked tattoos, hips starting to move a little. It was almost as if Victor could feel his gaze. When Andy's attention lingered on that hand and what it was doing, Victor lost his rhythm for a second. Andy caught his breath. "Oh yeah, baby." His voice went into the low silky tone that never failed with Victor. "Let me see it. I could watch that all day. Yeah, like that, I can feel it from here." He stroked himself, keeping time with Victor. His gaze traveled up, over the tense abs, past the no-longer-raw scar of the bullet wound on the upper chest, to the perfect mouth.

Victor had his teeth in his lower lip. He really wanted Andy to touch him, he'd make the guy pay for this later, but he was losing it. Breath fast and shallow, he kept going out of focus, even though Andy's gaze was locked with his now. "Next time I get my hands on you," he managed. Couldn't have moved off the bed right now for anything.

"Nothing stopping you." Andy's voice was breathless too. "Come on, baby. Come for me. Fuck, you're so fucking gorgeous, fuck that hand and *yes*."

Victor's head was back on the pillow, eyes closed, hand still, chest spattered with come. "Get in my mouth," he said. "Right now."

2

Andy levered himself off the door frame and took the few steps over to the bed. Set one knee beside Victor's head and fell forward onto his hands because he wasn't even balanced before that perfect mouth had him. Then he was on his elbows, eyes closed, vaguely aware that his other foot was still on the floor. Victor's arm was locked around a thigh and he was making hungry sounds that Andy would remember. "Jesus fucking *Christ*. Your mouth, baby. God almighty fuck!" Whether he collapsed or Victor pulled him over didn't really matter. His legs were across Victor's body and he was gasping into a pillow. They were both quiet for a minute. Then Andy said, "Did you get that hair for me?" and Victor laughed.

They had coffee in the sunroom, because they didn't have anywhere to be that day. There were still a few days when they had to report back to the set of 'L.A. Vice.' But the number of taping days was in the single digits now and very soon, or finally, they'd be done for good. Victor was wrapping up an almost ten-year run on the cop show, Andy nearly four. They might have worked through the end of this season if not for the shooting last September. That had been the final straw, a definitive 'enough' after years of threats and hostility because of their characters. Because of who they were and what they represented, as gay men in love. Andy knew that Victor still believed what they'd done had social value. Value enough to outweigh those years of stress. He did himself, though he personally wasn't sure the social value outweighed almost losing Victor to that bullet.

"What did you think of the schedule?" he said after a while. Almost the minute they wrapped their parts on 'Vice,' he and Victor were going out on an international tour to promote a movie. That was the only reason they had their phones out here.

"It's not that bad." Victor sipped coffee, enjoying the sun. It wasn't cold outside. The climate in the sunroom was ideal for nudity. "They spaced things out pretty well."

"The best thing about it is that's all we have to do. Get to the thing, do the thing, go wherever and sleep. Or find a milonga and dance till dawn and *then* go wherever and sleep."

"It'll be fun. Oh, fuck me." Victor's phone was buzzing; he had zero desire to answer it.

Andy picked up the phone. It was an unidentified number. "Victor Garcia's phone, Andy Martin speaking. This had better be important." He listened for a few seconds, held the phone away and gave it an 'are you kidding me' look, then put it back to his ear. His tone was still pleasant when he said, "How did you get this number? Well lose it, and go fuck yourself." He disconnected, blocked the number, and handed the phone back to Victor, who was laughing. "Somebody wants to sell you a sports car. You didn't want a Ferrari, did you?"

"That's a solid no." Victor glanced over, reluctant to ask, but knowing he needed to. "What's the latest on your pops?" Andy's father had recently had his second mini-stroke.

Andy sighed. "Mom says he's stubborn as a pig, which surprises exactly no one. The doctor said you have to stop smoking, he said I'm almost eighty why stop now, Mom said if you don't stop I'm going to divorce you."

Victor bit back a laugh. "But she won't."

"No, of course she won't, and he knows it. He did promise to go with her every morning for her beach walk when he's out of rehab." Andy rested his head on the chair's high back and gazed at Victor. "I'd better go over there as soon as the tour is over."

"What about those English guys you want to photograph?"

Andy really did want to photograph the guys in question, friends of a friend. Probably wouldn't have time later. "Okay, as soon as that's over."

Victor waited a few seconds to see if the health conversation was going to continue. "So you had your physical."

"Yep."

"What did your doctor say?"

"Said we want to put you on statins."

"Why the fuck would they do that?"

"It's the protocol." Andy made an impatient gesture. "I'm over fifty."

"You're fitter than I am." Victor was ten years younger, and he had to work to keep up with Andy. "That's ridiculous. They don't even have any evidence that shit does any good."

"Which is exactly what I said, and also gave him an earful about the side effects. Basically a big hellz to the no. You know last fall the guy at the hospital wanted to keep me on a heart monitor. They were like, it's your age, sir, shock can do funny things. Same thing Stan said, though I think he was talking about me passing out, not me stroking out."

"Don't even say that."

Andy turned his head, smiling. "I love you, catnip. My heart is fine as long as you're beside me."

"I love you too." A few more quiet minutes. Victor rubbed their dog's fluffy blonde belly with his toes. She did that catlike thing of stretching out all her paws, with a sound something between a sigh and a groan. Once they left the sunroom and actually started their day, Andy wouldn't stop being busy. He

5

couldn't help it. Victor wanted to make this peaceful moment last a little longer. "So you know I'm voicing a villain for that animated thing. Some songs to record. That'll get me out of your hair for a few weeks before 'Countdown 3' starts filming."

"I don't want you out of my hair. That's in town, though, right?"

"Right."

"Good. I might try to do something with dancing this spring." Andy was still watching Victor's face, so he caught the happy surprise there. He'd told his best girlfriend Dana, and she no doubt had told her wife Rory, but for whatever reason he'd kept the lid on it at home. He wasn't sure why. Victor would be a hundred percent behind whatever he decided to do. Andy couldn't help smiling again. "I guess I can't stay away from it after all."

"After the tango Olympics last year?" The movie they'd made together was wall-to-wall dancing. "After the way you slaughtered that thing at the premiere? Yeah, not surprised. I'm glad, though. Are you going to throw yourself on Dmitri and say find me a partner?" The thought was not entirely pleasant. Victor loved dancing with Andy. But the dancing he could do wasn't up to what he knew Andy could do.

"I'd dance with Dmitri," Andy said. Dmitri was a good friend; he also owned a dance studio, and had been quietly pestering Andy for years to get his ass into it as something other than the official photographer for the Underground Cabaret. Andy had thought that after the pressure cooker of 'Vice,' and the even-more-intense experience of the movie, Victor would be glad to work on something solo for a while. But his perfect Valentino face wasn't entirely supporting that conclusion. "I'd consider doing something with the Cabaret. I'm considering all

6

options at the moment. It's going to be so awesome dancing all over the damn place with you for six weeks."

Victor couldn't wait. "Like our honeymoon times three."

"I'm so glad you married me." Andy reached out a hand. Victor was close enough to catch it. "You about ready for breakfast?" Victor nodded, shifting forward in his seat. Andy didn't stand up, though. Instead he said, because he'd just been struck by inspiration, "I had this wild idea."

Victor settled back again. More talk was good. "What's that?"

"It would take a while to put together. A Broadway thing, like a concert, at Chrome." He was thinking out loud. "A little showcase for us, the two of us. Song and dance." Victor was smiling. "You like that?"

"I love that."

Andy leaned across the gap between them. Victor met him halfway for a kiss. Andy still had his hand. "I really love you. 'Vice' was stupid and that movie was tough but I don't want to stop doing things with you. You might need to take a jazz lesson or two. Would you do that?"

"For another show together, one that's all for us? You'd better believe I'll do that." Victor lifted their joined hands to his lips. "Do something for me?"

"Anything."

"Get yourself a new ring for this hand." He knew his tone was a little bit wicked. That ring Andy used to wear, before he joined the TV show, had driven Victor crazy. There was something about the smooth metal against his skin. He could still feel it sometimes. "And something for your wrist." The ring and the leather cuff had somehow made Andy seem slightly dangerous. Or maybe it was all in the way he used that long-fingered, surprisingly strong hand.

Andy pretended not to notice signs of returning arousal. *I could have you back in bed in another minute.* "Not another tattoo?" They had matching wristband tattoos on their left arms, dating back to their first vacation out of town. Andy only had two: the wristband and the delicate artwork at the base of his throat, also matching Victor's. Victor had lost one of his tattoos to the bullet wound. Andy knew he would get a new one sooner or later. He didn't especially want another one himself. "Because that shit hurts."

"You don't need any more of those. I've got you branded now." Andy laughed. Victor said, "Could be leather again. I liked that braided leather."

"I know you did." He was so tempted to go back to the bedroom. Some days it was like this, especially these days when neither of them were called to the set, neither of them had a meeting, they were free. There weren't enough of these days. Decision made, Andy stood up and pulled Victor to his feet. Victor stepped over Molly the dog because Andy was moving back, away from the windows, toward the bathroom door. "Silver or gold?"

"Gold. To go with our wedding rings."

"All right." They were crossing the bathroom now. Andy was walking backward, Victor's eyes telling him where he needed to go to avoid crashing. His legs contacted the bed and Victor stopped right up against him. They stood there for a minute, arms around each other, kissing like they hadn't seen each other for weeks. Then Andy had Victor's head between his hands, and seconds later both hands lightly around his neck. "You want to feel it here, don't you. Put that chain on and let my ring rub against it." Victor hadn't worn that chain for a while. Andy still remembered the first time he'd seen it, signaling 'bite here.'

"Oh God. Yes. The way it scraped." Victor shivered, from that memory and from Andy's voice. They were both fully aroused now, as if they hadn't done anything before coffee, or anything during the night. "Jesus, Andy. It's never enough. I never get enough of you."

"I know. I love it. I love you." Andy kissed him again, stroking his hands through Victor's hair.

"I love you. I wish I'd met you ten years earlier."

"I wish you had too." God, did he wish that. Andy bit gently where that chain should be, hands on Victor's hips now, thumbs stroking in, across and down. Victor had both arms around Andy's neck, one hand wound into the graying dark hair, his head tipped back and eyes closed. Andy's voice, that low silky murmur. "How do you want me now."

"Take me. Take me like you did that first night." Victor still thought about that, still fantasized about it. There were things to regret about that night, but he'd never surrendered like that before. He would never regret that.

"Jesus, Victor." Andy didn't argue. He wanted that too. He kissed Victor hard, then leaned down to open the nightstand drawer. Set the lube on top, pushed Victor toward the wall. "You turn me into an animal."

"I know. I love it." Victor was leaning on his elbows, Andy pressed to his back. Left hand closed around his throat and right hand cupping his balls. Victor closed his eyes, tense with arousal under that fondling, stroking hand. Andy's mouth was against his neck, on the side of his face. "I'll come on this fucking wall." It might have been a warning. Andy took his hand away. Then he was caressing with the lube. Victor's back arched, an invitation. Andy's left hand relaxed, sliding around to skim down his spine. "Jesus, Andy. Do it." Victor widened his stance.

Andy set his teeth lightly on the side of that strong neck as he engaged. He might have growled. Victor gave him some resistance and made a sound, half a laugh and half a moan. Andy's mouth on the back of his neck, teeth and tongue and hot breath. "Mmm, Victor. I love fucking a movie star." Going slow, working with their height difference. The heat, the pressure. Andy had one arm around Victor's ribs now and the other hand flat against the wall.

Another half a laugh, turning into some sort of wordless vocalization because Andy was all the way in. Victor tipped his head back, turning it enough for another tongue-tangling kiss. Then, "Yes. Fuck me. More."

Andy started to move. "Jesus, you're so hot."

Victor was braced now, taking it. "More. Nobody else." Breathless, gasping. "Oh *God*. Nobody ever. Only you."

"Only you. Always you." This was always fast, neither of them could make it last. "God *damn*. Christ you're so, not yet, *fuck*." Andy was gasping again, mouth against Victor's trapezius. "With me?"

"Always. Barely. Hurry." Victor was still braced on the wall. Andy withdrew carefully, turned him, kissed him. Then he was on his knees and Victor was in his mouth. "Jesus!" As hungry as the very first time. Victor couldn't hold it any longer. His back was against the wall and his knees were weak. Andy still had him. "Holy God, that mouth." A stifled laugh.

Andy let him go and sat back on his heels, catching his breath. Looking up at Victor's flushed face and sleepy eyes, thumbs rubbing over the gecko tattoo, and the rattlesnake. He pressed his lips to the list of dates that started just above Victor's knee. Key dates in their love affair, inked upside-down, ascending his thigh. "You are the most beautiful thing in the world."

"You are." They smiled at each other. Victor offered a hand. Andy got to his feet. One more kiss, and then they were stumbling to the shower. Ten minutes later, Victor was about to turn off the water when he felt Andy's arms around him again. "You've got to be kidding." A soundless laugh against his neck. Nothing else happened. Only the embrace, and Andy's face against his, for another quiet minute.

Then Andy let him go and reached past him to the controls. Handed him a towel, flipped the switch for the heat, and said, "I really love you."

"I know you do. I love you too."

Chapter 2

Victor had to find the right moment to talk to his friend Janis. She was in town with her tour manager Niall and his husband, novelist Geoffrey Anand, the guys Andy wanted to photograph. They were all staying out in Glendale with Janis' parents. And they were all busy; Geoffrey had three books under contract, and Janis was developing a new album. But she was the person Victor went to at the very beginning, after that first earth-shattering night with Andy, and she was the person he wanted to talk to now. *Ping me when you have a few minutes to talk?*

Her reply came promptly: *Are you on set?*

*Yeah but I don't have much to do. I'm still on desk duty*

*Uh right.* She suggested a time; Victor checked his schedule and confirmed. A few hours later she called. "What's up, Mr. Garcia?"

"Well, what's up with you? Fill me in." He listened with enjoyment while Janis raved about the music she and her collaborators were preparing. It helped that he knew them: cellist Isabelle Randall, who'd played on the cast recording for 'The Ghost of Carlos Gardel,' and their co-star Tomás Calderón. "You know you're going to have to give us Tomás for a minute. He's coming to Buenos Aires with us on the movie tour."

"Yes, and if I didn't think we were going to be playing there eventually I would be green with envy. He gave me half the tracks we're arranging, you know. I was like, what songs can we turn into tango that aren't tango to begin with, and he was all, well I like to play these. He's a hell of a piano player."

"Glad it's working out."

"So why did you really want to talk."

Victor bit his lip, glad they weren't in the same room so she couldn't see him stifle that laugh. This was one of those friendships where they had so little in common, but somehow understood each other completely. "I'm having a little bit of vertigo over Andy."

Janis made a confused Scooby Doo noise. "Something happen?"

"Nothing bad. We had a really good morning a couple days ago, and I fell down this rabbit hole of how many times I could have lost him."

"What the, do you mean physically lost him? Was there more scary shit? You told me about the time your cars got wrecked. I thought that was the worst thing until you actually got shot."

Victor was sitting in his dressing room, feet up on the counter, head tipped back to stretch his neck. "It was, but it wasn't. We agreed to never revisit the hate mail, but once you've seen it, it's hard to forget. It's hard to read that someone thinks you should be tied to a barbed-wire fence and used for target practice." He hadn't meant to say that.

"Jesus!"

"Sorry. Anyway. I feel fine now, my trainer is getting me back up to, well, almost full strength." His right side would need most of a year, he'd been told. Too much of the chest had been torn open.

"Don't rush it," Janis said. "You looked great dancing at the premiere but Geoffrey said Andy was watching you like a hawk."

"He always does."

"Somebody has to," she said dryly. Then, "Are you seeing a counselor?"

"We both are. I know it's helping. He's angrier than I am."

"Well, that asshole was trying to kill *him*, and ended up nearly killing *you*. I'd be fucking furious."

Victor huffed out a laugh. "Human flamethrower. He's still annoyed that he agreed to go to the Emmys and I wouldn't let him back out."

"You macho pendejo. I'll bet he gave you every opportunity to say, you know what, we don't have to do that."

"Mm-hmm." Victor heard Janis laugh. "Then his agent sent this thing about how if we didn't go, there would be news trucks parked outside the house all day, and I could hear him thinking oh the hell with it. He asked me if I wanted to go to any of the parties."

"Which obviously you didn't."

"God, no, I could barely walk around the yard. I was such an idiot." Janis laughed again. Victor was grinning. "But I got it done."

"Yes you did. Feeling better?"

"Yes ma'am. I think I just needed to hear that we're okay."

"Of course you're okay. But I'm not surprised you need to remind yourself from time to time. Now I am going back to the piano, and you probably have a P.A. hovering outside your door. Wrap that stupid shit up so you can go dance around the world."

"That's right. Take care and sing good, chica."

"I always do," she sang, and disconnected. Victor put his phone down, got to his feet, and opened the door. Sure enough, a P.A. was hovering.

Meanwhile, "You'd think all we ever do is fuck, the way I talk about him." Andy wasn't called to the set, so he'd been enjoying a free day in his usual way: working on a half-dozen projects. At the moment, though, he was relaxing on a lounger in the backyard. The remains of lunch were on a nearby

14

table; Molly dozed in the shade behind him. His friend Dana, who also had a free day, was on the neighboring lounger.

"You've always been like that," she said, stretching lazily. "It's surprisingly relaxing back here."

"The tap tap tap of the shingle guy is kind of pleasant, isn't it?" They were having the storybook-style triplex property next door completely renovated. The roofer was doing what amounted to an art installation over there, with designs woven into the custom-cut shingles. "Anyway, I can vouch for complete recovery. I was a little worried that he wouldn't be fully rehabbed for the tour, but he's in great shape now."

"Glad to hear it. Where's your first stop?"

"Berlin. I cannot fucking wait. We were talking about going there anyway, and then when the movie sold and they said hey we want to send you on tour we were like, all aboard." Andy glanced over at Dana. "They want us to dance."

"Ya think?"

Andy snickered. "Yeah, okay. So we're doing a couple of numbers. One of them has nothing to do with the movie. It started as a joke but then we were both like, hmm, and we talked to the promoter, and the people in Berlin said it was fine with them. I sure hope they understood what we were saying."

She cut her eyes over at him, noting his tone of voice. "What is it and what's making you nervous?"

"It's 'Mein Herr,' and what's making me nervous is it's Mein Herr. Like Liza Minnelli Mein Herr."

Dana sat up and looked at him for real. He did look nervous, but also excited. "Like your Velma Kelly?" He nodded. "You're doing it in drag?" He

15

made an 'eek' face and nodded again. Dana started laughing. "Are you going to get video?"

"We will definitely try. I know people will post phone videos, we're going to tell them, or we'll have the interpreter tell them, to knock themselves out. But we want one for ourselves and obviously we won't have someone there to tape it."

"Ask the promoter," Dana said patiently. "Why you always think you have to do everything yourself, I will never know. Well, actually I do know." Andy's second career as a commercial photographer had been cut short by unexpected TV stardom, but while he was doing that he was, in fact, doing everything himself.

"I know. I should be a little more used to it by now. Vicky and Sharon were giving me shit a year ago. I was over there bumming a slice of cake and they were like you know that place would deliver for you, right? And it honestly never occurred to me. Same as with the on-set meals."

"Rory told me she told you that and I thought, of course. But if it makes you feel any better I never thought of it either." Dana glanced at her watch and wondered if she should be heading home.

"Well, you have Rory doing her Feed All The People All The Time routine."

"Yeah, and it's a constant battle for me with the food. Not like you. If the day ever comes when you look like you need to lose a pound, I will assume it's the apocalypse."

"Also, quit looking at your watch. You could stay all afternoon and I'd be happy." Andy stretched, rolled his neck, and swung his legs off the lounger. He rested his elbows on his knees and gazed at his friend. "Victor was kind of asking me what I was going to do with myself after the tour."

"And what's the answer?"

"I'm going to print up more of the behind the scenes shit from 'The Ghost of Carlos Gardel,' including some pictures of Madame Director Tanith Salazar that she does not yet know exist, and chuck it all into a gallery." Dana was snickering. Tanith had been very single-minded on set; Andy probably had about a thousand good pictures of her. "Then I have a new photography thing in the works. It's not a big production. There's some prep work that can mostly happen while we're away, then one day of shooting."

"Glad to hear it. Any hints?"

"Our friend Janis, the jazz gal? Her tour manager and his husband. They're going to play Prospero and Ariel for me." Dana looked over with clear interest. "It was their idea. I was going straight to O'Toole-Sharif slashfic." Dana grinned, nodding. "Yeah, you saw them at the premiere. Aside from that, I have to get over to Miami for a minute to check on the parents. But."

"But what." Dana did not make any moves to go. She and Andy didn't get much one-on-one time. Being able to actually talk through an issue either of them was having felt like real luxury, and it sounded like Andy had an issue.

"So I thought after all those years of the TV show, and me bitching about it all that time, he'd be ready to solo for a while, right? And then we were talking and I realized he wasn't. Isn't. He's doing a voice project in town, and then he's got the movie shoot. The plan was for me to go out in June and do my little cameo and then hang out the way I did on number two in Miami. Oh, and I'm taking Molly this time. At the moment that's basically leaving the month of May that we're not together, which, you know, not a big deal. But." He stopped again.

"Andy." Dana waited. He didn't say anything. She knew this either meant he was still processing, or what he'd thought of was unsettling. "You know how much he loved doing that relationship stuff with you on 'Vice.' Right up to the movie, he thought that reunion scene was his best work. Like, ever."

Andy looked slightly surprised. "He told you that?"

"He told me that, Tanith that, his agent that. And he was a hundred percent non-conflicted about loving what you did in Tanith's movie, even after that curve ball you threw him. He said you took him places he never thought he could get to. He loves working with you. He wants maximum time with you. And I'm guessing now more than ever."

"That's what I realized. We're still seeing a counselor, but it's all, like, coping with real life and security issues and PTSD. We haven't gotten into how, or whether, our relationship might have changed." Andy didn't honestly think it had, but he might be kidding himself. He knew he still had some rage, couldn't imagine that Victor didn't have some dark stuff hanging out too, and couldn't help fearing one of them was going to let some of that shit out at a bad time. If there ever was a good time.

Dana was watching him think. "So? Has it?"

"I don't know yet. I don't think so?"

She heard the uncertainty. "You know," she said, "one of the great things about you guys is you both want what's best for the other. You're like Dmitri and Patrick."

"Or you and Rory."

"Okay." Dana smiled, accepting that. "Maybe that's how it always is for people who manage to latch onto the right one. Anyway, are you talking to your person about rage?"

Andy suppressed a cringe. "I am. It's on tape, after all. A few people have said, you were ready to set the world on fire, weren't you, and I couldn't exactly turn around and say oh no I'm fine."

"But not Victor?"

"He's not verbalizing about that. I'm pretty sure it's there." How could it not be?

"How's the security going to be on this tour of yours?" She saw Andy's face change and added, "You haven't thought of that?"

"Fuck me. No."

"Well, do me a favor and talk to the promoter. I would assume since the company releasing the movie is the same one you've been working for, they know all about your situation and have a plan for that. But I think you both need to *know*."

"Yes we fucking do."

"Okay. So back to you and Victor working together."

Andy latched onto the subject change with relief. "So my brain did one of its monkey jumps and went to, let's start putting together a Broadway thing. A concert, song and dance thing we could do at Chrome. No target date. A thing to work on. A thing to tie us together, so he would know I'm still all in with him."

"What did he say?" Dana loved the idea.

"Oh, he loved the idea. Even after I told him he'd need to take some jazz classes."

"But you still have a concern."

"Well, it's the history. My history. I've got basically two decades of Broadway or touring shows under my belt. I've done it all before. I've got ten years of experience on him no matter how you count it, simply because I'm that much older." Andy made a face. "We had a moment back at the beginning, when we were working on that Latin set at Chrome, his second show there."

Dana had, of course, seen it. She hadn't heard this story before. "What happened?"

"I told him what I wanted to sing, and he thought it was a joke, and I got kind of bitchy with him and said something about how I'd been doing this since whenever, and I hurt him. I had to work my way through all this stupid justification to find a real apology, which I wanted to give him, because I did not want to hurt him. I never have. But you know what a bitch I can be."

"You're much less of a bitch now." He never had been that much of a bitch, but when he went there it was memorable. Dana found it funny, because it was never directed at her. "Everybody I know thinks you're sweet."

"Well good, that's what I was going for, because I started hearing myself. Anyway, we got past it but I know he's going to remember that when we start working on stuff. He feels that inexperience. Comparatively speaking," he added, though he knew Dana already understood it. "And he never quite bought that I wasn't confident as an actor. A for-real actor."

"Well," Dana said, still watching him, "was that legit? Or was it your non-compete agreement?"

"It wasn't! I mean it was! It was legit! How was I going to learn how to fucking act when all 'Vice' gave me was sympathetic ear or loving wife or damsel in distress?"

"But then you turn around and pull that Alfredo Le Pera out of your ass, and you know it was a goddamned showstopper. What did your agent say?"

Andy sighed. "Raquel said, quote, I fucking hate you." Dana laughed. "That was after I told her to stop

20

sending me film and TV scripts for, like, a year." Dana was still laughing. Andy couldn't blame her. "You know for three years it's been nothing but the same. I fucking *cannot* with that shit anymore. And frankly, I didn't want to get a ton of scripts that would be like Le Pera, even if Raquel could have dug some up. I did not enjoy that. I still, ugh. Anyway we all know how many people haven't seen Tanith's movie. Most of them." If that was his defining moment as a film actor, Andy was glad most people hadn't seen it. The movie was doing respectable business in a few U.S. theaters, but it wasn't the kind of thing that got a wide domestic release. They all expected it to earn out its modest purchase price overseas.

Dana didn't say anything about the possibility that the film could become a cult classic. "If you don't want to do it, then don't do it. You don't need to do it. And I know you still think you shouldn't compete with Victor."

"He doesn't care. Or he says he doesn't. But he's Latino like me, and he's gay like me, and those are disabilities in this business, you know they are. He's basically the one gay Latino movie star, like, ever. I do not need to be out there in his way." Andy was saying more than he meant to. He shook himself, irritated, knowing Dana would get that he wasn't irritated with her. "He's more famous from that straight role in the 'Countdown' things than he ever would have been for 'Vice.'"

"So you're going to keep protecting his ego?" Dana was skeptical, and let it show. "Victor is tough. And speaking of ego, I don't think he would really appreciate knowing you're deliberately closing doors to do that. To protect him."

"But that's not why I'm doing it." For once there was next to no humor in Andy's voice. "It really isn't. Being a screen actor, I don't *like* it. I don't like the process. I don't like how what I do can get completely turned around or fucked over after the fact, before anyone else ever sees it." Dana couldn't help making a sound of agreement to that. "I don't like the distance from the audience. I don't like how it takes months or fucking years to know whether what you've done even has an audience. I like working on stage. Victor likes working on film." He had to check himself. "Okay, he likes the stage too. But he's got a real film career ahead of him, and he knows it, and he likes that."

Dana finally swung her legs off the lounger so she could lean forward, get her hands on his, and look straight at him. "Andy. It's good you're saying this shit. But you need to say it to Victor." He didn't say anything. She sighed, with a combination of exasperation and sympathy. "Sometimes you are such a *guy*. Did you not tell him you told Raquel not to send you anything? And that she didn't drop you as a client in spite of swearing at you?" That was a guess, but she could see in his face that she'd guessed right.

"No. You're right. I will. I want to do my own fucking stuff for a while, and if that means doing a one-man show of '42$^{nd}$ Street' here in the backyard then that's what I'm gonna fucking do."

"That's the spirit." She leaned forward and kissed him. "And now I should probably go. Because if I stay, I'll have another drink, and then it'll be dinnertime, and Rory will come over, and the next thing you know Vicky and Sharon will be out here, and Victor will get home and think what is the deal with all these women."

"That all sounds great, actually," Andy said, smiling. "I'll text mine if you'll text yours."

Victor picked up the text during a break while the crew was re-setting for another take. He didn't at all mind the idea of coming home to five of his best friends, and sent back a reply saying so. Then he spared a moment to consider how before Andy, he barely even had five friends – friends who truly knew him, friends he could say anything to – and appreciated that little miracle all over again. He still didn't know how he could have done things differently, aside from the mess he made of his first night with Andy. Being forgiven for that was another miracle.

On the way home, Victor had the usual excessive amount of email to get through. Messages from their business manager, from his agent, from their accountant, from their lawyer. Then it was on to the texts. There was one from his personal shopper Carina, telling him the things he wanted for their upcoming tour were all being delivered the next day. The message from his friend Tanith made him laugh. He sent back a reply: *Hi Tanith yes we're both loco. Did Andy warn you what we're doing in Berlin?*

She must have been home from work, or else hanging out at her job waiting for the worst of the getting-out traffic to thin out. A reply came back immediately: *NO he did not should I be worried?*

*I think you'll like it when you see it*
*No hints?*
*Nope*
*@%#$!*
*LOL. The promoter said the local people all said something that we are told means 'that's fine.' We're doing Por Una Cabeza for our first number. We*

*tweaked the Q&A a little to puff up the rest of the cast*

*You're a good team player Victor*

*Hey it wasn't a two-person piece. How's things with the Mouse, you still planning to keep on there?*

*Eh for some reason it's a lot easier to take with that kind of money in the bank. Also I'm teaching again this semester and don't have an immediate new project so why not hang out for a while*

*Well when you get a new project rolling, let us know*

*Duh*

*LOL say hi to Lieutenant Cutie and that alley cat for us*

*Will do. Abrazos*

*Y Besos.* Victor put the phone away. They were almost home. He wondered if a day would ever come when getting home to Andy didn't feel like a total blessing. "Hey guys." His security escort Stan and driver Jamil made inquiring sounds. "Have I thanked you lately?" They had almost certainly saved his life back in September, and probably Andy's too.

"Only every day, Mr. Garcia."

They were never going to call him Victor. They might have heard him rolling his eyes; there were snickers from the front seats. "I'm going to miss you when I'm off this show."

"We'll miss you too, Mr. Garcia."

Chapter 3
January 2019

Berlin was the first stop on their tour, which was one reason they'd thought of doing 'Mein Herr.' Once they were on the road, they wouldn't have time or space to rehearse a number like that. The week the tour officially started, when they still had a day of shooting on 'Vice' to do, Andy and Victor were up in the home studio running the routine. Or they had been. Now Victor was leaning on the wall outside the bathroom, mopping his face with a hand towel, still giggling. "This is the best thing ever."

Andy had a leg up on the barre, stretching, leaning over with his ribs to his thigh and smiling at Victor. "You and your fishnets fetish."

"If Berlin doesn't burn to the ground when you step on stage like that, it's only because it's January." Andy laughed. The costume was pretty darned effective if he did say so himself: shorts, halter top, garter belt and stockings, high heels and bowler hat like Liza Minnelli's. They'd already done a makeup test and he knew he could put it together in the few minutes they'd have after their first number at the Berlin premiere screening. Meanwhile, he was still in costume because he knew how much Victor liked it. If there were anything resembling a bed in this studio, that guy would be all over him right now. He changed his angle to stretch the front of his hip. That meant turning his back to his husband, leg still up on the barre but now extended behind him. He heard Victor make a yummy sound and smiled to himself. "You're teasing me," Victor said. Andy glanced over his shoulder, grinning. "I've got plans for you when we get off that stage."

"Why not now?"

"Because our last call day is tomorrow, there's a ton of shit to do, they're bound to keep us there late, we have to leave the next day, and you're gonna need a couple days to recover." Victor's voice had a husky quality that sent Andy right back to their first night. He lifted his leg off the barre and set his foot down, adjusting himself. Another glance over his shoulder, making eye contact, holding it as he turned around to rest both hands behind him on the barre. Knees together, feet beveled in those high heels, making his legs look as long as they possibly could. "Jesus, Andy. You're so fucking gorgeous."

"I know what you want to do. You want to fuck me like a cabaret girl."

"Goddamned right I do." Victor walked over, taking his time, towel draped over his shoulder. He stopped less than arm's length away from his husband. Head tipped back to keep that eye contact, because Andy in those heels was six inches taller than he was. He wanted Andy's hand on his throat, on his cock. But first he wanted to see him come. He said so, and Andy's whole body reacted. "You'll `be on your back with those legs in the air and I'm going to fuck you so hard they'll hear us in the street outside."

"God almighty, Victor." Andy was gripping the barre tightly, because his knees were a little weak. "I thought I was the one teasing you."

"You are." Victor moved in, put his mouth on the base of Andy's throat where the necklace tattoo converged on the letter V. He ran his fingers up the inside of Andy's thighs and heard his breath go out. "Maybe you should get another tattoo. Maybe you should have a whole line of these." He unbuttoned the halter top, drew a fingertip from the V to Andy's waist. Unbuttoned the waistband of the shorts, unzipped them, pushed them down. Put his hand on Andy's erection, straining against the dance belt. Then unhooked the garters and used both hands to peel off the dance belt. Andy stepped out of the shorts and the belt. Victor stood back enough to see him. The halter top hung open. The garter belt, stockings and shoes had him lightheaded. "Don't you move," he warned, and stepped back. He knew there was a camera in here, they'd taped the first run-through today. Andy stood obediently waiting, still gripping the barre, completely aroused. Victor found the camera, sitting on the counter of the kitchenette. He woke it up and said, "I could make a million dollars from this picture." Andy huffed out a laugh. Victor took some pictures. Then he set the camera on the desk, positioning it with care, and crossed the room again. "I can't decide," he said. "Hand or mouth."

"*Jesus.*"

"If I use my hand, I can kiss you." Decision made, he stepped in, took Andy in his hand, and invited that kiss. Andy didn't hesitate. Victor lost track of time. The kiss was so perfect he lost some concentration, too. But Andy was moving against his hand, he was vocalizing into Victor's mouth. Victor dragged himself back to consciousness. "In my mouth." He went to one knee, one hand on the barre beside Andy's for balance, because Andy was really too tall for this at the moment, but it wasn't going to take any time at all. Now that cock was in his mouth and Andy's body jerked.

"Oh God, Victor, fucking hell, goddammit." He was trying to hold on, trying to make it last a little longer because it felt so good and it looked so good. But it was no use. Victor did something with his tongue and Andy lost it. When he opened his eyes, catching his breath, Victor still had him. Andy looked down and watched as his husband slowly, lingeringly released him. Swallowing, catching the aftershock, smiling. He pulled himself to his feet, body tight against Andy's. Andy kissed him again, tasting himself. Finally took one hand off the barre and put it on Victor. "You're not done yet."

"I'm never done with you."

"What do you want, baby. You want some of that? My mouth?" Andy's voice was low. His lips brushed Victor's face.

"I can't decide. You decide."

Andy glanced over at the camera, a reflex. Now that he wasn't half out of his mind, he realized the red recording light was on. He almost laughed, and made up his mind what to do. He unbuttoned and unzipped Victor's pants, got a hand in there, heard the quick intake of breath. "Turn around, catnip." Victor did, leaning back against Andy's chest. Andy kept that hand on him, knowing they were angled just right for the camera. He stroked slowly, making the most of it. He had a feeling they'd both be watching this from time to time. It was going to be so decadent. His naked flank and hip behind almost-fully-clothed Victor, a long fishnet-covered leg, and that glorious handful. He couldn't wait to see it. "Now I know why you went commando today."

Victor laughed breathlessly. "When we came up here this wasn't the plan."

"Oh no?" Andy kissed him. "You knew I'd be in costume. Showing you my legs." One more kiss. "Teasing you." His other hand was on Victor's throat now. He never wondered why Victor liked this so much. It was the one overtly dominant thing Andy did, a thing he'd done on that first night without

28

asking if it was okay. Victor had been startled, almost resistant. And then he'd surrendered. *It's no wonder I never got over him.* Andy stroked down and up, cupping his jaw, turning his face for another kiss. "You and your perfect mouth. Your perfect cock. Wait till you see this. The whole world should see this. Oh, faster? You want it faster? You want to fuck my hand. Go, baby. Yeah. Oh, yeah." Andy kissed him again, drinking in Victor's muffled, urgent sound, and then it was over. He was gasping against Andy's face. "I love you."

Victor's eyes were still closed. He smiled. "I love you too."

Andy made sure Victor had his balance, then pulled the towel off his shoulder. "This was good planning." He wiped his hand. "What are you going to do with that recording?" Victor giggled. "Take it on location with you in May?" Victor laughed out loud. Andy started to giggle too. "Filthy motherfucker."

"I'll leave you a copy."

"Damn right you will."

They both agreed, later, that the two days in between Berlin and Stockholm were very much called-for. The travel time of course was negligible. Being able to sleep late had been a blessing. "I didn't need both days to recover," Andy pointed out, while they were getting dressed for the night's event. "You did such a good job warming me up."

"I didn't last as long as I wanted. Every time I caught a glimpse of one of those goddamned legs I was like, oh Lord." Andy laughed. "If there had been a mirror over the headboard you would hardly have even known I was there." Andy cracked up. Victor pulled a comb through his sleek black hair, smiling at his husband in the mirror. "I don't think anybody's going to see that video and not know what I wanted to do to you."

"Yeah, probably not." Andy stood back from the mirror, checked out the hair one more time. "This goddamned cowlick."

"I always loved that. The way your hair wants to break out and do its own thing."

"Easy for you to say. Yours stays where you want it. Eh. I'm starting to almost like the gray."

"I love it. I love everything about you." The escort was going to be there any minute, so Victor didn't do what he wanted to do. Instead he patted Andy's ass and said, "Watch out. Hair spray happening."

That night's post-screening performance featured the two numbers they'd be doing for most of the tour. And that night's venue didn't have a stage, so they did the dances on the auditorium floor. It ramped up from the first row of seats, with a wide but fairly shallow flat area right in front of the screen. "Jesus, good thing we've done this before," Victor said as they began. They had to tweak things, moving back and forth along that flat area to avoid the ramp. There were a couple of close calls. "Shit! Thanks honey." The projection-booth light was shining, casting their shadows on the screen behind them. The audience was a sea of smartphones, taking pictures and video all the way through. One person in the front row had a phone in her hand, but wasn't using it. She was watching as if she'd lived all her life to see this. "Do we know who that is?" Victor said quietly to Andy halfway through their second number.

"I don't think so." A few more bars. "She didn't say anything during the Q&A." They had some tricks at the end of 'La Cumparsita,' so Andy focused in.

After they hit their closing position, holding it for a few seconds before taking their bows, he saw that the person of interest was on her feet applauding. She showed no sign of being in a hurry to leave the auditorium. Their escort and the theater manager were standing off to the side. "She's heading over there. I'm getting really curious."

"Me too." One more bow, then they half-ran down the ramp and went to join their escort. After shaking hands with the manager, assuring him they'd had a wonderful time, and confirming they'd be out of there promptly, they turned to their escort. She was clearly waiting to introduce them to the other person.

"Mr. Garcia, Mr. Martin, this is Señora Caterina González Dávila. She is in charge of your appearance in Madrid and would like a word."

*So we didn't get back to the hotel until three in the morning because wine bar,* Andy wrote to their neighbor slash tenant Vicky. *We're due at Amsterdam venue in less than an hour and we are hating life*

Vicky's reply was predictably unsympathetic. *LOL serves you right*

*How's things on the B side?*

*Molly is moping. She's been curled up with the cats gazing mournfully at the door*

*Aw poor sweetie. Thanks again for babysitting*

*We like your dog. If you never come home there's going to be a cage fight with Rory to see who gets her*

*Bahaha any news on the disaster next door?* Turning that triplex renovation over to Paige, one of the incoming tenants, had been a gamble. So far it was not actually a disaster. Paige and Vicky's wife Sharon had bonded. Between the two of them, it was probably running more smoothly than if Andy had been there micro-managing.

Vicky confirmed it. *The disaster next door is not a disaster, they're getting shit done. Paige has all of the contractors eating out of her hand. Now get off the phone you have to be movie stars*

*Speak for yourself missy. OXO*

*OXO*


Andy got a text from Dana a few days after the Berlin video went live: *Hey big brother your neighbors are gung ho about your Broadway thing with Victor. btw that Mein Herr video was awesome. You were having some fun. Victor seemed to enjoy it too*

All he sent back was: *That hotel room will never be the same*

Andy didn't get a reply immediately. When he did, it came from Rory: *Uh wtf are you guys doing or maybe never mind. That text of yours ruined a take. Dana cracked up on set*

This time his reply came straight back: *wtf is exactly what we're doing. Making a little series of home movies*

*OMG LOL I want to know but I don't want to know*

*Well it started at home after a rehearsal with that number. Victor accidentally left a camera running*

*Oh yeah accidentally insert rolling eyes here*

*Bahaha anyway it was kind of inspiring. The next non-X-rated video will be going up soon. Madrid asked for Mano a Mano. We planned it this time*

*What else happened in Madrid?*

*Broke the desk in the room. Great episode though!*

*OMG LOL for real. R U srsly making a world tour porn movie??*

*Wouldn't you?* This time the reply was nothing but a line of eggplant emojis, which made Andy laugh so hard Victor woke up. "Sorry catnip. The girls wanted to know how the tour was going."

"I suppose you told them." Victor took the phone out of his hand, turned it off, and set it on the nightstand. "Get some sleep, hot stuff."

"Well, now that you're awake." Andy couldn't help giving it a suggestive spin, though he wasn't even half serious. The most recent episode had been fairly athletic.

Victor was laughing silently, one hand over his eyes. "I think you've worn me out, you nympho."

"But we haven't broken anything in this room yet." He only said it to make Victor laugh again, which it did. Andy leaned over to kiss him. "I love you."

"I love you too." Victor pulled him down. Andy let himself go, head on Victor's shoulder and an arm across his chest. A few minutes later, Victor was asleep again. Andy listened to him breathe, thought about dancing, and gradually went under.

February 2019

Buenos Aires was every bit as romantic as they remembered. Nothing much seemed to have changed in the fourteen-or-so months since their honeymoon, except for the fact that they were there to work this time. "We definitely have to come back here when we can stay a couple of weeks again," Victor said while they were getting dressed. "It's cool to be here with Tomás and the others, though."

"I wonder how the local guys are feeling about it." They'd done two rehearsals for this appearance. It was a big one. Andy and Victor would dance together twice, and their co-stars Tomás and Vicky were dancing twice. Then the four of them would dance with two local tangueros, re-creating a number from the film. "They seemed pretty chill this afternoon."

"I'm sure it helps that we can all talk. Well, all but Vicky." All five male co-stars of Tanith's movie spoke Spanish, but Vicky didn't. She was getting along fine thanks to the guys. Sharon was getting along fine thanks to Rosa, Tomás' wife, who'd made the trip to Buenos Aires with their son Fidelio so he could meet his Argentine grandmother.

"There is no sign that our locals are having trouble understanding Vicky," Andy said, then snorted. "Trouble keeping their hands off her, maybe."

"She said she thinks they view her as a challenge."

"Yeah, she also said if someone's hand lands on her ass one more time she's going to accidentally on purpose spike him with her heel." He straightened his collar, then turned to look at Victor. "For the record, I am having more fun on this trip than I think I've ever had in my life. You are spectacular."

"It's kind of great, isn't it?" Victor smiled at him from across the room. "Were you afraid we'd get tired of each other?"

"Fuck no. I'll never get tired of you." Victor crossed the room to kiss him. Andy held him close for a minute, strongly inclined to mess up their clothes and hair and everything else. "I remember that trip up the coast. At the time that was the best vacation ever. Then our honeymoon was the best. And now even though we're sorta kinda working, this is the best." One more kiss, then he reluctantly stepped back. They had a red carpet to get to.

34

It was a long evening, at the end of a long day. First the screening, then the performance, then a party for which tickets had sold out a month ago. They were all invited to a milonga afterward, and they all went (including Rosa and Sharon). It was very late, or very early, when they got back to the hotel. Victor double-locked the door and started to strip. Andy simply took off his shoes, threw his suit jacket on a chair, and collapsed on the bed. "Officially feeling my age, catnip."

"Good thing we have another night here. This project needs a Buenos Aires episode." Victor stretched out beside Andy and took his hand. Andy turned his head and smiled. Victor wriggled close enough for a kiss. "I love you."

"I love you too."

Andy woke up to broad daylight and a hushed exchange that he diagnosed as Victor and room service. He blinked up at the ceiling, then squinted down his own body. Still on top of the bedspread, still dressed, and apparently hadn't moved since he got there. He turned his head to see Victor, who'd thrown off the robe he must have had on to deal with breakfast. He was now wearing nothing, except for that silver chain he'd been wearing all the way through the tour. Andy stretched, squirmed a little, and sat up. "Wow. I really crashed."

"You don't do that often. Did this wake you up?"

"I don't think so." He swung his legs off the bed and stood up, rolled his neck, then walked over to his gorgeous naked husband. Ripped as hell from all that dancing, plus everything else they were doing. "You look good enough to eat." He gave Victor a kiss. "Mmm. Hold that thought." When he came out of the bathroom he was naked too. He threw his clothes at the chair where his jacket had landed the night before. "Is there anything there that I can eat off your ass?" Victor cracked up. Andy made a few progressively-more-obscene suggestions while he was setting up the camera.

"Before breakfast?" Victor said eventually, still laughing.

"This won't take long." Andy eyed him for a few seconds. "I'm feeling very energetic."

"Yeah, I see that." Victor stretched out on the bed, on his back, and got himself in hand. "Everything in frame?"

"Look at you. Yes. All of that perfection is perfectly in the frame. God almighty." Andy got on the bed, bent to kiss Victor (taking his time over it), then crawled down. "Want this."

"Jesus!" Victor took half a minute to appreciate being in Andy's mouth, but there was no way their position was an accident. He put his hand, and then his mouth, on Andy's cock. Enjoying the sounds of pleasure while making his own. They set a speed record. After a minute to recover, Andy patted Victor's leg. Victor sighed, stifling a laugh.

"What's so funny."

"I was going to say something about are you ready to eat now." Andy laughed. Victor rolled halfway over, kissed a thigh, and crawled off the bed to shut down the camera.

Toward the end of the tour, the nonstop travel was starting to wear them both out. That did not keep Andy and Victor from continuing to make home movies. "We can't stop now," Victor said reasonably. "It would look like we didn't enjoy ourselves these last couple of weeks."

"Which would not be true." Andy was flat on his

back in their Tokyo hotel, fully clothed. "I haven't been sleeping very well."

"I know. Any news from home?" He meant Miami.

"Pop is done with rehab. Mom is still bitching at him about smoking, as is his doctor. They're walking together every morning and they're going fishing a couple of times a week. She says at least that keeps him out of the social club where all he does is sit around and drink beer and smoke. Out on the boat he mostly sits around and drinks beer, but because she's there he doesn't smoke." Andy sighed.

Victor sat beside him and put a hand on his thigh. "He is almost eighty." His voice was quiet.

"He's had a good life, I know." Andy turned onto his side and curled around Victor, wrapping one arm around his waist. He spoke into his husband's hip. "Mom says she thinks he's trying to go fast. Not like his dad." Andy's grandfather had died a long horrible death of emphysema and dementia. "She says she won't be surprised if he has some kind of accident within the next couple of years."

"Accident, huh." Victor had his hand in Andy's hair now. "I'm sorry, honey." They didn't say anything else for a while.

Their duties that night included press, the screening, a Q&A, two dance numbers, and a short after-party. Then they went on to a milonga, but Victor could tell Andy's heart wasn't really in dancing. That was sufficiently unusual that he didn't want to force it. "I've got an idea," he said after a while. They were on the dance floor, Andy leading. He made an inquiring sound. Victor spoke softly against his face. "Let's go to a karaoke bar. You can scream a little." Andy half-laughed, then nodded.

Within thirty minutes they'd gotten a recommendation and their driver slash interpreter had brought them to the bar, where a late-night crowd of Japanese, mostly men, very refreshingly had no idea who they were. They both had to rely on their interpreter to find tracks they wanted to sing. "You're kidding," Andy said. "They actually have 'Paint it Black'? I am so totally doing that."

Victor chose 'Sway' and went up first. Ten minutes later Andy got his chance. Victor stood close to the small performance dais, watching the room while he took a phone video of Andy. *Yeah, you did need to scream*, he thought. Not that his husband was really screaming. It was closer to a growl. They might need to stay a while.

Two hours and three more songs later, Andy was ready to go. He looked pale and exhausted. Victor thought they ought to try and go straight to sleep. "We can always make our Tokyo episode in the morning." Except they weren't staying two nights, so they had to travel. They were going on to Kyoto, and then to Seoul, with no extra days in between.

"Eh. We can sleep on the train." Andy's normally-supple baritone was hoarse.

"Then let's try something completely different." Victor didn't say anything else till they were at the hotel, washed up, and ready for bed. He set up the camera. Andy sat naked on the end of the bed and watched. When Victor turned around he said, "Let's show the other part. The even more important part." All of their episodes so far had been about the fun and fury and joy of sex. This time he meant the comfort. Andy got it. He nodded, scooting back on the bed.

There was a lot of kissing. They both loved kissing. It was always part of foreplay, in these episodes. Tonight it was the main event. After a while, Victor sat up against the headboard and pulled Andy close to his chest, back to front. One arm around his ribs and the other hand working to give Andy relief. Still kissing, murmuring words of love. It didn't take long. Then Andy slid down to get his mouth on Victor. That didn't take long either. He stayed there, arms wrapped around Victor's hips, for a few silent minutes. Victor kept a hand on his back and didn't say anything about the overly-controlled breath, or the tears. He knew Andy hated to cry more than almost anyone, except maybe Vicky. He waited until Andy sighed, kissed his thigh, and sat up again with his back to the camera. Then he kissed his husband one more time and got off the bed to shut it down.

Chapter 4

They did sleep on the train. The next night's event was smaller, less tiring. Instead of dancing or karaoke they found a quiet sushi bar. Andy still didn't look rested, but at least he looked calm. "You're a genius," he told Victor on their way back to the night's hotel. "Last night was great."

"You didn't get much sleep."

"Neither did you. We don't have to leave that early tomorrow."

"Okay." Victor noticed the slightly suggestive tone. *Getting back to normal*, he diagnosed, and hid a smile. "What have you got in mind?" Andy leaned over and whispered in his ear. Victor bit back a laugh. What Andy had in mind was pretty much the polar opposite of the night before. It was a short episode. They got plenty of sleep.

On their way to the airport the next day, Andy showed Victor an email he'd sent. "I swear, I went to sleep right after this. Just needed to get it out of my head."

Victor read the email, which was about the photo shoot in the works with those English guys. "So what were the lines?" Andy pulled up a notes file and showed him. Victor read through the thirteen lines from 'The Tempest' and smiled. "That's going to be sexy as fuck. Do you know how you're going to stage them?"

"Want to help me brainstorm?"

"Love to." That kept them busy all the way to Korea. By the time they landed Andy's notes document included ideas for shooting the Ariel and Prospero solo portraits as well as the thirteen staged lines.

They were still talking about it on the way to their Seoul hotel. Andy was excited. "I'm starting to think this might be a big show. Maybe my biggest. There's so much more material. I can't stop thinking about other characters."

"Other models?"

"Yeah. I mean, if these come off like I expect, they would be the centerpiece. I wouldn't do so many lines with other characters. This thing is going to be its own thing. You saw them together at the premiere."

"Yeah. That Niall is an eyeful. I thought so back when we first met him. God, was it really only two years ago when we did 'Countdown 2'?"

"Losing track of time, movie star? You can have Niall if I can have Geoffrey. Jesus, what a cutie." Victor made a half-annoyed sound; Andy nudged him, smiling. "Not as cute as you. Nobody is. Anyway that's another thing to work on here and there. Hey, maybe I could get somebody to play Romeo and Mercutio. You know they had a bromance."

This went on all day. It was as if the project had gotten Andy over the hump of accepting what was going on with his father. Victor threw himself into it, because it was fun. He wanted to come up with characters they could play themselves. "I'll be reading those plays again while I wait for you on location. We could get that gal Charlie to take the pictures for us." Almost everybody they knew was capable of taking a decent photograph with a phone, but they were in touch off and on with another person who'd been a commercial photographer and whose work they appreciated. "That series she did with the local musicians was really good. Do you have a target date on when to hang this? It's going to take a

41

while to develop," Victor said while they were getting ready for the night's event.

"Most of the year, I think. I'll build the content first and then decide where and when to hang it. Because we have shit to do. I want to work up that Broadway thing with you. And I want to put together some dances with you. There's 'Milonga' again with the Cabaret in September."

"Gotta do it. What's the idea?"

"Love is Blindness."

"Not an apache, please." Andy laughed. Victor loved the sight of that. "Going to get Dmitri to choreograph for us?"

"Yeah, probably. And then there's 'Spy Games' in November." They made eye contact in the mirror, both immediately thinking of a dance they'd wanted to do years ago. "Mr. and Mrs. Smith. We could finally do the Assassins' Tango."

"Abso-fucking-lutely." Victor gave it a second. "Are you gonna wear fishnets for me?" Andy started to giggle. "Because you know your legs are better than Angelina Jolie's." A snort. Victor reached for him. His "God, I love you" was against Andy's throat.

Their escort's knock on the door separated them. "Jesus, catnip. Look at you." Andy bit his lip, trying to stifle more giggles. He helped reorganize Victor's clothes and hair. "Be right there," he said, projecting it to the hallway. "How do I look?"

"Like you've been molested." Victor set a fingertip on Andy's neck.

Andy adjusted himself, took a few steps, checked himself out in the mirror, shrugged at the love bite. "If the whole world doesn't already know we like to fuck, we're doing it wrong." Victor was still grinning when they opened the door.

Back to normal didn't mean totally okay. Victor checked with Andy before he posted one of his videos from the karaoke bar. "I won't if you don't want me to. Your folks will see it." He knew Andy was emailing with his mom almost every day.

"Yeah, I know." Andy looked around the gate area, where they waited to board yet another flight. "It's not like they don't know how I feel." Victor made a sound of assent. Andy turned his head to make eye contact. Tried for a smile. "You can post any or all of them as far as I'm concerned."

"All might be a little much." The one Victor wanted to post was the one that would be the most revealing. People would be wondering what the hell was going on. He'd had to think through why he wanted to post it, and realized it was because he wanted their friends ready to jump in and help Andy when he needed it, even if he didn't ask for it. Because he probably wouldn't. He wanted them to know Andy was going to need help, was what it came down to. "Okay, then. If you're sure."

Andy couldn't verbalize his appreciation, so he said, "I'm sure. I love you."

"I love you too." Victor didn't waste any time. The video was live before they boarded.

By the time they were strapped in, he had a reply from Dana: *Victor WTF with that video. Are we scrambling a rescue team?*

He hoped not, but he was grateful she asked. *About to get shut down goddamned planes Andy's dad is not doing well and this year's going to get rough. He's better now but he needed to scream*

*Thanks for the heads-up. I know you're taking care of him*

*Trying to. In the homestretch now. Hey we're brainstorming a new photography thing. Shakespeare slash or gender-bent or otherwise twisted, linked to the text*

*Ooh Rory wants to know if we can choose our own characters??*

A minute later the answer came: *Absolutely. Oh FML here's the phone police. Besos y Abrazos chicas*

*Back at ya especially hug the other one plz*

*Will do OXO*

As they both shut down their devices, Andy asked, "What was that all about?"

"About you, babe." Victor leaned over for a kiss. "We have good friends."

"Yeah, we do."


The last tour dates were in Australia. It was hot. "My internal thermostat is broken," Andy complained. "We went from winter in Europe to summer in South America and winter in Asia and here it's fucking summer again and goddamn." He was lying naked on the bed. They were finished, and he was glad. The tour had been so much fun, but they were tired. Victor had some time before starting that voice job when they got back to Los Angeles. Andy's tentative date for the 'Tempest' photo shoot was before that, but not immediately. "Can we take an extra day here?"

That sounded good to Victor. "To lie by the pool and rest? Sure. It's not like there's much prep for my thing." He already had the script, with the director's notes. "How about two? Two full days and nights, before we get back on a plane."

"Two days. Oh God that sounds great." They'd had multiple days between tour dates much of the way through, but at least one was usually lost to crossing multiple time zones. "Hand me my phone?" Victor did that. Andy sent a text to the promoter, and then one to their business manager: *hiding out in Sydney for extra 2 days, can you rebook the flight home plz and advise, TYVM.* "God I'm such a diva now." He dropped the phone somewhere on the bed and closed his eyes.

"Delegating like a boss." Victor had been sort-of planning to book them a massage. That was when they were going to travel the next day. Now they had this day, and two more days, and his husband was naked. *Never enough*, he thought, still amazed. He pulled off his tee shirt, shucked off his shorts, set a couple things ready (including the camera) and got on the bed. He straddled Andy's hips and enjoyed the resulting smile. "Keep your eyes closed," he said.

"What are you up to," Andy said lazily.

"You'll find out." Victor poured a little baby oil into his palm, capped the bottle and tossed it aside. Warmed the oil between his hands, then set them on Andy's ribs. He stroked up over chest and shoulders, down the slim muscular arms, to the hands Victor never tired of. Thumbs pressing into Andy's palms and the inside of his wrists. Heels of his hands slowly pushing up the underside of Andy's forearms, then hands wrapped around those arms above the elbows. Thumbs stroking up the inside of the biceps, watching the response. He bent and put his mouth on Andy's chest. Listened to the change in his breathing, the little gasp when tongue swept over nipple. Still there when his hands returned to Andy's, now massaging each finger. Arching his back to press the rigid cock against his. His own breath quickening. Teeth on a nipple now.

"*Jesus.*"

"Mmm." Victor couldn't make a word. Andy was lying completely still beneath him, except for that rapid breath. Victor wondered if they would both come from this. It was an experiment. He worked each finger as if it were something else, from palm to fingertip. Andy was breathing through his mouth, each exhalation slightly vocal. Victor's mouth still working on his chest, licking, sucking, biting till Andy made a desperate sound. He pushed up with his hips and pulled Victor's hands higher on the bed, stretching them up over his head, forcing him flat with his face against Andy's. Pressed together, it was too much; Victor had to move. Uncontrollable, hard, thrusting against Andy as if he were inside. Victor flung his head back, his whole body arching. As he felt them both come he uttered something between a curse and a prayer. Whatever it was, it was as loud as whatever Andy was saying.

"Holy fucking Christ," Andy said faintly, a fair amount of time later. Victor lay motionless on top of him, still pinioned. Andy let go of his wrists. They were somewhat glued together.

"Mmm."

"That was a thousand-dollar massage right there." Victor laughed silently. "Is the camera running?"

"Mmm."

"Good. I want to see that."

"Me too." Victor peeled himself off. It took him two tries to get on his feet and over to the camera to shut it down. He twisted his back, rolled his neck, scratched his belly. "How much do you think a porn site would give us for this masterpiece?" Andy laughed. "Maybe we could buy that shitty building on the other side of ours and tear it down."

"Stop. We haven't even finished the triplex." Andy sighed, stretching contentedly. "Shower before pool, or go down there like this?"

"Oh, honey, I think we need to shower." Victor leaned over to lick Andy's flat belly. He'd meant it as a joke, but after a minute he set his hands down and said, amazed all over again, "Or I could clean you off this way."

"Wow, you are really degenerate today." Andy lifted his head to watch, then propped himself on his elbows. "And oh my God, I really am a nympho. Turn that camera back on." One more swipe of his tongue, then Victor did. "On your front, catnip. My turn to give you a massage."

They didn't make it down to the pool until sunset. Dinner was delivered out there. Victor watched Andy eat, smiling. "It's unbelievable."

"I know." Andy set down his fork and leaned back. As usual, he'd put away half again as much food as Victor. "It's probably offensive."

"No way, not when I know exactly how you're burning it all off." Andy laughed. Victor drank some cold white wine, squinting up at the sky. "God, what a great day. I love you so much."

"I love you too. Think we can have a day like this here and there while you're on location?"

"I should have had it written into the contract." Victor put his head back and closed his eyes. *So tired*, he thought, *so happy*. Something he'd been thinking about since September finally crystallized. His agent had been sending him things; there were half a dozen potentials. None of them looked better than this. "You know what? After we wrap this summer, I'm taking a vacation. Like, no jobs. The next movie start date is looking like July of next year." It was going to be a romantic thriller, very different from the 'Countdown' series of action comedies.

Andy stared at his husband. He was admiring the perfect profile and the eyelashes, but also wondering if he'd understood correctly. Victor had taken breaks before, since they'd been together, but not long ones. Their summer trip four years ago had been the longest. Since then it had been a full schedule, never more than a month off at a stretch in between the months of TV or movie filming. Even those months had been interrupted with promotion, or fill-in work, or other business. Most recently, of course, with recuperation from a near-fatal bullet wound. All those sixty- and seventy-hour weeks. Andy always had his own projects, but always wished they could have more time together. He'd found Victor after so many years alone. "The whole time? This August to next July?" His voice must be communicating deliriously happy disbelief. He wasn't trying to mask it.

Victor opened his eyes and gazed back at Andy. "Think you can turn me into a real song and dance man with that much time?"

"Oh honey, it won't take that much time. Oh my God." Andy blinked, sniffed, swallowed. Nearly lost it when Victor set his hand on Andy's wrist, stroking up his forearm and back down to his hand. Their hands gripped hard for a few seconds, then relaxed. Victor didn't let go, though.

The next morning Victor came out of the bathroom, rubbing lotion on his freshly-shaven face, to find Andy sitting cross-legged on the bed with the laptop open in front of him. "You're not supposed to be working right now. It's wine-tasting day."

"Oh don't worry, I'm not missing that." They had a car coming to take them to an airstrip, where a private plane would fly them to Hunter Valley. "Look at this crazy shit that Red and Niall did." He turned the laptop around after tapping something.

Victor watched the video. It was a swordfight with dialogue, outdoors with the ocean behind them. "I'll be damned. Macbeth and Macduff." Their friend Red was a hunktastic action star with a long history as a weapons expert. Niall more than held his own with a broadsword. "You're going to grab some of that for your show, I suppose."

"Have to. Fucking have to! And now I want Red as Macduff solo and Mary as Lady Macduff, but in my version she doesn't die because give that bitch a sword." Victor laughed. Red's wife could definitely handle a sword. "You know it's the one Shakespeare play I've actually seen live on stage. I would like it so much better if she gets away with their boy. Shows up at the end when Macduff is busy handing Scotland to the other guy and thinks his life is over. Tweak the Lady's scene. It wouldn't even need any new dialogue, really."

Victor agreed. "Just a big, cathartic kiss. Though I'm sure Tanith would jump on writing it. Man, the audience would feel like all that angst was worth it, wouldn't they?" Andy made a sound of agreement. "You could get Theo to play the boy."

"Jesus, he'd be perfect." They already had tenants lined up for the triplex they were renovating. One couple had a mixed-race boy, seven and a half years old and bright. Andy could have gone straight into brainstorming mode, but they had time for that later. *So much time*, he thought, stunned all over again. He closed the laptop, stood up, kissed Victor, and said, "We'll watch that again later. It's kind of inspiring."

"Seems like everything is inspiring lately."

"You have a point. Well, you know they say use it or lose it. At this rate, we'll never lose it." Victor was laughing. Andy patted his ass. "Let me get my pants on and we'll go get drunk."

Before they left Australia, Victor spent some time composing an email to his agent about his plan for an extended break. Then he and Andy both got on the phone with their friend Rory to tell her they wanted to do things with the Underground Cabaret. "Okay," she said casually. Then, "How many things, all the things? Both of you? Are you not out of town? What's going on, are you okay?"

Andy made a 'what the fuck' face at Victor, who stifled a laugh. "Honey, we're fine. We're both fine. But we're tired, and Victor's going into that movie shoot, and then he's got another one starting next summer."

"I was like, fuck it," Victor contributed, and heard a sound of agreement from Rory. They were on speaker, not FaceTime, but he could imagine her face. She'd been bitching at Andy for years about overdoing things, and at Victor ever since the shooting. Plus, of course, she knew what was going on with Andy now. "We don't need the money. I don't want to cram another big job in there. And if I'm doing smaller things I want to do them with Andy, that's all."

"Okay. Okay." A pause while Rory collected herself. "So I'm assuming the 'Milonga' show in September."

"Right," Andy and Victor said together. Andy added, "And we want to do a thing for 'Spy Games.'

Mr. & Mrs. Smith. We wanted to do it way back at the 'Assassins' show but then fucking 'Vice' pulled Victor out of town."

"Those fuckers," Rory agreed. "What do you want for 'Milonga?' Because I'll put you down now and if anyone wanders in with the same song I'll tell them to try again."

Victor giggled while Andy said, "Love is Blindness. The Jack White track that Ricky and Anya used for their apache. It will not be an apache."

"Jesus, I hope not. I mean after seeing what you guys did with 'Mano a Mano' I think people would be calling 911 if you did an apache." They'd done a fight number in Tanith's movie that people talked about everywhere they went.

"Yeah, no. Ricky has fifty-plus pounds on Anya. My physical therapist would order a hit if I tried to do that shit with Victor."

"Do not do that shit. Anyway cool, so much cool, all the cool. What about next year?"

"Well, Dana told you about this Broadway idea, right?"

"Yeah. Is that for real?" Excited all over again.

Victor said, "Andy's going to put me through chorus boy boot camp." Rory laughed. "We were thinking maybe April. If we could get Chrome the week before Alison's showcase."

"Oh, *if* you could get Chrome." Rory's voice was full of sarcasm. "Would Tyrone and Terry find a date for you guys? Hmm, what do I think, I think hellz the fuck yeah. Whenever you want, basically. They'll have to price the tickets like one of those Virgin space flights or people will tear the fucking place down trying to get in." Andy and Victor both laughed. "Come to think of it, there's going to be a scalping situation if we advance-press your other things. Do you want to keep those on the down-low?"

Andy and Victor stared at each other for a second. Victor said, "Yeah. Keep us off the official cast list. We're doing this for fun, not to be pulling focus."

"We could put us on the table talkers and tease it without our names, like 'special guests,' on the main poster," Andy said. "The one at the club for the show nights. That way it'll be people who were going to come to the show anyway. You know you always sell out with 'Milonga.'"

"Okay. With you we already have six confirmed for 'Spy Games' too. What the fucking fuck, it's not till November, people are way ahead of this thing."

"Are a bunch of people using James Bond music?" Victor was grinning.

"Oh yeah."

"Great. Well." Andy glanced at Victor again; it seemed they had the main points communicated. "We're on our way back to L.A. tomorrow. First twenty-four hours home will be recuperating from that bitch of a flight and groveling to Molly."

"Molly's fine. She's been over here with me and the pack a lot."

"I know. You're the best. We'll get together for dinner soon, okay?"

"You bet. I'll tell Dana about the plan, she'll be psyched. Love you guys."

"Love you too." They all got off the phone. Andy set it aside, stretched, and threw a leg over Victor's. "It's too bad I can't do a show of stills from our porn tour." Victor laughed. "The world deserves to see you naked."

"You too."

"And legit post-coital." Victor waved a hand like 'stop.' Andy did not stop. "Hey, maybe you should check with the producers of next year's movie, find out if the accidental publication of X-rated photographs would void your contract." Victor was giggling. Andy was grinning up at the ceiling. If they hadn't both been utterly exhausted, he would have suggested turning the camera on again. Since they were, and it was three in the morning their time, he reached over and switched off the lamp.

Chapter 5

They did their best to sleep on the flight. In between catnaps, they talked quietly about the tour experience. All the screenings, performances, and after-parties had gone off without a hitch. Good transport and interpreters, acceptable hotels, and excellent security. They'd emailed with their counselor during the trip, confirming that they felt safe. "So how are you feeling about being home, catnip," Andy said about seven hours into the flight. "It seems like I've had more rage issues than you."

*You've got an extra trigger now,* Victor thought. "And you always have more insomnia than me. Monkey brain."

"Yeah, whatever. But seriously. No anxiety? Are you sure you want to do without a car team?" They'd had a driver and a security escort for years.

"The drama's dropped off a lot since last fall." It was as if the real violence had re-educated people who'd thought sending death threats wasn't actual terrorism. "We've got the on-site guy. We've got the surveillance. Let's try it this way for a while." Victor regarded Andy. He couldn't exactly say why he wasn't as angry as his husband. "I've had my moments," he said. "I mostly work it out in the gym. Maybe because it wasn't the first time. I was closer to dead in Mazatlán than I was last fall." The knife attack, when he was a teenager.

"Ugh." They gazed at each other. Andy knew that Victor's rage about that long-ago event had more to do with grief for his boyfriend, left dead outside a gay club, than with his own injuries. That thought led him to, "And you're mostly mad because that guy last fall was trying to kill me."

"Exactly. I'm not happy I got shot, it wasn't fun, but he didn't kill me. And even more importantly he didn't kill you." Andy made a sound of disagreement. Victor knew they would never quite mesh on this. "I love you."

"I know you do. I love you too." Andy took Victor's hand and kissed it. "If we get sick of driving again, though, I'm totally down with a car service. Maybe we could bribe Stan and Jamil to ditch the studio team and come work for us." Victor laughed. "So how do you like this ring." He'd chosen one in Australia, thinking it would be a great reminder of this fantastic trip.

"I fucking *love* it. That dreamtime inlay. Never take it off." Andy was laughing under his breath. "I like this thing, too." Victor wrapped his hand around the new cuff: a broad, supple braid made of many strands of thin crocodile-leather cord. It was held flat with metal clamps and closed with a pair of fold-over latches. "Should I guess why you got gray?"

Andy gave him a look. He'd stopped coloring his hair a year ago; it was now about twenty percent gray. His body hair wasn't there yet, but he could tell the day was coming. "You can guess but I'd thank you not to say it out loud." Victor snickered. "Yeah, you can laugh in ten years when we see what's happening with *your* hair."

March 2019

"Un-fucking-believable," Andy said, when Victor asked about the Tempest photo shoot. "They're going to be down here in a minute. Or thirty, or however long it takes them to bang. Probably not that long." Victor laughed. "I thought they were going to lose it before lunch." Andy was giggling now too.

"Yeah, from your text, I figured things were getting steamy."

"That Geoffrey. I'll show you the pictures. Like, here's Niall's face before Geoffrey did whatever he did, and here's his face after. That poor guy. He's trying to be a good subject, and I've got them right up against each other, and all they're really wearing is dance belts. Then here's Geoffrey with his hot little ass and oh my God." Andy laughed.

"I don't know why you say little, he's taller than me."

"Yeah, I don't know either. Fairly sure he weighs more than I do. Serious athlete, really, but he's so *pretty*."

"Shut up." Victor wasn't jealous. He was used to Andy being complimentary about other men, and they were always surrounded by good-looking men. If he'd ever thought Andy was seriously tempted, it would be different. He knew his husband never wanted anyone but him. "So you're happy with the work?"

"The work was great. They were in it. Took direction well, gorgeous to look at, the makeup was perfect, the costume pieces were terrific, and that throne of Red's really sells it. I wish there were some way to use that for other things in the series."

"It's definitely going to be a series, huh."

"Has to be. I don't know that I ever would have thought of doing something text-based like this, but you know how fast you were throwing me things in Asia. I'll bet we can cast the whole thing in about an hour, once we've read the plays and figured out what characters I should do. I know you said Rory and Dana are going to pick their own." Andy leaned against the kitchen counter, smiling at Victor. Dinner was waiting in the oven, wine was breathing, and once he got rid of the two Englishmen he thought they might play a scene of their own. It probably wouldn't be anything from Shakespeare.

"Yeah, for all I know they're going to go with Prince Hal and Falstaff. I listened to 'Othello' on the drive today," Victor said. He liked that Andy was saying 'we' about this project. "Not a fan of the storyline. I think Desdemona should kill Othello and Iago." He watched Andy laugh again. "Who could you see as that Desdemona? She has this line, 'Talk you of killing?' On the recording it's this tremulous, scared thing. But I thought, that's so Taxi Driver. That's, are you talkin' to me? Let's see who kills who, you jealous motherfuckin' meathead. She could be wiping a dagger on that stupid handkerchief."

"You're good at this." Andy stepped over to the control center, found a notepad, and wrote down the character name and the line. "I think we might have to have a Twister tournament. We know so many awesome women. Tanith could play the hell out of it."

"Anya," Victor suggested. "You know she's wanted to kill a few guys in her time. Or, like, every day." He watched Andy make another note. Briefly wondered where all these ideas were coming from. Dismissed it because they had other things to do.

The night before Andy left for Miami, Rory and Dana came over for dinner. There'd been a few texts back and forth about the whole video SOS thing, and everyone expected the subject to come up. They found other things to talk about for a while. Victor and Andy told tour stories, Dana talked about her TV show, and Rory talked about stage-managing the first Underground Cabaret show of the year. Halfway into their second glasses of wine, she planted her elbows on the table and said, "So, Andy. Your boy toy let us know you are looking at potentially a very shitty year."

"I figured he might have."

"Yeah. Since you very much suck at admitting you need help, or want help," Rory tried to look stern, "we'll be watching you like hawks and probably making epic pests of ourselves with preemptive or premature offers of help. Because we love you."

"I love you too." Andy had his elbows on the table now too, gazing back at her affectionately. "At the moment it's kind of a wait and see situation. After this trip I'll know if they've been selling me a load of bullshit." *Because neither of them can lie to my face.*

"You're still planning to go on location with Victor, right?" Dana was done eating. All of them were.

Andy drank the rest of his wine, thinking seriously about pouring a refill. He set down the empty glass with a sigh. "I'm still going to go. I'm still planning to do all the things I want to do with Victor. If something happens, I'll change the plans, that's all."

"And we'll do those things another time." Victor was watching his husband. "We'll get Dmitri to start us off on those two routines before I leave. We'll be able to practice while we're out at the Great Lakes. The shoot's supposed to wrap the first week of August."

"Plenty of time," Dana said. "And what about this whole Shakespeare thing?"

"We're going to mess around with character ideas on location," Victor said. "Once we're back Andy can start scheduling people."

"Did you see that video of Red's?" Andy asked. "The Macbeth swordfight?"

"Oh my God yes!" Rory looked delighted. "That looked seriously legit! Are you stealing some of that?"

"I totally am, they already said I could. Do you want to see the stuff I shot with Niall and Geoffrey? It's really gorgeous, I'm completely obsessed with it." Andy mostly made the offer to get everyone's mind all the way off the Miami situation, and it worked. He set up the laptop, then cleared the table and listened to the commentary. "So I'm looking at one or two lines to do with all the other subjects."

"Oh thank God," Dana said. "I can't believe there's another play where you could yank out this many lines and they would work so perfectly."

"I'm going to be learning a lot more about Shakespeare than I ever did before, that's for sure." Andy got the coffeemaker going and came back to the table. "But they look great, right?"

"Really great." Rory stood up, wriggling her back. Victor gave her a questioning look and she said, "A little stiff. You know, this whole over-forty thing is a crock." She rolled her neck. "But that reminds me. Did you guys actually make a, you know, episode every place you went on tour?"

Victor cracked up. Andy made a 'maybe' face. Dana said, "Why did that remind you of that?"

"Well, the reason my neck is stiff," Rory began, and Dana performed a swift 'say no more' gesture, trying not to laugh.

"Hey," Andy said. "If you're going to ask about ours, I think it's totally fair to ask about yours."

"We didn't spend six weeks tangoing around the world making a porno," Dana said, totally failing at not laughing.

Rory held up her glass, squinting through it at the light. "Because we are wasting our lives." She drank the rest of her wine.

Knowing their days on 'L.A. Vice' were coming to an end, Andy and Victor had decided to replace their cars, both wrecked by a vandal eighteen months ago. They'd delegated the job; car-shopping was very low on Andy's list of preferred ways to spend time, and Victor was more concerned with getting the job done than with doing it himself. Their business manager took care of it while they were on tour. Andy was satisfied with his new Subaru Crosstrek, and Victor loved his new Acura RDX. It almost made the trip to the airport tolerable. He pulled over on the curb at Departures and switched on the hazard lights. "Give me a call when you get in, okay?"

"You know I will. And I'll ping you as soon as I know how long I think I need to stay." Andy knew he had some heavy conversations to get through. He didn't want to rush them.

"Take as much time as you need, baby. I wish you didn't have to go." Victor meant 'I wish this wasn't happening,' and Andy knew it. "Give them my love."

"Definitely." Andy leaned over for a kiss. "Let's get my shit out. Like the new buggy?"

"I'm going to sleep with her tonight." Andy laughed. They both got out of the car. Andy didn't need any help but Victor was trying to get every last second with his husband. "I already miss you." A kiss before the rolling bag came out of the cargo area, and another once it was on the ground. Andy touched his face, leaned in for another kiss. Victor hugged him. "I love you."

"I love you too." Victor let him go, and Andy stepped back. "God I hate to leave you."

"I hate it too. Get moving." Victor watched him all the way into the check-in area. Then a cop beeped at him. He did a 'yeah, sorry' thing, got back into the car, and drove home.

Seven hours later, he finally got the call. He and Molly were cuddled together on the couch; he was reading, or sort-of reading, a script his agent had sent. Music was playing. It should have been a nice relaxing evening. When the phone rang he snatched it up. "Andy."

"Hi sweetheart. It's raining like somebody ordered an ark over here."

"Aside from that, how was the trip?"

"Eh. It was a cross-country flight. I'm heading over to the house pretty soon, having a snack here at the hotel first so I can legitimately tell Mom she doesn't have to cook. What are you up to?"

"Reading with Molly. She thinks this script is crap."

"Why are you even reading a script?"

"Because I read some Shakespeare earlier today and I was having ideas about your thing and thought I'd better step back." He was hoping Andy would tell him not to.

"Why would you do that?" Andy sounded surprised. "Don't do that. You're good at this shit. Have all the ideas you want. I want your ideas, okay?"

Victor was pleased, and let that come through in his voice. "Yeah, okay. So Parker sent me this thing, Pop Quiz wants to do a follow-up about the movie and the shooting and all that. Did you get anything on that?"

"Haven't checked. Hang on." Victor waited. He knew Andy usually started up the laptop as soon as he was properly inside a hotel room. After a minute, Andy said, "Sure enough. They say a sit-down, one-on-one thing. Is that what yours says?" Victor made a sound of assent. "Why the fuck wouldn't they want both of us. Well, huh. Do you want to do it?"

"Not especially."

"Which means absolutely not. Me neither, but one of us should, so I'll do it. Maybe it'll be Sherry again. Hey, maybe I can swing it over to being all about me and dancing, we can end the whole conversation about the shooting. I know you're tired of talking about it."

Victor really was. There had been far too many questions about that for the past six months. "If you don't mind, that would be great."

"Anything for you, catnip. I'd better get moving, though. Ping me anytime."

"I will. I love you."

"I love you too."

Andy was back in Los Angeles four days later, earlier than expected but none too soon. After a long embrace in baggage claim, he walked out with Victor. Both of them ignored the people whispering, pointing, and taking phone pictures. They weren't there for publicity. Andy waited until they were outside before he said, "We almost had a fight. Me and Pop. He was all, did you suggest your mother should move out of here when I'm gone, and I was all, yes Pop I did, because for one thing this street is under water at high tide and for another she is also almost eighty and in case you haven't noticed this place needs a lot of work. He got so mad."

"Thought it was a criticism?" They were in the parking deck now.

"Exactly. Which it kind of was. You know ever since I started making TV money I've been trying to get him to hire some of that work done. Told him I could help. He was always no, I can handle it. Well of course none of it ever got done." Andy made an impatient gesture. "If Miami takes a direct hit from another hurricane, their roof is going to end up in the fucking Bermuda Triangle."

"So how'd you leave it?" Victor glanced over his shoulder. Yes, there was someone walking the same direction, about twenty feet behind, carrying a gym-sized bag. *Just another traveler*, he told himself.

"We argued for an hour, we had a beer, he said yeah you're right. Goddammit." Andy stopped walking. He didn't shout, but he put all his stage training into his voice; his "What the hell do you want?" rang through the parking deck. He turned as he spoke.

The person following them jerked back as if someone had yanked on a leash. "I, what? I'm sorry, my car is this way. I wasn't trying to listen. I wasn't going to bother you." Andy stared at him for another second. Victor was staring at Andy. "Look, I'll go around this way. I'm sorry."

Andy sighed. "No, never mind. My husband got shot in the back last year. I'm a little touchy about people coming up behind us."

"Yeah, I get it. Um, I'll, yeah." The guy walked around them, giving them plenty of space, and moving as if he thought there might be land mines.

"Sorry."

"No, it's okay." The guy gave a half-assed wave and headed for a car. Pulled keys out of his pocket.

Got into the car. Andy and Victor were still standing there when he drove away.

"Are you actually okay?" Victor said quietly. He was having one of those moments of seeing Andy with fresh eyes, letting the soft-focus lens of 'friends, lovers, married' clear. Really seeing the fatigue, the grim expression, the need for some kind of violent release. Victor didn't think Andy had ever hit anyone in his life. Yelling at that guy was probably the closest he'd come.

Andy lifted his chin, stared at the concrete above them, took a visibly deep breath, let it out slowly. Then he looked back at Victor. "Not, actually. Let's get out of here."

They didn't talk much on the way home. The traffic was horrible, Victor needed to pay attention, and he wasn't sure how best to proceed with the next part of this. They absolutely had to talk, which meant his original intention of going straight to bed was on hold. After parking at home, he didn't get out of the car right away. "What do you need, baby." He thought he knew, but he needed Andy to say it.

Andy had his head back. He turned to gaze at his husband. After what seemed like a long time he said, "I need to hug my dog. I need at least one very large vodka martini. I need you to fuck me till I can't think. In that order, please."

"And after that, will you tell me what's going on?" His tone said he might not agree to that order of business otherwise.

"Yes."

"Okay, then." They went inside. Andy parked his bag by the stairs and spent a few minutes on the floor with Molly, who acted like he'd been gone for a hundred years.

He gave her a treat and petted her pretty blonde head. "You're getting old too, aren't you, best girl." He cupped her muzzle, noting the white fur. "Why can't dogs live as long as humans?" She licked his nose.

"I think there's a theory that they're too good for this world." Victor nudged his shoulder with a large, icy-cold glass. Andy took it, sipped, and nodded thanks. "She can't be more than seven. That's what the vet said, anyway."

"Yeah, I know. Good for a few more years, right Molly?" He hugged her again, and stayed there on the floor with her while he drank most of the martini. "Yes, I know, I'm guzzling. I didn't have one on the plane."

"Why not?"

"Didn't want to let my guard down." Victor was leaning against the kitchen counter, watching him. "You're not having one."

"I might later." He really wanted to ask, right now, why Andy was so upset. There had to be something more than what they'd already known. Andy had been there for him after his mother died, when they weren't even together. He'd said the right things, let Victor cry, stayed with him so he wouldn't have to be alone. And every day they'd been together since, Victor had wished he could have said something earlier. On their very first night. During the worst of that time, he might not have had to be alone at all, if he'd been just that little bit more brave. At least he was with Andy for this. "You know you can tell me anything, right? I'm always here for you."

"I know." Andy finished the drink. Handed the glass to Victor, petted Molly one more time, and got to his feet. "Whoa, yeah, that was strong. Perfect."

*You haven't eaten, have you.* "Go on up and get ready. I'll take Molly out for a minute."

"Get ready." Andy set a hand on Victor's shoulder, slid it up into his hair, lowered his head for a kiss. "Get ready for what?"

"Remember Berlin?"

"Oh." Not quite a smile, but warmth in those deep dark eyes, and another kiss. "I believe I do."

Chapter 6

Andy went upstairs slowly, feeling the vodka, and went into the bathroom. He was on the bed, naked, stretching, when Victor came up, carrying two full shot glasses. The lube was already out on the nightstand. He watched while his husband set the glasses on the other nightstand, then stripped.

Victor waited for a sign. He'd said 'Berlin,' and that meant face to face. He wasn't sure if that was too intimate in this moment. But Andy lay back, spread-eagled on the bed. *Okay then.* Victor was relieved. And also, inevitably, turned on. He had a hand on himself almost at once. A firm hand, stroking down to the head, squeezing. Then he picked up the lube and got on the bed, kneeling between Andy's legs. "You and your legs." Andy huffed out a breath, almost a laugh. Victor put his hands on those legs. Stroking from ankles to knees, fingertips reaching behind to the sensitive skin there. Then up the insides of the thighs to the groin, watching Andy's eyes half-close, watching the erection that rose as his touch swept near. He was dying to touch it. "Maybe tomorrow I'll touch that." Andy laughed under his breath, as Victor had hoped he would. "Get those knees up."

"Bossy." Andy bent his knees, tempted to lock his feet behind Victor's neck and pull him down for a kiss. But then this would be over too soon. He needed all of it, every second of it. Needed to be possessed, to feel Victor everywhere. His arms were spread wide on the bed, palms down.

"Yeah, you keep your hands out there. Digging into the bed. Hanging on while I fuck you." Andy's breath went out. Seeing his abs tighten made Victor even harder. He got some lube on his fingers and went to work. This wasn't what he'd imagined for the night, but it was what Andy needed, and it was impossible not to respond. He remembered to breathe so he could say, "What do you want now."

"Your cock. Fuck me. Jesus, Victor." Breathless, panting, desperate. Then "Oh *God*" as Victor engaged. Andy arched his back, offering resistance so Victor could go deeper.

Victor had his weight on one hand, the other arm under Andy's thigh, gripping his hip. Imagining how this looked, with Andy's foot on his shoulder. The other was hooked over the top of Victor's thigh. He was trying not to come too soon. Listening to Andy's vocal breaths, watching those hands. "That's how you want it? God you feel good." He was starting to lose focus. Pulling that thigh against him now. "Jesus Christ."

Andy was making sounds he almost never made, mixed in with, "Yes. God. Yes. Fuck. Oh Jesus, yes." Gripping the bed the way Victor had known he would, fighting for Victor's climax and against his own.

"Don't you fight me. Let me see that. Come on, baby, give it to me. Jesus you're beautiful. God you're so close. Andy, fucking do it, I can taste it from here, fucking *come* Andy, *yes*." Victor bit his lip, holding still as Andy's body spasmed, listening to his cry and watching his face. When he relaxed Victor put both hands down, felt Andy's feet lock behind his back, and let himself go. Fast shallow strokes as the tension coiled, then unwound in a surge. His harsh sound was echoed by a murmur from Andy. A hand in his hair while he rested for a few seconds, propped on his elbows, breathing fast. Then he kissed Andy's shoulder, disengaged and stepped off the bed, staggering to the bathroom. He was back a minute later to tidy them both up. "You okay, baby? That all right?"

"That was perfect." Andy was face down in a pillow. "I love it when you talk dirty to me." Victor lay down beside him and patted his ass, then stretched his arm across Andy's back to his shoulder. Caressing lightly with his thumb, waiting. They were both quiet for a while. Then Andy said, "What's that shit in the shot glasses."

"Taste it and find out."

Andy made a muffled, amused sound into the pillow, raised his head, looked over at Victor's smiling face. Rearranged himself and reached for the glasses. "Here." He handed one to Victor, then sipped, squinted, sipped again. "This is gin."

"Yes it is." Victor scooted up so he could sit against the headboard, beside Andy, still keeping their bodies in contact as much as possible. He sipped his own. It wasn't as icy cold as he liked it, but under the circumstances it was fine.

"Very good gin."

"Yes."

"I thought it was going to be some heinous schnapps and I was wondering why such a thing would be in our house. Why is it blue?"

Victor snickered. "Something about flowers. Infusion, I think they called it." They sat there quietly. Victor noticed that Andy had his eyes closed now. He kept sipping the gin, kept not saying anything. They heard Molly's toenails clicking up the stairs. "Hey Molly, come on in." She came through the doorway, sat down, and cocked her head. "Come up." Victor patted the bed. She trotted over and hopped up on the bed, curling up by his feet. "Good girl."

"She's the best girl. Did Consuelo leave us something for dinner?"

"Yeah, she did. Do you want to talk first?"

"Or we could keep drinking." Andy opened his eyes and set down his empty glass with a sigh. "Okay, I'll be a grown-up. So Pop had an angiogram. They said, you need a quadruple bypass or you're not going to make it to next Christmas. He said no surgery. Mom was there."

"When was this?" Victor was wondering about that 'next Christmas' bit. He had an idea but he didn't like it.

Andy confirmed it. "Before the first stroke."

"Fuck! And they just now told you?"

"I know."

"Why?" No answer for a few seconds. "Oh, for fuck's sake. Because of me."

"Because somebody shot you," Andy corrected. "Not because of you. You know they think the sun shines out of your ass." Victor huffed out a laugh, shaking his head. "Anyway long story short he's refused surgery, he's signed a DNR, and he's not expected to live out this year. And now that's all out on the table, we can start planning what to do with Mom."

"Baby, I'm so sorry."

"I am so grateful for you." Andy turned to look at him. "There may be times in the next few months when I don't act the way I should or I don't say the things I should. But I always love you."

"I know you do." Victor swallowed the last of his gin and set the glass down, patted Andy's thigh, and leaned over for the kiss they'd both been waiting for. "Mmm. So when are you talking to Pop Quiz?"

"Oh Christ, that's right. Day after tomorrow. I'm going to make a pitch for a dance partner."

"No kidding! You have a project in mind?"

"Yes, I was thinking about it in the hotel. The only reason I haven't said catnip would you do this with me is I don't know if I can even do it myself. It's ballet. It's modern, but it's ballet. I haven't done anything remotely like it for thirty years. It is extremely unlikely that anyone will take me up on this."

All of these qualifiers were making Victor very curious. "Well, what the hell is it? Have I ever seen it?"

"It's from Matthew Bourne's 'Swan Lake.' Did you ever see that?" Andy could tell from the blank expression that Victor hadn't. He smiled. It felt good. "God, I love you. You're so fucking cute."

"I'm forty-two, I can't be cute."

"You're cute if I say you're cute." Andy leaned over for another kiss. "You want to see it? It's on YouTube. We can watch after dinner."

Victor shook his head. "Tomorrow. Tonight you sleep. You're going to take one of those pills whether you want to or not." He could tell Andy was about to say something about the vodka and the gin. The OTC sleep aids weren't potent enough to worry him. "Purple haze, remember?"

Andy regarded him for a few seconds. Those were often enough to mute the monkey brain. And probably a better choice than another drink. "Okay. Let's go eat."

April 2019

A little less than two weeks later, Andy had a letter in his hand. "I am buggin' out," he told Victor. "I'm sorry, you're barely through the door. I'm so freaked."

71

"Why? What happened?" Victor could tell Andy wasn't freaked in a bad way. "What is that?" Andy handed over the letter. Victor scanned it quickly, then read it more slowly. He was smiling when he looked up. "You've got a prince."

"Should I call him?"

"Have you looked him up?"

"This is, like, brand new. Dmitri brought it over after dropping Simka at Grandma's." Vicky and Sharon's daughter was also Dmitri's daughter. "He told me how he got it, but I get the idea he hasn't worked with this guy himself."

"Okay. Dinner, then we look him up." They found a ton of good stuff, including an Underground Cabaret routine the potential prince (a guy named Zach) had done with their very own Rory, which they'd forgotten all about because it happened right when preproduction got rolling on Tanith's movie. He'd done two other things with the Cabaret. The manager of the West L.A. studio where he taught was a fan. Rory was a fan. The director of the summer pro shows was a fan. Victor couldn't think of a single reason why Andy shouldn't jump on this prince, and said so. Andy said he'd think about it, and then he distracted Victor by starting something that didn't require much thinking.

Two days later, Andy still hadn't called Zach, he was still dithering about the whole thing, and Victor said, "Will you *call* the guy for fuck's sake? Before I leave for this stupid meeting, so I can make sure you do it?"

"Gaahh, yes, okay!" Andy got his phone. Found the letter. Dialed the number, halfway hoping nobody would answer.

Then he heard "Zach Tyler Dance" in an indisputably live voice, not a voicemail invitation. If Victor hadn't been standing right there he might have chickened out.

Instead he put the call on speaker and said, "So I got this letter. It was handed to me by Dmitri Vasko, who got it from his husband Patrick, who got it from his colleague Paul, who got it from his husband Kevin, who works with a young lady named Karen Scott. Any of that sound familiar?"

They both heard Zach say, "Karen's my girlfriend." He sounded stunned. "She snatched that off my desk and said what's wrong with you and then left. I had no idea. Is this Mr. Martin?"

"Call me Andy. Tell me why this has come to me via such a circuitous route. Did you not really want to do it?"

"No, I did. I saw that piece on Pop Quiz and I wrote that, and then I was afraid to send it. Karen saw it on my desk and asked me if that was a copy, if I'd sent it."

"Am I to conclude that you have a problem with follow-through?" Andy saw Victor's face, which said '*He* has a problem?' and gave him a middle finger.

Zach said, "No sir. I really don't. I just have a problem with believing people want to work with me. I can't believe you called me."

"Well, imagine how I felt," Andy said, amused. "I throw my little pity party for Sherry, it goes live, and a week later I hear from someone saying I'll be your prince? It was either going to be the most fun I've had since Berlin, or calling in the anti-stalker brigade again. We looked you up. That was Karen you were dancing with, last May?"

"Yes sir."

"And you danced in 'Democracy.'" Andy's voice grew brisk. "I checked with Alison Jarvet about that, and the studio head where you work. They say good things about you. Our friend Rory approves of you. I was talking to Victor, waving this letter around, and he said will you call the guy for fuck's sake. So, what do you want to do?"

"I want to dance with you," Zach said. "I never thought I'd get a chance to do that piece. If you're serious, I want to do it."

"Even though I am almost twenty years older than you and probably in need of serious remediation?"

"Only sixteen." Andy laughed. The potential prince hastily added, "I mean, yes sir."

"Willing to work at my home studio?"

"Yes sir."

"I will text you my email address. Send me your schedule." Andy disconnected. "I wonder if he has any idea where the home studio is. We could be in fucking Pasadena for all he knows."

Victor had been trying not to laugh for most of the conversation. "Sir."

"Oh my God I *know*." They both cracked up. "Okay, well, are you satisfied?"

"I'll be satisfied if you put that smart mouth to work on me before I go." Andy, phone still in hand, got the other around the back of Victor's neck and pulled him in for a hard kiss.

"Two minutes," he said. He sent that text with his email address. Then he sent a text to his lawyer: *Need license to perform prince & swan pas de deux from Matthew Bourne's Swan Lake.* Then he set the phone down on the nearest surface and unbuttoned Victor's pants.

Andy was checking in with his mother daily by email, and occasionally by phone. That was mostly so she could put his father on the line, and they all knew it. He told them about the Swan Dive. "Yeah, so this guy saw my interview thing and said he'd like to do it with me. He said he never thought he'd get to dance the prince. And of course I never thought I'd get to dance the swan. So thanks again for dumping me in dance class all those years ago."

"We had to," said Ronnie. "You on a sports field was a tragedy."

Andy tried not to laugh, tried to sound offended. "If I'd had more than one week of soccer things might have developed differently." *God forbid*, he thought. "So I know you can't fly out here when we do it on stage, but I'll make sure you get the video, okay?" They talked a little more about that project. "I'm going to Michigan in June for the 'Countdown 3' thing. As soon as we're done shooting my cameo I'm going to fly down to see you guys again for a few days."

"You're leaving Molly with Victor?" Eva sounded like she knew the answer. She'd been delighted when Andy and Victor adopted the dog, who had predictably fallen in love with her on the one occasion Andy's parents visited them in Los Angeles.

"Yeah, she hates to fly. I thought seriously about driving up to Michigan now that I've got my new hot wheels. But road trips solo aren't as much fun as road trips with Victor. Hey Pop, speaking of."

"What?"

"I was thinking we could drive down to Key West while I'm there. Your old buddy still runs that fishing charter out of there, right?" *And I will make it worth his while to cancel anything else*, Andy thought. He was completely prepared to play the fame-and-money card in this situation.

"Yeah, he does. Yeah, that would be great."

"Okay then. Anything you need, Mom?"

"No, honey, I'm good."

Andy knew the real answer was 'the rest of my life with this stubborn old man, please.' They were telling the whole truth in their emails these days. "All right. I'm going to let you go. Ping me whenever, for whatever, okay?"

"We will. Love you honey."

"Love you too. Love you, Pop."

"Yeah, I know." He almost never said it, but this time he did. "I love you too."

Andy put down the phone. His father sounded wrong. Not for the first time, Andy considered abandoning the Swan Dive, abandoning the movie, dropping everything. He could simply go to Miami and stay there until the end. But there was nothing he could really do, and his father would be furious, and he didn't know if he could stand being away from Victor for however long it might be. So, not for the first time, he did some deep breathing to settle himself down, and went to find something else to do.

Halfway through April, Victor was done with his local job and Andy was getting physical therapy. "Ow."

"Sorry, Andy."

"Don't apologize, I know it's supposed to hurt." *Maybe not that much*, he thought, feeling sorry for himself, and then got over it. "Carry on." The therapist did, and it kept hurting, but when it was over Andy had full range of motion back in his ankle. He walked the therapist out and sent her on her way with a word of thanks, then turned back toward the house. Victor was lying on one of the loungers, wearing nothing but shorts and that silver chain. Molly was in the shade behind him. The scar was less noticeable now, or it would have been without the irregular border of what used to be a rainbow-colored stag's head tattoo. "That's a nice tan you're getting."

"Thanks. Want to work on yours?"

"I think that's a fine idea." Andy went to the table behind the loungers, with a quick detour to pet Molly. Vodka and orange juice were set out next to a bucket of ice and a clean glass. Andy assembled his drink. "How many of these have you had?" Victor snorted and held up a single finger. The middle one. Andy stifled a giggle. "Enjoying your mini vacay?"

"So much. Is Zach back tomorrow?"

Andy set his glass down on a side table, pulled off his tee shirt, and stretched out on the other lounger. "Every other day till we do this thing. Can you believe he had the audacity to say if we don't do it that often he doesn't trust me to keep doing the work?" He picked up the glass again for a well-earned drink.

Victor didn't answer that directly. Of course he could believe it. Andy was having to work out more at the gym, and eat a lot more than he wanted, and even though he was loving this project he was bitching nonstop. "He doesn't want you to drop him."

"I'm not going to drop him!" Andy set his glass down with an exasperated click. "I *can't* fucking drop him, he's literally hanging on my fucking neck." Victor laughed. "Shut up. I know it was my own fucking idea. What the hell is wrong with me." He was laughing now too.

"Nothing's wrong with you. Anybody looking at you would think you're twenty years younger than you are."

"If I dyed my hair again." Andy accepted the flattery otherwise. The gym was a pain in the ass but he couldn't object to the results. They were quiet for a while, enjoying the sun and the sounds of progress from the renovation contractors working next door. The last time Andy checked, they were almost done with the flooring. Today's soundtrack sounded like maybe baseboards and casings. He swallowed the last of his drink, at least until the ice finished melting. "So did you read another play for me?"

"I'm working on the Henry plays. I don't know if any of those are going to be fun for this purpose. We might want to stick with the fiction plays."

"God knows there are plenty of those. I read 'King Lear' after reading that novel 'If We Were Villains.' Great book, you'd love it. And that play is definitely one of the better ones."

"Had an idea for that?"

"Dmitri and Patrick as Kent and Lear. Do you remember?"

Victor turned his head, making eye contact but only half focusing. Trying to remember the National Theatre Live screening they'd been to the previous year. He'd been convalescent, and it was a long night. He couldn't swear he'd stayed awake through the whole thing, even though it was Sir Ian McKellen. "Kent is the good guy, right?"

"The hero, I'd say. The one trying to keep the whole shitshow from falling apart."

"Okay." They stared at each other for a few seconds, both thinking. "So if that's a slash pairing, it needs to pre-date the story." Andy smiled, and Victor knew he was on track. "Before Lear loses his mind. Before he's a toxic asshole." Andy laughed. "Because Patrick would have words for us if he thought you really saw him as a toxic asshole."

"Yeah. The image would have to show why Kent tries so hard. The love they had before. Kind of elegiac."

"Is there a line for that?"

"'My life I never held but as a pawn to wage against thine enemies.' It's not a statement of love the way a lot of them are, but it's this deep loyalty." Andy swirled the ice cubes around in his glass, tempted to get a refill. *Do not turn into an alcoholic.* "And then there's a line after Kent is in disguise, to get back on the inside, right? And Lear says 'Thou serv'st me, and I'll love thee.'"

"Oh man." Victor winced. "That's like a knife in the gut, isn't it? Kent is doing this all for love, and the old bastard doesn't even recognize him, but he says he'll love him. Jeez, Andy."

"I know! I'm a sick son of a bitch!" Andy swirled the ice around again. "I know Dmitri can give me the perfect look. Wounded pride, broken heart. Maybe with Patrick turned a quarter upstage, hand on Dmitri's shoulder, this kind of dismissive, oblivious 'good boy' thing." Victor made a sound of approval. "I will owe Patrick an apology. It's really about his look, you know? That amazing hair of his." Dmitri's husband Patrick had a full head of silver-gray hair. "It'll be sexy as fuck in the first one, and then we can make it all rumpused and raggedy for the second one. Maria will have a fit when she sees him." The makeup artist he'd hired for the Tempest shoot had already said she'd love to work on any more like that.

"Put it that way and you won't have to apologize. You should let him know far enough out so he can let it get long." Andy giggled. "So, two images. Telling the whole story. Wow." Victor emptied his glass. "Have you ever gotten Patrick in front of the camera before?"

"No. I don't know if he's going to be flattered or horrified."

"They got that portrait done," Victor pointed out. "He is not a shy guy. He'll probably be all, why couldn't I be Prospero." Andy laughed. "So when do I get to see you and Zach do this thing?"

"Well, do you think the production will cut you loose for a minute so you can see us on stage? Alison offered us a slot in the May showcase."

"Or more accurately Alison begged you to do it." Andy couldn't hide the quick smile. Victor stood up, took the two steps over his husband, and leaned down for a kiss. "I'll do my best to get here. I'll shut down the production if I have to. But if that doesn't work, can I see it before I go?"

"Of course you can." Andy gave his hand a tug. Victor sat beside him. "Come in while we're running it tomorrow. We might have to do it twice," he warned. "Zach has a guy crush on you."

"Maybe. He's completely infatuated with you."

"Well of course he is. I'm the swan." Victor leaned in to kiss that laughing mouth. What started as simple affection quickly turned to something else. The kiss got hot and deep. Andy wasn't laughing anymore. They each had a hand in the other's hair. Victor had his other hand braced on the back of the lounger; Andy's was high on the inside of his husband's thigh. Victor moved his mouth to Andy's neck. Andy took a breath. "God almighty, Victor. We'd better get inside before any of those contractors decide to ask us a question."

"What, you don't want to do this out here?" Victor cupped Andy's cock. If this wasn't broad daylight, his hand would be inside the shorts already.

"Yes, I do." He really did. He wanted that hand, or that mouth, or whatever else Victor had in mind.

"But if we're going to put any porn on the internet I want to see it before it goes up." He located his tee shirt and pulled it over his head. Victor collected their glasses and they went inside. Molly followed them in. "Jesus I'm glad Consuelo isn't here today. It would be embarrassing to walk through like this."

Victor set the glasses in the sink, then locked the back door. "I wonder what it is about you," he said, stepping close to Andy. Backing him against the counter. Leaning in to put his mouth on that neck, his hands on those hips, pressing his own close so they could both feel the mutual arousal. Flat against each other, the way they'd wanted to be outside. "How can everything about you be so perfect." It wasn't really a question. He knew the answer. Everything was perfect, because everything was Andy. He moved his mouth up and across, into another deep and hungry kiss.

Andy wrapped one arm around Victor's back and set the other hand on the side of his neck. He let his ring rasp against that chain and felt Victor shiver. He slid his other hand down, into those shorts, pulling Victor tight against him. "Are we doing this right here?" he murmured, low and silky. "Like this?" Victor moved against him as if they were naked. Andy wanted that. "Take off my shirt." He lifted his hands, let Victor do that. "Take off those shorts." He got out of his own at the same time. Now they were skin to skin, a full-body kiss. Andy had his hand on Victor's neck again, metal against metal, and felt the reaction. It was irresistible. He went slowly to his knees, letting his mouth travel down that warm skin, listening to Victor's choked breath and the non-word he produced when Andy's mouth closed around him. The profane, desperate words that followed. *God, I love you*, Andy thought, eyes closed, savoring every second of the few minutes before Victor climaxed, one hand wound in Andy's hair and the other grabbing for the edge of the counter.

"Jesus!" Victor gasped for breath, looking down at his gorgeous husband. "Now you." He put a hand down, Andy grasped it, and Victor pulled him up. He didn't go down immediately. He took Andy in hand and kissed him again, working him nearly to climax before settling on his knees to finish the job. When it was over he stayed there on the floor, leaning his head against Andy's thigh. Andy had a hand in his hair. It was a few minutes before Victor looked up and said, "Never enough."

*Jesus, you're beautiful.* "All you have to do is kiss me." They smiled at each other. "I'll get the vodka if you get the juice." They put their shorts back on and went out to clean up.

Chapter 7
May 2019

Andy knew it was going to suck being home alone. It always did. But, as he told Dana, "It sucks extra hard now."

"Because you were all over each other for six solid weeks, and then it was still all-access here in L.A. for two months. What did you expect?" Her voice was sympathetic, but also a bit dry.

Andy glared at the phone. "I expected it to suck! Just not so much."

"Well, you know you can always come over here. Or we can come over there."

"I'm mooching around the B side like a stray dog," he admitted. "Every time they leave the front door open. I'm a mess. If this thing with Zach hadn't come off, I'd be in Michigan already."

"It's only a few more weeks. How's the Swan Dive going, anyway?"

"God, I love it. When the prince first made contact I thought, well he called my bluff, let's see. Then Sergei said he'd come out to teach it to us, and I thought okay. Then Zach turns out to be strong like bull and a really good trainer, and boy does he want this to work."

"No ego problems?"

"That guy barely even has an ego, as far as I can tell. He's awesome. I kept thinking, those first couple days when Sergei was here, he's going to crash. He's going to hit the wall. He's going to say what the fuck were you thinking, this is insanity. Instead he's like, one more time."

Dana heard the admiration in his voice. "That's what Rory said about dancing with him last year.

You know he's the one who got Mike Borodin rehabbed after 'Democracy,' when he had that stress fracture."

"I did not know that. Why did I not know that?"

"Because Victor, and the premiere, and the tour."

"Oh yeah. I actually heard from Mike after we got started on this. He said if nobody else had offered, he would have."

Dana hadn't heard that. "Aw, what a sweetie."

"Yeah but thank God for Zach because he's physically perfect for it. Mike would have made me look like a crone."

"That sounded kind of diva, Andy."

"I am going full diva for this. You know the story of the Bourne staging, right?" Dana made a sound of assent. "Okay, well. Zach has a body image problem because he *doesn't* look like Mike. Or me," he added. "He's a beautiful mover, but he's not the typical ballet boy. So he fully gets the wanting to be the swan thing. Mike already is the swan. He could dance it like a dream, I'm sure. The two of them should do it sometime."

"But not this time."

"Nope. This time is all about me me me." His phone's alarm pinged. "Ugh."

"What was that?"

"Time to eat again. If it wasn't for that one thing at the end, I could do this in my normal state. He's all, sir, you know this position is designed to minimize the stress on you but I'm still really heavy so please go lift a lot of weight because if I break your neck I'll never forgive myself."

Dana was cracking up. "Is he that heavy?"

"Not as heavy as he thinks he is, and it's all muscle and bone, but he's maybe ten pounds heavier than me. Normal me, that is."

"How sore were you the first couple of weeks?"

"Oh my *God*. Agony. I've got foam rollers in every room. I'm getting massages twice a week. But I have to say there's some satisfaction in going beast mode for once in my life."

"You? A beast?" Dana couldn't keep the skepticism out of her voice.

"I'll send you a selfie. And then I'll go and have the latest muscle-gain mini-meal. Jesus, I can't wait to live on fish tacos and champagne again."

"Go do it. We'll see you soon."

"Bye." Andy stripped down to his briefs, went to the master bathroom, and took a few mirror selfies to show off the new body. *Not bad for fifty-two*, he thought, and sent the best to Dana. Then he put his pants back on and went to eat. The next time he checked his phone there was a text: *Has Victor seen this yet? Because wow*

Andy giggled. *No*

*You may have to make a new episode when he's in town for the performance*

*Oh I plan to*

*LOL*


When Victor actually got a look at Andy with his clothes off, he said, "Holy shit."

"I hope that's a holy shit of approval and not of horror." Andy wasn't really in any doubt. Especially after Victor got his hands on him. "Uh, catnip, the performance is tomorrow and there are certain things I should not do." Victor didn't say anything. He kept doing things. "Oh, but," Andy grabbed for his train of thought, "we can do that."

About ten minutes later, Victor said, "I meant to say hi, sweetheart, I missed you." Andy cracked up. "You said you were working out. I knew you were working out. But damn." Victor peeled himself off his husband, shook himself like a wet dog, and looked around the room. "Oh really?"

"Dana's suggestion."

"No it was not."

"I promise. I sent her a selfie." Andy watched Victor go over to the camera and switch it off.

"You were already, what, eight pounds up when I left?"

"It's hard to see it day to day, I know. That look on your face was awfully gratifying."

Victor laughed. "You have to admit you made quite an entrance." Victor's flight got in at a horrible time for traffic, so they'd agreed a car service would pick him up instead of Andy. He'd walked into the quiet house, greeted Molly, and gone looking for his husband. Hearing the 'I'm up here' from the bedroom, he'd already been expecting some kind of reunion fun. He wasn't expecting the Olympian hotness leaning on the bathroom door frame.

"I'll make a couple of entrances tomorrow." Andy sat up.

Victor knew exactly what he meant. He couldn't wait. But he only got these two nights, and then it was back to work. "Do your fishnets still fit?"

*Oh really*, Andy thought delightedly. "I don't know. Let's find out."

"What, right now?"

"You've been gone for three weeks. If you need a little more recovery time we can eat first." With that gross insult, Andy went over to their huge walk-in closet and found the garter belt and stockings. Not the tights, because those had to come off for fun. "Yep, they still fit." He put on some high heels and walked back into the bedroom. The camera's red light was on again. Andy struck a pose.

"'How do I love thee? Let me count the ways.'" Andy sprawled on the couch in the green room, makeup smudged, covered with sweat, pants molting, feathers everywhere. Zach was looking at him with concern. Andy grinned, tired and happy. "You were great, Zach. This whole thing was great. Thank you so, so much. I hope every company in the country sees the video and thinks, shit, why is that guy not working with us."

"Thanks, Andy. Um, I think people are waiting for us out in the house."

"I know they are. Throw me a bottle of water?" They got themselves out of costume, cleaned up, and dressed. Andy's phone had been buzzing nonstop ever since he turned it on. He didn't bother looking at the messages because the people he most wanted to talk to were all right outside. Zach waited so they could walk out together.

There was an hour of meeting and greeting and congratulations, then a small mob of press outside the club. Andy singled out Sherry Martinez, the Pop Quiz reporter who'd set the whole thing in motion for him, while he and Victor waited for Zach and his fiancée Karen to join them. Then the four of them gave good face for about ten minutes before making their way through the mob to the waiting limo. Andy and Victor were home less than half an hour later. "So," Victor said, after they were undressed and while he could still think, "are you glad you did it?"

"Honey, I'd be glad for no other reason than that you came home to see me."

"When will you join me?" Those three weeks apart had felt more like three months. Victor knew it was because of the tour, and the following two months at home together. He'd been sending a ridiculous number of emails and texts, ostensibly about Shakespeare, simply because getting a reply to each one made Andy seem closer. He'd emailed their counselor, too. Her response amounted to 'what did you expect.'

Andy wished they had more than one night before Victor was gone again. He wished he didn't have anything else to do, that he could go with his husband tomorrow, instead of another two weeks from now. "There's Janis and her concert next week, and then I have the opening for the Tempest show at that gallery. The minute that's done, I'm on a plane with Molly."

"No chance I can get back for the concert. Tell everybody I'm sorry to miss it." He really was. Janis had been a backup musician for those two sets Victor did at Chrome, back in the day. Now she was a Grammy-winning recording artist, about to head out on a world tour of her own, promoting the album based on tango. "Tell her I've pre-ordered the album."

"I'll do that." Andy had his mouth on the back of Victor's neck. He nibbled on that silver chain. "You wore this just for me, didn't you."

"Every time I wear it, it's for you. You wore the jewelry for me."

"You'd better believe it." His wedding ring, the Australian ring on his right index finger, and the crocodile cuff. Both hands were on Victor, wrapped around from behind as they both knelt on the bed. Andy brought his right hand up Victor's side, keeping that cuffed wrist in contact with skin, loving the way his neck relaxed against Andy's shoulder. He raised up a little, wrapping his left arm over Victor's chest and changing their angle so he could kiss Victor's mouth. "God, this mouth of yours."

"You liked it yesterday." Victor was breathless, swamped with desire.

"You liked mine." They'd gone sixty-nine without discussion, Andy on his back with those high heels planted above the headboard. "Still want me to make an entrance?"

"Jesus, Andy. On my back. So I can see your face when you come."

Andy really hated dropping Victor off at the airport again. He knew he would. They talked about it on the way. Victor confessed to a record-breaking rate of self-abuse. After laughing, Andy confirmed that he'd been doing the same thing. "We had all that time, and it was like even on days we didn't fool around we *could* have, right? Then you're off in Wisconsin or wherever the fuck and I might not even be actively horny, but just thinking about you being there and me being here, it's like, gaahh."

"Exactly." Victor was smiling. "Sleeping with you, sitting around in the morning with you, hugging you, kissing you. I miss it all so much. And since nothing I can do to myself adds up to any of that, I spank the monkey."

"Like a couple of goddamned teenagers." Andy kissed him, because they were together and he could. "Thank you for being here. It was so great to know you were out there."

"It was so great to be here. I really wanted to see you do it on stage. You were gorgeous."

"Thanks sweetness. It felt good. I mean, it felt like torture for six weeks, but doing it felt good. Being able to do it. I had my doubts there for a minute."

"You played it off pretty well." A car honked behind them. "I do not want to get out of this car."

"Go be a movie star. I'll be there before you know it."

"I love you so much."

"I love you too. I'm not getting out of the car with you because if I hug you I might not let you go."

Victor nodded. He felt the same way. He reached between the front seats for his overnight bag, opened the door, then leaned over for one more kiss. "Hurry."

The movie shoot was going well, but Victor was counting the days. Even after that talk, he didn't know why it was so bad. Jonathan and Loretta noticed, maybe because he kept prolonging their regular evening get-togethers in the hotel bar. When there was still a week to go before Andy would be there, he finally thought *I have a problem.* He emailed his counselor Robyn again, asking if they could do a phone session. "I don't know what's going on," he said when they connected. "Since that thing in September, we've been talking about anxiety and whatever in the context of safety. Everything's fine with that. There is like zero threat level out here, our manager says the chatter is basically all green, Andy says there's absolutely nothing doing at home. It's not about safety. Why am I so freaked out?"

"There was a chance this would happen," Robyn said. "I think it's important for you to remember the scope of what happened to you in September. You say you're not anxious about your personal safety, or about Andy's. But because he's not there with you, you are anxious. Now connect that to September."

"When I got shot." She didn't say anything. Victor took the next step. "When I got shot because I put myself between my husband and a gun." Robyn made a sound that meant 'keep going.' Victor said

90

the thing he hadn't said before. "When I made a split-second decision based on the fact that I would rather die than live without him. Oh, fuck."

"And that hasn't actually changed, has it."

"Of course it fucking hasn't. So all of this mess in my head is that same thing? I'm living without him and I hate it, even though I know perfectly well he's alive and safe and on his way to me?"

"Victor. You've consistently downplayed the severity of that injury. Some part of you knows how close to dead you were. It's been less than a year, you've been working almost constantly since then, you did not take the time to process. I'm frankly amazed you've kept up with our sessions at all."

"You thought after the tour I'd bail out, didn't you."

"One of you was admitting to rage and anxiety. The other one wasn't."

"I'm still shielding," he said, on a sudden realization. "There's this whole category of stuff I could never tell anybody. I could not open up. I could not show weakness. I'm still not used to the fact that his love is unconditional."

Robyn didn't let him past that one word. "Do you think it's weakness?"

"No, I know, it's this Latino macho bullshit. Like going to the fucking Emmys less than a week after the shooting."

"Well, I wouldn't have put it quite that way." She sounded as if she might have wanted to laugh.

"Andy was so pissed. I said I wanted to go at a moment when he was so mad he went straight to, let's show all those motherfuckers. And then I wouldn't let him back out. We had people over that night, everyone was like were you out of your fucking mind. Walking the red carpet, you asshole."

He was laughing. It shouldn't have been funny, then or now. He couldn't help it. He'd survived, they'd both survived, and showing those motherfuckers hadn't made anything worse. Might have made things a lot better. "I was on that painkiller high, like, clearly it was not beyond me. Don't mess with Mexico. Whatever. I'm still glad we did it."

"Yes, I'm aware. How are you planning to handle it when Andy goes to Miami?"

"Because I can't be falling apart like this every time he has to live life out of my sight?" Victor sighed. "I'm going to lose him. I know it. He's ten years older than me. This business with his father is, like, *beating* at me because I see Eva about to lose Ronnie and I'm already imagining that same pain."

Robyn repeated the question. "How are you planning to handle it?"

"I am going to do my workouts, and do my relaxation shit, and talk to him every day and tell him I love him. So that no matter what happens he will know that I do."

June 2019

The end was in sight, and Andy was on the phone with Rory. "You're going to be out of town for ages," she said with disapproval. "Did Dana tell you she had to go back East too?"

"No," Andy said, wondering what that was about. "Something happening?"

"Family wedding. I was invited but when we saw where and who Dana said I didn't have to go. It was the branch of the family that starts speaking in tongues when they see my tattoos. So I wondered, since we're both home alone, if you want to come over for dinner. Bring Molly," she added. "I'd like to see you before you leave."

"I'd like that too. Tonight?"

"Sure!"

"What can I bring?"

"You, your dog, and whatever you want to drink."

*Which would be everything*, Andy thought. "I'm trying not to become a full-blown alcoholic, so how about some Pellegrino."

"That works," said Rory, immediately changing her plan regarding wine. "If we don't drink a bottle of wine we can have chocolate mousse, right?"

Andy laughed. "Yeah. I'll bring some of that, too." He rolled up at Rory and Dana's cottage at five. The front door was standing open and the pack was out in the yard. Molly jumped out of the car and went into a reunion frenzy with Precious the Malti-Pom, Oscar the dachshund, and Spike the cat. "You act like you haven't seen them for years," he said, amused. He took the carton of Pellegrino and container of chocolate mousse inside. "Hey cherubim! You leave the door open like that and all kinds of misfits can wander in. Where the hell are you?"

"Up in the loft, be down in a second." It wasn't a second, but no more than twenty before Rory ran down the stairs. "Hey! Wow." She studied him for a second. "You look great."

"Don't sound so surprised." He hugged her. "That thing with Zach was hard work."

"That was so completely beautiful," Rory said. "I knew it would be, but still. Worth the pain?"

"Every bit of it. But God, I never stopped eating. I haven't weighed this much maybe ever. Victor was like, whoa." Rory giggled. Andy stood back and showed off a little. He'd put on fifteen pounds of muscle for the performance. "He said, will your fishnets still fit, and I said, let's find out." Rory laughed. "Anyway I'm sure it'll come off fast, there's no way I'm keeping up with that. I'd be back to my old ways already if it weren't for that cameo."

"Oh, you're going to be the big tough grizzled boat captain, right."

"Thanks," he said with a hateful look for the 'grizzled' part. "I knew you were going to give me shit about that."

"Well, you didn't tell me you were growing a beard," she pointed out. "You're lucky the critters still knew who you were."

"They didn't even notice I was here. Molly was like hi guys tell me what happened! And they were all oh my God let us tell you what happened!" Rory laughed again. "Victor doesn't know about the beard." Andy made an 'eek' face.

"Please. I'm begging you. Be ready to take a picture of his face when he sees you." Rory looked around for her phone. "Can I send one to Dana?"

"Sure, why not." So they did that, and they laughed at the text Dana sent back, and they did a lot more laughing (even without wine) while Rory happily delegated operation of the grill to Andy. Then she started telling him about some of the submissions that had come in for the Cabaret's June show. "Is anyone actually doing 'Rodeo'?" Andy asked. "And are you doing anything?"

"Yep. I'm breaking out the strip and the tease again for 'I Cain't Say No.' There's a lot of business with petticoats." Rory took the tongs out of his hand so he wouldn't drop them. When he finally stopped laughing she said, looking satisfied, "This one may be the pinnacle of my achievements in striptease. Tomás and Vicky are doing 'Don't Fence Me In,' the David Byrne one. There's a ton of great shit going in.

The A-team is doing the Hoe-down from 'Rodeo.' Zach, Hiro, Ricky, Willem, and Mike."

"Fuck, I wish I could see that live."

"Mike choreographed it since Zach was busy with you. He's also doing 'They Call the Wind Maria' with Paula and the Kung Fu Flyers. Oh, and Sam and Mateo? They're doing 'The Good, the Bad, and the Ugly.'"

"Fuck! God damn this movie!" Rory laughed. Andy attended to the grill for a minute. "Last month we got a pretty good start on our two things for later this year. That was fun. Dmitri hooked us up. And Victor took a few jazz classes so we put some of that flavor in."

"Cool. Did he like it? Well, he likes dancing with you."

Andy gave her a sideways smile. "Yes, he liked it. We haven't even really started talking about what we might do for our Broadway thing."

"Plenty of time," Rory said, watching him, knowing there was so much subtext. She took another picture while he wasn't paying attention.

Much later, when the dishes were done and the kitchen was clean, Andy turned around to look for Molly. "Oh."

"Yeah." Rory was leaning on the counter. Molly was on the big dog bed with Spike. The other dogs were on the small bed. All of them were snoring. "It's kind of a shame to wake her up."

"She had all the fun today. So did I."

"If we'd been drinking we'd have an excuse for me to say, crash here tonight." She was watching him again. "Are you flying out tomorrow?"

"No, day after."

"Then crash here tonight."

It wasn't that late. The two residences weren't very far apart. Andy was coping pretty well with being alone at home. But not so well that the offer didn't strike exactly the right chord. "Got a spare toothbrush?"

"Okay," Rory said after a while, in the dark. "I have known you for, what, twelve years. I can't believe this is the first time we've slept together." Andy giggled. She added, "Good job not braining yourself coming up the stairs."

"It's a good thing we weren't drinking," he said. "I might not have been so alert to the clearance deficit. Thanks for this, by the way. I've been hanging in, but it's tough being home alone right now."

"I figured. I'm guessing there's no good news."

He sighed. "Well, since at this point what Pop wants least out of life is to die in a nursing home, then the fact he's not likely to is good news. It's these little strokes, though. Not enough to kill him, just enough to scare the hell out of Mom and fuck him up that little bit more. What he wants is the massive heart attack."

Rory slid her hand down his arm to his hand. He gripped her fingers. "I've always contended that a massive heart attack is the best way to go short of an actual nuclear bomb."

"Maybe so. A few minutes of pain and then you're done. None of this godawful years of torture bullshit." After a moment he said, "It does make me think, what else do I want to do in life. If eighty is the outer limit for being able to really do stuff, I've still got almost twenty-eight years to get shit done. And Victor will be only seventy. That doesn't sound so old now."

"Seventy is the new fifty. Look at Clint Eastwood. Richard Gere. Patrick Stewart. You're as fit as any of those guys were at your age, and better looking than all of them."

"You're biased." His tone was amused.

"Well, sure, but you're objectively good-looking and you know it. Remember when you were living with us and I was giving you shit about, well, everything. Did you know I took pictures when we were out on shoots?" She probably wouldn't have said that if they weren't here in the dark alone. She was a little surprised that she said it now.

"You took huh?"

"I sneaked phone pictures. Of you. When you were shooting 'City of Angels.' I was in love with Dana but I totally had a crush on you."

"Say *what*?" It was almost a squeak.

Rory laughed silently. "You were *gorgeous*, Andy. And you were so funny, and smart, and talented. You're still all those things. It never surprised me that Victor fell so hard for you. I couldn't believe nobody else did for all that time."

"Well, neither could I." Now his voice was dry. "In a city like Los Angeles, you would think the dating pool would be a little deeper."

"You didn't stick with anybody very long. That did surprise me. Because I knew you wanted to be with someone."

"I wanted someone like Dana." He knew she would understand what he meant. "I kept meeting people, but it never took long to figure out if something was going to work. It was never enough. I was never enough."

"Okay, what." Rory was annoyed. "How much else could someone fucking want?"

97

"That's what I thought!" He got a laugh with that. "But come on, you know what I mean. I wasn't the right age, or I didn't make enough money, or I wasn't tolerant about drugs, or I didn't want to swing. Lived in the wrong area. Drove the wrong goddamned car. Whatever. A lot of guys liked me, or at least they wanted to fuck me, but they wanted that plus a lot of other stuff. Victor's the first one who ever came in and said, you are everything I want."

"Well, thank God for him."

"I think that every day." They were quiet for a while, getting drowsy at last. "You'd better send me those fucking pictures." Rory snickered. She did send the pictures, the next day. Andy allowed himself to appreciate his forty-year-old face. It was, objectively, good. And now it was finally almost time to go. *Hi catnip had a sleepover with Rory. She says hi. Can't wait to sleepover with you. I love you, see you tomorrow*

He got a reply a few hours later: *Were you that shitfaced or was she being mama bear?*

*Mama bear. We didn't drink AT ALL, and put away that surprised face*

*Can't wait to see you and show you my O face*

*That's my favorite face*

*I know it is. I love you*

*Love you too. Get some sleep, you're gonna need it XOX*

Chapter 8

June 2019

Andy almost wished Victor could have met him at the airport, but apparently everyone in the state knew this movie was filming and was excited about it. A security escort collected him and Molly, delivering them to the hotel. Then they had to wait what felt like forever before Victor was due back from the day's filming. Andy tried to come up with some way to surprise him with the beard and finally settled for ambushing him in the bar. He had a few words with the bartender and waited for the text he knew would come when Victor got up to the room and found Molly but not Andy: *Hey baby where the hell are you I was hoping to have you in bed by now*

*Miss me? I missed you too. I'm down in the bar*

*You know I've got booze up here*

*Was not shocked to see that. Come on down, I have a surprise for you*

*Be right there.* Andy closed the text app, opened the photo app, handed his phone to the bartender, and got into position. Victor was looking for him as soon as he came through the door. Andy was in a dark corner, turned half away, trying very hard not to laugh. Victor didn't spot him. He went up to the bar and said something to the bartender. Andy approached from behind him. He pitched his voice low and silky the way Victor liked it. "You lookin' for trouble?"

Victor turned toward the voice, already smiling. Then he stared at the face and his expression changed to astonishment. "What the *fuck*."

That was completely satisfactory. "Think it's a good look for a boat captain?" Andy shut down his smile and narrowed his eyes a little, as though squinting into the wind. He hid his own astonishment at the unexpected but unmistakable reaction. *Holy shit he's turned on*.

"It's a good look for any fucking thing," Victor said finally. His voice was husky.

Andy sucked in a breath. Now he was turned on, too. He turned his head toward the bartender, holding out his hand, and failed to speak. The bartender set the phone in his hand. Now Andy managed a "Thank you," and tipped his head toward the door. Victor didn't say anything else, simply followed him out.

They didn't speak until they were in the elevator. "My God you look like Sean fucking Connery, with better hair." Victor grabbed him. They were still kissing when the doors opened on their floor. They stumbled down the hall, passing the security guy who hadn't recognized Andy at first, and to the door of their room. Victor's hand was shaking as he pushed the key card into the lock. He was completely floored by his own reaction. *Never knew I had a thing for beards*. He'd never seen Andy with more than a couple of days' growth. They were through the door. Victor double-locked it, said "Hi Molly" through the open door to the connecting room, and pulled Andy toward the bed. "Off. All the clothes. Off."

If he hadn't sounded so desperate Andy might have been amused. As it was, he had barely enough time to start the camera he'd set up before Victor was stripped and throwing back the bedspread. Andy got naked as fast as he could. Then they were kissing again, Victor's hands were all over him, they were on the bed, and now Victor's mouth was all over him. "Jesus, Victor."

"This body, holy Christ I've missed you." Victor wanted to keep kissing Andy, wanted to keep his mouth on that cock, wanted everything. He settled for a hand wrapped around both of them, his other hand holding himself off the bed. Andy was flat on his back with one hand clutching Victor's hair and his legs locked around Victor's thighs. They were both moving, both vocalizing, both out of control. Victor went first, losing his grip, and lunged for Andy's mouth again.

Andy pulled him tightly against his own body, loving those thrusts and that convulsion, letting it finish him. "God *damn*." They breathed together for a minute. "That felt like a fire hose." Victor snorted, then laughed silently into the side of Andy's neck. "Happy anniversary, honey."

Victor lifted his head. "Oh shit, it is, isn't it?" Seven years from the day they'd met. He kissed Andy again, rubbed his face against the surprisingly-soft beard. "I should send Tanith a thank-you note."

"I already did. I said, thanks for hiring me to do those pictures for your play way back when, and she wrote back with speaking of pictures I'd like to have a word with you about the stuff you hung in that gallery." The behind-the-scenes photos at the movie premiere had mostly been of the actors, in rehearsals or on set. The ones that had gone into the gallery show included a lot of photos of the crew. All were flattering, because Andy wasn't interested in making people look bad, but the collection made it clear how high the stakes were for everyone involved. "And I said now nobody will look at the timeline and say oh they must have thrown that together." Andy stroked the hair back off Victor's face. "We seem to be glued to each other."

"Works for me." One more kiss, then Victor shifted sideways and onto the bed. 'Glued to each other' was a good metaphor, not so great as a practical matter. "So when did you decide to go all Ahab on me?"

Andy snickered. "Well, I didn't bother shaving for a couple of days, or like four, and then when I saw how grizzled it was coming in I thought, huh. For the part," he explained unnecessarily.

"Not going to keep it?"

"I wasn't planning to, but then I wasn't expecting you to react like that." He was grinning at Victor's almost-embarrassed expression.

"Who else has seen it?"

"The girls next door. Rory, at our sleepover. And she sent a picture to Dana." Andy turned onto his side, propped his head on his hand, and gazed at his beautiful husband. "You look fantastic. Having fun?"

"Yeah, we're having fun." It was true, and thank God for that. If the shoot hadn't been fun, being without Andy would have been infuriating. "This is the silliest thing ever."

"Hey, you wrote it." Victor shook his head, smiling. He and his co-stars had written the treatment, not the full screenplay. Andy leaned in to kiss him again. "We're rehearsing my thing day after tomorrow, shooting day after that, according to the email I got. I get the idea they don't know I actually know how to drive a boat."

"Well, it's not on your resumé."

"Jeez, maybe it should be. I might consider doing something if I got to be out on the water. Wait, what am I *saying*, three days from now I'm going to be all, never again." Victor was laughing. "Speaking of boats, though, I'm taking the parents down to Key West when I go out there. It might be Pop's last chance. He sounded like shit on the phone. He's had another mini stroke."

"Oh, hell." Victor had been hoping the elder Mr. Martin might make it a little longer. "I'm sorry, honey."

"Yeah, me too. On the plus side, we're all saying things we've been needing to say, and he's probably not going to end up like his dad in a nursing home forever." Andy almost added 'and we'll be able to do our things,' but it sounded really wrong in his head. He hated that he was going to lose his father. He also would have hated having to cancel or postpone doing things with Victor. They were never going to have enough time to do everything they wanted to do.

Victor might have read his mind. He brushed his knuckles over that mind-blowing beard. "I'm so glad you're here. We're on our own for dinner tonight. Jonathan asked if you might want to get together with him and Loretta before you go to Miami."

"Love to." Andy leaned in for one more kiss. "I should take Molly for a walk. You want to order for us?" He sat up.

"I'll do that. Hey."

"What?"

"I love you."

Andy smiled. "I love you too." He swung his legs off the bed and went to get ready to take Molly out. They returned to the room before dinner arrived. After they ate, Andy handed his phone over to Victor. "Rory had a little confession moment while I was over there. It seems she had a crush on me back in the day. Took some pictures."

"When was this?"

"Twelve years ago."

"I don't know if I can take you at forty. You're killing me right here and now." Victor opened up the photos and scrolled through them slowly. "Yeah. Wow. No wonder."

"No wonder what?"

"No wonder she had a crush on you. Why didn't everybody?"

"That has *always* been my question for the universe!" When he got the phone back, Andy looked at the pictures the bartender took downstairs, laughed his ass off, and sent one to Dana and Rory. Their replies made him laugh all over again. Then Victor took the phone away, read the texts, made some threats, and took him back to bed.

During a break in rehearsal on the boat, Andy got his phone out for a couple of selfies. He sent one to his agent Raquel without comment. If anyone had asked him why, he would not have known, or maybe admitted to what he knew. Then he put the phone away and got back to work. On the return trip to the hotel he was checking messages when a reply text came in: *I fucking hate you*

*LOL what*

*Do you have ANY IDEA how many things have come in that I would have loved to send you?*

*No and don't care I have personal shit going on*

*Okay yes I know. So why did you send me this Old Spice Sex Machine picture?*

Andy almost dropped the phone, he was laughing so hard. Victor took it out of his hand and read the exchange. "That's a pretty good description. Why *did* you send it?"

"Well." Andy took a moment to compose himself and his thoughts. "Because of what's happening with Pop. Because I thought maybe it was stupid to slam that door when I'm still young. Or at least not incontinently old."

*Thank you Jesus*, thought Victor. "Anyone who can fuck like you is not any kind of old." They both heard a snort from the security guy in the front passenger seat. "Are you going to tell her you might consider something for around the time I start my thing next year?"

"Do you think I should?" Victor gave him a look. Andy shrugged. "Maybe if it was filming in England too. Because I don't want to be on the opposite side of the planet from you. Like, ever."

"I don't want that either. Tell her." He handed the phone back to Andy.

Andy read the exchange again, starting with the selfie. It really was pretty good. And not every part would be as boring as what he'd done on 'Vice,' or as stressful as what he'd done for Tanith. After close to a year of doing exactly and only what he wanted to with Victor, he'd probably be ready to try something new. *Hi Raquel thanks for the compliment. V agrees with you btw. He has a new thing starting next July in England. I would consider something same time same place. No sweet tame bartender tho I am OVER IT*

The reply came immediately. *I'm on it*

They had their dinner with Jonathan and Loretta the night after Andy's scene wrapped. Victor was on set for that, but the other two weren't. Jonathan spent most of the week finishing up some scenes on the Mackinac Bridge, and Loretta was filming a cat-and-mouse chase at Niagara. They all told stories for hours. Andy got caught up with Jonathan, who he hadn't seen since they were all in Miami two years before. That set off a round of gossip about mutual friends.

Loretta said, "It was nice meeting your friend Jim at your premiere. Do you see him often?"

"Hardly ever," Andy confessed, feeling slightly guilty about it. "I used to see him all the time when we were both working on the Cabaret shows. Then 'Vice' happened and we couldn't really go anywhere without the whole Secret Service deal, and he lives out in the Valley, and ugh."

"That doesn't mean anything to Loretta," Jonathan said. "She's only been in L.A. a couple of times." He lived there too, in a downtown loft. Loretta was still based in Miami.

"Okay," said Victor. "Well, imagine you're trying to get from Miami Beach to Fort Lauderdale at rush hour. Now imagine it's less than half the distance and takes more than twice as long. That's getting from West L.A. to the Valley, or vice versa." Loretta made an 'ugh' face.

"We still email." Andy continued to feel guilty. "Jim's out and about a lot. He still does video for dance events, and since Tanith's thing he's gotten some more gigs on indie films."

"He was nice," Loretta said. "Tell him I said Hi. And tell your parents I said Hi."

"I'll do that. Send me a sexy selfie for Pop."


The next night, Victor was in the hotel bar with Jonathan and Loretta when a text came in from Andy: *Hi catnip, we're heading for the Keys tomorrow. Everything good?*

Victor signaled the others. Loretta waved him away. He didn't actually leave, but turned his attention to the phone. *Everything's good except I miss you. How'd Ronnie like that picture from Loretta?*

*A LOT*

*LOL good. What are you doing tonight?*

*Dinner with Alonzo. His hubs Enrique just left to take his nephew to Puerto Rico for the summer, they're building houses*

106

*Good for them*. Victor was conscious of a totally unexpected pang of jealousy. When they'd been in Miami before, Alonzo had been 'my friend from my past life.' Only later had he learned that Al had actually been Andy's boyfriend back in the day. He told himself to stop it. *How does Al like your beard?*

*Shocked and appalled*

*How did your mom like it?*

*Shocked and appalled*

*LOL and Ronnie?*

*Laughed his ass off, which is the main reason I haven't shaved it yet. Don't worry, I'll let it grow again because I like the way you like it*

*Hmm maybe for Love is Blindness*

*Okay but not for the other one because I don't think I can pull off a drag routine with this*

Victor laughed out loud. *Are you really going to do it that way?*

*You said you wanted me to. You don't ask for much*

*I love you*

*I love you too. Be in touch once we get down to Key West*

Victor took a moment after they signed off. Thinking about that flash of jealousy, thinking about Andy with the beard and Andy in fishnets and heels, and feeling lonely.

"Everything okay?" Jonathan was watching.

"Yeah, sure. What'd I miss?"


Two more nights, two more text exchanges because that was easier than calling, and then Victor picked up a text in the middle of the afternoon: *Sweetheart if you can possibly get here I really need you we lost him*

107

Victor went straight to the location producer. They'd just wrapped a scene, they were ahead of schedule, and everybody liked Andy. They said they'd rearrange a couple of things and let him go.

He got to the little house in Shorecrest at half-past two in the morning. A light was still on. He'd texted from the set, from the airport in Buffalo, and again when they landed in Miami. Andy's reply to the last had been simply *door will be unlocked thank you I love you*. Victor walked into the quiet house, locked the door behind him, and set down his overnight bag on a chair in the kitchen. He was about to go looking for Andy when he heard that voice, a soft 'hello,' sounding hollow. Victor remembered that feeling. "Hi honey. I got here as fast as I could." Andy walked into his arms.

There wasn't anything that needed to be decided. There wasn't anything that couldn't wait for daylight. So they went straight to bed, where Victor held Andy while he cried, and then loved him until he could sleep. They were both awake again before eight, when the scent of coffee filled the house. Andy lay on his side staring at Victor. "They let you go."

"They might have realized I would come no matter what they said."

"Where's Molly?"

"Loretta's taking care of her. You want to talk about it?"

"Not yet." Then, after a moment, "Yes."

Victor had Andy's left hand in his right. Their feet were touching under the sheet. The ceiling fan turned slowly overhead, morning light was slanting through the shutters, and there was a cricket singing somewhere in the room. He remembered those details later. "I've got you," he said softly.

Andy's eyes flooded again. For once he didn't

try to hide it. "It was best-case scenario, really. We had two great days out on the boat with Bobby. Then yesterday morning Mom came to my room and said baby, he's gone. He went in his sleep. So I went to find the manager, and she called the people who had to be called. Mom and I went back to her room and sat with Pop. The manager brought us coffee with rum in it." He smiled a little.

"It's good you were here."

"Like you and your mom. Knowing it's coming doesn't really help, does it."

"No." After a moment Victor said, "Do you want to tell our people yet?"

"Let's wait. There's not going to be an autopsy or any of that. No funeral. Only a memorial service. Once that's set up, we can tell people." Andy watched as Victor sat up, reached for his phone, and sent a text to Jonathan and Loretta. He showed it to Andy: *Will send details on memorial soon appreciate keeping it quiet till then thanks.* Andy sat up, leaned forward to stretch, stayed there with his ribs on his thighs and his hands gripping his ankles. "That was just right, what you did last night. Everything you do is right."

"I've fucked up a time or two."

"So have I. Thanks for coming." Andy sat up again, twisting his back. "God I need to work out. I feel like a bag full of coat hangers." He heard a stifled sound and turned his head. Victor was trying not to laugh. "You'd be doing me a favor if you laugh."

"If you say so. Want to go get some coffee? With or without rum?"

"Maybe without rum today. Who needs rum when I have you." Victor scooted over, wrapped himself around Andy from behind, and kissed his cheek. Andy tilted his head back and rested his forehead against Victor's. After a minute he patted Victor's arm. They untangled themselves and got out of bed.

Victor stayed as long as he could, which wasn't long enough for him to be at the memorial. By his last night there, Andy and his mother were doing okay. Sufficiently okay to be arguing about where and when Eva would be moving. Sufficiently okay that when the house was full of Ronnie and Eva's friends, and Andy's friends from way back, both of them were able to smile and laugh and talk about the good things.

Nobody paid much attention to Victor, aside from greeting him, asking how he was doing, thanking him for being there. It had been a long time since Victor was the afterthought in a room. He didn't like it. He was aware of not liking it, told himself to button it down, made a mental note to talk about it with their counselor sometime.

Then Alonzo was shaking Andy's hand again, hugging him again. Both hands on Andy's clean-shaven face, a kiss on the forehead. *Fucking Alonzo*, Victor thought, envious because Alonzo had known Andy so long. He reminded himself that they weren't together. They'd been a couple off and on for five years, but Victor already had more of Andy than Al ever had. They'd never lived together. Al was married too, fifty-five and balding and starting to show a little bit of a belly. Andy loved him, Victor, and there was no reason to doubt it. There never had been.

Al said something. Andy said something back with a warm look. Then Al kissed him on the mouth. Closed mouth. Nothing unusual in this place, at this time. Victor had to turn his back, monitoring his breathing, slowing it down and shoving the surge of sick rage back in its box. *What the fuck is wrong with you.* He was facing somebody, somebody who said something, and Victor managed to respond in a way that must have seemed normal, or at least socially acceptable.

He thought Andy hadn't noticed. The house was so full, so loud, so busy. And the next day, Victor had to go back to Buffalo. There was a lot of rum the night before; Andy was asleep before Victor got in bed. In the morning he was already out in the kitchen with Eva before Victor woke up. It would have been good if they could have made love before he left, but they were out of time now. *We'll figure it out*, he told himself, not examining that 'we.' They had plenty of time before the movie shoot was over.

"I'm working on Mom. Pushing for Marina del Rey," Andy said while they were waiting for Victor's car to show up to take him to the airport. "But I probably won't get her out of Miami. She's got a lot of friends here."

"Into a condo, though, right?"

"Yeah, we've reached agreement on that. This house, for fuck's sake." Andy rolled his eyes. "There's such demand for housing, someone would buy it. But I feel like selling it is doing a disservice to the buyer. Nobody should even be living in this neighborhood."

"You could tear it down. Sell the bare lot. They'd have to build to the new code."

"And if nobody thought it was worthwhile, it could go back to nature. Good idea." Andy leaned over to kiss him as a car rolled in outside. "There's your ride. I'll be back in Buffalo as soon as possible."

"Don't hurry. Stay as long as Eva needs you." Victor didn't especially want to say that, because he needed Andy too.

"Honey, she's already tired of me. She needs some time to herself. Have I mentioned I love you? I love you. Get out of here before I make you miss your flight." Andy hugged him, kissed him, and sent him on his way. Watched him go, realizing Victor hadn't said 'I love you' back and wondering about that 'don't hurry.'

"Is everything okay?" Eva's voice, behind him. Andy turned around and made a 'what do you think' face. Eva shrugged. "I know, I know. Did you boys just say you think we should tear the house down?"

So Andy went back inside and they argued about that for a while. But it was a full moon, and that night the tide flooded the house. Eva was sweeping water out the front door when Andy squelched into the kitchen. "Really, Mom."

"I know, I know. Can you stay till we find me a place to live?"

There were a million texts and messages; it was even worse than after Victor got shot. Andy worked his way through all of them. He took charge of things, bullied his mother into eating, made sure neither of them drank too much. They both went out to walk on the beach. Andy carried a trash bag and picked up litter, bitching about what pigs people were. It made Eva laugh. The memorial made them both cry. "But it's good," Eva said afterward. "It's good he went that way. Before things got too bad."

"When he was happy," Andy said. "He had a good life with you."

"Yes he did." Eva leaned on him. "He was so proud of you."

"Jesus, Mom, stop it." They left the social club. Ronnie hadn't wanted any kind of religious thing. There were hands to shake, more hugs. Andy wished Victor were there to deal with the press lurking out by the street, and for ten thousand other reasons. He said what he needed to say, arm around his mother. Then he signaled his driver, and they escaped.

Chapter 9
July 2019

Andy landed in Buffalo with a long progress report to give Victor. They'd texted every day as usual, spoken on the phone regularly, and both said 'I love you.' Andy could tell something was wrong, couldn't imagine what it was, and was getting annoyed about it. *My father just died, goddammit, and what the fuck is your problem.* He couldn't say that. Didn't want to say that. Couldn't help thinking it.

The first week back was mostly okay. Molly was delighted to have both her humans. Jonathan and Loretta were attentive and kind. Andy came to the set some days, went out on the lakes some days, stayed in the room sometimes to follow up with various people and various projects. Victor made time for them to practice their two routines for the Underground Cabaret. They did some more brainstorming about the Shakespeare project. They had slightly careful sex. Andy let Victor take the lead, grateful for the kisses and touches. He wasn't feeling quite himself and didn't want to deal with whatever wasn't right. He got an interesting email from his 'Tempest' photo subjects Niall and Geoffrey, and didn't even mention it to Victor. The level of tension was sufficient that he thought it might set something off. Andy couldn't summon the energy to have a fight. He never liked to fight, always avoided it if he possibly could, but he was starting to think they were about to. About to have their first fight now, of all times, when he was tired and sad and only even where he was because he wanted to be with Victor.

Then the production moved to the Poconos, and the lid came off. Victor had a few long hard days. He was tired and cranky and very much aware that he was the problem. That made him defensive and snappy. At dinner, when they were both in their bedroom and Molly was in the room next door, Andy said, "Mom sent a picture of her new place. Alonzo helped her get moved in last weekend. Do you want to see?"

Victor set down his wineglass a little too fast, hitting the edge of his plate. He managed to catch it before it spilled, but that second of gracelessness set him off. "Could you not talk about him like he's part of the family?"

Andy's breath went out as if he'd been punched. He sat back, slowly refilling his lungs, eyes narrowed. *That hurt*, he thought almost calmly, *and why did you say it.* "He is part of the family. Mom's known him for as long as I have. He was my boyfriend. My lover. You knew I had lovers before you. I was forty-six fucking years old, Victor, when you showed up and said you wanted me." *After you landed in my life like a falling star and tore me open because you couldn't be honest with me or the world or yourself.*

"I did want you."

*Oh, past tense now.* Andy breathed through his mouth for a few seconds. "What exactly are you saying, Victor."

Victor pushed his chair back and stood up. "I'm saying don't rub it in my face. I didn't get your life. I didn't get to fuck whoever I wanted, whenever I wanted, as long as I wanted." He turned away sharply. He couldn't look at Andy. Not at that face, pale under the tan, eyes wide and wet. He couldn't believe he'd said those things. Had never recognized that resentment. *He gave me a fucking year, it's my own fucking fault, Jesus Christ what have I done.*

Andy studied Victor, standing with his back turned, vibrating with some powerful emotion. He was too angry himself to go on with this. Nothing was likely to help right now, except maybe space. "I am going next door," he said quietly. He couldn't quite keep the bite out of his tone. "Don't come in."

Victor didn't say anything. He thought if he tried, he'd break down. He heard Andy stand up, the soft clink of tableware as the chair was pushed aside. Heard him cross to the door and go out. Heard him speak to the security guy outside. Then the door to the adjoining room opened, and closed. Andy spoke to Molly. Victor remained standing, shaking, blinded by tears.

Andy curled up on the bed with Molly. She was doing that telepathic dog thing, as if she knew something was wrong. He was pretty sure he knew what set Victor off, and very sure if he'd tried to talk it through it would have turned into a genuine fight. *Got out, yay me.*

At the same time he was congratulating himself, he was wondering if this had been inevitable. He and Victor hadn't dug deep into the history. Maybe they should have, but there was never time. Or there was time, but it would have been taken away from one of the ten thousand things they wanted to do together that there already wasn't time for. They'd skated around it, for more than six years now. Would it help Victor to hear about Andy's past? About the long string of lovers, casual and not-so-casual? About the guy who beat him up twice in high school before Andy managed to turn that around, the guy who was still enough of a friend that he'd come to the

116

memorial? Would it help him to know about the long stretches of being alone, when being alone had seemed preferable to trying again? Maybe it would, Andy realized. He might have played that down. Might have thought it would make Victor feel like Andy wanted him so that he wouldn't be alone, not for himself.

Maybe Victor didn't realize that Andy had that same thought occasionally. He always dismissed it, because there was no chance Victor would be alone unless he chose to be. But because of the way they'd met, because of that first wonderful night and the disastrous morning after, because of putting Victor through that year of 'no' – even though it really meant 'not yet' – maybe Victor felt he was still being tested. As though his long-delayed coming-out made him untrustworthy. "Why are humans so complicated," Andy said to Molly. She licked his face. "Yes, we should be like dogs. I couldn't agree more. Thank you for being a huggable size."

He didn't expect to sleep. Simply lay there with his arm around Molly and his face against the top of her head, hoping he and Victor could fix this. He wished they had two dogs because he knew that guy needed something to hug right now, but it couldn't be Andy. Not till they were really ready to talk.

Somehow Victor got through the night without banging on the door, begging Andy to let him in. He had his own key, of course. He wasn't going to use it until he was invited to. Didn't know what Andy had said to the security guy, didn't want to admit they'd had a fight. *That wasn't a fight.* He was thinking of the morning after their first night, when he'd told Andy they couldn't see each other again. When he'd lied about why. Not even realizing until much later that he'd prayed Andy would take charge the way he had in the night. Make him talk, make him tell the truth, make him stay.

He couldn't tell Jonathan. Couldn't tell Loretta. No one else there was a friend, not that kind of friend. All their friends were back in Los Angeles. He couldn't get to sleep, had to somehow, he had a six o'clock call for another heavy day of filming and they had no time to spare now, because of his trip to Miami. *Thank God I went*, he thought, even though that trip had precipitated all this.

Eventually he turned off the room lights and got down on the floor in the dark, stretching, breathing. If he couldn't sleep, at least he could stay loose. The makeup people could fix his face in the morning. Tomorrow's work wasn't action. If he was slow it wouldn't matter. When the knock came it was still much too early to try to reach anyone in L.A., but if he sent a text now, maybe he'd hear back when he had a break. So he wrote to Dana: *Help, I've fucked up in a big way, tell me what to do*

There was no return text when Victor checked at noon. None at three, or at six. Finally, at nine o'clock, when they wrapped for the day, he was exhausted and hungry and dreading going back to the hotel, a message: *Four women here think you need to be kicked in the balls for about an hour*

He was in the trailer, letting the makeup person clean him up. *What did Andy tell you*

*Something about blaming him for having a life before he knew you existed. Trying to think if your timing could have been ANY FUCKING WORSE*

*I know, I'm totally in the wrong, he did not do anything wrong and he never has. Jealous asshole was jealous. How can I fix it?*

118

Four messages in quick succession, all from Dana's phone. The first: *This is Rory. Fuck you. You need to grovel a fuck of a lot.* Then: *This is Vicky. Do not even think of trying to excuse your behavior. Apologize.* Next: *This is Sharon. Talk to your counselor and figure out why the fuck you did that. Then apologize again. And grovel some more you prick.* Finally Dana again: *Whatever you do, DO NOT LET HIM LEAVE until you sort this out. Have you talked to him at all today?*

*I texted him six times saying I'm sorry. He didn't answer and now I'm terrified. I've been working for fifteen hours haven't slept what if he left while I was stuck out here.* He was hyperventilating a little.

"Mr. Garcia, are you all right?"

"Could you please have someone call the hotel and make sure Andy's there?"

She looked like she thought he was losing his mind, but she poked her head out of the trailer and spoke to someone. Victor sat there clutching his phone. After another minute the makeup person – *her name is Melissa, say thank you* – finished up. "I'll go see if they've heard anything."

"Thanks Melissa." Victor closed his eyes, waiting, wondering if his whole life, his whole *world*, was falling apart.

"Mr. Garcia?" Victor looked at the door. Melissa was there. "Mr. Martin left a message saying he'd have dinner ready for you."

"Does that mean he's there?"

"Oh. Yes, he's there, he's waiting for you."

Victor almost cried. He blinked, swallowed, sucked in a breath. "Thank you. I'll be out of here in a minute." First a text to Dana: *Thank God he's still here, I'll see him in about a half hour. Thank you and the girls for advice, I will follow all of it OXO.* Then

119

the text to Andy: *I'm so sorry sweetheart, please forgive me, I'll figure my shit out. I never meant to or want to hurt you. Please stay. Please don't leave me. I love you so much.*

Andy read Victor's last text and frowned. He called Dana, who he knew was standing by. "Why does Victor think I might leave him?"

"Well, you haven't talked to him all day and he hasn't seen you for twenty-four hours and that's what you do."

"The fuck?" He had no idea what she meant.

"Andy, remember back at the beginning when you cut him loose because he'd never had a real relationship before? Your husband is well aware you have a history of leaving. You would not have been single otherwise." Dana was Andy's number one fan, and she was squarely on his side in this. That didn't mean he was perfect. For full disclosure, she added, "Also I may have said don't let him leave. Meaning don't let you leave."

Andy didn't say anything for half a minute. He was flashing back to the night he'd asked Victor to marry him. Victor had said, later, that he would have asked Andy himself except, oh shit. *He thought, or was afraid, that I'd get bored.* As if that were possible. "Goddammit."

"How angry are you?"

"Right now? Not very."

"Good. I don't think Victor's angry at all. I think he's very afraid."

"Well yeah, if you said that, he probably immediately went to me packing my bags." Andy was a little annoyed about that. The thought hadn't crossed his mind. But fair was fair. Dana had mostly seen him in the 'failing at love' stage of life before

Victor. He hadn't, as a rule, talked about those failures seriously. It was so much less painful that way. He sighed. "Do you and Rory ever get into it?"

"Once in a while. Usually about trivial shit, and then somebody makes a joke and we get over it."

"And then what do you do?"

"Get jiggy." Andy laughed, as she knew he would. "Is this actually the first time you've had a fight?" He made a sound of assent. Dana said, "Probably overdue. Look, it's up to you how to handle it. But if you know what the trigger was, and you know it's something you can deal with later, maybe skip straight to getting jiggy."

"I know what the trigger was."

"Can you deal with it later?"

"How much of a beating did you girls give him?" As soon as he heard all four of them were in the room, Andy had started feeling a little sorry for Victor.

"We kicked him around pretty hard."

"Then I'll deal with it later. I'd rather get jiggy." She snorted out a laugh. Andy half-smiled. "Thanks for everything chica. Hugs all around."

"Let us know how it goes."

"I will." Andy disconnected. There was time to take Molly for a walk before the caravan returned.

He was set up in their main room when Victor came in. He looked exhausted, hollow-eyed and afraid. "Catnip," Andy said, "come and hug me now."

"Oh God." Victor sort of collapsed into Andy's arms. "Thank you for staying."

"I was not going to leave you. Never crossed my mind. The only reason I walked out last night was because you weren't rational and I was furious. One of us was going to say something unforgivable."

121

"I thought I already did."

"No, not quite. I mean, some of it was true. You didn't get my life." Andy did not point out that Victor got shot because somebody else didn't get Andy's life.

Victor heard it anyway. He'd heard it all night. The thought that the same darkness could have festered in his own heart was sickening. "You don't rub it in my face. I shouldn't have gotten bent about Al. I'm so sorry."

"I forgive you." Andy felt the quick intake of breath. He stood back a little, enough to get his hands on Victor's face and make eye contact. "I do. I love you. If you'll talk to our counselor about this, we don't ever have to talk about it again."

Victor's whole body sagged with relief. "I will. I promise."

"I think we *should* talk about it, mind you." He had to say that. "But not right now. Have something to eat, for Christ's sake, you look like you're about to faint." It was a cold meal, because it had been a hot day. Andy cut Victor off at two glasses of white wine, and only had one himself. He sent Victor in for a shower while he pushed the room-service cart into the hall and went to check on Molly. The security guy said he would take her for a walk after his relief came. Andy thanked him and opened the door to their room. "Oh." The security guy made an inquiring face. "It might get a little loud in here." A stifled laugh. Andy went in and double-locked the door.

He was sitting up against the headboard, naked, when Victor came out of the bathroom. The robe was over a chair a second later, and Victor was on the bed with his arms around Andy's waist and his head on a thigh. Andy dug a hand into his damp hair and tugged gently. Victor looked up. Andy said, "Don't you ever look at me that way again."

"What way?"

"Like you think I'm going to hit you."

"Is that how I looked?" Victor wriggled closer and sat up. Andy's hand slid to his neck, tracing around where that chain should be. Where it would be again as soon as they were done filming. "Maybe I thought you *should* hit me."

Andy made an annoyed sound. "What possible good could that do? Plus I'd have messed up your pretty face, and the producers would have put me in a cage, and the tabloids would have gotten hold of it. What a fucking disaster that would be. And besides, I probably would have broken my hand because what do I know about hitting people."

"Have you ever?"

"No. When I was getting beat up I was like this." Andy did a cowering thing with his arms protecting his face.

"What's the worst you ever got hurt." It wasn't quite a question. Victor barely knew why he asked. He still had his arms around Andy; now his face was against his husband's chest. An arm came around his ribs. Every little extra bit of skin-to-skin contact felt so good.

"You've taken a lot more damage," Andy said softly. "The guys who beat me up in New York cracked a rib. I went right back out on stage the next night, black eye and all."

"The show must go on."

"Yes it fucking must. So." He got his free hand on Victor's side, pushing him up and over. Victor looked up at him, surprised. Andy leaned over, planting his hands on the bed on either side of Victor's head. "You didn't sleep last night, did you."

"Couldn't."

"Yeah, it wasn't good next door either. I had all day to nap, though. Molly thought I finally turned into a real dog." Victor smiled. "I'm going to wear you out now. You're going to sleep."

"I'm not called till ten."

"Yes, I know." Andy lowered his head and rubbed his face against Victor's. Didn't kiss him, not yet, not on the mouth. Everywhere else, though. Hands and mouth all over that glorious pliant body, turning him, moving his arms and legs to get access to every inch of skin. Victor tried to get his hands on Andy a few times, but kept failing. Finally stopped trying to do that, and started trying not to come until Andy kissed him. He was dying for a kiss. Andy knew it. When at length he spoke again, it was to say, "How do you want me now."

"Any fucking way," Victor said. "Only kiss me."

"Are you going to come when I kiss you?"

*Oh Jesus.* "Uh," Victor managed. Andy laughed against his skin. Then he had Victor flat on his back again, lube in his hand, slickening himself and pushing between Victor's thighs. Stretching out on top of him with his mouth against the necklace tattoo at the base of Victor's throat. Victor felt teeth, strained against him, clutching at him. "God, Andy, *please.*" They moved together. Andy was making the same kind of noises Victor was. Victor was past thinking, beyond a sort of hazy surprise that he hadn't gone over yet. Then Andy's rhythm changed, he made a harsh sound, and finally, finally, he was kissing Victor. He uttered something, not really a word, absorbing Victor's spasm and the breathless cry.

Then he let himself go, saying "*Love* you" against Victor's mouth. Cock throbbing, mind blank for a moment. He'd gone harder than intended. He wasn't going to apologize. At least he wasn't inside. He pushed up a little, felt Victor's rib cage expand, saw the tracks of tears running down from his closed eyes. *Fuck.* Andy moved, detached himself, slid off to the side. Still with a hand on Victor, still with their faces close together. "Sweetheart. Did I hurt you?"

Victor shook his head slightly. "You kissed me." He was sweaty and sticky, and his back was aching. From fatigue, and from being pinned down during that climax. He needed to stretch. Didn't want to move.

"I always will." Andy kissed him again. "Be right back." He didn't want to move but his movie star deserved some after-care. He pried himself off the bed and went to the bathroom, came back with a warm damp washcloth to wipe off Victor's belly and legs. Gently applied a little oil to both of them. He felt a hundred years old, and he'd never seen his husband look so tired. Once he was in bed again he kissed Victor's cheek. "Going to sleep now?"

"Mmm. Did you actually bite me?" A faint smile.

Andy checked the damage. The answer was yes. "Didn't break the skin." He touched the marks on Victor's chest, collarbone, neck, mouth. "Melissa's not going to be in much doubt what you were up to tonight."

"What *I* was up to." Victor turned his face into the curve of Andy's neck, pulling their bodies close together again. "I love you."

"I love you too. Go to sleep."

The day of catnaps didn't keep Andy from sleeping. He woke before Victor. *Hmm, how to get out of this situation.* They were very tangled up. That didn't happen often, but after the past forty-eight hours it wasn't too surprising. He managed to extract himself without waking his husband. Went to the bathroom, placed a quiet call for room service, got more or less dressed. Left a note and went to take Molly out. When he brought her back, Victor was up and moving. Molly acted like she hadn't seen him for weeks. "This dog," he said, amused. "You are why people love dogs." He got down on the floor with her for a minute. "Always so happy to see me. Best girl." Still hugging Molly, he looked up at Andy. "I wish I could stay here with you today."

"You have to go be a movie star." He touched Victor's bruised mouth. "I really did a number on you last night."

"I wanted it."

"Yeah, I noticed." Someone knocked on the door. Andy went to answer it, and let their breakfast come in. Once that was managed, Victor stood up and went to wash his hands.

While they ate, they talked about the schedule for the last four weeks of filming. Victor was hoping Andy would stay for the entire time. They had two weeks more in the Poconos, then two weeks in the Catskills. "It should get easier pretty much by the day," he said hopefully. "Most of the action stuff is done."

"Well, you've got plenty of sneaking around to do." Andy thought about the shooting script. "Car chase, right? Some business in the lake."

"Always with the water on this series." The first movie had required action scenes in and around Long Beach. The second had extensive action out on the water around Miami. This time it was lakes. "At least this lake shouldn't be as cold as Michigan."

126

"Or Superior. Did I show you the face Molly made when she stepped into it?" Victor shook his head. That had been one of Andy's side trips, a 'see every Great Lake' thing. Andy went to get his phone. He pulled up the picture of a very shocked and betrayed dog. Victor stifled a laugh. "I sent this to Niall and Geoffrey. They got in touch after their book came in."

"That was nice of you, to put that together and send it. I don't know where you found the time."

"Well, my red-hot lover was out of town," Andy said lightly. "All I had was the Swan Dive to keep me busy." Victor rolled his eyes. Andy checked the time. "They have a contact there in the art business. He's also in the porn business, but on the legit side he says he wants to bring the Shakespeare show to London whenever it's done."

Victor sat back, surprised. "Well, wow. That's kind of cool."

"That's what I thought. Those guys showed him their book and apparently he said some nice things."

"I'm sure he did." Victor tilted his head. "Porn, huh."

Andy read his mind. "I'll show you his website when you get back tonight. It's amazingly classy." Victor laughed. Then there was another knock, and it was time for him to go. Andy said, projecting it to the hall, "He'll be right out."

Victor stood up, ran a hand through Andy's hair, bent and kissed him. "I love you. Thank you for last night. Thanks for staying."

Andy caught his wrist. "Hey. We are married. We stay, okay? That's what that means. I love you." Victor kissed him again. "And don't worry, I'm here for the duration. Go do your thing."

Chapter 10

Andy didn't want to talk any more that night.
Neither did Victor. Instead they looked at the porn
site, liked it enough to subscribe, got inspired, and
wore each other out. It was two days later when
Victor said, "I owe you such a huge apology."

"You've *been* apologizing."

"I don't even know how to. I don't want to
justify that awful shit I said. Vicky told me not to."

"What did she say?" Victor didn't answer, only
got his phone and pulled up the whole exchange.
Andy read it, thought *oh crap*, and said, "Now I feel
like a dick for not answering your texts. I'm sorry. I
wasn't trying to scare you. I'm sorry I did."

"I deserved it."

"No," Andy said, handing the phone back and
getting Victor's full attention. "No, you did not. You
said stuff, you regretted it, you apologized. Me not
answering was a dick move. By the time you sent that
first text I'd been thinking all night and I thought I
knew what set you off and I thought I knew how to
solve it. But you were working, and it wasn't
something we could solve via text, and I'm basically
a bitch. So I didn't send back even a simple, you
know, thanks for the apology we'll talk later."

Victor looked away. "I was so scared."

"I didn't mean to scare you. Look, I was hurt. I
wanted you to suffer a little. But not like that, so I'm
sorry. Come on, let's do this." He gestured to the
couch. Victor sat down. "There's a thing I thought of
saying to you way back on that first vacation, when
we went up the coast. When we got these." He lifted
his left hand, the one with the stylized eagle-feather
wristband tattoo. "As usual, we got busy doing other

things and I never did say this. But listen." He paused, gaze locked with Victor's. "You are the one and only, the one I wanted all my life, the one I will never leave." Victor's eyes were wet. So were Andy's. "Never. I love you."

"I love you." Victor's voice was husky, but not in the way that signaled arousal. Neither of them moved.

Andy cleared his throat, taking a moment to call up the thoughts he'd had recently. "We never talked much about my history. Maybe we should have. But we have time to deal with it now so here we go. I was with a lot of people. Not an egregious number of people, but from fourteen to forty-six is a lot of years. I left all those people, or they left me, for a lot of different reasons. When I left it was because I knew that person wasn't right for me. That's exactly what's *supposed* to happen." He thought Victor didn't quite understand. "Hang on." Andy went to the room phone, called down for a bottle of rum, and then leaned on the wall to wait for it. "Okay, case in point. Alonzo. We hooked up after I left someone I'd lived with for a while. I left that guy because he cheated." Victor's eyes narrowed. "Yeah, fuck him. Al and I never lived together, we weren't even in the same city for the whole time we were hooking up. We never knew each other in Miami, we met in New York, but when he moved back there he wanted me to come too so we could be together. I didn't want to live there again. Whenever I had to stop dancing, I wanted to be somewhere no-one knew me as a dancer."

"Honey," Victor said, suppressing a smile, "you fucked that up."

"Jesus, I know. It's all your fault, and thanks for that by the way."

"You're welcome. I left people too. I left them the way I left you, after one fuck."

Andy gave him a look. "That wasn't one fuck."

"No, okay. That was a whole night, the best night of my life. I hated walking out of your place. I sat in my car and thought, I have to go back up, would he even let me in, how the fuck do I excuse that. Explain that. I couldn't think of a way. There was my mother, dying back in Mexico, and she didn't know."

"I understand. I truly do." They gazed at each other for half a minute. Then the knock came, and the rum. Andy thanked the person delivering it, and double-locked the door again. He poured them each a couple ounces and handed a glass to Victor. "Salud."

"Salud." Victor sipped, grimaced, sipped again.

"So sweetheart." Andy sat cross-legged on the bed, staring at Victor. "I understand why you weren't out. You had a family reason, you had a cultural reason, and you had a career reason. You were eighteen years in and starting to get noticed. Not only fully employed, which is rare enough for someone like us, but noticed. When we first met I thought Jesus, what a fox, but I didn't even consider trying to vibe you because I was there to do a job and so were you."

"You didn't have to vibe me. I was looking at you with those lights in my eyes thinking, you know, why now. Why this one. I might never see him again. It was a horrible thought."

"And then you decided to get that tattoo."

"Somebody referred me to Lola, and there you were."

"At a funeral for a fucking cat." That event had been a community send-off for a respected adversary, rather than a beloved pet.

Victor almost laughed. "Standing there in those shorts. Looking the way you do, with that floodlight from the side of the building. It should have looked like a prison yard and instead it was like you were in a spotlight. I couldn't stand it. I couldn't resist. I had to try."

"And because I'm a tramp I took you right upstairs."

"You took me all right." Victor sucked in a breath at the memory. Then, because if they kept going this way they were going to be in bed again and they still had words to say, he tracked back. "Okay. So the reason I never had a relationship was because I put my career and my family first. I only fucked people I didn't care about, people who didn't know me. I felt like I couldn't risk getting to know someone, letting someone know too much about me." Except by the time he'd left he'd handed Andy his whole life. "Until you."

Andy remembered that too. "I told you not to sign that photo release."

"Maybe I thought if you blew it open, I deserved it. Maybe I wanted you to, so I would have to face it once and for all." Victor saw in Andy's face that he'd already thought of that.

"You were under a lot of stress. It's a very rare person who can be celibate. I couldn't." *Not until I had a reason to be.*

"How often," Victor began, then stopped.

Andy read his mind. "How often was I with someone only for sex?" Victor nodded. "A lot. It was always out in the open. Like, I can't stand doing this for myself for another day, are you okay with that. And occasionally the guy would say no, fuck off. But most times he'd say that's fine, me too. These were

131

mostly guys I already knew. I wasn't finding a new guy every time."

"I never went back to anyone. I was afraid if I did that, it would turn into a relationship, and it would blow open." Victor sighed.

There was something Andy thought he needed to suggest, even though he really hoped the suggestion would be rejected. "Do you want to open it up?" Victor looked startled. "I mean, if I live as long as Pop that's twenty-eight more years of only me. If you want to look outside for a while. Maybe you need another year."

Victor felt cold. "What are you *saying*."

"If you want to see other people. So you don't feel like you're missing out. You can do that. As long as you play safe. I want you all to myself, I always have, but only if you're happy that way." Andy hated to say it. Had to add, "One-time offer, though, catnip."

Victor stood up, paced halfway across the room and back. Went to the rum bottle and poured some more, tossed it back, coughed. Set down the glass carefully. He didn't know how to feel. Knew the offer had to cost Andy. Didn't know if Andy had any idea how much it hurt to hear it. "Can you honestly think I want anyone else?"

Andy breathed for the first time in what felt like a year. "No, I don't honestly think that. I'm sorry, I know that pushed a lot of buttons. I hate the very idea of it. But I needed you to reject it."

"You sadistic son of a bitch." Victor came over fast, wrapped his hand around the back of Andy's neck, and went in for a hard kiss. "I reject it. I reject the fuck out of it. I want you, always you, only you. You're everything." Andy dropped his glass. It rolled off the bed and hit the floor with a clunk. Neither of them heard it.

Andy caught up with Dana while Victor was out on location the next day: *This time zone thing is a pain in the ass, are you working?* She shouldn't have been working at all, but her stupid show had been especially stupid. Some essential material for the coming season had to be shot during what should have been everyone's summer break.

Her reply came right back: *Nope, on set but nothing to do for two hours at least. There seems to be a problem with the guest star*

*What kind of problem*

*The can't remember shit kind of problem*

*LOL sorry to hear that. So the boy toy and I have patched it up. Tell the others plz*

*Glad to hear it, will do. Some talk and not only action I hope*

*Lots of talk. Serious talk.* Andy thought briefly about summarizing it, decided that could wait till they were all face to face and possibly shitfaced. *Bottom line, he was tired, I was self-involved. This was at least half my fault*

*Andy you just lost your father, give yourself a break*

He was relieved to get her permission. *Yeah okay. Anyway things are good here. Did you and Rory decide on your Shakespeare characters yet?*

*We are leaning toward Midsummer Night's Dream because fairies*

*ROFLMAO naked fairies?*

*Uh let me read the thing again. You made those guys look so gorgeous*

*They are already gorgeous and so are you & Rory. Oh and when the whole thing is done, I may get*

*to take it to London. The Tempest guys know a guy*
*How fuckin cool is that?!*

*I know!!* Andy giggled, wondering if he should tell her the guy ran a porn site. That should maybe also wait until they were shitfaced. *I need to get in touch with the guy actually. So I'll let you go. Hope your guest star locates a functioning brain cell*

*If he doesn't we're going to be here till midnight. OXO*

*OXO yourself.* Andy disconnected, took off his reading glasses, and looked around to see what Molly was doing. Not surprisingly, she was napping, in the shade of a big evergreen behind the hotel. He was on the deck by the pool, under a patio umbrella. He squinted up at the sky, which seemed to be threatening rain. If it rained, the day's shoot would have to shut down, and Victor would be back early. The downside of that was they'd have to either cram the rest of today's work into another non-rainy day, or push the schedule. "Do not rain," he told the sky, and set down his phone. Molly raised her head when he spoke. "Hi best girl. Keep on napping. I'm going inside for a thing, be right back." As if she understood, she put her head down. Andy laughed to himself and went in for his tablet and a cup of coffee. When he returned to the deck, Molly came up to join him. He gave her a treat. "You are the greatest dog in the history of dogs. Yes you are. Yes you're a good girl. You're the best girl. Thank you for the kisses." Andy wiped his face. Molly settled behind his lounger with a contented sigh. He woke up his tablet and found the email from the porn guy.

Dear Mr. Martin,

Upon receipt of your subscription I took the liberty of contacting Mr. Niall Phelps, who assures me that your email address is in fact that

134

of the artist responsible for 'A Tempest.' Brilliant work as I'm sure you know. Have Mr. Phelps or Mr. Anand hinted at my thoughts anent bringing the work to London?

I have recently taken action to drag my mode of conveyance of filth at least two steps from the gutter. I can provide references from the legitimate art world. Not to put too fine a point on it, I want to be in business with you. Should this be of interest you may reach me at this address or at the number given below.

Yours most sincerely,

Reggie Galant

Niall and Geoffrey had, of course, been in touch. According to Geoffrey, the AT YOUR SERVICE website had recently undergone a major transformation. He also said that he and Niall were engaging Reggie to paint a portrait, which told Andy a lot. It was one thing for a writer of M/M romantic suspense to give an interview to a gay porn site. That had probably been a good business move. To then follow up by writing 'letters from the road' for the site's subscribers implied that Geoffrey liked working with Reggie. The interviews Geoffrey and Janis had given the site indicated that all three of those friends trusted the guy. Andy had enjoyed working with Geoffrey and Niall. Therefore, in the spirit of 'if they like him I'll probably like him,' he wrote back.

Dear Mr. Galant,

Thanks very much for your letter. Niall & Geoffrey did confess to showing you 'A Tempest.' Did they mention those pictures are going to be the centerpiece of a much larger show? My husband and I have been developing the concept and I'll start shooting when we get back to L.A. next month. All based on text from the plays, characters slash or gender-bent or otherwise twisted.

Incidentally Niall's Macduff is in London right now with his lady to help a local company develop the Scottish play complete with that sword fight. I threw them an idea that I think they're running with (has to do with Lady Macduff). I hear that's on the boards in October. Anyway whether they run with my idea or not I'm going to grab them as soon as they're in Los Angeles again and stage it my way. If you get a chance to see it I'd love to hear about it. I know N&G will be on tour with Janis by then.

Victor and I are very excited about hanging the show in London. He'll be in England next July to shoot a movie, my agent is trying to get me something at the same time. If that doesn't work out I'll be there anyway. Could go on about this for hours but won't. If this is a good time to chat feel free to text me.

Cheers, Andy

If Reggie wasn't busy there was a good chance he'd reply quickly, so Andy put his head back and closed his eyes, thinking about Red as Macduff and Mary as his lady, Dana and Rory as naked fairies, Dmitri and Patrick as Kent and Lear. He and Victor had a long list of other characters for the project, some already cast. They hadn't quite decided on their own. While Andy was working on the Swan Dive, Victor had been sending him completely insane suggestions. The last play Andy read was 'The Merchant of Venice,' and that gave him what he thought was the best pairing. Maybe he'd spring it on Victor tonight.

He was almost napping when his phone buzzed. He blinked, remembered where he was and what he'd most recently done, and picked up the phone. *Mr. Martin delighted to hear from you. I've seen that swordfight and while I regret that Mr. Phelps won't be on stage with Mr. Warner, I shall certainly go to see the play. Also very interested in this bit about Lady Macduff. What did you propose? Yrs R. Galant*

Andy put his reading glasses back on and replied: *Hi Reggie, call me Andy. I suggested Lady Macduff doesn't die. If you see Red's wife you'll know why. It would take a regiment to put her down. Find 'Green Darkness' videos via Underground Cabaret Dance Theater*

*I will do, the minute you decide you've had enough of me. How big a show are you proposing?*

*At least fourteen other pairings, a few solos. Some of the pairings may be only a single image, some may be two. Already working on a pairing from Lear, two images. Had to give advance notice on that because my Lear needs to let his hair grow*

*Well if that isn't tantalizing I don't know what is. Is this one of your dance friends?*

*No he's my accountant but he's married to a dance friend.* Andy took a moment to imagine the reaction.

*I'm quite sure no-one on earth wants a picture of my accountant. Will you and your smashing husband appear in the show? I'll confess I've recently secured a copy of your recent film*

*Yes we're planning to be in it. Have to get him to sign off on the characters. How did you like the movie?*

*Between you and Ms. Vaughn I've now taken a deep dive into tango. Can't dance a step but nor can I stop listening. Perishing to paint you, frankly*

Andy wasn't expecting that. The R. Galant paintings offered through the site were all more or less erotic, but not explicit. The kind of thing, actually, that he'd love to have. They had another offer to paint them, from someone whose work they liked but whose style didn't bring the heat. *What did you have in mind?*

*God's teeth do you mean to say you'd actually contemplate it?*

Andy laughed. *What are you doing for Niall & Geoffrey?*

*After the wedding scene, in morning coats at the Oxford station. In return G is sitting for a nude*

*I like your style. Let me talk to V about that. He always says we don't have enough pictures of me*

*I'd agree with that*

Andy wondered what Victor would say if he suggested sending one of their porn clips to this guy. Or extracting an image, or two. He giggled to himself for a few seconds. Then he forwarded the selfie he'd taken out on the boat, during rehearsal for his cameo.

The reply made him laugh out loud again. *Bollocking hell you might have warned me, a shock like that could kill a man*

*V likes the beard*

*Of course he bloody does, who wouldn't? Is it a fixture?*

*Did it for this movie. Based on reactions it will have regular return engagements. The only thing he likes better is, well, find our Mein Herr video from Berlin*

There was a nearly-six-minute delay before the next text from Reggie: *Christ on a plank*

Andy cracked up. Molly came around to investigate. "Molly, don't tell Victor but I'm teasing a pornographer. Oh hell I'll show him the whole thing later anyway. Oh my God." He giggled some more. Finally he wrote: *Sorry, had to laugh for a minute*

*Gave me time to tidy up*

*LOL.* Molly stuck her head in between Andy and the phone to see what was happening. He couldn't stop laughing.

*I don't suppose you'd consider an interview for the site? I could link out to the movie's page or anything else you like*

*Will show this to V tonight and if he laughs too I'll be in touch about interview. We haven't done much press since the tour*

*My dear man I've just found a story regarding your recent loss. Sincere condolences and hope I haven't offended*

*Not in the least, I needed a laugh like that and hey, I started it*

*Well that's true*

Andy snickered again. *My dog wants some attention so I have to go. Nice chatting with you*

*You as well.* Andy disconnected, set the phone down, and sighed. For a few minutes he'd almost forgotten about his father. "Well, Molly. I said you wanted some attention, which is almost always true. So let's go for a walk, okay?"

He showed the whole exchange to his husband later, with reassuring results. "Do the interview," Victor said after handing back the phone. "You haven't done one since your thing with Sherry, aside from that little bit after your performance."

"Well, and a minute outside Pop's memorial. Anything you want me to keep quiet about?"

Victor was now on his back on the bed, head and shoulders hanging down off the side, trying to release the tension that always seemed to settle between his shoulder blades. He lifted his head to study Andy for a few seconds. "Maybe don't mention we made a whole porn movie. A one hundred percent plot-free porn movie." He put his head back down, listening to Andy laugh.

"Yeah, ours is one hundred percent porn. I'm going to tell somebody you need a proper massage. And after dinner I'll work on you a little."

"Yeah. Work on me." Victor's tone was slightly suggestive.

Andy gave it right back. "I'd work on you now if they weren't knocking on the door any minute with our food."

"Maybe it'll be cold food again." Another laugh. "You want to give me a hand up from here?" A second later Andy was straddling his thighs, linking arms, pulling him up and into a kiss. They stayed there until the knock came. "God, I hope that's cold food."

Andy had something else he wanted to run by Victor, but he waited until after dinner, and after working on Victor's neck for a while. "How's that, baby."

"That's better. Much better, thanks." Victor was now face-down on the bed, naked.

Andy rested a hand on his ass. "You're still getting a proper massage tomorrow. Short day, right? Back here by four?"

"Right. And the day after, we're off to the Catskills."

"Can't wait to see you and Loretta doing some dirty dancing."

"You should teach us how to do that lift." Victor sounded drowsy, which wasn't actually surprising.

"I could try." That was not the first time he'd heard the suggestion. He kept hoping it wasn't serious. He'd only done the lift himself once, and that was a long time ago. "So before you fall asleep on me, I had a little too much time this afternoon after that whole thing with Reggie and I had some sick ideas and I did some stuff. I promise I won't do anything with it unless you say it's okay. But God it was fun, and that would be why I basically pounced on you and let your food get cold."

"I didn't mind," Victor pointed out, somewhat more alert. "I don't recall objecting at all." He rolled over. Andy's hand stayed on him. "Are you going to pounce on me again?"

"I shouldn't." Andy retrieved his hand. "You need some rest. Anyway I went to a few of our episodes and pulled some images. Non-explicit. I kind of want to send them to this guy."

Victor was fully awake now. "Why?"

"Because you're beautiful. Because I love the way you look when I'm kissing you. Because us kissing set off an explosion, but we both survived, and now every time we kiss for the world to see it's like this giant 'fuck you' to everybody who thinks we shouldn't." That wasn't everything. What Andy had in mind was a photo essay that could go on the public part of the site. Only kisses. But those videos had always been intended to be private, so he wouldn't take it any further unless Victor said he could.

After a moment Victor said, "Show me what you did." Andy went to get the laptop. The videos themselves were behind several layers of security, but the new files were under a single password. He only had three images so far. Going through the videos took time. One was from Australia and showed Andy on his back with Victor a millimeter from kissing him. They were framed from the chest up, lying in a patch of late-afternoon sunlight, both in need of a shave. Both smiling, with their eyes open. The second image was from Japan, that very late night after karaoke. Sitting up with Andy in front. Framed from the ribs up, showing how Victor was holding him. Both with their eyes closed. Andy's head tipped back, faces turned toward each other, Victor's mouth lightly on his. The third image was from their 'Mein Herr' rehearsal, arguably the one that started the whole X-rated project. Andy hadn't been in makeup, but he'd been wearing the hat because it was a prop for the dance. He'd pulled a frame from near the beginning, after Victor had him exposed, before it got to the point where their expressions alone were explicit. They were framed from the waist up. Victor's head was tipped back in this one because Andy'd had those high heels on, his own head bent for that open-mouthed kiss. "Jesus," Victor said after a while. "No wonder you pounced on me." Andy laughed. "Are these so hot because I remember exactly what we were doing?"

"Well, we could ask Reggie."

Now Victor laughed. "Do you want to do a whole photo essay like this, is that what I'm hearing?" Andy nodded. "What would you call it?"

"Probably 'Besos,' don't you think?" Victor seemed to agree. "So you don't mind if I run this by him?"

"No, I don't mind. These are great." He stifled a yawn. "Not bored. Only tired."

"Get ready for bed, sweetness. I'll tidy this up." Andy leaned in for a quick kiss.

Chapter 11

Andy spent most of the next day working on the photo essay. It was late in the afternoon before he remembered the Shakespeare idea. They were mostly packed for the next day's move to the Catskills, and Victor was getting a massage. "So what did you do today," he said after he was face-up on the table.

"Worked on those photos for quite a while. Dug around on Open Source Shakespeare in 'Merchant of Venice.' I think I may have our characters."

"Oh yeah?"

"Antonio and Bassanio." Victor made an interested sound. "There are words of love but there's also this heavy subtext. Antonio is willing to ruin himself for Bassanio. A lot is implied."

"Yeah, it is. You have the line? Or is it more than one?"

Andy referred to his notes. "A couple jumped right out at me. Bassanio, 'from your love I have a warranty.' And Antonio, in the same scene, it's 'do but say to me what I should do,' like God, anything for you. Which is basically how I feel about you." Victor laughed under his breath. The massage therapist did a good job of pretending not to listen. "But there's also Bassanio doing the lady and the tiger thing with Portia, 'my blood speaks to you in my veins." Victor made a yummy sound. "Then in the big quality of mercy scene Antonio goes 'say how I loved you, speak me fair in death.' I kind of like those better."

"I do too. Do you know how you want to stage them?" Victor already had an idea. "If people know the play they'll be all wait, what? But I think Bassanio making some passionate approach and

143

Antonio kind of oh my God, is this for real, is he talking to me."

"In other words, exactly how it was at the beginning." Andy's voice was dry. Victor laughed. "Okay, great. I'm sure you can think of some tragic scene for the Antonio line."

"We need a third person, someone to be Shylock with the dagger. You with your chest bare. Me kneeling, our hands clasped, this desperate kind of eye contact. Like, if this is our last moment, please see how much I love you."

"God, you guys," said the massage therapist. She sounded so distraught that both men laughed. "You're making me cry. You need to stop talking about this," she told Victor. "Till I'm done."

"Sorry." Andy leaned over to kiss him. "I'll go take Molly out."

There were a lot of extras to wrangle for the Catskills part of the shoot, and more than a dozen supporting actors. Victor and Loretta had multiple scenes to shoot together, Jonathan was in the mix, and before long all of them were thinking they would never get done in time. The whole setup was so entertaining they didn't really care. "If we have to stay another week to wrap this thing, are you going to be able to hang out?" Victor asked, about four days in.

Andy looked up, surprised. "If I was frowning it wasn't because I'm ready to go. It was because my Botox is wearing off." Victor laughed. "Reggie is, quote, gagging for it. He wants that photo essay and he wants it now. I told him I'd do the interview as soon as I'm done with that. I've been in touch with a bunch of our potential subjects for the Shakespeare thing. Tanith is pestering me. I have too much to do right here, once we're home it's going to be like we kicked open an anthill." He swallowed some wine.

"What's Tanith pestering you about?"

"Her big dance concert. She's been working with Alison on this noir nightclub thing. Everybody is in it. Apparently Tina, the second camera person from the movie?" Victor nodded. "She started drawing this graphic novel and Tanith wrote the script, and a couple of the characters are based on us. Well, the look is based on us. Tanith says this concert is like a staging of musical scenes inspired by the graphic novel, but there might be a movie in it. So she really wants us to see it live on stage if possible."

"Well, there's no way this nonsense will go three extra weeks. Go ahead and get us some tickets to closing night and then you can tell her we'll be there." Victor finished his dinner and sat back. "Based on us, huh."

"Yeah, but we're bad guys. Like, really bad guys, and we get killed early on. She said it's 'Dick Tracy' meets 'From Dusk Till Dawn.' And the cherry on top is, Vicky kills us." Victor laughed again. "She's Santanico Breathless Pandemonium Mahoney. Except of course she will not be singing in the movie." Victor cracked up. Vicky had many talents, but singing was not among them. Andy finished his wine, grinning. "I cannot fucking wait to see this book."

"Jeez, me neither. The one she had out last year was gorgeous. What's the latest from your mom?"

"She's pretty well settled in. A couple of her friends live close by, they get together. She's meeting people. You think we could go out there for Christmas? And then I could go back in April for her birthday."

"Sure, of course." Victor had a thought.

Andy read his mind again. "After our Broadway thing."

"It's about time we decided what we're going to do for that, isn't it?"

"Plenty of time, catnip. Let's focus on these two dances for the Cabaret, and getting your movie done. When's the big dance scene?"

"Tuesday. Loretta really, really wants to do the lift." They'd referenced a scene from 'Dirty Dancing' (and 'Mrs. Maisel') by having Victor and Loretta undercover at a Catskills nightclub, pretending to be performers, and forced into dancing on stage. Victor and Loretta both knew how to dance, so the salsa choreographer hadn't faced much of a challenge. But if you were doing a scene like that, everyone wanted the lift, and she hadn't put it in. Something about potential liability. They'd argued to no avail.

Andy had always known he would give in if they persisted. "Then I guess we'd better get out in the lake tomorrow." He located his phone and sent Loretta a quick text. A few minutes later the phone buzzed. He picked it up and laughed. "She says why not tonight."

"Well, why not tonight?" Andy made a 'really?' face. "Yeah, really."

"Okay. Put that wine down. No, Victor, you can finish it later. Believe me, you're going to want it." He took the glass out of his husband's hand. "Get in your swim trunks."

They met Loretta out on the dock twenty minutes later. She was in a boogie-boarding wetsuit, so excited she was bouncing. "Oh my God Andy, I've always wanted to do this. Can I do it? Will I kill Victor?"

"We are going to go slow," Andy said. "I don't think you'll kill Victor. You are going to crash a lot. Ready for that?"

"Yes, Andy." She stood there with clasped hands, looking very serious.

"Okay, let's do the plane first." Andy put three beach towels down on top of each other, and a yoga mat on top of those, for a cushion. Victor stretched out on his back, and they worked on the flying position until Victor consistently had the hand placement and Loretta consistently held her balance, even when Victor went from bent to straight arms. "That's so good, you guys. So his hands will be right there all the way. You jump straight up, he'll carry you the rest of the way, you dive over his head. The hard part is stopping the dive at horizontal. Everybody in the lake." Once they were all in the water he gave them the same disclaimers they'd already heard about a dozen times, warning them that Loretta would be slippery. "That suit will help a lot but you're probably not going to get it tonight, okay?"

"Okay." Victor and Loretta both looked disappointed.

"Don't feel bad. This isn't easy. Let's focus on getting the elevation here where there's a safe place to fall." *Sort of safe*, Andy thought, cringing at the potential for disaster. They really wanted to do it, though, so he carried on.

Forty minutes of splashing, shrieking, and laughing later, they all hauled out onto the dock. They were resting there when they heard Jonathan. "Nobody told me there was a pool party."

"Jonathan, Andy is trying to teach us the lift. I am so, so bad." Loretta's voice was husky from shrieking.

"She is not bad." Andy was flat on his back on the dock. He'd done his share of lifting, getting Loretta to really commit to the jump, challenging her with his extra two inches of height. "This shit is fucking difficult."

"Yes it fucking is." Victor was sitting cross-legged, rolling his neck.

"I'm sorry I'm so heavy," said Loretta, who weighed about a hundred and twenty pounds.

Victor gave her a look. "You are not heavy. That's not why we're crashing."

"Did you really think you'd get it in one night?" Andy sat up. "And with a very not-the-best coach? We can work on it some more tomorrow."

Jonathan said, "Same time?" Everybody else looked at him. "Well, I could spot you. Then Andy could watch and see where the problems are."

"If you could help spot them, we could do this in the gym with the crash mats." Those were in place for fight rehearsals. Andy would have suggested it already if he hadn't thought it was a really bad idea to risk Loretta and Victor both falling. "And with their shoes on."

The following night, things improved fast. In the well-lit gym, with crash mats and a tall strong spotter on each side, Loretta and Victor both had more confidence. They actually got up to the lift four times. "That is amazingly good!" Andy said, when he finally made them stop for the night. "Next time you'll be able to hold it."

"Are you sure," Loretta said, wincing. "Ay, my hips. It's a good thing I'm not in a swimsuit for the rest of this thing."

"Sorry about the bruises, honey." Victor had a few himself.

"What the hell is going on in here?" They all looked around, as guilty as teenagers caught with a bong, to face the location producer.

"Um, we're practicing?" Victor said. "For the dance scene?"

"Ms. Bautista, are you injured?"

"No! I'm fine. I'm tired, that's all. We're done here, sí?"

"Sí amiga, go take a hot bath and get some rest." Victor kissed her cheek.

The producer let her go, studying the three men with narrowed, suspicious eyes. "Mr. Morris, I don't believe you and Mr. Martin are in the dance scene."

"Nope." Jonathan didn't give her anything else.

"Andy was giving us some professional pointers," Victor said, reminding the producer of his husband's bona fides. "And Jonathan didn't feel like staying in his room alone. Right, Jonathan?"

"Right." He said the one thing the producer would probably appreciate. "Hey, it's better than all of us being in the bar."

She gave him a sideways look and flapped her hand. "Fine. Whatever you're up to, at least everyone's still walking. But get out of here now." They all made cooperative noises and headed out.

They didn't say a word until they got up to their floor of the hotel. "Oh my God you guys, I haven't felt so busted since my mom caught me with a six-pack." Jonathan was laughing as quietly as he could. Andy and Victor were cracking up too, stifling it. "You think you can get it tomorrow? If she catches us again, you're toast."

"We'll get it tomorrow," Victor said.

Andy said, "You'd better."


Victor had a break the next day. A morning scene with Jonathan went perfectly and wrapped early, leaving him with hours before he had another scene to do with Loretta. It wasn't enough time to go back to the hotel and molest Andy, so he only sent a text saying how much he'd like to. Then he composed a text to Dana and their other three best girlfriends: *Hi girls. I know Andy's been in touch. He's been apologizing as much as I have but I know I've still got some penance. With you too because I worried you. I'm sorry. I've been in touch with our counselor to let her know what happened and will follow up when we're in town. Thanks again for being there for us. OXO*

He wasn't really expecting a reply. Vicky and Sharon were probably at work; Dana and Rory might be doing any one of a dozen things. But he got a text back from Vicky: *I'm skiving off work today for a rehearsal. Dana told us you guys straightened it out. Sorry we smacked you so hard*

*Don't worry, I felt like I deserved it*

*Eh maybe not. Dana had us a little worked up. You know when she calls Andy big brother she really means it*

*Yeah I know*

*But I was there when you saved his life. I mean not that exact second obviously but I saw him covered with your blood, and Stan there trying to plug that godawful hole in you, so I know how much he means to you. Whatever was going on this summer, I know you'll solve it. Sharon too*

Victor had to take a minute. He hadn't expected this level of absolution. *Thanks for that chica. We are blessed to have friends like you. Oh FML here's that damn producer again, back to work for me OXO*

*Stay out of trouble. Don't drop Loretta*

*OMG you're not supposed to know about that LOL*

*I don't know nothing, get off the phone OXO.* Victor put away his phone, feeling like a great weight had been lifted off his heart.

The following Tuesday, Andy left all his other projects and went to the club location with the crew. He had to see if Victor and Loretta pulled it off. All he took with him was his camera. The location producer gave him another suspicious look when he ambled in. "You're not in this scene." There were already close to fifty extras milling around, in colorful summer-resort evening wear.

Andy was in jeans and a tee shirt. "No I'm not. Do you mind if I hang out and watch?"

"You have to be outside the main doors, behind camera three."

"That's fine. I won't get in the way." He'd been on set so much with this production, he could almost read the director's mind. "Pictures okay?"

"Don't post anything."

"I won't." With that, he strolled off to the craft services area to see about some coffee. Behind his casual face, he was nervous. If this went bad, it was probably his fault. If one of them got hurt, it was definitely his fault. If they crashed in a non-damaging way that they could use for comedy in the scene, which he knew they were prepared to do, he could live with it. Any other kind of crash, not so much.

Fortunately, they didn't crash. Nobody was expecting the lift, that was for sure. There was a genuine gasp from the crowd of extras when they made it, and genuine cheers at the end of the dance when they took their in-character bows. They got offstage while Andy was busy texting Dana: *OMG Victor and Loretta totally nailed the lift and even if the rest of the movie sucks this is AWESOME.* He looked up and the location producer was standing there, arms crossed, tapping her foot. "What?"

"Did you have something to do with that?"

"With what? Did something happen?" She gave him a hateful look and stalked off. *Dana this producer knows I was in on it. She wants to cut off my head and use it for a punch bowl*

A reply pinged in: *Eww gross Andy are you laughing your ass off right now?*

*Yes but on the inside for plausible deniability oh shit they're setting up for another take*

*Fingers crossed. Did you get video?*

*You know I did. TTYL OXO*

*OXO*

They did the dance scene twice more, after a lengthy conference with the director and producer, who was on her phone the entire time. Probably with a lawyer. Whatever everyone said, the outcome was that the dance was performed with the lift. Andy suspected the third take was punishment, or maybe they were hoping for a good outtake for the special features. The second and third times through, all the production assistants had eyes on the extras, because more than one oh-so-casually had a phone out and nobody wanted this to leak. Andy took some stills. Somehow Victor and Loretta managed not to crash, though it was a near-run thing on that third take.

After that it was time for the lunch break. Andy deliberately stayed away from Victor because he knew if they got caught talking about the dance, which they would have, they were all in big trouble. They exchanged some nonsensical texts. Andy found Loretta and avoided her laughing eyes while sincerely congratulating her for her sensational performance. He called the hotel and arranged for flowers to be sent to her room, and for some therapy gear to be sent to his and Victor's. Then they had a backstage dialogue scene to do, which also went for three takes. Andy found a place to lurk back there, halfway listening to the dialogue and halfway concentrating on watching them move. They both looked fatigued, but not damaged. He finally relaxed.

"Fucking hell, my back," said Victor, much later.

"Actually hurt, or just tired?"

Victor winced his way out of his jeans and shirt, trying to tell the difference. "I don't know. Probably tired. I can't believe we did that with less than a week to train." He checked himself out in the mirror as if he thought he should look different. The tank top and briefs didn't tell him anything new. The body underneath said 'I hate you.'

"I can't either. Lie down, I got you something." Andy waited for Victor to arrange himself face-down on the bed, then laid the already-warm electric heating pad on his husband's back. He listened to the whimper of pleasure and got to work massaging Victor's legs. "You were fantastic. Truly, truly great."

"Did you get video?"

"Yes I did, and some bitchin' stills. You want Molly?"

"So much."

"Hop on up, Molly. There you go, good girl." The dog lay down next to Victor. He draped an arm over her back. "I can't believe those fuckers made you do it three times."

"I can't either. What's for dinner?"

"A very antioxidant super greens salad with filet Oscar and as much red wine as you want."

"I love you."

"I love you too." He leaned over to kiss one of those bare legs. "Let me know if the heat is too much."

"Mmm." Victor fell asleep almost instantly. Andy turned the heating pad off after fifteen minutes and sat beside him, checking email and catching up with people, until Victor stirred again.

Andy heard the sounds of imminent dinner in the hall. "Good timing, catnip."

August 2019

The night the shoot wrapped went very late. Not because filming ran long, but because there was an epic wrap party. They'd essentially been filming the thing backward, so the scenes in the Catskills were all in the first third of the movie; the tone had gotten progressively lighter and sillier. Jonathan's character had met the woman who played his love interest in the Poconos and Niagara, whom he'd had to rescue in Michigan as part of the big dramatic climax. Loretta and Victor's characters had established the relationship they'd started in the previous movie, complete with love scenes, misunderstandings, and a low-voiced but operatic Spanish-language argument out on the dock. Two of the bad guys had been dealt with, three more had gotten away to create mayhem later in the story. All five of those actors were still on location the last day, though all of the extras had been released. Somebody put on some music, and nobody shut them down.

Andy and Victor sneaked out at about two in the morning. Back in their room, Victor said, "That was fun. If they never do another one that'll be great for all of us to look back on."

"You don't think they will?" Andy was doing the bare minimum of tidying-up, because they weren't checking out the next day. The security guy had walked Molly and she was on the couch, half-snoozing. "You know this thing is going to make money." The first two certainly had. Andy kind of hoped they would do another one. This one was the first that would have Victor's name above the title with Jonathan's. And about a million times as many people would see this as had seen 'The Ghost of Carlos Gardel.'

"Yeah, it'll make money. You never know." The co-stars hadn't tried putting together a new treatment this time, or maybe it was more accurate to say 'yet.' Jonathan already had a contract for something that started the following March, Victor had his thing starting in July. "It couldn't start filming until eighteen months from now, earliest."

"It'll take them that long to develop a script." Andy went to the sliding glass door and stepped out onto the balcony, listening to the sounds of the Eastern forest. "It's nice out here."

"Yeah, it is." Victor stood by the bed for a moment, looking at his husband's naked back and those long bare legs. He should have been too tired to be thinking what he was thinking. But they didn't have to get up early, or at all. "I'm so glad you could be here."

"Me too." He was also glad when Victor came up behind him, put his arms around Andy, and kissed the back of his neck. Andy wrapped his arms over Victor's. "I'm still trying to get my head around you not working for eleven months."

"Me too. I've never not worked for that long."

"Me neither." Andy turned his head for a kiss. "We're still going to be busy as hell." Victor laughed under his breath. They did have a lot of stuff in the works. "We're taking Loretta home with us, right?"

"Yeah, I don't like the sound of that ex of hers. I wonder if Jonathan would like to hang out a little. Maybe we should try to do another treatment."

"You totally should. You know he's going to be in town." Andy turned to face Victor, going for a long hug. Soon there would be kisses, but right now he wanted the hug.

"How are you doing, baby." It was quiet.

A sigh. "I get the emails from Mom and it's always this jolt. This, not exactly a surprise, just oh yeah, Pop's not there anymore. She'll never be telling me what he said or what he did. Once in a while there's a hint. Like, I went this place your father used to go, I saw his friend so-and-so, we had a good talk. I don't know how she does it."

"It was that way for me, for a while. Tía Susana would write to me and there was nothing about Mama and I'd be like why, and then I'd remember." They were quiet for a minute. "I hope we make it for fifty-four years."

"I would literally be one hundred years old."

"So?" Victor leaned back a little to smile at Andy. "It's a nice round number." Andy was gazing at him with something like sadness. Victor's smile faded. "I know. We'll never have enough time. Infinity wouldn't be enough time. I'm sorry I ever wasted a second of it."

"You didn't. We haven't. Kiss me."

Chapter 12

Andy probably would have sent the email to Reggie anyway, but maybe not right then. He'd pulled the image that first day, after Reggie said that thing about a painting. He was sitting on the couch in the room, laptop open, Molly snoozing beside him, watching Victor sleep. Thinking of the time when Victor had surprised him with a framed 20x16 photograph of the two of them, a photo that a friend had taken during their first trip together. It hung in their bedroom now, and it always would. But there were other walls, and he didn't really think either of them would ever get tired of being reminded of the tour.

He opened the image again. It was a still from their performance of 'Mein Herr,' in Berlin. One of the showiest poses, when Andy had his upstage leg on Victor's shoulder. His upstage arm was extended up and back; Victor's upstage hand was braced on Andy's ribs. Victor's weight had been split, with his downstage leg back, standing far enough away that Andy's downstage leg was at the same angle. Their downstage arms were linked to stabilize the position. The overall shape was of the letter 'X.' *You had me*, Andy thought, remembering how many times they worked that through to fix the balance points. He wrote:

> Hi Reggie I've been thinking about the whole 'paint me' thing and have a counteroffer. Specifically, 'paint us.' I want to give V a present. If you can work from a photo I'm attaching one. Name your price.
>
> Cheers – Andy

He attached the photo and sent it off. It was already afternoon in London. He set the laptop on the side table and stretched out (to the extent he could) on the couch, rearranging Molly along his side. The next thing he heard was "You're going to regret sleeping there."

Andy pried himself out of the pretzelated position he'd settled into, laboriously sat up, twisted his back and rolled his neck. "You are so right. Fortunately we don't have to travel today. Maybe they can find us another massage person."

"Why were you on the couch?" Victor poured them both coffee. Apparently room service had delivered while Andy slept.

"Woke up, had some thoughts, wanted to deal with them. Didn't want to wake you up by crawling back in bed."

"I wouldn't have minded." He never did. "In fact, for the record, I like it when you wake me up. Because that means I get to go to sleep with you again." He brought the coffee over to the couch, sat beside Andy, and kissed him. "Good morning."

"Good morning. God, thanks for this."

"You're welcome. Happy first day of vacation." They smiled at each other. "What do you want to do today? Aside from a massage."

"Lie by the pool. Eat breakfast. Fool around with you. Not necessarily in that order."

"That's kind of a full agenda for the first day of vacation." Victor was grinning. "Should we start with breakfast?"

"Probably, yeah. You're going to need your strength." The day's program ended up being: breakfast, fool around, shower, pool, massage, an early dinner with Loretta, fool around again. Andy crashed first, and crashed hard. Victor quietly got himself packed and ready for their departure, then took care of most of Andy's stuff. He was curious about the early-morning thoughts, but they had plenty of time to talk about that.

*So much time*, he thought while he was walking Molly. So many days to look forward to that could be almost exactly like this. Maybe they really should buy the neglected property on the other side of their duplex, tear it down, put in a guest house and a pool. Be obnoxious Hollywood millionaires. It was only a single-family home, and their other two properties already served five households. No one could reasonably object. That was something else to talk about. Eventually he lay down beside his sleeping husband, and simply gazed at that beloved face until he fell asleep too.

Victor, as usual, managed to nap on the flight home, reclining in the semi-private first-class seat with Molly in his arms. After almost ten hours of sleep, Andy couldn't have napped if someone had offered him money for it. He'd checked his email before packing up his laptop. Not too surprisingly, there was a message from Reggie:

> My dear sir,
> Your proposition is most welcome. Nearly any proposition from you would be. Leaving that aside, price is a function of size (size does matter). And that said, yes I can work from a photo, yes I'd bloody kill to paint that picture, and when do you want it.
> I don't suppose you've much need to economize but the price is also very much negotiable if a limited-edition print run could be made available through the site. Your husband is

not the only person who might like that image on his wall.

Will look forward to your thoughts on these variables.

R. Galant, still hyperventilating

Andy replied by text, after consulting his records regarding the surface area of various bedroom walls and after Victor and Molly were in nap mode: *Hi Reggie size would be 30x40, when would be Christmas, and print run depends on what V says. I want this to be a surprise so can't answer that yet. Quote me as if no prints, and then if he says prints are OK we could work out a royalty*

A reply came back fast with a quote Andy thought was more than fair. It even included shipping to Los Angeles. By the time Victor woke up, the deal was made. Andy was reading some Shakespeare. He'd chosen one of the funnier plays, just in case Victor caught him giggling.

The 'Countdown 3' production had run over, but not by a full week. Victor, Andy, and Molly were home and officially beginning their very extended vacation only six days later than expected. Their first night back, Andy and Victor settled Loretta into the guest room, went upstairs with Molly, pulled the door closed, and cracked up. "I feel like in loco parentis," Andy said.

"You're loco all right. You're not old enough to be her father."

Loretta was thirty-four, so, "Horrifyingly, I am. But seriously. I hope she closes her door. I'm thinking, how loud can we be before she hears us? Am I going to start to say something really vile and then choke?"

Victor giggled. "Maybe you'll like keeping it quiet. Didn't you ever do that thing where you're messing around and someone's in the next room and if they catch you you're in a heap of trouble?"

"Well, sure." Victor laughed again at Andy's isn't-that-obvious tone. Then he stopped laughing because Andy's hand was in his hair and they were kissing as if they'd been separated for months, instead of embarking on this wonderful, glorious almost-a-year together. Victor broke for a breath after a few minutes, staying close with his face against Andy's. "You still like the beard, huh."

"Oh my fucking God."

Andy laughed under his breath. "I need to get a haircut."

"Don't do that either." Victor kissed him again, hard enough and long enough that he almost forgot what he meant to say. "Go full Renaissance for me."

"Oh, for Antonio? I'm not sure they actually wore their hair this long." Andy stopped talking because they were on the bed. Victor was stretched out on top of him, elbows planted beside his head, both hands in that hadn't-been-cut-since-May hair, making sounds into Andy's mouth and moving in a way that said they might have waited too long to get their clothes off. *Oh no you don't.* Andy exerted himself a little and rolled them over. Once he was on top he tore off his shirt, unbuttoned Victor's, then put his mouth on that tanned chest. Spared a glance at the silver chain, thought *later for you*, and headed south. Unbuttoned, unzipped, pulled the jeans off and then the briefs. Heard the hungry, desperate sound. "Jesus, Victor." Replaced Victor's hand with his own, and then with his mouth.

"Fucking Christ!" Victor surged up, felt teeth scrape, heard Andy's apologetic sound, didn't care.

The heat, the pressure, the tongue. "God *damn* oh my *fuck* Andy —" The next sound wasn't a word. It wasn't quiet, either. Andy held him in his mouth till the end. Victor felt his throat work and surged again. Then he lay there gasping, breath gradually slowing and evening out. "Was that as loud as it sounded in my head?" Andy laughed, mouth still on Victor, and finally let him go. He brushed his bearded face against Victor's groin, heard a muffled whimper, and smiled to himself.

"Yes it was. You have officially blown our cover. Or I have." He watched Victor laugh silently. "What do you have to say for yourself, Mr. Garcia."

"I'll say anything you want."

"Tell me what you think I should do with you now. I have a few ideas of my own."

"I'll bet you do." Victor had his eyes closed, but he felt Andy get off the bed. Heard another pair of jeans hit the floor. Heard the nightstand drawer open. "Are you going to get in me?"

"Yes, I think so. This way?"

"This way. I want to see your face."

"I want to see yours, too. I want to watch you watching me fuck you." A cushion hit the bed. Victor still had his eyes closed. "Push up, catnip." Victor arched his back, lifted his hips. Andy got the cushion under him. "You look like someone who spent three and a half months making an action movie. Pretty ripped, there."

"Speak for yourself." Victor had his eyes open now, because Andy's hands were on him, and he wanted to see everything. But Andy was sitting back on his heels between Victor's legs. "I can't see you."

"See what? This?" Andy raised up, watching Victor's eyelids come down, his lips part, his breath catch. "You want me to fuck you with this?"

162

"Jesus, yes." Andy stayed where he was, one hand working Victor with the lube until he was half-hard again and Andy was about to explode. He bent to put his mouth on Victor's thigh, felt both legs jerk, listened to the sounds of renewed arousal as his mouth traveled from one leg across the groin to the other. "Andy. You're killing me."

"Well, how do you think I feel, looking at all that." A hand on himself now, plenty of lube, and a push. Victor moaned. Andy felt a little light-headed. *I might not even get in before, hell.* Victor arched, pushing back, taking him. "My fucking movie star." Deeper, faster, panting.

"Yours."

"Jesus, Mary, and Joseph." Victor half-laughed. "We are a blasphemous pair of filthy fuckers." Victor laughed out loud. "Oh damn don't do that, don't laugh."

"Don't make me laugh. God *damn* Andy."

"Yes. God damn me. Holy fucking hell, no, Jesus *God* I love you, I want to fuck you all night, I can't." Andy bit his lip, pulling Victor's thighs tight against him, watching his husband's ecstatic face and rigid cock. "I want to fuck you till you come again. Come again. Victor."

"Andy. I love you. Touch me."

Andy changed his hand and arm configuration because he really wanted to see that. Right hand on Victor, wrapped around Victor. Holding still inside Victor because those hips were moving again and there he went, Jesus, "God, you *beautiful* thing." Andy's voice on top of Victor's cry. He hoisted Victor up, reaching under for that cushion and shoving it aside. Then they were down and flat, Andy tight against Victor and thrusting hard, coming hard, saying something loud and unbelievably vile that

Loretta would surely hear. Finally spent, Victor's legs crossed behind his back, gasping into each other's mouths. They were both quiet for a few seconds. Then Andy performed a slow backward collapse, disengaging, ending up on his back, stretching out his legs. "I should clean us up."

"Eh. We can get in the shower."

"You first." Victor was apparently close enough to bite an ankle. "Ow." Some more activity, Victor finding the cushion and tossing it somewhere. An offended snort from the floor. "That was Victor, Molly, he'll apologize later."

Victor was laughing. "I can't even see her."

"Then you shouldn't be throwing cushions."

"Sorry, Molly." A soft thump as Victor's feet hit the floor. He got his hands around Andy's ankles and pulled him around to the edge of the bed.

"Jesus, you *are* strong."

"Says the guy who lifted me off the bed."

"Only half of you." Victor laughed. Andy was smiling. "You were power-lifting Loretta. You're such a movie star. That scene is going to absolutely kill."

"I wonder which take they'll go with." To Victor, it was a toss-up. The director might choose the first take, which had been closest to perfect in terms of execution of the whole dance (including the lift). On the other hand, he might choose the third, when they'd almost whiffed it. Victor'd had to do a half a turn with Loretta in the air, setting her down with a degree of haste that almost certainly read as 'near disaster.' Which would be perfect for the storyline, and by then the extras were expecting the lift to go well, so when it had looked as though Victor might drop her there had been an audible reaction. "They didn't let me see the rushes."

Andy sat up, finally. "The third time was funny as shit. It wouldn't have been funny if you'd dropped her, but because you didn't." He shrugged. "Or more accurately, if she'd overshot her position. You weren't dropping her. It was a balance thing."

"She was great. I love her."

"I know, I do too. Hope she isn't down there going, oh my God, how long can I tolerate that kind of racket." They both giggled. Victor gave Andy a hand up off the bed and they headed for the shower.

"A week to rest," Victor said lazily a few days later, when they were all in the backyard, lounging in the sun. "And get those routines back in our heads here at home. Then it's into the studio with Dmitri for 'Love is Blindness,' right?"

"Right." They were on the double lounger. Andy had Victor's hand in his. "I've got our costume managed thanks to Kenji, and he's going to do Shylock for us. Charlie said she could shoot our lines. We'll get that out of the way and then I can start scheduling the others."

"Patrick looks like the Armenian Ricardo Montalban."

"Wrath of Sarkisian." They both giggled. "I think Dmitri digs it. Have you decided what you want to do, amiga?"

Loretta knew all about this project by now. She was putting herself through Shakespeare boot camp. Her high school hadn't taught it, she'd never read any of the plays, and had seen only one film adaptation. She was mowing through Andy and Victor's DVD library while she read the plays. "Do you already have Viola?"

Andy sat up a little and looked over at her. *God you're cute*, he thought. She was lying on her front in

165

her bikini with her hair up in an octopus clip, e-reader in front of her, and reading glasses perched on her nose. He let go of Victor, fished his camera out from under the lounger, and took a few pictures of Loretta. "No, we don't. Did you find a good line?"

"I think so, but it's not twisted." She looked worried.

"It doesn't have to be. We've got Macbeth and Macduff straight out of the play. There's quite a few of these that are going to be played straight."

"Oh good."

"So?"

"'I am not what I am.' When she is Cesario."

Andy was pleased. "Oh lord yes. See, Shakespeare already twisted that one for us. Historical costume?"

"Oh, yes please." She looked excited. "I can put the picture in my portfolio?"

"Of course. Hey, holy shit, that reminds me."

Victor looked over; he thought he was completely up to date on Andy, but possibly not. "What?"

"Raquel sent me this thing. A historical thing for next summer, an English production. Filming partly in England and partly in Spain. It's about the siege of Badajoz, during the Napoleonic Wars, which I knew absolutely zero about until I saw the script."

"Oh *that's* what you were muttering about last night! I was like, Bada-what?"

"I know about that," Loretta said, surprising them both. "We didn't study it in school but I read about it in a romance novel. The hero was there and he had, like, PTSD. His dreams were so horrible and sad, I had to look it up. Are you going to take the part?"

"Well, they want me to do a couple of scenes on video. I'd be playing a Portuguese, meaning a good guy."

"An officer?" Victor was thinking he'd love to see Andy in uniform. It might have come through in his tone; Andy shot him a laughing look. "Do they want an accent?"

"Apparently the baseline is Spanish-inflected English. Which I can do, especially if I study with Nick for a minute." One of Andy's friends was English. "Anyway so the idea is I send in the video and if they like it they'll ship me some costume, and if they like the look it's mine."

"And that would be while I'm doing my thing?" Victor was delighted. Andy nodded. "That is awesome."

"Wikipedia says there was a TV movie about this back in 1994. I'm going to try to track it down."

"Do you want to read this book?" Loretta asked. "I have it here in my e-reader. It's really good, I read everything this person writes."

"Tell me what it is, I'll get my own copy." Andy looked around for his phone, found it, and pulled up his Amazon app.

"It's 'Summer Campaign,' by Carla Kelly."

"Great." Andy squinted at the screen and did things. A few minutes later he nodded with satisfaction. "Thanks, chica. I'll read that tonight." He set down the phone, looked with disapproval at his empty glass, and went to get a fresh drink.

A couple days later, Andy realized he had the house to himself, and felt not relieved but abandoned. "Molly," he said, "there was a time when being alone at home was all I wanted. Now I hate it with the fire of a thousand suns." He petted her head for a minute.

"Guess what we're going to do? If she's home." He found his phone, dialed, waited. "Hey there. Victor just left for a two-hour session with our counselor. He's dropping Loretta off at the spa. Are you free? Could I bring Molly over to play with the pack? Well of course I'd like coffee, when do I not like coffee. See you in a few minutes."

He parked in front of Rory and Dana's cottage fifteen minutes later. The front door opened and three small animals dashed out. Andy got out of the car. Molly jumped out right behind him and started running around with the others. He watched them for a minute, smiling, then transferred the smile to Dana. "So where is the cherubim?"

"She's at Dmitri's, and then she's going to the gym. What's up? Come on in."

"You finally got a break," he said, following her in. "That show of yours is stupid." She made a sound of agreement, leaving the front door open, taking him through to the dining den. "Jesus, it smells good in here."

"Rory made cookies before she left." There was a plate on the table with the coffee things. "You are amazingly hairy." Andy tossed his head queenily. Dana grinned. "It's really kind of hot."

"Victor likes the beard. He's all, don't cut your hair. It seems to be a year for embracing the grizz."

"I had to start with mine." Dana was philosophical. "I realized it wasn't only the not-getting-as-much-sun thing, though that was part of it, so I've been making time to get outside. Plus some color."

"Highlights?"

"Shaya goes through with a crochet hook and separates the gray chunks and turns them blonde again. Between the Botox, the facials, the gym, the hair, and the imminent neck lift and eye job, I'm officially high maintenance."

"Neck lift? You're only forty-six."

Dana shrugged. She wasn't committed to it. But, "The face is the only part of me I can't maintain in the gym."

"It's still way better than average. I think you're more beautiful now than you were when I met you."

"Aw, thanks. I was thinking next summer for that, if this stupid show will wrap the season at a normal time. But maybe I'll let it go a while longer. Anyway. How are you doing? How do you like having Miss Cuban America in the house?"

"She's so fucking cute. She didn't grow up like us, with books. She's mainlining Shakespeare, we talk about it constantly. Victor has more of the academic view, his high school was about ten times better than mine for that shit. I sit there with the internet open looking up commentary so we can figure out what the dude was actually saying with this line or that. And in exchange, she turned me on to romance novels."

Dana laughed. "No kidding? I love a good romance novel. Rory and I have a keeper shelf up in the loft."

"Do you read the dirty parts to each other?"

"Yes we do. So Victor is doing some time with the therapist, huh."

"Well." Andy ate a cookie. "We almost had another fight because he wouldn't stop apologizing. I was like, dude, I was every bit as bad with my silent treatment. You forgive me? Okay, well I forgive you. He's working on it. We're talking a lot."

"Still getting jiggy, I presume."

"Oh my God." Andy's expression was eloquent.

Dana snickered. "Back at the beginning with me and Rory, when I wasn't working full-time, it was so great. We could fool around and then, like, stay in bed. Talking or napping or listening to music."

"That's exactly what it's like. We have so much time. We're still kind of looking around going, don't we have something we have to do? And we don't! We have all this shit going on, but absolutely none of it is mandatory! It's fucking *bizarre*!" He made big eyes at Dana. "Anyway yes. We're having a lot of great sex. Poor Loretta." Dana cackled. "But we're also having these hours of kissing each other and holding each other, and there's no hurry. It's never like, let's get to the main event because ten minutes from now we owe somebody something. It is sensational." He drank some coffee, ate another cookie. "You changed the colors in here."

"We had the red and pink look for a long time."

"It looks almost underwater now. Moody. Are those the same chandeliers?" A cluster of small ones over the dining table, all painted in shades of blue and green.

"Yeah, we told Lucy what we wanted to do and she said cool, I'll come get them. By the time the new drapery was done, they were ready. When Rory saw the pearls and shit she swooned a little."

"Our girl is a sensualist at heart."

"Mmhmm. So." Dana ate a cookie. "I presume you actually do have ten thousand projects going."

"Pretty much, yeah. Still waiting for you girls to tell me what Shakespeare characters you're doing."

"Well, what are *you* doing?"

"Antonio and Bassanio. That's one reason for the hair situation." Dana laughed again. Andy was grinning. "He came up with the staging in about five seconds. I was sitting there going yep, sounds perfect,

170

okay. It's going to be sexy as fuck for the Bassanio line, and full heartbreaker for the Antonio line."

"Any hints?"

"Those *are* hints." There was a slight rumpus of toenails, and then all four animals swarmed into the den. "Hello pretty girl. Did you have fun with the littles? What can I do for you? Oh of course, well, always. Such a good girl. Yes you're the best girl. Jesus Molly you saw me a few minutes ago." He was laughing, wiping his face. "This dog, I swear."

"I know." Dana had her hands full with the two small dogs. Spike the cat was on the table investigating the cookies. "Get your ass down, you little shit." She goosed him gently. He gave her a *pro forma* hiss and jumped onto the cushioned bench, where he washed himself vigorously. "You look really great. You've been sleeping."

"And eating. Not like this spring, that was extreme, but it seems Consuelo is enjoying having Loretta around. They're always in the kitchen conspiring. I call Mom up and tell her what they made. It's always a good conversation starter."

"How's she doing?"

"Lonely. Sad. Missing Pop." Andy wasn't making eye contact. "I asked her if she wants me to come out and she said, not until Christmas, I need to get used to it. Her complex has all these activities. She's doing everything."

"Still seeing old friends?"

"Oh yeah. Well, you know. She's lived in Miami all her life." Andy slumped against the wall, gazing at Dana. "There are times I think I should have gone back there to live."

"You had a good relationship with him this way."

"Yeah. Probably a better relationship than if I'd been there. He was a stubborn old goat." He drank the rest of his coffee, then admitted, "I would have resented it. I know this was better."

"Your life would have been smaller there. And you wouldn't have met Victor."

"God, I know. I look at him sometimes and think, what if. Who would I have settled for, so I wouldn't be alone forever."

Dana drank coffee, watching him over the rim of the mug. "Was there anyone here?"

"Not really. My best bet might have been Sergei. I could have moved to Las Vegas, if it got bad enough here." *If I didn't have Victor, if I didn't have a home. Surrounded by friends finding love while I didn't.* Dana might have seen all that. Andy shook himself a little. "Sergei and I were never together. There wouldn't have been any baggage. It was always this, well, maybe. You know?"

"Yeah, I know. There were a few well maybes back in the day."

"Of course there fucking were. Little blonde hottie." Dana did a 'stop it' thing, but she was smiling. "Anyway I *did* meet Victor, thank all the gods, as Tanith would say. So instead of becoming bitter and hateful in my lonely old age, I get to fuck like a tomcat and brag about it to all my happily-married friends."

"And also, of course, live in a castle." Andy performed a gesture saying 'exactly.' Dana offered a refill. He nodded. She poured. "I'm still jealous of that sunroom."

"You should be."

Chapter 13

Victor stared at Robyn. As usual, she appeared totally relaxed. Attentive, calm, and neutral. "Doesn't any of this get to you?"

"Victor, you're not telling me you murdered someone and hid the body. You have some issues, we're talking about your issues, and you're going to solve those issues. Because you want to. What gets to me is if someone comes in here to talk about their issue but they don't really want to solve it."

He laughed under his breath. "Yeah, okay. So when Andy and I talked about this I'd already figured out part of the problem. Two parts of the problem. I mean, the source. Why I was resentful, why I was jealous. I still haven't figured out why I would lash out at him like that. I spent so many years suppressing, why couldn't I hold it in." He thought for a minute. "Because I don't have to?"

Robyn did a 'possibly?' thing. "You trust him."

"I do. I always did, even when it was potentially career suicide to trust him." He didn't say anything for a while. Robyn didn't push. She never did. Sometimes simply being in that room with someone who was waiting to hear what he had to say was enough to get him to the next words. Even though he always had that at home, especially now. Now that they had so much time. "Our first night was eight hours long. We haven't talked about that, have we?"

She shook her head. She knew how he'd met Andy, and how he'd made the pass that took them to bed, and how he'd fucked things up almost immediately. "Tell me if you want to," she said after a moment of silence.

That was all he needed. "We had sex three times in those eight hours. We slept together, we talked, we kissed so much my mouth was sore the whole next day." *I was sore all over*, he thought. "We were naked. That was only the third time in my life I was naked with a lover, and the first time I spent a whole night with a man."

Robyn had heard about Victor's experiences with women. He'd told her he felt like the sex was the price for actually sleeping with someone. "That must have been profound."

"I was almost crying when I walked out of there. I was like, how can I leave, I have to leave, this was the worst thing I've ever done. His face, my God."

"When you told him you had to go?"

"When I told him I shouldn't have been there." Victor pinched the bridge of his nose, took a deep breath, let it out slowly. "Sometimes I feel like all I've ever done is hurt him."

"Victor."

"I know. I know it's not true. And he's taken a swipe at me a few times. But you know, he's always so far out in front of me. He's got those extra years, all that experience. He hears himself and he fixes it. I don't always hear myself."

"You'll get there."

"So the first time. Are you sure about this? I can't talk about this without getting graphic. I don't want to gross you out."

"Victor, I do court-ordered counseling."

Ugh. "Right. Okay. I had him on his back on the couch and we were about to do it. He had one foot on the floor and the other up on the back of the couch. I was about to turn him over. He said, uh-uh, I want to see your face. For a second I was like, what? Because I never did that before. Not face to face. He told me

174

where the lube was, and that alone made me feel like an idiot. I knew we needed it. Anyway he pulled me down and kissed me again, and hooked that foot over my back. When I got in, being able to see his face, my God. Being able to kiss him while we did that. It was the most intimate thing I'd ever done in my life. I didn't even know what I was feeling. I was never in love before. You could have told me that was what it was, and I would have said, no, you're loco."

"Even your first boyfriend?"

"Oh hell no." Victor smiled. "He was great, we had a great time. He was such a pendejo. He was a liar, he drank like a fish, he stole things. Funny as hell, terrible temper, always in trouble with his mouth." His smile faded. "I still hate that he died. It wasn't his fault or my fault, neither of us did anything to deserve that. Nobody deserves that."

"Did you ever feel that you did deserve it?"

"No. I was in the closet for Mama, not because I hated myself."

Robyn nodded, making a note. "What happened next?"

He knew she meant with Andy. "Did a little cleanup. Went to sleep. When we woke up he said he was hungry, so we went in the kitchen and then it was like one in the morning, right? He didn't ask me to stay, but he didn't tell me to get out, either. I didn't ask. I just didn't leave. Didn't want to leave. After a while we started kissing again. And then we were back on the couch doing sixty-nine, and I'd only done that twice before, and Jesus. Even with condoms, with that mouth, my God." Victor could tell Robyn was trying not to laugh. "Yeah, I was never so glad as when he said we didn't need them anymore. We were both clean."

"When was that?"

175

"Early, like a month in, after we cooled off enough to talk history and open up the charts. I won't lie, I was worried."

"Because he was older?"

"That, and he'd been in New York in the Eighties."

"Had you been with other people in between?"

"Neither of us was with anybody else after that first night. It was sixteen months from the first to the second. He said he'd always been super careful because when he moved to New York it was right in the middle of the AIDS epidemic. Everyone was careful, unless they wanted to die, or unless it was too late for them."

Robyn made a movement, almost a shudder. "Were you that careful?"

"Before? No, I was lucky. Lucky there was hardly anybody I *could* be with. I wasn't picking people up at random." But this was about him and Andy. "He took some pictures. He asked, and I was in this kind of dream state. We slept again, and then we were kissing again. I stopped thinking about the next day, about what happened next. When it started to heat up again he didn't even ask. Put me up against the wall and was getting me ready. I'd taken it before, a couple times. Didn't a hundred percent like it. Even so I was like, well, okay. Anything. Anything he wanted. And then he did this thing."

After a moment Robyn asked, "What thing?"

"Wrapped his hand around my throat. I was like, what the *fuck*. Almost scared, you know? Wasn't expecting that, or anything like it."

"Did you think he was going to hurt you?"

"Wouldn't have been the first time." For some reason it seemed important to say, "I kind of expected it. Taking it, that can hurt. He's taller, he's got ... well, use your imagination." Robyn did laugh then. "Anyway. There I was, braced on the wall. I could feel his ring against the side of my trachea, right here." He touched his neck. "Then his lips were against my face, this brush of a kiss. I realized he wasn't gripping." Victor showed Robyn the difference between curved fingers and the way Andy's hand was. A dancer's hand, strong, but graceful and open. "You've seen his hands. He stroked down my neck, then back up to cup my jaw." He did it to himself, showing her. "He turned my face like this and kissed me, and I fucking melted. He said something." He thought back. "What did he say? Really low, really soft. What was it. Can't remember." Victor let his hand fall, shaking his head, half laughing. "Anyway, he dances, he still does the morning class thing. I go out and watch sometimes, do part of it with him. He makes that shape with his hand and it's like I can feel it. Never fucking fails."

"So is that why you signed the release?"

He thought about it. "Because he could have hurt me, and didn't? Maybe. Yeah, maybe so."

"You put your life in his hands."

"Literally. And I know that's part of why what I did hurt him. It was giving and taking away at the exact same moment. But he forgave me. He always does. Because he loves me." *And I don't deserve it*, he started to think, and then corrected himself. That was a reflex, based on nothing but fear, fear that had no foundation. He loved Andy with everything he had. Andy knew it. "And I deserve it. I deserve to be loved."

Robyn permitted herself a small smile. "Good work today. Same time next week?"

"Yeah, thanks." Victor got himself together and went out, still wondering about those words he couldn't remember. Wondering if Andy would. They'd said a lot of things to each other that night, and it was years ago. It bothered him that he couldn't remember something from that night, from that moment.

He went to collect Loretta from the spa at The Grove. They picked up a few things from the farmer's market, taking a chance on a moment of normality. She was dressed casually, wearing sunglasses and a hat, looking like a pretty but probably-not-famous Los Angelena. People did the 'hey isn't that' thing, turning to look at Victor, but he was unshaven, and with a woman. It seemed that was sufficient camouflage. In any case, they got out before it turned into a mob-the-celebrity scene. He listened to her chatter all the way home. Parked the car, spoke to their security guard, and said, "I'm going to get a little sun while I still can." Loretta said something about studying and took the market things inside. Victor went up into the home studio to change into shorts, then back outside to lie on the big double lounger and wait for Andy to get home. He was warm, somewhat drowsy, lying there with his eyes closed when he heard the sounds of a familiar vehicle, and the familiar light-footed stride accompanied by the patter of Molly's paws. "Hey there."

"Hey yourself." Andy leaned over to kiss his gorgeous husband. So did Molly, before going to her usual spot behind the lounger. "Dana fed me cookies. She said please take some home with you so I don't eat all of them, so here."

Something landed on Victor's chest. He smiled without opening his eyes, lifted the small package off and set it by his hip. "I was talking to Robyn about our first night. Something's bothering me."

"Oh yeah? Can I help?" Andy stretched out beside him, certain that Victor's choice of the double was some kind of invitation. It usually was, especially after a session with the counselor. They didn't always talk to each other about those afterward, but they almost always wanted to be close.

"The third time, after the pictures, when you put me up against the wall. You did that thing with your hand."

*Oh*. Andy wondered if his husband had gone into detail about the sex. If so, that was interesting, especially in view of their mutual insatiability this year. He was positive it was linked to the shooting. Everything seemed to be, and he knew they had to air it all out sometime. But maybe not today. "This thing." Andy did it to him.

"Jesus, Andy." Instant arousal. Never failed. Then that mouth on his again. Victor reached for him, got an arm around his neck for a long, enthusiastic kiss. When Andy shifted away Victor opened his eyes. It was not nearly dark enough to be doing this outside. Not dark at all, in fact. Andy was smiling at him. "What did you say? You said something right after that, before you started to get in. It's really bugging me that I can't remember."

"Ah. Let me think." Andy stared back at him. He had Victor's hand, absently stroking the inside of his wrist. "There were a lot of things I was trying not to say. You were so beautiful, that whole night was such a dream. At first I thought, you know, this was going to be a casual thing. Serendipity. Make the most of it."

"That's what I thought too. But the first time was magic, and I didn't leave. Then the second time was magic, and I couldn't leave. When we started again you seemed different, like you were going to take everything. And for a minute I thought I was about to pay for the rest of it. Then you did that thing and I was like oh my God, how. Help me Jesus." He smiled a little.

Andy kissed him again. "I was going for everything. I was like, God damn you for being this way and never being here before. By that time I thought there was a chance this wasn't casual." He leaned his head against Victor's and spoke very softly. "It didn't feel casual. And the way you reacted when I did that … the only word I ever found for it was surrender."

"Mmm."

"I said, how can you be so perfect." Victor made a small, pained sound. "You were. You are. It wasn't only the sex, you know it wasn't. Not then any more than it is now."

"I know." Victor set his free hand on Andy's face, stroking a thumb up his cheekbone, then running his hand through the shaggy hair and down his neck. "I wish I had been a little bit braver."

"So do I. But you were brave enough to come back. For all you knew I was going to throw a drink in your face, make a huge scene, blow your cover and ruin your life." Andy kissed him lightly, smiling again.

"I knew you weren't going to do that. You had four months and a photography exhibit you could have used to do that."

"I'm still dying to put some of those pictures up on a wall somewhere. Not to mention a few I've taken since then." Victor giggled. Andy felt relieved. "How do you think Reggie would like those?"

"Let's wait till we need a good scandal to jump-start our careers," Victor suggested.

"Or until we redecorate. We could put a mural of you in the guest bathroom." Victor laughed. Andy kissed him again. "Let's go inside, I'm hungry." He sat back, swung his legs off the lounger, and stood up, holding out a hand for Victor. "I love you."

"I love you too."

"Don't forget those cookies."

Toward the end of their second week back, when Andy and Victor were starting to be almost accustomed to not having anything they absolutely had to do, being free to do nothing if they so chose, they were starting down the stairs from doing something other than nothing when they heard Loretta talking. They glanced at each other, quickly deducing that she was in the living room, on her phone. They hung back for a second because they heard their names.

"Oh my God yes. I know. Andy came out on location with this beard and ay papi." She laughed. "No no no. He never wanted a woman in his life. You should have seen Victor though. Oh my God and the producer. The production assistants, everybody, it was hilarious. No, everybody's that way about Victor too, oh of course me too. Since the first read, I was like wow. For a minute I thought, hmm, and then Andy came to Miami and I thought no. No no no. I would never. They're so in love. Oh my God they're all over each other. Yes! I can hear them on the other side of the house. I get so hot. It's terrible, they can be in the fucking kitchen talking about, you know, fucking *salad*, and their voices change. Yes they both have a sex voice, you would die. Oh yes. I'm, my God, find me a man. I don't know anybody here except their friends. Everybody's married! Except this one guy, I met him at the movie premiere last winter. He was so nice. He doesn't live close by. I don't know, he was single then. No! Oh my God you're so loco." She laughed hard. "Throw me a bone, oh my God."

Victor and Andy couldn't look at each other. They would have cracked up for sure. Andy had a hand clamped over his mouth. Victor was halfway through the bedroom doorway because he didn't know if he could maintain.

"No I'm not going to call Ernesto, he can fuck himself with a chainsaw, that piece of shit. I don't know, I'm wearing out my vibrator." She laughed again. "Oh yes. That's the only thing. I'm busy learning Shakespeare. We have dinner with their neighbors a lot. They're all in and out of each other's houses all the time, it's just like we were growing up, it's nice. We're going to a show next weekend, one of the neighbors is in it. That woman who was in the tango movie. Oh she's amazing. There's an after party, all their hot dancer friends will be there. God in heaven, *somebody* has to be single. Yes, maybe I can find a man there. Light a candle for me." Another laugh. "Sí sí chica. I'll talk to you soon. Besos a ti."

Andy and Victor crept back into the bedroom, easing the door shut, as Loretta was winding up the call. They went through to the bathroom, closing that door behind them too. Victor turned on the shower. Then they laughed, trying to muffle it with bath towels. "Oh Jesus," Andy said after a while, splashing water on his face before he turned the shower off again. "Well, that answers the question of how non-obvious we are. Not at all."

"Do I have a sex voice?"

"Oh, honey, do you ever." Andy said that in *his* sex voice, which got a laugh – and a hot look – from Victor. "I guess I'd better locate my phone and send a text to Jim. If he's not already planning to be at this thing next weekend, clearly he should be."

"See if he can come to dinner this weekend," Victor suggested. "We could get Tanith and Sid, Tina and Reza. Have a little movie-making chat fest."

"And it won't be so obvious if he's not the only guest. Brilliant strategy." Andy kissed him. "We should go downstairs. I do not know how I'm going to look her in the eye."

"Oh, like you didn't know she can hear what we do up here."

"All of it, apparently. She's been so politely oblivious." Andy checked himself out, noted the love bite on his neck, gave Victor a look. "I really am so in love with you."

"I know. I'm so in love with you, too." Victor kissed him again and opened the door. They went downstairs, and everybody managed to act normal. They talked about the costumes their friend Kenji's shop was working up for Loretta as Viola as Cesario, and for Andy and Victor as Antonio and Bassanio. They had Maria the makeup artist lined up. This was all scheduled for the following week. "Get on the phone to those people about this weekend," Victor reminded Andy. "You know they're all busy."

"Yeah, okay." Andy found his phone in the control center off to one side of the kitchen and composed a group text. After he sent it he glanced up at Loretta. "We're inviting some people over from last year's movie. Tanith and some others. Apparently they're all sort of working on this new thing she wrote for Tina."

"Tina the camera woman? The one who got the Eisner award?" Loretta had done her homework on their colleagues, even though her own part in 'The

Ghost of Carlos Gardel' was simply to dub Vicky's lines for the Spanish-language markets.

"That's right. She's doing another graphic novel which is actually the inspiration for this show we're going to see next weekend. So we thought it'd be fun for you to hear about that."

"Oh yes. Thank you!" She went and got herself a glass of water, leaning against the counter to drink it. She looked like she wanted to ask something. Victor made a 'what's on your mind' gesture. "I loved doing that dance in the movie. I haven't ever danced like that before. Do you think I could take some lessons while I'm here?"

"Jesus, yes," Andy said. "We should have thought of that ourselves. Dmitri's studio is less than fifteen minutes away."

"Tomás works there," Victor said. "Vince works there, you met him at the premiere. They have a lot of great teachers. Want me to take you over tomorrow, show you where it is? Then you could take Andy's car whenever you want to go."

"Hey!" Andy tried to sound outraged. Loretta and Victor both laughed. "Fine, whatever, take my car. Let's see about some dinner."

Chapter 14

It was a full house that Saturday; even Tanith's husband Sid, an LAPD lieutenant, was free to join them. Vicky and Sharon came over from next door, so every seat at the table was taken. "Mother of God," Andy said, "would you *look* at these women. You're all going to be out under the piazza lights later so I can take some pictures."

They had some catching up to do. Tanith talked a little about the most recent class she'd taught. Sid told a story about a recent case. Vicky and Sharon told stories about their little girl. Victor and Loretta described their dance shenanigans on location. Reza, who'd been Tanith's cinematographer, talked about the house he and Tina were renovating. Tina ranted about her day job doing computer animation. Jim had a story about a recent indie film shoot he'd worked on. Andy told everyone about his FaceTime dialogue-coaching sessions with his friend Nick. "He assures me that my English accent is approaching respectability," he said, with the accent.

"That's not bad at all," Tanith said. "But keep working on it." He made an offensive gesture and she laughed. "So obviously Tina and Sharon saw 'Diamond Dogs' at the dress rehearsal. Sid's seen it all in fragments on the Dropbox. Vicky's in it. Are the rest of you coming next week?"

"I think that's a yes," Victor said. "Are you going, Jim?" He knew perfectly well that Jim was. Andy had been in touch to say 'get a ticket if you don't already have one,' and of course they'd secured one for Loretta.

"Yes, I'll be there. It's going to be weird seeing a show at Chrome when I'm not taking video." Loretta

185

obligingly asked him about that, so he started talking about how he'd been doing video for the Underground Cabaret for eight years; how he'd pitched Andy to them for their posters; how he'd met Andy in the first place. "I was doing second assistant to the third assistant director on a production with a lot of moving parts. Andy was there, why were you there?"

"Jesus, I can hardly even remember that far back. That was like two thousand six. Before my first exhibit. I'd only been out here for a year or so, I was still scratching around for any kind of photography job. I was doing continuity. They had really overdressed sets and a fuck-ton of costume and somehow with this huge crew they didn't have enough people to remember where all the shit went or whether the collar was buttoned or unbuttoned, so they yelled for help. A friend of a friend was involved somehow and told me about it. God that was a mess."

"Jim, how old were you then?" It was Tanith asking, for a reason nobody cared to investigate. She probably, being Tanith, had read the room and determined that Andy and Victor were trying to do a little matchmaking. Jim and Loretta were, after all, the only unmarried people there.

"I was twenty-five. A few years out of college. Getting my ass kicked by Hollywood."

"Welcome to the club." Tanith drank some wine. "It took me till age forty-two to get noticed."

"So I've still got four years." Jim smiled.

"Stick around these people," Vicky said. "All kinds of crazy shit happens."

"Yes." Sharon topped up a few wineglasses. "Crazy shit. Like buying a triplex you didn't even need."

"We needed it not to get torn down and a six-unit piece of garbage put up by some money-launderer," Andy said. "Our life would have been hell for years, or more like forever. Fuck that."

"Also it's a cute building." Victor was smiling.

"It's cute *now*," Sharon said. "Paige and the gang really love it. That was a good thing you did."

"It was all their idea. I might have left it vacant." Andy shrugged. "We had a minute to deal with it."

"I remember you said that," Tanith said. "Your minute kind of went sideways on you."

Victor leaned back, still smiling, a little smug. "We've got another minute. I'm not working till next July. We're going to be dancing, Andy's working on this big new photography thing, and we're going to put together a concert."

There was a chorus of "No shit!" "When?" "Where?" from everybody but Vicky and Sharon. Sharon said, "Your Broadway thing?"

"That's right." Victor glanced at Andy. "We'd better get our set list ironed out. Decide who's singing what. Get Valerie started on the arrangements."

"Monday morning," Andy said. "Deal?"

"Deal."

"Well," Tanith said, "maybe this is the point where we talk about Tina's thing."

Tina shook her head. "Your thing."

"You started it."

"You wrote it."

"God help me," Reza said. All the other men laughed. "Is there coffee?"

"There is coffee," Andy said. "Let's get that rolling."

Not much later, everyone was taking turns looking at the proof of Tina's new graphic novel. "It was Vicky," she said, "which Vicky knows. After I saw her on set. I'd had this idea for a noir thing ever since 'Agent Carter' got cancelled."

"So full of rage," Tanith said.

"All the rage. Anyway, so that one image was really the first one. Vicky in the suit with the revolver, the cigarette and martini glass. I know you don't smoke," Tina said, semi-apologetically, "but this is set in the forties and everyone did."

"If we make a movie," Tanith said, "there are tobacco-free cigarettes."

"Anyway I had some other stuff but it wasn't until I saw these fuckers do their fight, you know we watched that fight like a thousand times while we were editing, that I got more of an idea about a story. But it wasn't coming the way 'Nightingale' did, and Tanith was right there, and she can write, so I threw it at her and ran away." Tina shrugged.

"I'd've loved to get you on the stage for this," Tanith said, looking at Andy and Victor. "But I knew it wasn't possible so I didn't even bring it up. And what you'll see is really only a dance concert. It's great, and we're totally taping it, but what's on the stage isn't a movie. This book, I think, is potentially a movie. I wrote the script as if it were a movie. There's a ton of guys in it."

"They all die," Sid confirmed, "all but two."

"Because we are bloodthirsty bitches," Vicky said with satisfaction. "And I kill you guys first because you're the baddest bad guys."

"Take off the head and the rest of the monster runs around blind." Sid drank some coffee.

"So why this next?" Victor was watching Tanith.

"Well," she said, "after Reza handed me the first few drawings, because Tina was too chicken to do that, he said the art wants what it wants. That was

188

during our last week of filming. I was mostly out of my mind. All of you had completely *blown* my mind. When we did my little play all those years ago, my God." She shook her head. "It was so small, but it felt huge to me. Our schedule was so tight. There was no time to let it breathe and grow, and I didn't dare let go of any of it."

"Plus of course there was a murder investigation going on in your last week of rehearsals," Sid murmured.

Tanith shook herself at that memory. "By the time we did the movie I'd had the 'Green Darkness' experience, where the dancers changed the Grendel character and it got so much richer. Anyway I had that in my head when we started the movie, and I wasn't afraid of letting it shift. The songs were the songs and the words were the words but you guys all created those characters in a very real sense. That was art happening right in front of my eyes. So when Reza said that, and I'd seen that incredible drawing of Vicky, I thought, oh fuck me here we go again."

"That's pretty much exactly what she said." Sid was laughing along with everyone else.

"Anyway long story short, if a movie happens, I am going to grovel as much as necessary to get you to play my baddest bad guys."

Victor and Andy looked at each other. If they got killed first, the parts were likely to be small. The time investment wouldn't be a burden. The question was whether Tanith would get this rolling when they were both available, because if the movie script was like the book, they were on-screen together in every one of their scenes. "You know we'd love to work with you again," Victor said after a moment. "I'm down with getting villainous."

"And as long as I don't have to be hateful to Victor ever again, I can cope." Andy had his hand on Victor's thigh under the table. "You might need a time machine, though."

Tanith sighed. "I know. Either that or a permanent set that I can cycle folks in and out of. Conceivably we could take a year or more to film it, as people are available."

Tina stood up, with an air of tabling this discussion. "Where's the bog?"

"Over this way." Victor stood up too, directing her to the guest bathroom. Then other people were up and moving, a few people got fresh beverages, and the subject was definitively changed. Andy herded the women out to the patio for a quick photo shoot. When they all were back inside there were three separate conversations happening, and nobody seemed to notice that he was doing something on his phone.

Eventually Tanith and Sid started to make going-away noises, and that set everyone else in motion. Jim went first. Vicky and Sharon were next. Tina and Reza took off shortly after, leaving Tanith and Sid with the hosts and Loretta. "Tina's pregnant, by the way," Tanith said. "Reza already said he would be happy to work with Jim again. You could let him know sometime."

"Okay." Andy looked slightly shifty.

Victor said, "What are you up to." It was so clear that Andy was up to something, it wasn't even a question.

"Well, she said that about a permanent set. And I had a thought." He pulled out his phone again, woke up a text exchange, and handed it to Tanith. She read it, looked up and stared at him, read it again, handed it to Victor. He read it and laughed. Andy said,

"Well, come on. It has sixteen-foot ceilings, it's air-conditioned, it's secure, there's a bathroom and there's parking."

"What are you talking about?" Loretta looked deeply confused.

"My friend Nick," Andy said. "The guy who's teaching me to speak English so I can tape that audition. He has a studio rentals business, vintage and antique furniture. He has this huge warehouse out in the Valley."

"And apparently he's willing to squeeze his shit together so one end of the warehouse can turn into a semi-permanent movie set." Victor was shaking his head.

"Well, like he says. A rental is a rental," Andy said reasonably.

"I cannot with you," Tanith said. "Okay. One screenplay coming up. Sid, let's get out of here before something else happens."

"Yeah. Good idea. Thanks for dinner, guys." There were handshakes and hugs, and then Victor and Andy were alone with Loretta.

"This is what he did all the way through that movie," Victor told her. "Somebody would say, we have this problem, and he would say, well here's how you fix it."

"It's no wonder you love him," she said. "Do you have all those shows she was talking about?"

"Yes, we do. Catnip, why don't you steer Loretta that way while I get this cleanup started."

They spent most of Sunday doing not much. Victor was finding it unusually easy to talk Andy into spending an hour on the lounger, or listening to music, or watching a movie. They had a great excuse to simply hang out and consume entertainment:

Loretta kept finding things in their collection that she'd never seen or heard. Molly was delighted to have an extra human around, and especially to have her own humans both there so much of the time. She was with Andy and Victor in the sunroom on Monday morning, when they settled in with some coffee to figure out their Broadway concert.

"We need to send Sharon some flowers," Andy said, about two hours in. "I would never have thought of putting a mini fridge and a coffeemaker upstairs, but this shit is lit."

Victor laughed. He was also a fan of not having to go downstairs for a beverage or a snack. Especially now that they were confining all their love play to the master bedroom. "Thank God our house guest is an adult."

"For real. An adult who can drive." Loretta was making regular, if tentative, forays into the maelstrom of Los Angeles traffic. She was showing no sign of wanting to go back to Miami. They'd promised they'd start taking her out dancing once she had a few more tango lessons. They had also suggested to Jim that *he* should take a few dance lessons. "Okay. So we have a lot going on here."

Victor studied the list. He read it out to Andy. "Is that what you have too?"

"Yep. Eighteen numbers, counting 'Mein Herr' for the encore. 'At the Ballet,' we need to line up two more singers to do it with you, and two more dancers to do it with me."

"That's a lot of dancing. Two rumbas together, plus 'Hot Honey Rag' and 'Mein Herr.' Then you've got your tap extravaganzas to 'Lullaby of Broadway' and 'Let's Misbehave,' and the ballet thing. This is going to be a hell of a show. Who are you thinking to dance with you?"

"Mike and Zach, probably. I'll bet I can bribe them to choreograph it." Victor laughed. Andy was grinning at him. "Jesus, I can't wait to do this. I need to get back in tap class, stat."

"And I need to get back in jazz. Dmitri can give us the rumbas. Who do you want to choreograph the Hot Honey? Tomás?"

Andy set his notepad down on the table between them and shoved a hand through his hair, which he still hadn't cut. Victor watched that hand move, the Australian ring flashing, and thought *yum*. Then he tuned back in to what Andy was saying. "Yeah, he'd be good. He can give it some of that tango flavor. And we can ask Dmitri for some tango in the rumbas, too. This is going to be so much fucking fun."

"You know what's funny? How we ended up with so many of the same things before we even started comparing lists. Did you ever play Julian Marsh?"

"No. I was in the chorus for a while. They might take me seriously for it now. If the show is ever casting here I might go out for it." Andy stood up, stretching his back. "I want to watch every one of these shows again."

"Me too. Are there any we don't have?"

"Not really. Nothing essential, in terms of creating references. I don't even *want* to reference 'Phantom,' ugh. Let's pretend all that is, is a nice sweet somewhat-over-the-top love song."

Victor watched Andy, now bending over to touch his toes, pet Molly's head, and then fold himself even further. "I should stretch more."

"Yes you should." The voice issued from between Andy's knees. He unfolded slightly to shoot a sideways look at Victor. "I could help you with that. I could help you with that right now." He

193

straightened up, expecting some kind of flirty or dirty comment from Victor.

Instead he got gender-bent Shakespeare. "Age cannot wither him, nor custom stale his infinite variety." Victor said it softly, registered Andy's expression, and stood up. "God, when you look at me that way." He stepped over Molly, laid a hand on Andy's bearded face, and kissed him.

About fifteen minutes later Andy said, "I wish there were some way to actually quantify how much I love you. Because it seems like it's more all the time. I keep thinking there has to be a limit, and then the next day it's like okay, another record shattered." Victor was smiling against his skin. Lying in Andy's arms, sweaty and satisfied. Andy's hand was stroking lightly, lazily, up and down Victor's arm. Victor's hand was behind Andy's neck, still closed around a hank of hair. "You know my hair hasn't been this long since I was actually in 'Hair.'" Victor laughed silently. "I forgot how nice it could be to have my hair pulled." Victor tugged on it again. "Maybe you should let yours grow too."

"Maybe I will. Maybe I won't cut it till it's time for Broadway."

"I'd like to see that." Andy moved his head, and made a sound of protest. Victor let go of his hair. Andy kissed his forehead. "Now that you're all relaxed, let's get down on the floor and stretch. And then one of us needs to put some pants on and take Molly outside."

"Counteroffer. Let's put on warmups and both go out. We can stretch on the patio and then lie on the loungers for a while."

"I accept." Andy patted him. "Let's get moving."

The topic of the property next door came up that night. It wasn't posted for sale, but Victor hadn't been able to dismiss the idea. "It's awful, and it's in awful shape. The people in there have either been there forever, or they're renting and don't give a shit. If they've been there forever they're probably a million years old and either don't want to fix it up, or can't afford to fix it up. If we got that, we could have a pool." He'd saved his best argument for last. From the look Andy was giving him, he should have led with that.

Loretta certainly thought so. "Your own pool? Oh my God I would never leave." Both men laughed. "Are you going to build a new house?"

"We may have to," Victor said. "For a bunch of reasons. But there are a lot of reasons why having a spare house could be a good thing. Between us we almost always know somebody who needs a short-term rental."

"We could see if Paige wants to take point on it again." The idea had been too much back when they were on tour. Now, the more Andy thought about it, the more he liked it. Maybe their real-estate guy could find a way in. "Ping Elliott. See what he can find out. Because the second you said 'pool' my inner goldfish went yes please."

Andy knew he was going to laugh about this later. They were supposedly on vacation, and here they were planning a concert, rehearsing two dances, discussing another real-estate deal, anticipating another Tanith project, and launching the Shakespeare photo sessions. Their own went off without a hitch. Loretta looked great for hers. Dmitri and Patrick were scheduled for the first week of September. Dana and Rory still hadn't decided what they wanted to do. Andy nagged Rory about it: *Make up your alleged minds*

She wrote right back: *Kiss my grits*

*LOL you know I'll put you in no matter what but I've got other people pitching things too now that the word is out. If somebody else comes in ready, don't come crying to me about how those were the characters you really wanted*

*Gaahh whatever okay*

*I would have expected someone with an English degree to be a little more decisive about her text*

Rory sent back a sticking-out-my-tongue emoji, and followed it up with: *Speaking of English have you done your audition tape yet?*

*Tomorrow*

*Is Victor reading the scenes with you?*

*Of course*

*Well knock em dead*

*Thanks chica. Go make up your mind now plz*


The following Sunday found Loretta, Andy and Victor seated at a lounge table, about a dozen feet back from the stage at Chrome. A couple of security guys from the company they used were discreetly nearby. The club was packed, the noise level was high, and Loretta was not sure about the show's signature cocktail, a Black Widow martini. "It's black?" she said. "How is it black?"

"Don't worry," the server said. "It's dark rum and crème de cacao with a little food coloring. Not squid ink."

She laughed. "Oh my God that's what I was afraid of. Okay." They all ordered the same thing. "I think I see why this cocktail, though," she said, looking over the show's program. Act I started with

'Someday I'll Fly Away,' by Nicole Kidman; Act II ended with 'Bad Girls,' by Pussy Riot.

"Yeah, this is not a case of needing a bunch of dialogue to tell the story, is it?" Victor was smiling. "Sixteen numbers though, wow. That's a big one."

"Everybody we know is in this damn thing." It was a slight exaggeration, but Andy was full of righteous envy. "I wish we could have done it. I want to dance every one of these songs with you."

"Especially 'Bad Girls,'" Victor said. Andy caught his eye and smiled. "That's definitely a song we should dance to."

"Yes it is, sweetness."

Not too surprisingly, they loved the show. Nearly every male dancer they knew appeared at least once. There were three who had through-lines. One was Charlie's husband Sacha, in a cross-dressed role. The second was Tomás. They inferred from the graphic novel that he would be playing a lounge pianist, in love with the lounge singer. Here he seemed to be a sort of pet for the merciless women in charge, led by Vicky. The third was Andy's prince Zach, who had a recurring role as a seducer before being assassinated. Every other man in the cast was also shot, strangled, poisoned, stabbed, or otherwise exterminated before the end of the show. Every female dancer was getting a spotlight moment.

Victor and Andy were cracking up at how many ways the choreographers had come up with to introduce and then end characters. "Vicky is enjoying this an awful lot," Andy said at intermission.

"So is Anya. What did she say about Desdemona?"

"She said, the second this fucking show closes. Those exact words," Andy added, listening to Victor giggle. "Terry's going to be dead Othello and Ricky will be dead Iago."

"Can't wait to see that. Loretta, what do you think so far?"

"I need to take more lessons!"

So many people were dancing at the after party, the club opened up the curtain to make more space. Andy and Victor took Loretta to join a crowd of cast members on stage. They each danced with her once before Ricky cut in. After a while they saw her over at the bar, talking to Jim. "I love you," Victor said. He was in Andy's embrace, dancing slow tango to something fast.

Andy turned his head for a kiss. "I love you too." He made eye contact for a second, to see if Victor's statement was part of a conversation, or simply a gift. Apparently it was the latter. Andy kissed him again, and kept dancing.

When they finally got home, very late, they steered a woozy Loretta into her room, took Molly out for a few minutes, and then went upstairs at a slower-than-usual pace. Washing up was leisurely too. They were both tired, but pleasantly so. The whole day leading up to the show they'd had next to nothing to do. The night before, they'd gone to bed early and slept late. Lying in bed together now, with Molly stretched out on the floor – she almost always came up to the bed at some point, but had been their dog long enough to know that she might want to wait a while to join them – Victor said, "I felt like I could have danced all night. I didn't want to stop."

"It was the best milonga ever, wasn't it? All kinds of different music, everybody there somebody we know. Little miss cutie was having fun."

"She's a good follower. I was thinking about the times we went out dancing before. Way back. Before you were on the show. And that time in Oregon."

"Oh my God, Oregon." They'd been in Eugene, pausing their return from vacation to put in their offer for the Faux Chateau. There was a dance studio across the street from their hotel. When they went over to see what was happening, it was an Argentine tango class and practica. "We should go back there someday."

"We could do that whole trip again someday."

"Stay longer everywhere." Andy was smiling, and he could tell even in next to no light that Victor was too. "Do the whole Shakespeare festival in Ashland."

"Jesus, yes. You could take your show up there."

"Holy shit, yeah! Goddamn, Victor, I keep thinking we've planned things out so far ahead we'll never catch up and then here's something else." He leaned in for a kiss. "Table that idea. We'll discuss it after you're done with your English movie. Oh, and by the way, it's *our* show." Another kiss. "You've been an idea machine. All the staging you come up with, it's great."

"It's writing, kind of," Victor said, almost hesitantly. "Taking one of those lines and thinking of who we're putting in the role and then coming up with the scene that makes it work. I really like it."

"I can tell." They were lying close together, skin to skin, both mildly aroused. It always happened when they were this close, especially if they were kissing. Andy knew he could turn this into lovemaking with a word, or a touch. But somehow the whole evening had felt like lovemaking. And they had nothing to do the next day. Nothing but what they wanted to do. Glorious, amazing, incredible *nothing.* He changed position, settling them in a way he knew worked for sleeping. Kissed Victor's forehead. "I love you."

Victor let himself relax against his husband. He could have initiated something. All he had to do was put his hand on that long lean body. But this felt so good, and there was always tomorrow. "I love you too."

Chapter 15
September 2019

It seemed that their not-so-subtle maneuvers had achieved their immediate aim, namely getting Loretta and Jim to go out on a date. At least one date. Andy resisted the temptation to interrogate her; he had photographs to take, and more photos to plan.

Their friend Red Warner, currently in London being Macduff, never had collected the dragon-bones throne Andy'd used for the Tempest photo shoot. It was locked in the storage shed, in the garage. Andy opened up the shed, studied the throne, remembered how heavy the fucker was, and did not try to move it by himself. Instead he went next door and wheedled the three men living in the triplex. "You're all so much younger than me," he said, trying to look pitifully old and frail.

The 'so much younger' part was true; they ranged in age from thirty to forty. The 'old and frail' act got a lot of rolled eyes. All of their tenants had seen Andy and Victor in 'The Ghost of Carlos Gardel.' The middle guy, Sandesh, had worked on the movie as Tanith's production assistant. He said, "With all due respect, give me a break. Who brought it downstairs?"

"I'd rather not say," Andy hedged, because the answer was 'me and Adrian the security guy' and he frankly didn't want to admit it because he still couldn't believe they hadn't both been killed. Getting it *up* the stairs had been 'Red and Adrian,' a combination Andy had underestimated.

Now one of the guys asked, "Where do you want it? Back upstairs to the studio?" The others winced at the prospect.

Andy said, "Nope! Under the pepper tree, please." He and Victor had gone over their staging ideas for Kent and Lear several times. All of the Shakespeare images were going to be processed, with layers of effects. The Lear line would be shot in the studio, with a neutral backdrop so Andy could layer in the suggestion of castle walls. For the Kent line, they'd both agreed that an overtly sensual starting point would provide the best context. He directed the other guys as they lugged the throne out of the garage across the backyard, bitching all the way. "It's a beast, that's why I came crawling to you. About four feet in front of the trunk, please, on this side so the wall is behind it. Awesome. Thank you so much."

"Let us know when you want us to put it back," Sandesh said, shaking out his hands.

"Soon," Andy said. "Patrick and Dmitri are coming tomorrow. Thanks a lot, guys. We're grilling on Sunday, so come on over." He walked them all out his back gate, took a moment to appreciate having useful friendly tenants, and then went to think about things for a while.

With the throne in place, he could finish designing the scene. He'd decided to shoot that line at night, and with the effects he was planning there wasn't much else to add to the set. He got himself a drink and positioned a lounger so he could sit and watch how the evening light changed, and how the throne looked after the piazza lights switched on. After a while he went up to the studio and found the velvet wizard's robe he'd used for the Tempest shoot, draping it over the back and arms of the throne. *There we go.* It softened the lines, making it not so obviously dragonish. Imposing, but more sensual. He folded up the robe, but didn't go in the house. His better half was in there being a writer; Andy was content to take a little me time. He was still outside when Victor came looking for him. "What are you up to? Oh."

"I didn't move it myself."

"Glad to hear it. Thanks for not asking me to help." Andy snickered. "Jonathan's getting the four-one-one from Loretta about the whole Jim thing. He'll be heading out pretty soon."

"How's it going?"

"The outline's pretty much done. It was coming almost as fast as the last one." Victor sat beside Andy, squeezing onto the edge of the lounger. "We can't quite decide where to set it, though."

"Starting from the honeymoon hell idea, Niagara and the Poconos were a gimme. Can't do that again. Would you stay with the love interests?"

"Oh yeah," Victor said. "Me and Loretta, anyway. Don't know about Jonathan and his lady."

"He wasn't a hundred percent comfortable with doing that, was he."

"Well, he was single when we wrote the treatment for number three. By the time we started filming he wasn't." Victor twisted his back, rolled his neck. "And he's not as cool about it as you."

"Well, doing a straight love scene while his girlfriend watches is different. So tell me what you've got."

"Let's get on the double, so I can stretch out too."

"Yeah, good idea." They moved the single lounger back into position, then settled themselves on the double. A few minutes later, while Victor was starting to talk through the outline, Jonathan came out. He brought Molly with him. She greeted Andy and Victor with her typical where-have-you-been excitement. "Hey pretty girl. Hey there big guy. All caught up with Loretta?"

"We're all caught up. This is such a nice backyard. Holy shit, what is that?"

"That is the Beowulf death throne that Red Warner built five years ago. We used it for my Tempest photo shoot, and I'm using it tomorrow for King Lear. What king are you going to be?"

"Eh?" Somehow Jonathan hadn't heard about this.

"What's your favorite Shakespeare play?"

"Coriolanus."

"Jesus, why?"

Jonathan laughed. "Because I loved what Ralph Fiennes did with it. That was sick."

"Those modern militaristic settings really work, don't they? The Lear we saw last year did the same thing. Patrick Stewart's Macbeth, Ian McKellen's Richard the Third." Andy was eyeing Jonathan. "We don't have a bad guy yet."

"Coriolanus is a bad guy," Victor agreed. "You've played bad guys."

Jonathan snorted. "I played nothing but bad guys for ten years." He'd been recruited to play a bad guy, at the height of his career as a professional wrestler. Nobody had expected him to steal every scene.

"This show concept is Shakespeare with a twist. If we found you a line that put you with that other guy, the one Gerard Butler played, implying there was something sexy going on, would you be cool with that?" Andy would go with a solo image if it meant getting Jonathan in the show, but remembering that film adaptation had inspired him.

"Sure, yeah. I've done stuff like that before."

Victor remembered an early low-budget action movie with some homoerotic subtext that wasn't terribly 'sub.' "Yes you have."

"Who would be Aufidius?"

"I dunno." Andy thought for a few seconds. "Hey, how about Mike Borodin? He worked with us on the movie last year. He's your same height, blond, straight. He's a dancer but he's great with character. I'll send you links to a couple of his things. He's tough as nails. Got broken in half in a car accident and never quit."

Jonathan clearly liked the sound of all this. "Sure, yeah. I'll be in and out till we get this treatment done, so keep me posted. I'd better get out of here now, though."

"Thanks for this," Victor said, standing up to shake hands. "This shit is fun to do with you."

"Same goes. Talk to you soon." Jonathan headed for the back gate. Victor stretched his back again.

"You need a massage, don't you," Andy said. "Call your person."

"Yes sir. I need dinner, too." Victor pulled Andy up off the lounger. "Go put away your wizard robe, I'll get things started with Loretta."

After dinner, Andy sent Jonathan the promised links. Then he and Loretta started debating what movie to watch. Victor broke in with, "Honeymoon in Vegas? Is that what you just said?"

"Yes," Loretta said. "Don't you like it?"

"I love it. Put it on. Holy shit." Victor had his phone out, texting Jonathan. "Las Vegas, Andy. For 'Countdown 4.' We could do a whole helicopter thing at the Grand Canyon."

"Oh shit." Andy was giggling. "Car chase up the Strip. You have to. Have to!"

"We could steal so much shit. This movie. 'Diamonds Are Forever.' 'Casino.' 'Swingers.' This is so money." Victor was giggling too.

Loretta said, "I want to be a showgirl. Or a drag queen. 'Miss Congeniality 2.' Oh my God, no." Now she was giggling. "Andy, *you* have to be a drag queen."

He laughed out loud. "Oh, I really do. Where do you get any fucking water in Las Vegas? All these damn things have water."

"Bellagio," said Victor and Loretta together. "Oh my God," Loretta added, "in the fucking *fountain*. Would they let us?"

"Honey, for the right money, they'll let you do anything. Okay. Who gets caught backstage and has to disguise himself as an Elvis impersonator? You or Jonathan?"

"It should be Jonathan. I got the backstage thing this time around. And could we get Lucas?" Victor was thinking of one of their co-stars on Tanith's movie, who actually played an Elvis impersonator on a streaming series set in Las Vegas. He glanced at his phone; the reply text from Jonathan was simply a thumbs-up. "Loretta, honey, we may actually have to write this whole thing."

The next day, Andy was going through Open Source Shakespeare and said "Holy shit" out loud. He sent a text to Jonathan: *Hey buddy there is an Aufidius speech in Act IV that is like whoa. I mean WHOA. Okay with you if we use something from that for your image with Mike?*

A reply came back fast: *what speech?*

*Scene 5 right after 'I know thee not' where CC does his do me a favor and kill me thing*

It was a few minutes before Jonathan wrote back. Then: *Whoa is right. I did not remember that*

*So is that too far over the line? I'd want to get physical with the staging*

*No, it's great. Go for it. Those videos were pretty whoa too*

*Awesome URA rock star TTYL.* Andy disconnected and made some notes. He could not fucking wait to see what Jonathan and Mike did with 'Let me twine mine arms about that body.' Or 'I have nightly since dreamt of encounters 'twixt thyself and me.' They might have to do both, because damn. He pulled up Mike's number and sent a new text describing the project and proposing the role.

It was almost three o'clock before he heard back: *Hi Andy sorry I had to wait till lunch hour and then look it up. I'm down for it. Do you have anyone doing Hamlet and Ophelia? Because I mentioned to Paula and she said Ophelia should have lived, Hamlet would have too because she would have knocked some sense into him*

*She is absolutely right and no I don't have anybody down for those roles. Get in Open Source Shakespeare and find me a couple of lines that work for them both surviving!*

*On it, thx Andy.* He set down the phone, because Dmitri and Patrick would be there in an hour and he had shit to do. Then he picked it up again because he'd had another brainstorm and was too excited to wait: *Hi Charlie saw Sacha in 'Diamond Dogs' and am dying to have him model for me. The Shakespeare project. Rosalind. Should have thought of it eons ago. Have him ping me back plz? Thx!* Now he could concentrate on Kent and Lear.

Andy shut down with difficulty that night. There was suddenly a lot going on with the Shakespeare

207

project. Half a dozen sets of costume were in production, he had several more characters scheduled to shoot, the Kent and Lear pictures were absolutely killer. Victor had been asleep for an hour when Andy thought *goddammit just write an email and get this out of my head.* He copied, watermarked, labeled, and compressed one of the photos of Dmitri and Patrick first. It was his favorite for the Kent line, showing Patrick on the throne but turned to profile, Dmitri standing alongside, their foreheads tipped together, right hands clasped and held to Dmitri's chest. His eyes were downcast; Patrick's gaze was on Dmitri's face. Andy knew they were going to love it.

Hi Reggie I would apologize for wee-hours communication except thank God for time zones I don't have to. Shakespeare thing is on fire. Also I've been cast for a thing shooting in England and Spain same time Victor is out there for his deal. So we will both be there next July, in an official capacity meaning we'll be doing publicity, and I'm going to have a fuck-ton of artwork. Attaching a sample of Kent/Lear from today. Haven't heard from Red and Mary regarding their upcoming stage thing, assuming no news is good news and that is still a thing. Hope all is well in the porn and painting biz. Cheers – Andy

He would have tried to get to sleep, except a reply came back before he shut down his tablet.

Good morning Andy. It's a bit early for me but no more than I deserve since I neglected to go out carousing. Thank you for the smashing picture (even without effects). Is that the bugger's natural hair?? As one who commenced shaving his off at the first sign of gray, I salute him. In more ways than one.

It so happens the company in question has opened rehearsals. A broadsword fan-club assembles every time they run the fight. Ms. Vaughn & Co. are of course away for their tour, but rumor has it Mr. Phelps gave the company's Macbeth considerable grief, of the 'why are you so much better than me you twat' variety.

Madame Warner is a stunner. They engaged Mr. Anand for the tiniest re-write of her canon scene, and to write a brief reunion at the end. The company has already pre-sold six weeks out and doesn't know what to do with itself. They've binned Hecate and their Lady Macbeth is said to be delivering a perfect performance. I shouldn't be surprised if the RSC sends a scout.

The porn business is, shall we say, on the rise. The traffic on your photo essay is breaking records. People are begging for prints. I am working on your picture and expect to deliver ahead of deadline. Hope all is well with you and Mr. Garcia, it's lovely looking at you both every day. Yrs – R. Galant

*He is such a flirt*, Andy thought, amused.

Hi Reggie I wish to fuck we could get there to see Red and Mary on the boards. Have already suggested they get the company to film it. Will nag some more and will underwrite the goddamned thing if necessary. Did you put an ad on that photo essay? If not, you should. Make some money and you can take us out for drinks when we're in London. Re: prints I'll consult V and advise. Had better sign off now though, if he wakes up and catches me online I'm in the shit.

If you wanted to hand-deliver that painting we'd both love to meet you in person. Cheers – Andy

Smiling at the thought of Reggie in Los Angeles, Andy finally shut down and went to sleep.


Two weeks later, weeks full of dance rehearsals, photography, and speed-writing 'Countdown 4,' Victor woke up when it was still dark, which was unusual. Molly wasn't curled up by his feet; Andy wasn't by his side. He blinked, frowned, noticed a faint light through the half-closed bathroom door. And then, now that he was listening for it, heard a soft low voice. "Yeah, I know. Me too, Mom. Most of the time I'm living life and things are fine. But sometimes it hits me. Of course it's terrible for you. You lived with him for fifty-four years. I only lived with him for eighteen. Who said you should be over it? Well, fuck them. It's barely been three months. Tell them, my son Andy, the movie star, says go fuck yourself." A soft laugh. "Yeah I know. But it sounds better than my son Andy who's married to a movie star. Oh, he's great. He's perfect. How did you like those pictures? I don't know if he's going to let me cut my hair for a while. Yeah, I'm getting all desperado up in here. I'll send you the link as soon as this new dance is done. He's killing it. We never had so much time to work on one before. He's doing stuff he thought he couldn't do. Well yeah, of course I knew he could do it. He's a talented son of a bitch. So is that one guy still trying to get in your pants?" Another, less-soft but muffled laugh. "Oh shit Mom stop, I'll wake him up. Yes it's the ass-crack of dawn on this side of the continent. No, it's fine. We're on vacation, I can nap all day. Call me anytime. No, I mean it, any damn time. I love you too."

Victor was sitting on the side of the bed in his robe, cherishing those casual words, waiting for Andy to finish talking. As soon as he did, Victor went through the bathroom and into the sunroom. It wasn't full dark. The sun would be up in an hour. The light from the phone was less noticeable out here. Molly looked up and thumped her tail. Andy gave him an apologetic smile. "Sorry."

"Not a problem." Victor leaned over for a kiss. "Everything okay with your mom?"

"Eh. She's how you'd expect. Okay most of the time, fucked up some of the time." Andy rested his head on the back of the chair. "When's the last time you saw John?" Victor's father, who still went in to work every day at his car dealership near San Diego.

"It's been a while. I was thinking I should go."

"Isn't his birthday in October?"

"Yeah. He's going to be eighty-two, can you believe that?" Victor was standing behind Andy now, hands on his shoulders. He dug his thumbs into those tight trapezius muscles and felt Andy start to relax.

"I didn't realize he was older than Pop."

"His other son is your age." Not 'my brother,' because by the time Victor came to the United States both of John Larson's other children were already grown and out of the house. They knew each other, they were all friendly in a careful sort of way, but they weren't family.

"Do not tell me John is a great-grandfather already." Thanks to having Loretta in the house all this time, Andy had recently realized that he himself could, technically, be a grandfather.

Victor laughed softly. "Not yet. You want to go down there with me? Couple of days at the beach, go into Escondido, take the old man out for a birthday dinner?"

"Sure. That would be great." They were quiet for a minute. "Trying to decide if I should make some coffee or go back to bed."

"If you can't decide, there must be something on your mind. You won't sleep anyway. How about I make some coffee, and you get ready to tell me what's on your mind. Then maybe we'll go back to bed." He squeezed Andy's shoulders and went into the bathroom to set up the coffeemaker. "Remember what a scene Patrick made about these bathrooms?"

Andy huffed out a laugh. "Didn't stop bitching for weeks. He still wants his own sunroom." He stayed where he was, curled up in his chair, while Victor came to the sunroom door, collected Molly, and took her down the outdoor stairs to the backyard. By the time they returned, the coffee was ready. Andy accepted a mug and another kiss. "Thanks, sweetheart. I'm really okay."

"I know you're okay. Let me be nice once in a while."

"You're almost always nice."

"I thought I was perfect."

Andy laughed into his coffee. "I've been telling you that for years." He uncurled himself, setting his feet on the ottoman. Pointing, flexing, curling his toes. They all cracked. "Yeah, fuck you, feet. I was thinking about something Pop told me on the way to Key West." Victor didn't press him. "We were talking about their trip out here, for the wedding. When they met John, and everybody else. Mom started by saying how glad she was that we got married then, when they could come. And then of course she said she was glad we got married at all, after living in sin all that time. Pop was cracking up. Then he starts talking about, I guess this was before the ceremony because after that it was party all night,

212

he wasn't super clear about the timeline. Anyway he said, okay, from here on out this is Pop talking." Victor made a sound of comprehension. "Me and John were talking about our boys. He said how proud he was of Victor, my son the movie star. He said he had a picture in his office at the dealership that Victor signed to him. Says 'para mi padre.' Every time he saw it he was like, I made that. How the fuck did that happen. And I said, shit, me too. I look at Andy and some of the shit he's done and I think, how did me and Eva do that. I drive a bulldozer and she's a waitress and we made that? Hard to believe." Andy sniffed, swallowed, took a breath. "And then Pop said, he said this to John, when they said they bought a house and then we saw the pictures and of course it's this fucking castle, I thought, well it figures."

Victor laughed, wiping his eyes, because he hadn't heard any of this before. Hadn't heard that his father was proud of him, or that he said that to other people. Didn't know that the autographed picture was in his office for the world to see. "Thanks for telling me that."

"I wish you could have had John in your life when you were a kid."

Victor sighed. "I saw him once a year. It was a hell of a lot better than nothing. It was more than a lot of kids got whose fathers were right there in the same town."

"He cared about your mother."

"Yeah, he did. He cared about both of us. He made sure I got everything I needed, and a lot of what I wanted. But I know what you mean. It's not the same."

"It's not the same. That's something else I got that you didn't get." Andy finished his coffee. "I

213

must have been nine or ten before I fully realized what a problem it was."

"What do you mean, problem?"

"I mean, by then it was crystal clear I was this way. They put me in dance at age six, for Christ's sake. I just couldn't give a fuck for all the guy things. Cars? Sports?" He made a *pfft* noise. "They tried me in soccer for a minute. I was like, what in the hell is the point of this." Victor laughed again. "I was about music and dancing and theater. I liked to hang out with girls because they were bitchy and giggly like me. I'd hang out in the kitchen at everybody's house, gossiping with the big sisters and doing bachata with the aunties. Most of the boys were okay with me because I wasn't feminine. I was foul-mouthed and I made them laugh. I could run really fast. I could take a fall. I could get over a fence like nobody else. But sports, no. I was like that girl in 'Clueless,' no balls flying at my face, please. Until later." Victor snickered. "But yeah. When the other boys had been in sports for a couple of years, it started to get obvious that Pop was working pretty hard to create a normal for me. To find me that safe place where there would be others of my own species. The great thing was he never acted like it was this chore. This imposition. It was just, this is my son and this is what he needs. I got to tell him how much I appreciated that."

"What did he say?"

"He said, what the fuck else was I supposed to do? You're my son." Andy wiped his eyes. After a moment he went on. "You know he solved the thing in high school. There was this one kid who beat me up twice. The first time I went home and I had the bloody nose and the black eye, and Pop was really pissed off. He asked if I wanted to learn how to fight.

214

I said I wanted to learn how to not fight. So he came up with this plan. He said, if it happens again, try this."

"What was the plan? What happened?"

"Oh, the guy did what these guys always do, pulled in a couple of other meatheads and cornered me. Started slapping me around, throwing a few punches. They were getting a little carried away. So I go, in my head, Pop this had better fucking work, and I say is this really worth your time? Is it not kind of unrewarding? It's not like I'm putting up a fight. It's not an achievement, is what I'm saying. He didn't know what the fuck to do." Andy was starting to laugh at the memory. "He was like, are you seriously trying to talk your way out of this? And I was like, well, obviously. Wouldn't it be so much cooler if you were at an actual boxing gym with other guys who like beating things up? Because I know a guy."

"Jesus Christ. Did it work?"

"Hell yeah, it worked. He was all, there's a gym for that? Dude ended up getting a boxing scholarship to college. We're still in touch. He came to Pop's memorial."

"What about the other two meatheads?"

"Oh, you know, they were followers. They followed him to the gym but they couldn't actually take getting hit so they found someone else to follow. Dumbasses." Andy thought about going to get some more coffee. Morning had officially broken. "Not long after that I started to get my height. I looked like a fishing pole, but I kept getting taller, and I learned how to move a little bigger. The rest of high school was fine."

"I was a scrapper."

Andy glanced over, smiling. "You got in fights a lot?"

215

"I was a mean little bastard. Anybody said anything about my mother, he was in the shit. Anybody fucking with a girl, he was in the shit." Victor was gazing out at the gradually lightening sky. "I was an altar boy too. I was in the church."

"Anybody mess with you?"

"No. Our church didn't have that. Somebody up the chain must have known what to look for and cared enough to keep it out. There were a couple of characters used to hang around the church school, expose themselves. We used to throw things at them. We weren't scared."

"What was the best thing about living where you lived?"

"The ocean," Victor said immediately. "I could never live far from the ocean."

"Yeah, me neither." Andy leaned forward, stretching. Trying to remember if they had any unbreakable things that day.

Victor must have read his mind. "We don't have anything scheduled. Want to take a vacation day? Go to the beach?" Andy turned his head and smiled. They were still sitting there, because there was no hurry, when Victor noticed activity in the yard. "Well, I'll be damned," he said softly.

"What?" Andy turned to look. "Oh, Loretta, you naughty girl." It was Jim, going out through the back gate. "Do you think he made her wait all this time, or is this just the first time he's stayed over?"

"Maybe the first time he's stayed over and we were out here to see him go." They both giggled, delighted. "Let's go downstairs and give her some shit."

Chapter 16

Loretta was, of course, in the audience when Andy and Victor performed 'Love is Blindness' at Chrome. She was there both nights: on the first night, sitting at a lounge table in the second row with some of their neighbors; on the second, sitting alone at the bar. Chrome's manager Terry swung by to help her maintain a buffer zone. The club was packed to capacity, with a standing-room-only crowd in the downstairs lounge. The word about the celebrity performers had gotten out quickly. Victor waved to Loretta as they took their bows. "It was nice of her to come again tonight," he said, giving Andy a sidelong glance.

"Oh, yes, very nice. Has nothing to do with the fact that Jim is here and that he's staying for the after-party." Andy was grinning. "Let's get off stage." They went off, the curtain went down, and they fetched up beside Rory at the panel.

She was speaking through the panel mic, inviting the rest of the second-act cast to the stage for the curtain call. People trooped past them, going out through the curtain for another bow. Eventually they all came back across the stage, returning to the green room to change clothes or otherwise get refreshed. "Okay. Half an hour to party time. Can't wait to see the video," Rory said. "That's the only sucky part of running the show, all I've got is this little monitor. How'd it feel?"

"Felt great." Andy had his arm around Victor. "This guy is fun to dance with."

"It is a much less terrifying routine than Ricky and Anya's apache was. What gave you the idea for that flying thing?"

"The Swan Dive," Victor said. "I figured if Zach could get him in the air, so could I."

Andy squeezed him. "Felt challenged."

"Inspired by slinging Loretta around." Victor was smiling. He was deeply satisfied with what they'd done.

"Bet you never thought you could do that a year after getting shredded," Rory said. "When are you going to get some new ink?"

"When I make up my mind what I want." Victor turned to Andy. "Let's go freshen up and dance some more."

Andy kissed him. "Okay." Then he leaned down to kiss Rory. "See you later, kitten face."

"Dinner, our place, soon." Rory started shutting down the panel.

When they went out into the house, they found Loretta still at the bar, talking animatedly with Cabaret regulars Mike and Paula Borodin. "I loved your piece so, so much. How did you find that music? Nobody else used music like that!"

"Nobody ever has," Paula said. "We heard it on this classical channel on Sirius one time when we were on a long drive. I was like wait a minute, that's 'Buttons and Bows,' which is a song I hate. One of those super-sexist standards," she told Loretta, who clearly didn't recognize the title. "Totally infantilizes women. Anyway I scribbled down the name of it and we looked it up."

"Because the second she started glaring at the display I thought, uh-oh," Mike said, smiling. "It's by a composer with our same last name. We meant to do it last year, but then I had that stress fracture."

"No one would know," Loretta said. "How you can dance! You're both wonderful! Victor," she said fondly. "You and Andy, oh my God, I could watch you all day."

"Well, you can't," Andy said, "because we're going to dance with you. Where's Jim?"

"He's packing up. No, here he is."

"Hi guys," Jim said. "Hi Mike, hi Paula. Another great performance. When are you going to kiss that law firm goodbye and go pro?"

"Probably never," Paula said. "We've got a groove. Where does a going-on-forty-year-old get to do work like this?" They were all aware of the shoveling-out procedure, Chrome staffers gently steering general-admission customers up and out of the downstairs lounge. Only those with the gold wristbands would be staying for the after-party.

"No one would know," Loretta said again. "You are beautiful on stage, los dos. I have such an envy."

"You're getting there," Victor said. "I'll take you for a spin as soon as they get the riffraff out." Andy and Paula laughed.

Jim said, "Guess I'll have to wait my turn. She'll get a better dance from you anyway."

"You need more practice, that's all," Andy said. "Dance with me. Oh, don't give me that look. I never made a pass at you."

"You totally did!" Jim was laughing.

"Okay once, the first time we met. Nothing ventured. He had all his hair then," Andy told Loretta, who snorted and covered her mouth for a second. Victor and Mike made eye contact and both tried very hard not to laugh. Paula wasn't even trying.

Jim had a disbelieving face on. "Jesus, Andy!"

Loretta bit her lip and said, "Tu cabello está bien."

"My hair is on its way to hair heaven." Jim didn't look too troubled about it, possibly because he was standing very close to Loretta and she had her fingers tucked into the waistband of his pants.

"Listen, we have music. Let's go." Victor gave Loretta a hand down from her barstool and led her across the room, heading for the stage steps. The curtain was open again, making more space for dancing. Mike shook hands with Andy and Jim, and took Paula that way too.

"Okay, kid. Lead me." Andy gave Jim an expectant look. Jim made an 'oh my God' face, gave a slight and trepidatious nod, and headed toward the steps.

"You're too tall for me," Jim said about two songs in.

"Height is irrelevant, as I'm sure Tomás has told you. Victor dances with me when I've got high heels on." Jim snorted. "You're doing fine, you know, considering."

"Considering I have two left feet."

"Considering you only started taking lessons a month ago, you moron. Loretta seems to like you a lot."

"I was so surprised she even remembered me." Jim glanced at Andy, who was apparently busy watching the entire space around them. "How many eyes do you have, anyway?" Andy laughed under his breath, but didn't say anything else. "She wants me to write to her after she goes back to Miami."

"You going to?"

"Well, yeah. I'm crazy about her. She's incredible." After a moment, he added, "I can't quite believe this is happening. She's so out of my league."

"That's what I thought when I met Victor. It was very Notting Hill for a minute there." Jim got the reference; he nodded. "The funny thing is, he felt the same way about me." They were into a third song now, and Jim hadn't crashed yet. Andy said, "You're doing awfully well. Dance with her next. She's insecure, you know."

"Why?"

"A lot of bad men. Disrespect. Not being valued as a person." Andy gave that a few seconds. "As soon as they get done writing that first draft, she's going home. Give her a reason to come back."

"I'm sure going to try."

"I did the whole in loco parentis thing with Jim," Andy told Victor later, when they were up in their bedroom stretching.

"Were you like, what are your intentions?" Andy snorted. Victor was smiling, leaning over a leg. As always, Andy had better extension. "I'm gonna catch up with you one day."

"Don't you challenge me, sonny." Andy shifted, going into a full split, and Victor made an annoyed sound. Andy laughed.

"You're such a dick."

"I *have* such a dick." Victor cracked up. Andy was trying not to. "Anyway not exactly. He said she asked him to write to her, I said are you going to, he said yes. Then I told him she's planning to go back to Miami when you guys finish the first draft, and to give her a reason to come back."

"You think she will? God, I hope so. It would be so great to have her out here with us." After a second Victor added, "I mean, not literally with us. I'm ready to start fucking you in the kitchen again." They both started giggling. "And in the living room. Over the dining table. On the stairs."

Andy fell out of his position, laughing. He folded his legs and scooted back against the wall. "All of that, yeah. Maybe she'll move in with him."

"She wants a baby."

"Oh, really? Huh." Andy hadn't thought about that. Enough of their friends had kids that it wasn't a totally out-there concept. "Maybe the kid would get his eyes. Jim has pretty eyes." Dark blue, with dark lashes. "She said her mother has blue eyes."

"What if he doesn't want kids?" They stared at each other for a moment. Victor changed position, sitting cross-legged in front of Andy. "Well. All we can do is wait and see, I guess."

"And let them both know we're behind them either way." Andy leaned forward for a kiss. "Let's get ready for bed."

Victor got to his feet. "Molly's way ahead of us."

"She's been looking at her watch for the last half hour, going will you turn off the light please." Andy accepted a hand up from Victor. They both petted their dog on the way to the bathroom.

October 2019

The writing team called it at the end of September. The screenplay wasn't polished, but it was complete. They met up one more time to read it through. "I can't believe we did this so fast," Jonathan said.

Loretta made a *pfft* sound. "I can't believe we did it at all! The first time, it felt like a game."

"Well." Victor regarded them both. "I think we make a great team. Do you want to send it to the producer now, or wait till we hear about the rough cut on number three? Or maybe we could have Tanith take a look at it."

"Oh yes," Loretta said immediately. "Would she look at it? She could tell us if we are out of our minds." Jonathan laughed. "God in heaven, I never typed so much in my life."

"We owe you," said Victor. "Doing this by hand on legal pads would have been a pain in the ass." Loretta's phone buzzed. She glanced at it and grimaced. "Aren't you going to answer that?"

"It's my mother," she said. "She will say when are you coming home, why are you wasting your time in L.A., don't you know there is work for you here. She is my manager," she told Jonathan. "I think I have to fire her. There will be such a fight. She wants me to do local things, little things, so she can keep me close."

Victor had already heard about this. "You know if you want the big roles, you're going to need to be out here," he said softly. "You have friends here. She doesn't need to worry about you."

"Gracias, Victor. You and Andy and Jonathan are the best friends. All your friends are wonderful. I don't know if I want the big roles. But I can do better than being a spokesmodel." She sighed. "I do need to go home. I have things to finish there."

"And I actually need to go home." Jonathan stood up, stretched, offered a hand to Victor. "This has been great. I never would have thought I'd be co-authoring an actual screenplay. I barely graduated from high school."

"You have good ideas," Victor said. "And you know about story, and character, and action."

"What does Andy think?"

"Andy said, only for you and this genius nonsense would I consent to having my ass waxed. Again." Loretta and Jonathan cracked up.

"You shared the ass-waxing thing, didn't you," Andy said later, because Victor kept snickering.

"You seriously can't expect a person to play a drag queen with a hairy ass."

"You don't have a hairy ass," Victor said, barely keeping it together.

"But I'll be wearing a *thong*, Victor."

"Oh Jesus, stop."

Andy did not stop. "You of all people should know that fishnets do not provide good coverage. Inappropriate hair situations are instantly public knowledge." He bit his lip, heroically suppressing a giggle as Victor bent forward, hands pressed to his face, shoulders shaking. "Would you like me to go put some on and remind you of this?"

"God in heaven, yes."

The first thing Andy and Victor did after taking Loretta to the airport was text their housekeeper Consuelo and give her the rest of the day off. The second thing was to go home, ensure the place was empty, and take off all their clothes. The third thing was to defile some of the rooms they hadn't defiled for two months. Several hours later, Victor got a hand on the back of the couch and pulled himself out from under Andy. "God almighty. That was epic."

"Thank you." Andy wriggled until he was face-up. Victor was sitting more or less upright; Andy's legs were across his lap. "And thank you. That was epic."

"Is there anything we have to do for the rest of this week?"

"No." There might have been, but Andy couldn't care at the moment. Victor patted his thigh. Andy smiled up at him. "Maybe dinner with Rory and Dana."

"Their place?"

"Yeah. Remember she said so, after Milonga?"

"Oh yeah. I was so caught up in the writing gang." Victor was thinking about going to the kitchen for a drink. Instead he found himself petting Andy's legs. "You've got quite a tan."

"You too. We've been spending a lot of time outside. I'm trying to remember if I've had long pants on during daylight hours, like, at all." He shifted, enjoying that light touch. If Victor didn't stop, they were going to be back in business very soon.

Victor didn't stop. His hand moved to the untanned region, tracing the edges of the tan line, teasing the smooth pale skin. Andy inhaled, made a pleased sound, and parted his legs. Victor found new areas to explore. They were both aroused again. "I knew it would be like this," Victor said softly.

"It's always like this. The only thing better than looking at you is kissing you."

"Get that leg over me." Victor shifted forward, turning toward him. Andy lifted a leg and put his foot behind his husband. Then he wrapped his hand around Victor's wrist and pulled himself up so they were sitting face to face.

A couple more minor adjustments later, Victor was leaning on the back of the couch, Andy was straddling Victor's lap, and they were kissing. Deep, slow, with his hands in Victor's hair. Victor had his hands on Andy's hips, moving in slow figure eights, front to back. Andy broke the kiss for a moment, gazing at his husband's face, into those hot sleepy eyes. "I love you so much."

"I love you."

"Can you believe we still have nine more months of this?"

"I bet I'll feel exactly this same way on the day before we leave for London."

"What way." Andy said that with his mouth against Victor's face, right hand on his neck, letting the Australian ring rasp against that silver chain. His left hand was clutching the back of the couch, because Victor had a hand between them now. Playing with both of them, with his other hand on Andy's ass. "Jesus, Victor."

"Exactly this hot for you. Every time like it's the first time. Can't believe I've got this gorgeous man in my hands." Victor's mouth on Andy's clean-shaven throat now, Andy's head tipped back. "Loving the taste of you. The scent of you. The way you move, my God, Andy." They were both moving, only a little, but they couldn't help themselves.

Andy was gasping into Victor's hair now, arm wrapped around his head. Focused on the hand between them. "Jesus *fuck*, Victor, get us both and I'll come, I swear to God, let me feel you. Oh yeah, you sweet thing, you're close. Tighter. Jesus. Are you going to give it to me, come on, come on baby, *yes,* fucking *hell*."

Victor's teeth were on Andy's shoulder and he was breathing hard. He listened to Andy's breath settle, timed his own to match. Andy shifted, relaxing his arms, bringing his hands back to Victor's face. Stroking his thumbs over those elegant cheekbones, going in for one more kiss. Victor opened his eyes. "Never. It's impossible."

"What's impossible?" Andy kissed him lightly.

"That there could ever be anyone more perfect than you. I love you."

"I love you."

"It's a good goddamned thing this slipcover is washable." Victor smiled as Andy slid off to the side, giggling.

"It's a good thing we have two of them." Andy managed to get onto his feet. "God. I could use a drink."

"Me too. Give me a hand up."

"Since you just gave me a hand up? Sure thing."

Victor was slightly concerned about their dinner date with Rory and Dana. Aside from brief meetings at Chrome for the Swan Dive, 'Diamond Dogs,' and 'Milonga,' they hadn't spent any time together since spring. It left him feeling almost the way he'd felt the very first time they all had dinner together. That had been early in his actual, in-the-open relationship with Andy. After the Year of Maybe was finally over, after they'd said 'I love you,' but before Andy's longtime girl friends had officially approved of him. He wasn't really trying to conceal his nerves, so he wasn't surprised when Andy said, "This feels familiar, doesn't it."

"Too familiar. I feel like I'm going to meet my parole officer."

Andy huffed out a laugh. "How do you know what that feels like?"

"Hey, I've done my research. Remember how long I was on 'Vice.' We had all those LAPD consultants."

"You ever miss that?"

"Fuck no." He really didn't, even though the series had been good to him. Getting that role had been a huge deal. If he hadn't already been established in it, coming out could have tanked his career. If Victor hadn't had a good reputation with the production company, they would never have considered taking Andy on; he'd barely even worked in TV before. And the whole reason had been to break the huge taboo about a gay relationship, expressed physically, in primetime. That first kiss had set off an explosion. In a way, they were still recovering from it. "I feel like we're not really done with it yet," Victor said after a moment's thought. "Not until we've fully processed what happened last fall. Maybe I'll miss it when that's all some kind of hazy memory."

That got a skeptical snort from Andy. "I don't think anything about that is ever going to be hazy. I'll never forget what it felt like." *Awful*, he thought. The moment of incomprehension after Stan said 'Gun,' being knocked off his feet by Victor at the instant they heard the shot, landing flat on his back with Victor on top of him. So horribly still, for what felt like forever. "You're talking about that with Robyn, right?"

Victor glanced over from the driver's seat. They hardly ever talked about it themselves. "Yes. That and a lot of other things. Things about Mama, and John, and what happened with you this summer. We're making progress there."

"Good. Well, if Dana and Rory start in on you tonight I will play the diva card and shut them up. It's my own fault. I went running to them."

"So did I."

"But I shouldn't have. I'm sorry for that, too. I'm a grown-ass adult and I should have known better. Now they'll always think of that."

After a moment Victor said, "I appreciate that. Dana did scare the shit out of me."

"I told her that. She wasn't very apologetic." Not at all, actually, but that was Andy's fault too. Granted, he was still raw from Miami at the time. Nonetheless, he'd been a little too operatic about the whole thing, given the relatively minor offense. *Minor in retrospect*, he thought. *Should have put him face-down on the bed and dealt with it the old-fashioned way.* The thought made him snicker.

"What's funny?"

"Thinking I should have never left the room that night. Should have thrown my weight around a little. You wouldn't have been in any doubt how much I wanted you. How much I always have. I should have backed you up against the wall and said," dropping into his sex voice, "you know what, you're right. All you get is me from here on out. Get on that bed and let's see how you like it."

"Jesus, Andy." Victor squirmed in his seat, grinning. "This car doesn't need a stick shift." They were still giggling about it when he parked at the cottage.

Rory opened the door, saying, "Hi guys, good to see you. I made cookies."

"She wasn't supposed to," Dana said as they went in. "It's pot roast, and there's wine, and cookies mean my ass is back in the weight room in the morning."

"Your ass is always in the weight room," Rory said. Victor and Andy exchanged a glance, mutually decided that everything was cool, and went on through to the dining den.

"So did you reach critical mass with the hair?" Dana asked once they'd progressed to the coffee and cookies portion of the evening. "It really did look hot."

"Yes it did," Victor said, doing something to Andy under the table.

Andy stretched elaborately, settling one arm over Victor's shoulders, murmuring something to him that Rory and Dana couldn't hear. Then he said, "It'll be back eventually. I'm doing our routine for 'Spy Games' in drag so the next couple of months will be about less hair, not more." Victor snickered. "Temporarily, catnip. I promise."

"Victor, quit molesting Andy, the kids can see you." Both of the small dogs were on the bench with Rory and Dana. Spike was on a cushion not far away. Dana put her hands over the dachshund's eyes. "Don't look, Oscar. Guys, we may have to ask you to assign us characters for the Shakespeare thing. We cannot get our story straight." All of them seemed to hear that at the same time. All of them started laughing. After a minute, she said, "Okay yes. Phenomenally poor choice of words. Could you?"

"If you really want us to, yes of course," Andy said. "I promise it won't be straight." He seemed to lose focus for a moment. Then he blinked and said, "So guess what new craziness we're launching."

"Jesus, you don't have enough to do?" Rory drank some coffee, watching them. Whatever they'd been talking about in the car before they arrived was obviously still on their minds. "And speaking of enough to do, would you like to be excused for a few minutes? Because you could go out back in the bamboo grove and do whatever you're already halfway doing, and we could get the kitchen cleaned up."

"And then we could have a conversation in which everyone is paying attention." Dana wanted to be annoyed but she couldn't. Victor was giggling, Andy was grinning, and the whole vibe was so ridiculously normal that she finally got over that summer's scare. It was one too many, she realized. They'd almost lost Victor for real, could have lost both of them, and not until Victor's panicked text came in had she really understood how vital that relationship was to her own sense of well-being. "Rory, my darling little cherubim, let's address some housekeeping. Gentlemen, get out or get yourselves in order."

Victor and Andy took a second to silently consult, silently agree 'later,' and separate, following the women to the kitchen. "Give us something to do," Andy said. "That isn't that."

Dana laughed under her breath and patted her wife's ass. "Honey, take a load off. You did all the hard work. I'll wash, Andy can dry, and Victor can tell us more about how they're utterly failing at being on vacation." Rory went to sit in the reading chair, instantly joined by Spike the cat.

Both men were smiling. Victor said, "We are *totally* failing. Neither of us has ever done it. Maybe by the time we go to Europe we'll figure it out." He thought through the list of projects, most of which their friends already knew about, and remembered what they hadn't mentioned yet. "On top of everything else, we're trying to buy the property on the other side of us."

"No shit!" Rory was fully surprised. "I thought you would have been sick and tired of real-estate shenanigans after you finally got that triplex squared away. I mean, we did that renovation last year for the gang in the big house and I never want to see another contractor again." Their cottage was on the same lot as a full-sized house, currently shared by two families.

"Well, actually." Andy wiped a wineglass, hung it in the under-cabinet rack, and went on. "The whole triplex operation was so painless, it's almost like it never happened. Paige was on it from day one, Sharon was a very capable second brain, we weren't even there for six weeks, and by the time we were really paying attention the worst of it was over. But Victor had this idea while we were on location."

"It had to do with a pool," Victor said, and both women made sounds of instant understanding. "Because we were both loving the hotel pools this summer. And that house is an eyesore."

Dana said, "Yes it is. And you clearly can't put a pool in your own backyard. Yours is party central."

"Right." Andy hung up the last wineglass. He and Dana had always been good at cleanup duty. "We asked Elliott, the guy who handled both our other things, to bloodhound the situation and see if the owner had any interest in selling." He eyed the plate of cookies, took one for himself, and offered the plate to Victor. Victor delivered a cookie to Rory, handed one to Dana, and set the plate down with a sad look. Andy stifled a laugh and did not say 'you know we could burn that off later.'

"And?" Dana ate the cookie, momentarily regretted it, decided it was worth it.

"And it's this older couple, not super old but retired, they've lived there for thirty years. They have a kid who lives in Monterey and wants them to move up there, but they would have to build something. And the kid doesn't have room for them to live with him and store their stuff. So they're looking at renting in a very not-inexpensive market for however long it takes them to build in a very not-inexpensive market." Andy took a breath.

Victor finished the story. "So Elliott made the approach and they told him all this. He said, how much would you need, because my client is motivated. And *they* said, is it the guys next door?"

"Uh-oh." Rory glanced at Dana.

"No, it was good. Elliott said he didn't answer straight off, because we asked him not to say it was us. But instead of hanging up on him they said, because if it's those guys we wouldn't mind seeing the place go to them. So let us get back to you after we talk to our kid. And that's where it is right now."

Dana was impressed. "Do they even know you?"

"Well, we didn't think they did. But I guess, you know, they've been there this whole time. Saw us fix up the Faux Chateau, and then the Sleeping Beauty." Andy ate the last cookie, because he could see that Dana wanted it and that she would hate herself for eating it.

"Thank you for eating that," she said. "Are you thinking it's another rental property?"

"Well, ideally," Victor said. "Because then a big chunk of the cost is covered. But it would have to be someone who's okay with us being in the pool all the time." Rory snorted. "Us and probably all our friends."

"Probably," Dana said. "We had a minute of thinking we could put a pool between the cottage and the house. But the logistics were like, oh my God."

"They're going to be bad enough if this comes off," Andy said. "But we're willing to tear that house down if we have to."

Chapter 17

A week later, while Andy and Victor were down in Escondido taking Victor's father out to dinner, they got a text from their real-estate guy Elliott: *House next door available. Sending email. Asking price based on recent comps plus two years estimated rental expense.* Andy saw the message after they returned to their hotel at the beach. "Honey, looks like you might get your pool."

Victor read the message over his shoulder. "Our pool. Open up the email?"

Andy got his tablet out, opened his email, and pulled up the message. The number was on the high side, but they'd expected that. The proposed vacancy date was earlier than they'd expected. "We can afford it, right?"

"Oh, definitely. Especially if we get a tenant." They brainstormed for a few minutes. Once the former owners were safely away, they could get an inspection and see if the house was salvageable at all. If so, they might need an architect to look at it to see if there was any possible way to make the thing less of an excrescence. "I guess that's what we get for buying a castle," Victor said, smiling. "Now everything else has to live up to it."

Andy was studying the street-view photograph Elliott had attached. "You can't even really see the goddamned thing behind those fucking cedars. All you can see is dingy beige stucco, and brown trim, and that shitty little excuse for a window. Is that a picture window behind the cedars?"

Victor squinted at it. "Could be."

"I am so not a fan of brown asphalt shingles. It can't possibly be two stories, can it?" The shape of the house was so obscured by overgrown trees, it was hard to tell. Neither of them had thought to take a picture from the back. All they had really been aware of was a desolate, empty, large yard in between a shabby fence at the alley side, and a row of arbor vitae up by the house. "You know, these people should be living in a condo, not a house. They clearly are not gardeners." Andy wasn't either, but at least he cared how the outside looked. Their own backyard was very low-maintenance, designed for entertaining. The front was a shallow formal garden with turf bordered by lavender at the sidewalk edge, and white Iceberg roses up by the house. "If the front matched the cottage garden Paige is doing at the Sleeping Beauty, that could be cute."

Victor made a sound of agreement. He was still thinking about how tall the property was (or wasn't). "If it's sound, maybe we could pop the roof. Build up. Make it another duplex. The top unit could be our private guest house, for when friends are in town, and the bottom could be for the regular tenant."

Andy was watching Victor think. *You are so cute.* "Remember how much it cost to re-do all the systems and shit at the triplex."

"Yeah, I know. Let's run this by Patrick and his team. If the studio picks up 'Countdown 4,' and if I get the same rate for that, it would be a wash."

"If they pick it up based on your script," Andy pointed out, "you're going to get paid more. And I really don't think they'd bring you back and not give you a raise. You got quite a bump from two to three, and not all of it was because of your story credit."

"And I want it." Victor was grinning. "I want that pool."

"I want it too." Andy laughed. He was so excited. "God that would be awesome. Maybe we could plant our own bamboo grove."

When they put in an offer on the Faux Chateau there were a lot of hoops to jump through. They hadn't been married then, for one thing. On this one, the banks and lawyers took about five minutes to say 'okay.' Andy couldn't wait to tell somebody, so he texted Rory: *We got the house*

*Cool!! How bad is it?*

Andy almost wrote 'we need explosives' but settled for *Salvageable*. He expected her to reply with something snarky.

Instead she wrote *Will you teach me to swim?*

*How do you not fucking know how to swim?! You grew up in San Diego!*

*Yeah okay but we didn't have a pool and none of my friends did either*

*Did you not swim in the ocean?*

*I got wet in the ocean. I did not swim*

Andy was amazed that he never knew this. *Honey you're going to be the cutest little feathery mermaid when I get done with you. btw thanks again for dinner, we'll experience the joy of bamboo some other time*

*ROFLMAO*

*And incidentally you and Dana will be playing Tybalt and Romeo. Govern yourselves accordingly*

*Uh what*

*I'll send you the lines later. Besos y Abrazos chica*

*Y lo mismo para ti*. Andy disconnected, highly satisfied. He and Victor had combed the complete works for a slash pairing that hadn't already been done (or at least claimed), that was also gender-bent, and that would therefore sufficiently spank their friends for taking so damn long to make up their minds. Victor devised the staging for the lines in about five seconds. Andy was already itching to shoot it.

Victor had scaled back to one-hour sessions with Robyn after a few more late-night and early-morning talks with Andy. He was being more open about his insecurities; Andy was breaking off pieces of his own protective shell. "I never realized how much we were both hiding," Victor told Robyn. "It always seemed like we were completely open with each other."

"History can hide for a long time when the present day is action-packed," she said. "You two haven't had this kind of time before."

"It's so unbelievably great. I always felt like, I don't want to miss a thing. There's so much there. He's so complicated. But yeah, we were always so busy. We're still busy, but we get to do a lot more together. Going to the gym, going to the beach. Taking twenty minutes or an hour, or two hours, to simply sit and be together and talk, it's such a luxury. I was at a meeting the other day and mentioned I was taking time off, and this one guy said ugh, how can you stand it."

"What did he mean?"

"He meant both things. Taking time off, not working, but also being with Andy so much. I didn't want to ask, but I thought, don't you want to be with your wife? Do you work so you can avoid her?"

"It's not uncommon."

"Ugh." He made a face. Robyn suppressed a smile. "I think we're doing the right thing. I think we needed this."

"I think so too."

"It all comes down to time, doesn't it. I'm never going to get enough with him, enough of him, because we found each other so late." Victor sighed, trying to relax in the big wing-back chair. "I'm trying not to wish, you know? Not to be resentful about what we can't have. I want to make the best of it."

"How do you think all this relates to what happened this summer?"

"Now I'm starting to think it was all about the shooting. About being so close to losing it all. I think that triggered me in a way I didn't even recognize." Robyn didn't say anything, simply waited. Victor let the words come. "Me being jealous of people from his past is nothing more than me wishing I'd been there instead. It's got nothing to do with Alonzo or any of those other guys. But there was also this thing, you know, he had so many people when Ronnie died. When I lost Mama, I had Tía Susana back in Jalisco, and that was it. My cousins, none of them really knew me. I'd been away for almost twenty years. Here in L.A., nobody really knew me except Andy. I think me going off in July was because of that. You had all those people, and all I have is you. I would have laid down my life for you, and if I'm not enough for you I am nothing."

Robyn let that sit for a minute. "Do you still feel that way?"

"No. It's not even true now, it's a holdover from back then. I've got more friends than I have time for. We were talking about it, though. About the actual event, which we haven't talked much about up to now. I said some of this stuff, pretty much exactly. He said, do you remember what I said the morning after? And I kind of didn't. I was drugged up, not really in my right mind. I know I told him why I did it. How I saw Stan looking behind us and knew, like I

238

could see it, where the gun was. And I launched because I could not let him die. He said something then that I didn't really remember. He reminded me. It was, if he had killed you, do you think I could live with that for one fucking day."

"So then what happened."

"Well, there was some crying." Victor half-laughed. "We've both been doing more of that this past year than I think we ever have. He said, if I lost you, I would survive because of our friends. They wouldn't let me not survive. But there would be this giant hole where you used to be. Nothing and no-one could fill that. I wouldn't even try. You are my one true love." Victor swallowed, took a deep breath, and blinked away tears. "He said, I would be walking around without my heart for however long it took me to actually die."

Robyn reached for the Kleenex box, took two for herself, and passed the box to Victor. After a few minutes she said, "Well. What did you say?"

"I didn't try to say anything. I was a mess. I took him to bed."

"Did that work?"

Victor coughed out a laugh. "Yeah, that worked."

"So what's next?"

"Well, we're rehearsing this new dance that we'll perform in November. In December we'll start working with our arranger on this concert for April, and we're going over to Miami to see Eva for Christmas. Andy's brushing up his tap, I'm taking jazz lessons. A couple of friends are doing choreography for us for the April thing. We bought the house next door. That'll be a long-ass project, but there's not much we have to do personally aside from write checks."

"You bought another house." Robyn's tone was rich with disbelief.

"Well, it was an eyesore, and we want a pool." He could tell she was trying not to laugh. "We'll probably have tenants again. That's if we can turn this shithole into a duplex."

"Is it that bad?" Victor got his phone out to show her a picture of the house next door. All the encroaching trees had been cut down so the inspector could actually see the place. It looked wretched. "Oh," Robyn said. "Well, the picture window will be nice." Victor snickered. "What happened with your screenwriting project?"

"My friend Tanith, the one who wrote the movie we did last year, she took a look at the script for us and said it didn't suck. So as soon as we get some feedback on the rough cut for number three, we'll probably toss ours at the producer. The earliest we could start work on it would be a year from now."

"You two are never going to run out of things to do, are you." Now she sounded amused.

"Not for a while, anyway. And if we do, we can sit by the pool until something comes along."

October 2019

Ten days before Halloween, it was another quiet evening after another low-demand day. Consuelo had left hours ago, before Andy and Victor went back in the house from their afternoon practice in the home studio. Vicky and Sharon came over for dinner, and to make the men laugh with stories about the rehearsals happening at Shall We Dance for the upcoming Cabaret show. "Well, you know Tomás never stops having ideas," Vicky said. "Our thing for 'Milonga' was fun but with this theme being 'Trick or Treat' it could have gone a couple different ways."

"A whole lot of ways," Andy agreed. "Any idea what the balance is? Rory wouldn't cough it up. Some years it's like a freak show, some years you think, okay, if this wasn't a bar we could totally have kids in here."

"What did you do with all that candy, anyway?" Sharon was referring to the photo shoot for the Halloween poster. Andy had put the four scantily-clad Underground Cabaret principals in a plastic kiddie pool and covered them with candy. "And thank you for not giving any of it to us, by the way."

Victor said, "He filled up a few piñatas and gave them to Tasha to take over to Theo's school. They had to do the whole disclaimer thing about peanuts and tree nuts and whatever."

"So then I felt bad and put together one with zero allergenic candy contents," Andy said. "The four sensitive kids can bash away at that one."

"Anyway, it seems like the lineup is mostly freaky with a little bit of cute. Anya and Ricky are doing a thing. Dmitri and Hiro are doing their 'Toxic' thing again, everybody begged them to. Sam and Mateo are doing 'Dragula.' Mike and Paula are working on something I haven't seen because they're keeping it over in their local studio. Oh, and Stacey's back, which will definitely be a treat."

"No kidding! That's great!" Andy was sincerely pleased to hear that. Stacey had been with the Cabaret for nine years, but had taken a long break from performance after having a child. "Is she doing aerial silk again?"

"That's what I hear. Some kind of blues song about being tied up." Vicky rolled her neck, well aware that she hadn't yet answered the unspoken question of what she was doing. "You're dying to know, aren't you." Both men laughed. "We're doing

241

'Devil Inside.' It's fast as heck. And a lot less tango than I'm used to with him."

"I'm guessing it's closer to the freaky end of the spectrum. Can't wait to see it."

"There's something else you're going to want to see. The girls from 'Diamond Dogs' came in with a group cabaret routine that's really something. I only even know because Rory let me see the submission tape. It's one of Tanith's songs, 'Speak No Evil.' I hear she re-wrote the lyrics, she wants to use it when she does the movie."

Victor was a little hurt. "She didn't ask me to record it."

"I thought she was going to. She said something about it last month. Maybe it got away from her?" Vicky looked guilty. "Annette said they've been using a backing track, no vocal. Look, hold on." She stood up, went over to the B side, and quickly returned with phone in hand, texting: *Tanith WTF Victor never heard from you about that song and we're talking about Halloween and DON'T KICK MY PUPPY*

A reply came quickly: *FUCK that totally got away from me SHIT it's next week groveling in 3 2 1*

Victor's phone pinged a minute later, over at the control center. Vicky was still standing, so she went over there to fetch it. He read the text out loud. "Sorry Victor I'm teaching again and forgot all about asking you if you could record a song for me. It's super short notice but I'll pay for the studio time and Valerie etc if you're available. Rewrite of Speak No Evil. Can do?" He looked over at Andy, who appeared to be fairly pissed-off. "You know what all she's got going on."

"There are these magical tools called calendars, Victor." Sharon and Vicky gave each other an 'oops' face, because Andy didn't get mad very often. He caught them doing it. "Don't worry, I won't bitch at her. I am keeping score, though."

"You always do, honey." Victor took a look at their calendar, then wrote back to Tanith: *I have unbreakable appointment Westside Thursday 15:00 otherwise can be where you need me when you need me*

*I'll get on to the studio and Val in the morning and let you know ASAP. Session will be ASAP. IOU and truly sorry for being an airhead, I never wanted anyone but you for it.* Victor didn't read that one out loud, but he showed it to Andy. "It'll probably happen. I'm flexible."

"Getting more so all the time," Andy murmured.

"And on that note," Sharon said, "we'll clear out of here. Nina Simone's been with Paige and Maya for hours and they're probably coming up with some rationale for a goat."

"No goats," Andy said with alarm. "Absolutely no goats. I draw the line at chickens, that is the livestock limit."

"Yeah, you tell Paige where I come from, we eat goats." Victor watched Vicky and Sharon laugh. They headed out through the kitchen door to go collect their daughter. Andy and Victor cleared up, tidied the kitchen, then leaned on the counter and stared at each other. "On the one hand, I'm glad she wanted me. On the other hand, I'm like fuck."

"Exactly," Andy said. "What if you decided you couldn't stand being idle, and ran off to do that play in San Francisco?" Neither of their agents had stopped sending them things. "This last-minute shit isn't going to fly. We pulled 'Carlos Gardel' together that way but only because we all knew it was fucking happening."

243

"Well, she knows we're doing 'Spy Games.' She would know I wouldn't ditch on you. But I'll have a word with her. Remind her how far out we've got stuff scheduled." Victor shifted closer, letting his body rest against Andy's. "I love that you're mad about it." Andy huffed out a laugh. "I'll find out what else she's got going on with this thing. Remind her it's the both of us, which means two schedules to work around."

"Remind her about that shared calendar. Sandesh and his tool kit. Imagine what a clusterfuck last year would have been without that." Andy put an arm around Victor, kissed the side of his face. "I'm glad you're getting to record that song again."

"Jesus, yes. Maybe she dropped the rap part."

"Jesus, yes." They both snickered. "Let's take Molly out, then take a nightcap upstairs."

"I've been wondering," Victor said later. They were lying in bed, doing the unhurried cuddle thing that had gradually developed over the past few months. Andy had his head on Victor's shoulder, an arm across his chest, and one leg between his husband's. Sooner or later things were likely to develop; they nearly always did. But for now, it was another sweet quiet moment.

"What have you been wondering, querido."

"When you did those photos for Tanith's play. When we met. It never occurred to me that you lived at the Brewery. I figured she brought you out there because we already had the space."

"There were all kinds of rehearsal things going on back then. That room got used a lot. It's not as often now that there are some newer spaces around town that have sound and lights, but I hear they still get the lower-budget productions in there." Andy glanced up for a second, then laid his head down again. "I'm not sure Tanith even knew I lived there. Jim referred me for that job. She found him through the showgirls, because they'd done a couple of Cabaret things at Chrome and he was there taping." Another quiet minute. "I almost gave you my business card. I never heard of you before. Didn't watch the show."

"You watched it after."

"After our first night, yeah. I wanted to hate you. I was like, please let him suck. Please let that bastard be only a pretty face." Victor laughed silently. "Obviously that didn't work out. I knew you were good because of that fucking play."

"My part was so small."

"Yeah, but you killed it. What made you go out for that, anyway?"

"I'd done a few stage things, a few musicals. My only bad guy was Billy, from 'Carousel.' I hate that show."

"God, I do too. A few good songs, but the message blows."

"Right? Forget passion, forget dreams, this tiny life is all you get. And you'll never walk alone, because we'll be up your ass every goddamned second of the day." Victor felt Andy laughing and tracked the conversational thread back. "For Tanith's thing, it seemed like with such a small cast, there was a good chance I could get noticed. And it was a different part for me. I'd done bad guys on TV plenty of times but they were, like, fill in the blanks bad guys. Oh we need a bad guy here, you know. That guy Ivory, he was a piece of work. I had a whole back story for him in my head. Why he would run a club like that, why it would be this friendly neighborhood dance hall with entertainment, and then

245

after hours it goes all the way dark. I asked Tanith how she came up with that."

"What did she say." Andy's voice was soft. He loved hearing Victor talk about his work.

"She said she wrote the first version after reading this series of books about a vigilante. The Evan character wasn't a cop at first, and Jenny's character wasn't the girl's mother. She was one of the entertainers. I'll bet Tanith's going to pull from that for 'Diamond Dogs,' the movie version."

"And we're coming from Tina's drawing. That whole straight-razor thing gave me a little chill."

"God, me too." Victor was petting Andy's arm, fingers lightly brushing up and down. "Reza better be glad he's not in this one." Andy snickered. Tina had used Reza's face for a character in her Eisner-winning book 'A Nightingale Sang.' He'd survived in that story, in a 'to be continued' kind of way. "When you found out about that show. Tanith's play. Did you wish you were in it?"

"No," Andy said. "I was fully off-stage. Even if I hadn't been, there was no dance chorus. She had the showgirls and the social dancers."

"You could have played Ivory."

Immediate disagreement. "Oh no. Not then. I could do it now." Another minute, enjoying Victor's touch. "The last thing I'd done was 'Chicago.' I told Rory, when I was living with them, I regretted doing it. Even though it was a great experience, for a good cause. It was like tearing the scab off. I was really serious about never again."

"Sorry about that."

Andy turned his head, kissed Victor's chest. "I was so far gone over you, you could have suggested going out on a cruise line as a song and dance team and I probably would have said yes."

246

"We could still do that." Victor felt Andy laugh again. "We could be Gene Kelly and Donald O'Connor."

"Fred Astaire and Judy Garland."

Victor snorted. "Bing Crosby and Danny Kaye." They were both giggling now. "So how short is your skirt going to be for Spy Games?"

"Wouldn't you like to know."

Victor's hand moved south, to the top of Andy's thigh. "This short?"

"Oh, you'd like that, wouldn't you."

"I sure would. I'd sneak in there and put a lock on the green room door so I could put you on the couch after dress rehearsal."

"You've put me on that couch before."

"Yeah, with that goddamned unlockable door, all those people outside. How bad did I want to pull the couch right in front of that door so nobody could open it."

"Damn, why didn't I think of that? We totally could have done that." Andy shifted his position, lying on his side so Victor had better access.

Victor shifted too. On his side so they were face to face, so he could kiss Andy. "God, I love you."

"I love you too." Another, deeper kiss. Lingering. Andy's hand on Victor's neck, his wedding ring rasping against the chain. Feeling Victor shiver. "You and your metal fetish."

"Mmm." Victor had his mouth on Andy's neck now.

"What if I told you it's a long skirt."

"Mmm?"

"Long enough to hide the knife strapped to my thigh. Right here." He moved Victor's hand. He wasn't really going to be wearing a knife. Or at least, he hadn't planned to. "You sick bastard."

247

Victor was light-headed with arousal. "What *is* it with you. God." Andy had his hand between them now. "How are you, oh Jesus, ungh. How are you doing that routine in a long skirt." He managed the question with what felt like the last rationality he might have for a while.

"It's slit," Andy said, and caught Victor's hand again. "Up to here." Then he was on his back, laughing, Victor's mouth open over his.

Chapter 18

Andy was up in the home studio the next day, working on a set of the Shakespeare photos, when he got a text from Victor. Rolling his eyes, he picked up the phone. *Hey baby got the arrangement and shit, studio tomorrow to record, the rap is gone*

Andy wrote back *Thank God. That would not have worked in a 1940s story. Why are you texting me instead of coming back here?*

*Because I was thinking about last night and got all worked up and I know you're working*

Andy switched to voice. Victor picked right up. "When have I ever minded being interrupted? By you," he added, because other interruptions were annoying.

"Well, the thing is, I got so worked up it's kind of a done deal."

Andy laughed for about a minute. "Maybe I should show you the sketch of this dress. Get you worked up again."

"Or I could come up there and get *you* worked up."

"I'll bet you could." He knew it. He was half there already. "I could give you a hint."

"Go on."

Andy had a feeling Victor was on the move. "You know how Dmitri stole some choreography from the Girl Hunt Ballet."

"Yeah? Oh wait a minute. Oh my fucking Jesus."

Andy was giggling. He disconnected, set down his phone, and pushed away from the desk. A second later Victor was at the top of the studio stairs. "Well, if it worked for Cyd Charisse."

"Are you wearing *that* dress? Holy Mother of God."

Victor had that hot-eyed look. Andy stretched out a graceful hand, palm down, as if expecting his husband to kiss it. "And the gloves." He rotated his wrist, did a 'come here' thing with his fingers.

About fifteen minutes later, Victor lifted his head and said, "When did you get a chaise longue in here? I was just here."

Andy stretched luxuriously. "When I scheduled Juan and Charlene for Antony and Cleopatra." And because after all this time he had finally decided they needed a soft surface in the studio, he'd bought it instead of renting it. Clearly, his timing had been exceptionally good. "They delivered this morning. The quilt was Charlie's suggestion."

"Oh was it now."

"Apparently there are a couple of these in their house. She and Sacha do things on them."

"She told you that?"

"She didn't have to. The way she was blushing was a dead giveaway." Victor laughed. "It's a good size, isn't it?"

"Perfect size. Like you." Victor sat up, blew out a breath, shook his head. "Never fails. You are the *sexiest*." He regarded Andy for a moment. "What color?"

"The dress? Red, of course. I want to make sure people get the reference."

"Are you doing the cloak thing too?"

"Oh yeah." Andy sat up, stretched again, and realized he was hungry. "Isn't it time for some food?"

"Yeah, it is. Hope you were at a good stopping place."

"I was getting stuck. This was a perfect stopping place." He patted Victor's hip. "Let's go eat, and then when I come back I can finish this set."

Victor leaned over for a kiss. "I love you."

"I love you too."

The next day, Victor had one of those moments of seriously missing their transport team. He was stuck in traffic going over Coldwater Canyon, and because he was driving he had to pay attention. *This is a pain in the ass*, he thought, and then laughed at himself. People did this every day to get to their jobs. He was only going to a recording studio. He'd downloaded the backing track and synched it to his phone so he could listen (and sing along) in the car. The melody was the same, but there were enough changes to the lyric that the extra practice was good. Plus, of course, there was now a sung bridge instead of that rap thing.

The first person he saw at the recording studio was Valerie. "Hi Victor! God it's forever since I've seen you." She hugged him, then stood back and studied him. "You look amazing."

"Thanks. Being on vacation agrees with me, I guess. You look good too. How are things with you and Russell?"

"We had a two-week vacation in Vancouver in August. It was the *bomb*." He laughed. "We both love it up there in the summer. He's still good at his job, I'm staying busy. Tanith's lucky I had today free."

"Yeah, me too. I'm going to bust her chops about it."

"You should. I certainly did. Anyway, so you had a little time to work with the track?"

"All the way over Coldwater." She made an 'oh my God' face. Victor said, "So is Madame Director here?"

"She is not, yet. There are actually reasons why she's scatter-brained." Valerie filled him in about some personal stuff Tanith had going on.

Victor conceded that the reasons were valid, but as much as he liked Tanith, he didn't want to set a precedent of being too easy to get. He would rather have been at home with Andy today. "Okay. Is she going to be here to hear this? Because I'll drop everything else once, but not twice."

Valerie made an 'eek' face. "Trust me, she knows. She promised she'd be here. I'm going to call her now. Do you need to warm up?"

"No, I'll go do the comfort things and stretch a little. Wait for you inside?"

"Yeah, that's good." Valerie got her phone out. Victor went down the hall. A trip to the bathroom, a drink of water, and a few minutes chatting with the sound engineer while he stretched. Checking his phone to see if there was a text from Andy, smiling at the *did you wish you still had Stan and Jamil?*, sending back *God did I ever, fuck L.A. traffic*

*Fuck it ever so much*, Andy wrote. *Is Tanith there?*

*On her way. She had Reasons*

*Eh whatever. Be safe coming home*

*Always. Be thinking of other ways we can defile that chaise longue*

*Oh honey I already have a list*

*LOL XOX*

*XOX*. Victor put the phone away because he heard two female voices. He looked up and confirmed that Tanith was there, talking to Valerie. "Hey ladies. Let's get this show on the road."

252

He texted Andy again before leaving the Valley, and got the idea his husband would be in the home studio again when he arrived. So after parking, and saying hi to their security guard, he went straight up. Andy was working on the computer, but clearly had heard the door open and Victor's footsteps coming up the stairs. "Hi catnip," he said, pushing the chair away. "Good session?"

"Good session. What have you been up to?"

"Oh, you know. Deciding which two pictures of these gorgeous humans should get the treatment. Deciding what I wanted to do with my gorgeous husband the next time I saw him." Andy stood up, took the two steps necessary to get his arms around Victor, and kissed him. "How is it you always look better? I mean I see you in the morning and I think, okay he's perfect. Then I see you in the afternoon and I think, yep, even better. Either I have no short-term memory or you really do get more beautiful by the minute."

Victor was laughing. "I feel the same way." He kissed Andy again. "You still have champagne up here?"

"I do. Are we celebrating?"

"We're always celebrating. What did you decide to do with your husband?"

"Well," Andy said, with his mouth close to Victor's face and his voice at its lowest and silkiest, "I thought about bending him over the back of the chaise. Or letting him bend *me* over the back of the chaise. Or doing sixty-nine on the chaise. Or reclining like a pasha while he puts his mouth on me. Or getting my mouth on him and making him say really filthy things."

"Jesus Christ, Andy." Every one of those suggestions sounded good to Victor.

"But first, let's pop a cork." Andy kissed him again, hard, then let him go.

Twenty minutes later, Victor was on his back on the chaise, naked and close to begging. Andy's mouth was everywhere except where Victor was desperate for it. "No you don't," Andy said. "Hands off." Victor whimpered. Andy took another mouthful of champagne and went back to Victor's chest, letting the bubbles pop against a nipple, feeling his husband buck underneath him. Andy licked up the spillage and smiled, even though he was so turned on himself that the movement of Victor's hips was nearly enough to send him over.

"You vicious bastard." It was faint, breathless, half a laugh.

"You want that on your cock?"

"Oh *Jesus*." The thought alone had Victor squirming.

"Are you going to come when I do that?"

"Fucking *hell*."

Andy picked up his glass, sipped more champagne, set down the glass again and moved up to Victor's mouth. Kissed him with closed lips, then opened his mouth to share the champagne. Victor's body was tense beneath his, those hips moving again. Andy took a breath and said, "No. Sorry, catnip. Making you wait. Don't you move." He pushed up onto his knees, pinning Victor's arms and legs with his own hands and feet. "Mother of God, if the world could see you like this, every fucking body would come."

Victor was too out of his mind to laugh. He thought if Andy said one more word he'd lose it. "Your mouth."

He couldn't wait any more. Had to see it, feel it, taste it. One more mouthful of champagne, and then his mouth on Victor, tight. Andy pinned his thighs down and listened to the desperate profanity until he finally let him move, let the champagne run down, took that climax in his throat and made his own sound of satisfaction.

"Holy *fuck*." Victor caught his breath, looked down his body at Andy. Half on and half off the chaise, slowly releasing Victor, making eye contact. "Jesus!" That aftershock. Andy sat up a little. "You saved it for me. Get in my mouth." Victor pried himself off the chaise, pulled the quilt after him, got on his knees. He kept one hand on the seat as Andy moved closer, one knee on the chaise and the other foot on the floor. Rings flashing as he swept his hands through Victor's hair. "Fuck my mouth, Andy, give it to me." It didn't take long.

A few minutes later they were both sitting on the floor, on the quilt, side by side. Refilled glasses in hand, backs against the seat of the chaise, leaning on each other a little. "You are a pushover for novelty," Andy said after a while. Victor snorted. "New piece of furniture, and it's our honeymoon all over again."

"Our porn tour." Victor turned his head, frowning a little. "Did you tape that?"

"What do you think?"

Victor looked around. Sure enough, the camera was on the desk, and the red recording light was on. "You know, I'll bet most people make one or two sex tapes and then they're like, okay, did that, moving on." Andy laughed. Victor got to his feet, walked over to the camera, and turned it off. "We are a couple of perverts." Andy had almost stopped laughing, but that set him off again. "We actually *watch* these things." Andy waved at him like 'stop.' Victor did not stop. "We *rate* these things."

"Hey, some days we feel like Buenos Aires, and some days we feel like Amsterdam." Andy giggled again, wiped his eyes, and hauled himself to his feet. "Look at it this way, the likelihood that either of us will ever need Viagra is really low."

Victor laughed, then winced. "Ow."

"What? Oh." Andy touched the bruise on Victor's lip. "Sorry about that."

"Well, I told you to. Odds were in favor of you going hard."

"I was hard all right. Thanks for not biting me." A light kiss. "Do we have to do anything for the rest of the day?"

"I don't think so."

"Let's go watch a movie with Molly." But before that, Andy had to take a minute, or three, for a long silent hug. *This man*, he thought, *my love.*

Andy hadn't exactly forgotten about their friends Red and Mary, and the whole Macbeth situation in London. But they'd been sufficiently busy that he hadn't followed up with anybody. It was Monday, and they didn't have a thing they needed to do before getting ready to go out to see Vicky (and everybody else) perform at Chrome. It was warm, so they were out on the loungers. Molly was in her usual spot behind them. Victor was reading; Andy had been reading, but was now looking at email. "Our friend the pornographer says that the revised Macbeth is smashing all records for that company."

"They probably don't usually have an American action hero playing Macduff."

"Playing anything," Andy agreed. "Not to mention the most-commented-upon swordfight in the history of the internet."

"Is it really?"

"Apparently so. The Niall and Red version, which must chap that guy's ass." Victor laughed. He felt sorry for the actor playing Macbeth. Andy didn't, much. "Come on, he's lucky he has the part. Niall could have said, you know what Janis, I'll catch up with you and Geoffrey after it closes, have to tread the boards now."

"He didn't want to be an actor."

"I know. He doesn't want that life."

"He's got his hands full with Janis."

"And his mouth full with Geoffrey, no doubt."

Victor snickered. "So what have you told Reggie lately?"

"Not a lot. I sent him one of those pictures of Dmitri and Patrick and he swooned so much I thought I'd better not send him any more."

"Who's still outstanding?"

"Well, since I got Antony and Cleopatra this week, I think I'm through until Red and Mary come home. Nobody else has come knocking saying can we do this or that, and I'm out of ideas, and you haven't thrown me anything for a while."

"We got so many more than I expected. It was fun."

"Yeah, it was. Anyway, I've been pretty much choosing the gallery images along the way. Now it's time to do the processing. And now that I know how many it is, I can start thinking about when and where to hang the show."

"That gallery where you had 'A Tempest' is too small, huh." Andy made a sound of assent. Victor looked around for his drink, realized the glass was almost empty, and went to get a refill. "More water for you?" He refilled Andy's glass too, set down the pitcher, and had a thought. "Were you working on a show when we met?"

"When I did Tanith's pictures? Yeah, I was."

"Did you not do a book for it? I only remember seeing one from spring twenty twelve."

Andy's usual thing was to print up a single book with all the images from a given shoot, highlighting the ones he'd printed for hanging. Only occasionally did he design and print a book for the public. "The spring show had a book. The fall show, after I hung it, I thought it was too depressing. So I didn't do my usual thing, much less one for sale."

"What was the subject?" Victor sat down, elbows on his knees, studying his husband. Andy didn't usually do depressing things.

Andy gazed back at him. "Empty theaters. I'd taken it down a week or so before we met again."

"Oh." *Say no more*, Victor thought. No wonder Andy hadn't kept working on it. At the time, that must have felt like opening a vein. He wanted to apologize. Something in his husband's expression told him he shouldn't. He tried something else instead. "Ever think of revisiting that?"

"Well, I never did before." Andy thought about it. "In view of subsequent events, I might feel differently about those images now. There's a lot of promise in an empty theater."

He might have hesitated to suggest another project for his husband, but he knew this one wouldn't take much time. Andy had a template for those archive books. Plus, he wouldn't be surprised if some of that material would be a good tie-in for their Broadway concert. "I'd like to see them."

"Then I'll throw together a book." Andy smiled, leaned across the gap between the loungers, and kissed Victor. "I love you so much."

"I love you too. You're literally the most interesting man in the world. Even when you don't have the beard."

"I don't always print a book," said Andy, striking a pose, "but when I do, it's a dirty book." Victor laughed. "Is it time to shower?"

Chapter 19

October 2019

They took a livery car to Hollywood, since experience had taught them that driving themselves would be a pain in the ass. The last time they'd done it, it had taken them more than twenty irritating (and anxiety-inducing) minutes to get from the club to their car. This way, they could be picked up within feet of the entrance, with a driver and the Chrome doorman to deflect paparazzi or other celebrity hounds. "You know what's nice," Andy said on the way. "I've been hanging around this place so long that Tyrone and Terry don't give a shit about me. They're like, oh it's you again? I suppose you want a loveseat up front. I mean," he added, glancing over at Victor, "most people only give a shit about me because I'm married to you. Mr. Movie Star."

"Yeah, whatever." Victor waved that off. Maybe once the new 'Countdown' premiered, with his name above the title, he'd start feeling like he actually was a movie star. "Is Jim here tonight?"

"He said so. Maybe we can catch up at the after-party. Loretta hasn't had much to say lately."

"I know. I told her Tanith didn't hate our script and she sent back a thumbs-up, and that's basically all I've heard."

"Hope that ex of hers isn't causing trouble."

"Me too." Victor wasn't sure whether that guy was actually dangerous, or simply a loudmouthed asshole. "And I hope Jim is keeping in touch."

"Me too." There were enough people coming to the Cabaret shows in hired cars these days that nobody really noticed them going in. Andy exchanged greetings with the longtime doorman Julio as they passed. On the inside, he took a moment for a fresh look. "I remember what this place looked like when it was still called Level. Did you ever see that?"

"No, what was different?"

"Well, for one thing, Tyrone didn't have that space." Andy pointed across the catwalk. "No ground-floor lounge. You came through the door and there was a wall. Went straight downstairs. The upstairs bar, this part where we can see down into the performance space, that all came after he got the ground floor." They headed downstairs. "They had a removable dance pole on the stage, instead of out here separate. Jeez, hardly anybody even uses it anymore."

"Dana's kind of retired, huh."

"She was just learning pole when we were roomies. Michelle was doing it, this other chick in the original company did it. Then that chick got a job in Miami, and then Michelle started doing ballroom."

"It looks kind of wicked here anyway."

"I'll bet bachelorette parties still get some use out of it." Victor laughed. Andy was grinning. "And bachelor parties, probably. That was that same year," he realized. "The year we met."

"Was it really?"

"They had this huge grand re-opening show. That was such a good poster, if I do say so myself. 'Blue,' you remember that one?"

Victor definitely did. "You had that one up on your wall on our first night."

"Yes I did. You liked it. Figures, since Michelle had that fishnet catsuit on. I didn't know about your fetish then."

"I didn't even know I *had* a fetish till I saw you doing that 'Chicago' thing. Damn, I wish I'd seen that on stage."

*I wish you had too*. They took their seats. Andy checked out the table talker with the mini poster and the show order. "Sam and Mateo are opening. Stacey's closing Act One. The cabaret group is closing the show. Fuck, I don't want to wait that long to hear you sing."

"You've been hearing me sing," Victor said, amused. "I'd've thought you'd be sick of that song by now." He lowered his voice, even though the noise level in the club was high enough to cover ordinary speech. "What's our position for 'Spy Games?'"

"We're opening." Andy shot him a look. "I told Rory about the whole costume thing and she said, well, I guess we'll need to start you over at the bar, won't we. And I said, well shit, maybe so."

"When was this?" Victor was half-laughing. "Because we'll need to work out how we get you up on the stage."

"This was, like, yesterday. Okay, so." Andy looked around; a server was there. They ordered some drinks, and the themed menu items, and then got back down to business. "They have the new spotlight, you know, that swivels out into the house. So they'll bring up the light for you on stage, start the music, and then hit me with the spot. We already had the first eight bars for the introductory bullshit."

"If you're vamping your ass off by the bar, I'd better keep still on stage. Don't want to pull focus."

"Sweetness." Andy gave him a quick kiss. "You can smolder up there. Anyway, I get the cloak off, get to the stage, maybe a couple of the guys give me a hand up so I don't break an ankle."

"Oh, as if." Victor thought *no time like the present* and said, "I had a thought about footwear."

"Oh yeah?" Andy turned to give his husband his full attention. They'd danced 'Mein Herr' with complete success despite the height difference. But this dance was different; there was a lot of work in closed hold.

"When we're practicing, it feels fine. I don't mind that you're six foot four with those high heels on. And I sure love the way it looks. But when I looked at the video and there's me five ten, I thought, there are some people who might laugh at that."

Andy waited. There was one super easy way out, which was to jettison the drag component and dance it as two men. Their normal two-inch height difference was negligible on stage. They could mask it entirely if he wore flat shoes and Victor wore Cuban heels. He'd do that if Victor was feeling like the fun factor wouldn't make up for the potential laughter. All the same, he didn't want to suggest it. "What's your thought, sweetheart."

"I really want you to do it in that dress. What if I got some boots? Like platform boots?"

*Yes*, Andy thought. He knew his face was saying the same thing. "I personally would fucking love that. You would need to get them, like, immediately. Practice night and day. They're going to feel really heavy. You won't be able to feel the floor the same way."

"But there's not a ton of complex footwork for me. Nowhere near what we had last time. Where would I go? To find that shit?"

"I know a place. We can go tomorrow. Get you straight to work. Then if you absolutely hate them after a week, we can revisit. Because I can lose the dress."

"No," Victor said. "If I can't get the hang of the boots, I'll just have to look really mean."

"You can do that." Andy kissed him. "Wow, honey, maybe someday I'll get *you* into some fishnets." He got his phone out and sent a quick text to Rory: *We had a thought for our number next time, we're going to work out the getting on stage part. And I think don't announce us, okay?* He knew she was stage-managing 'Spy Games.'

The reply was immediate. She was undoubtedly backstage right now, getting ready to perform. *You want to surprise people?*

*With any luck it'll take them a minute to even realize it's us*

*OK I'll do the usual sit your asses down and prepare to enjoy thing, then we'll take the house lights down so you can get in position. I'll ask Terry to let you change in the office and make sure they keep a seat open at the bar*

*Thanks chica*

*You realize second night is going to be a fucking madhouse*

*Eh well the price of fame*

*LOL enjoy the show TTYL.* Andy showed the exchange to Victor, then put the phone away. "I'm looking forward to seeing what the fuck she does with 'Paint it Black.' She wouldn't tell me if it was jazz or striptease." The lights dimmed, giving people a chance to organize last-minute drinks and their seats, and then the show started. They thoroughly enjoyed the first act, joining the standing ovation for Stacey in her comeback number on the aerial silk. There were a few friends in the house to chat with during intermission. Then the lights went down again for Act II. Rory was opening the act.

"Wait one goddamned minute," said Victor, very softly, when the vocal came in. He turned his head; Andy was staring back at him with a very 'what the fuck' expression. It was definitely Andy's voice. He shook his head a little, like 'I have no idea,' and they both turned back to the stage. It was a jazz routine, and it was tricky. Nasty, growly, something they hadn't seen from Rory before. They both loved it. So did everybody else, apparently; there was another standing ovation.

As soon as they sat down Andy had his phone out again, texting: *WTFF! Cool as hell but how?*

Her reply took a few minutes. Andy watched the next number and waited for the phone to buzz in his hand. *How is more like ow I am getting too old for that shit. Tanith had video of you at Springbok karaoke that time. Danny peeled you out of there somehow and remixed it for me*

*You are all sneaky fuckers. Also don't say old you're the same age as V*

*Yes I know and you don't see him doing that shit do you*

Andy snorted. *He wasn't a gymnast missy. Great job TTYL*. He handed the phone to his husband, who also snorted at the exchange before handing the phone back. There were two more numbers, and then the finale. The cabaret team entered while the stage was black; each woman was hit with a mini spot as the song's intro began. Then Victor's voice came in with the new lyrics for 'Speak No Evil,' still a boogie-woogie hymn of non-repentance. There was a perfectly-synchronized first verse, using cabaret chairs. On the second verse, the dancers blended cha-cha and jazz. They were making the most of their costumes, fringed bodysuits over fishnets and lace-up mesh dance boots. On the bridge they went into a stepping section that got the audience worked up. The last verse was a return to tricky, trampy cabaret jazz. Most of the people in the club had probably never heard the song before, but judging from the standing ovation, they liked it. "That," said Andy after the curtain call, as the applause died down and he turned to Victor, "was objectively cool as fuck. I almost forgive Tanith for the last-minute recording session."

Victor grinned. "It's so much better now," he said. "If we ever do a little jazz set here again, I'm totally doing that." Somebody overheard that and asked them about the song. Victor explained that it hadn't been released yet. There was some discussion with a growing number of other audience members; people had recognized them now. Before it got too intense, Terry was there with another Chrome employee, quietly suggesting that these two celebrities should be given some space. Before long, the shoveling-out procedure was underway for the after-party. Victor got his phone out to text Tanith: *Hey chica I don't know if you're here tonight it's kind of a mob scene but new Speak No Evil went over big. People want to download. If Val can get you produced and released you can probably make a buck to spend on that movie*

*I'm upstairs and they only want it because you sang it. I'll talk to Val. Btw rewriting In The Night too and I'll want a version from each of you because leitmotif for every one of your scenes. Shared calendar will be a thing within next ten days TYVM can't stay for afterparty but talk soon.* Victor put his phone away because the performers were out in the house, and the party was starting. They knew everybody who'd been on stage, and most of those people's friends. Even after the music started, a whole gang was hanging around the bar and talking instead of dancing. Victor only realized how late it was getting when he looked down the bar and saw Vicky with Sharon, imminently leaving. It was a work night for both of them. He waved as they headed out, then looked around again, trying to spot Jim. Andy was talking to him on the other side of the room. Victor made his way over there. "Hey Jim. What's new?"

"Not much," Jim said, "except I'm worried about Loretta. I was telling Andy."

"We haven't heard much from her." Victor and Andy exchanged a glance. "Is it that Ernesto douchebag?"

"Yeah, I think so. I got a message today from a new number. She changed it. She shut down her social media too. There was some of that if I can't have you nobody will bullshit."

"Fuck!"

"Yeah." Jim looked upset. "I asked her if she wanted me to come out. Haven't heard back yet. I don't know if that would make things better or worse."

Another silent consultation between Victor and Andy. Victor said, "You being there might escalate the situation. On the other hand, it might not. And if you being there made her feel safer," he stopped. Shrugged.

"I don't know how much use I could be," Jim said. "I'm not a big tough guy. I don't know how to fight. But at least I could be *there*."

"Sometimes that's enough," Andy said. "My mom has a one-bedroom condo with a big-ass couch. She knows Loretta. I know she'd be happy to have you stay while you figure things out. If that doesn't include you staying with Loretta."

"I think I'm going to go. Tomorrow," Jim said. "I have a job starting on the fifteenth that I can't really afford to blow off, but maybe by then this will be resolved."

"Okay. I'll text you Mom's number and her address, I'll get in touch with her, and we'll tell Loretta you're on your way. And you call us if there's any fucking thing you need, right? Weapons, attack dogs, assassins."

Jim huffed out a laugh. "Let's hope it doesn't come to that. Thanks, Andy. Thanks, Victor. I'll text you when I touch down." They all shook hands. Jim went to speak to a few more people. They saw him head out shortly after.

That conversation took a lot of the fun out of the evening. It was a little too close to home, in more ways than one. They made the rounds, congratulating performers again and resolutely dropping no hints about 'Spy Games.' Everyone there seemed to know they would be dancing in it. Everyone promised not to spill the beans. "Somebody's totally going to spill," Andy said on their way out. "We might actually want to hire security for the trip next time."

"Or maybe that's the Loretta situation talking." Victor thought about it, though, on the ride home. Once they were safe inside, with Molly walked and the doors locked, he said, "No. Let's tell the car company to send a team. If nothing happens, which it probably won't, it's only a few extra bucks. And if something happens there'll be another pair of eyes and hands to help us deal with it."

Andy brushed a hand through his husband's hair. Kissed him, and said, "Thank you."

The next day they were back in Hollywood at Molest Shoes, and Victor was cracking up. "Oh my *fuck*," he said. "How does anybody walk in this shit? Dude, help."

"Call me Rowena. Get your weight back over your heels, sweetness," said the sales diva. "Hips forward, shoulder blades in your back pocket. Oh honey yes."

"Mercy me," Andy said, somewhat faintly. "I could die happy if I saw you in the lace-up thigh-highs. You have no idea what those are doing for your ass."

"He really doesn't," Rowena agreed.

"Shut up!" Victor couldn't keep a straight face. He walked around a little, paying attention to his alignment, trying to ignore the yummy noises. After a few minutes he started to get the hang of it.

"Get him those ankle boots, please? The ones with the buckles." Andy was truly enjoying this.

So was Rowena, who knew exactly who they were. "Is this for a purpose other than fun?"

"Yes it is." They were alone in the store, so Andy told him. "A dance thing. I'm in drag and he's not, but we want to minimize the height difference because it's not a comedy routine."

"Not that it would be funny," Rowena said gently, with a face that said 'except it totally would be.' Andy managed not to crack up. "The ankle boots. Coming right up." He gave those words a special emphasis, and shot Andy a speaking look. "Do not even go near those," he warned, seeing Victor heading toward something that appeared more stable and also more Frankenstein. "You are not permitted to wear those. Oh no honey. Walk away. Yes, walk *that* way."

Andy giggled along with Rowena, watching Victor move. He was actually handling the seven-inch heels really well, considering. "Come over here, baby." *Uh-huh*, he thought, when he saw Victor's eyes widen at the fact that he was now looking down at Andy. "How do you like that?"

"Uh." Victor was not sure if he should be honest here. Then he realized Andy was shaking with silent laughter, and said, "Yes, okay, I like it. I like being taller than you. The shoes themselves are a nightmare. I can already feel the cramp I'm going to have. Is there any possible way I can dance in these fucking things."

"Give it a try." So they did a little bit of tango around the store, and it went better than Victor expected. Andy had to help him out once or twice, when a direction change got hung up due to the heel-management situation. Andy had his hand around the back of Victor's neck. He played fair and didn't let his wedding ring rasp against the chain. "You are so sexy," he said softly. "You always are. You're such a good sport. You're so much fun. How much do you hate those shoes."

"I hate them a lot less when you're telling me how great I am." Victor turned his head a few degrees for a kiss. "What do you think."

"I think we get this style, because walking in these will be good practice. But with the chrome platforms, because those are bomb. And we also try on those boots with the buckles. Those aren't as high."

"I won't be as tall."

"Your calf muscles might thank you."

Victor couldn't argue with that, so he went over to a chair and carefully lowered himself into it. "Jesus, my knees. How do women do this?"

"With a lot of bitching," said Rowena. He had the boots ready. When Victor got them on and stood up, he was surprised. The sales diva wasn't. "Not as bad, are they?"

"Not nearly. Is that why you gave me the high ones first?"

"Yes, honey. Take a spin around the dance floor."

Victor took that literally, going back to Andy and trying some more tango. "Okay," he said after a while. "I would not call them comfortable but I think they might be manageable. How do they actually look?"

"Wicked," said Andy and Rowena together. Then Andy let him go, turned to the sales diva, and said, "I really really want to try on the lace-up thigh-highs. I have no excuse on earth except you have them." *And I want to see Victor's face when I walk out in those.*

"Do you have panties on?" Rowena said doubtfully.

Victor was laughing his ass off as he headed for the chair. Andy managed, with a heroic effort, not to laugh too. Of course his jeans had to come off to try those on. "Yes."

"Okay then. What size."

"The right size," Victor said, performing another careful sitting-down maneuver. He left the boots on to educate his feet while his husband did whatever craziness he was doing. He and the other guy had disappeared. A few minutes of low-voiced conversation later, there was a cackle of laughter from the dressing room. Victor got his phone out and put it on photo mode. He heard the heels clicking on the tile floor and looked up. "Holy shit."

Andy was holding his phone too. He took a picture of Victor's expression, then struck a pose. All he had on was the boots, briefs, and a long-sleeved thermal knit shirt, barely long enough to cover his ass. "What do you think?"

"Buy six pairs." Victor took a picture. Andy did a slow turn. "Holy Mother of God." Rowena cackled again. Victor took another picture. "Seriously. Get them in every color." Once they were on their way home again (with both styles of boots for Victor, but only one pair of thigh-highs), he said, "I had no idea I had this kink."

"It's a very harmless kink," Andy said reasonably.

"Did you ever really do the drag thing?"

"That's what's hilarious! I never did! I learned how to dance in heels for 'Chicago.' If you hadn't gotten so out of control over that, I might not have ever thought of doing Mein Herr the way we did."

"And if we hadn't done that, we wouldn't be doing this. You are following my kink." Victor started to giggle again. "Oh shit. Who knew. And now I've fucked myself because I'm gonna have to dance in heels too."

"Give it the week," Andy said, smiling. "It is not a requirement, no matter what faces that little diva made. You're still going to be sexy as fuck and the man in charge if you're five foot ten."

"The man in charge, huh." Victor was regretting that he had an appointment to get to. He might have put Andy in those thigh-highs for a minute.

Andy was also regretting that appointment. He used some of his alone time to tease Reggie. He hadn't done that for a while. This time, he forwarded a selfie he took in the dressing room: *Hi Reggie. Rowena was selling me these awesome boots. If you come to LA maybe I can introduce you*

It was late evening in London, but a reply came back immediately: *Are you in fact trying to kill me*

*Boots or Rowena?*

*Either or both*

*He likes dark-skinned men with English accents.* Andy wasn't making that up. The little diva had pinups of Chiwetel Ejiofor (in the 'Kinky Boots' movie) and Matt Henry (in the 'Kinky Boots' stage musical) in the back.

*Perhaps I should hand-deliver that painting*

*Perhaps you should. How close to done?*

*Very close. It's been a pleasure. How goes Shakespeare?*

*Waiting only for Red & Mary to get their asses back to LA. Scouting a gallery here for January*

*Does that mean I could preview?*

Andy knew he had Reggie now. *Yes it does. V & I are going to Miami 18th December, here till then*

*Will make arrangements and advise. Do take care of those smashing legs*

*We will.* Andy signed off, switched numbers, and sent a text to Red requesting an ETA. He was so very tempted to spill the beans to Dana and Rory about Victor's shoes, but he didn't want to jump the gun on that. They'd find out soon enough, if it worked out.

He almost spilled it a couple of days later when he was on the phone with Dana. Her series was about to wrap for the mid-season break; she and Rory were discussing how to use the time. Andy told her about the many rounds of inspections on the new old house, and about some meetings they'd had with their contractor (their neighbor/tenant Paige) and the engineers. He made a joke about never running out of things to do, and figured she would give him a little of the same old shit about failing at vacation.

On the other end, Dana wondered which of the men was actually driving all this activity, and if they'd thought about why. "Andy, doing every single fucking thing it occurs to you to do will not actually make you live longer. It will not give you more time.

The only thing that will give you more time is doing *less*."

Andy started to say something reflexively bitchy and then stopped. "Give me a second."

Dana was amazed. "Are you actually thinking about that?"

"I would be if you would shut up. I love you," he added, knowing she already knew that. Because she did, Dana didn't say anything. It was close to half a minute before he said, "Is that what we've been trying to do? Pack so much in thinking we're buying time?"

The 'we' was unexpected. That meant it was both of them, and it was a relief because it meant she was right about the why. "Haven't you talked about this with your therapist?"

"Not exactly." Edged close to it, maybe.

"I understand, you know. You waited a long time for him, and then you almost lost him. He never had anyone before you, and then he almost died. You must both have moments when you think, we have to do this now because we may not have tomorrow."

Andy was silent for another half a minute. He could have said, you know how we are together. Could have said, we're taking all this time off. And it really was both of them; Victor never stopped either. "I hear you."

"Remind me what you have between now and the end of the year."

"Only 'Spy Games,' and going to Miami. Oh, and the painter guy from England is coming out for a few days in between, we're going to have a little party while he's here. I'll send you the info."

"Okay. A two-night performance, a house guest, and a trip to see your mom. Do me a favor and don't add anything to that, would you? I happen to know, because I'm in it, that Tanith is contracting her new movie. I also know that you guys are in it, which means you're going to be even more insanely busy starting in January."

"Ugh, I know. You're right. It's," he stalled for a second. "It's because everything he does is so great, and he never says no, and I wasted so much fucking time." He'd never said that out loud, he'd even denied it, but on some level he felt every day before Victor had been wasted. He said it in a rush, speaking only for himself, even though he knew, he *knew*, Victor felt the same way. He didn't dare say anything else.

Dana heard his voice go wrong. After a second she said, "Andy, you haven't wasted a minute in your whole life. If you dropped dead right now you would have accomplished more than most people would in a hundred years. Everything you've done with Victor is great, yes. But just being together, it's *important*. My therapist told me that. You know I never really had anyone before Rory. I didn't have any bad habits, but I had to learn how to be with somebody. And sometimes it's the only thing that saves a shitty day. Getting home from the set and there she is with the pack, and something smelling great in the kitchen, and a smile. We sit in that reading chair. If we were praying people, that would be what we give thanks for. It's not for the shows we've done or anything like that. It's that we're together. Don't be afraid to give yourselves those moments."

Andy let what she was saying sink in, promising himself he'd take it out later and think about it. For the moment he checked his breathing, decided he could speak without betraying himself, and said, "I promise I won't start any more fires before the end of the year."

"All right then. I'm going to ask if Rory wants to go back to Guam to see her granny. Give Victor a kiss for us."

"Give the cherubim one for us. Bye chica." Andy disconnected. Then he tipped his head back and blinked hard, pinched the bridge of his nose, and thought, *she is right*. He wasn't sure why these words at this time had knocked him sideways. Dr. LaSalle would probably say 'because it's something you already knew.'

It was something he'd have to catch over and over again. His heart believed they were forever. If his brain didn't quite, for a very good reason called 'a bullet,' he could at least act like it did. Everyone told him he was a good actor. Maybe if he was convincing enough, Victor would begin to believe in their forever too.

He started that night, after dinner. Victor said, "Are you going to read? Because if so I might work on the laptop for a while."

Andy wasn't sure if reading counted as doing something, but he was fairly certain him reading while Victor worked did not count as 'being together,' not in the way Dana meant. So he said, "No, why don't you put in a movie and let's cuddle." That never felt like wasted time.

Victor looked surprised, and also pleased. "Okay." Ten minutes later they were stretched out together, watching 'Galaxy Quest' for the umpteenth time. Molly was on the couch with them, and it was heaven.

Chapter 20

November 2019

Victor spent the rest of the week in one or the other pair of heels. There was nonstop bitching. They rehearsed their 'Spy Games' number with his regular shoes, in his Latin shoes, in the lower heels, and in the sky-high heels. Andy advised on posture, kept his opinions about heel management mostly to himself, and freely shared his opinion of how the heels affected Victor's walk. They were both in the main house on Saturday morning, sitting at the dining table catching up with messages after breakfast, when a new email came in. Victor frowned at it. "This is unexpected."

"What is it?"

Victor glanced up. "Message from Tanith. She says, there is something wrong with this screenplay. Your action thing was good. Can I turn this over to you for a week, I think I'm hitting the beats but in between there is dead space."

"She wants you to script-doctor it? Wow, that *is* unexpected. But kind of gratifying." Andy picked up his coffee mug, registered with displeasure that it was empty, and stood up. "Want some more caffeine?"

"No, thanks, honey. Too much makes me jittery and then I fall over."

"No you don't." Andy brushed a hand through his husband's hair as he went to the kitchen.

"She attached the document. I wonder if she knows I can barely type." He was gratified though. Before, Tanith had said 'it doesn't suck.' Now she said 'it was good.' So either she really wanted his help, or she'd downplayed her assessment before, or both.

"The girls next door could give you a lesson. They both do like a hundred words per minute." Andy was fairly speedy himself, but he wasn't about to touch this project. He'd be helpful when it came time to compose the shots. Till then, he was keeping it zipped. "Vicky might have thoughts on that too. Isn't she one of the stars?"

"Well, I guess we're about to find out. Let me ask Tanith if it's okay to show her." He sent a reply text, then leaned back in his chair, stretching his legs out in front of him. "Every time I see my feet I'm like, what the fuck."

Andy smiled. "Are you starting to not notice them?"

"Actually, yeah. Except when I go to the john and then I'm like, how far down is that damned thing." Andy giggled as Victor's phone pinged. "She says might as well, this is all her fault anyway. Damn, we're a little cranky over in the Valley this morning." He stood up, noted that he hardly even had to think about how, and went out the front door.

The entry door of the B side was closed, so he knocked. He heard Vicky saying something, probably to Sharon, then as she approached heard "How many times have we told you La Provence will deliver that cake?" The last word sounded like a genuine question, because she had the door open and was staring up at him. "The fuck?"

"Mom said it! Mom said it!"

Victor bit his lip, trying not to laugh as he heard Sharon (also apparently trying not to laugh) start to explain (again) to Simka why grown-ups sometimes used bad words. He said from on high, "Hi Vicky. Do you have a few minutes to talk about a screenplay?"

She recovered. "I think we need to talk about why you're six and a half feet tall all of a sudden."

She looked him over with interest and growing glee. "Sharon, do I have an hour or so to talk about a screenplay?"

"At least. I'm going to take Miss Smarty Pants for a walk over to Grandma's."

"Okay. Give Miriam my regards. Careful crossing the street. Love you honey."

"Always. Love you too."

Vicky stepped out, closing the door behind her. "Let's talk about this screenplay. Is it Tanith's thing? Wow, your ass is phenomenal."

"Isn't it?" said Andy through the open door from the A side. "Want some coffee?"

"Yes please."


Andy didn't ask about the screenplay until Sunday night. By then, Victor and Vicky had put in about twelve hours on it. Sharon had come over to drag her wife home for dinner, and Victor was lying on the couch bitching. Not about his feet, for a change, but about his back.

"Well, you've been hunched over the laptop for the better part of two days," Andy pointed out. "Tonight you need to seriously stretch, and tomorrow we need to seriously rehearse."

"You're right, I know. Do you want to hear about this thing at all?"

"Do I have to be hateful to you?"

"Nope, and I'm not hateful to you either."

"Okay, good. Are we singing or dancing on screen?"

"Singing offscreen, dancing on screen. Not with each other, because forties straight club setting, but eye-fucking each other while we dance with other people." Victor couldn't help smiling about that. He couldn't wait to play it.

Andy couldn't either. They'd done some good eye-fucking on the TV show. "Okay, great. Then is it the straight-razor thing?"

"It sure is."

"Yikes, okay. What else would I want to know?"

"I guess that's it." Victor was still smiling, looking up at Andy, very much appreciating that his first concern was how they would be, together, in their scenes. "Did you hear back from Red?"

"They're flying in today. I'll shoot those at the end of the week. We'll re-purpose some of the other costume for Mary, and of course Red's got his own shit for Macduff."

"Which line is it for him? Oh yeah, 'my wife kill'd too.' He got great reviews."

"Yes he did. He said getting that message from Niall was such a kick in the head. He'd never done any of the plays before, not as an actor. Only on the crew. I'm sure his agent is having a continuous screaming orgasm."

Victor laughed. "Is Raquel still trying to get you to take something between now and July?"

"Yes she is. Presumably Parker's the same. Why they won't take no for an answer, I'll never understand."

"Well, they get paid when we do." Victor wriggled a little, then sat up. "I think I'm hungry."

"Good, I've been waiting for that." Andy gave him a hand up off the couch, then couldn't resist stepping in for a kiss. "Gee this is fun." If he hadn't been truly hungry, he would have done something more.

"It is fun." Victor bent for another kiss, one hand on the side of Andy's neck, still amazed. They fit together differently, but they still fit together. "Your mouth is every bit as nice from this angle."

"Mmm. Better stop that if you're hungry."

"How hungry are you?" Victor couldn't seem to stop kissing his husband. He had his hand on Andy's back, fingers running up and down the indent of his spine. He walked backward slowly, bringing Andy with him, around the end of the couch. Sitting on the back of it, with his feet on the floor and Andy between his legs. Pressing him close for another open-mouthed kiss. "Jesus, Andy."

"Maybe we'd better do this first." Andy unbuttoned, then unzipped two pairs of jeans. "God almighty, how you feel." They didn't stop kissing until they were both spent and gasping. After a minute Andy kissed Victor's cheek and said, "Did you even think about walking backward just then?"

"No I did not." Victor glanced down at the seven-inch heels. "Tomorrow's rehearsal should be interesting." He patted Andy's ass. "And now I'm even hungrier."

"Me too." One more kiss, and then they headed for the kitchen.

The next morning they finally both heard from Loretta, in a long email ranting about her ex and raving about Jim. A few updates had come in from Jim, most of them of the minimally informative 'not sure I know what's happening' variety. After that email Andy and Victor both thought Jim probably was sure now. "I'm going to have to check in with Mom," Andy said. "I know he was there for a few days. If he got out the door without telling her everything, she is not the woman I grew up with."

"Want to call her now? Then we can go practice." Victor turned the kitchen over to Consuelo and got out of her way. "Let's go upstairs." He led the way without even thinking about his shoes.

Consuelo gave Andy a 'Still? Really?' kind of look that had him stifling laughter all the way upstairs. It was the buckled boots today, which were probably the ones Victor would wear for their performance. Andy could not help but think that he was actually starting to like them.

Andy was, as usual indoors, barefoot. So when he took the last step and fetched up beside Victor, he had to look up a little to make eye contact. "You are really digging this, aren't you," he said.

"Consuelo thinks I'm insane."

"I think you're the hotness." Andy ran his knuckles up Victor's torso, from his navel to the hollow of his throat, and brushed his ring against the chain. "Why don't you think about that while I talk to Mom." He swept his thumb across Victor's mouth, then dodged away. "Oh no. If I don't catch her now she's going to be out beating the pants off her neighbors at bridge." He heard Victor mutter something about 'pants off' and thought, *soon*, heading straight to the sunroom. "Hi Molly, you feeling all right? You didn't join us for breakfast. My good girl. My best girl. That was a long walk yesterday, huh. Lazy old lady. Yes pretty girl, go back to sleep." The creak of rattan, a minute's silence, and then "Hi Mom." Victor was on the floor, stretching. He took his shirt and the shoes off, thinking about this apparently insatiable desire. He'd had the idea that with all this time together, they'd eventually cool off. Neither of them were. He tuned in again. "Glad to hear it. Yeah, we got an email from Loretta this morning and it sounds as though things have resolved. Apparently getting a visit from the FBI calmed that dickhead down. He was like, it was only on the internet, I was just messing around, I didn't mean it. He posted this long-ass apology.

Loretta linked to it. Yeah, we read it. Sounded pretty sincere. Said things about how someone messed with his own sister online and he should have remembered how it made her feel. Said he was getting counseling. Promised to respect Loretta's request and stay away. So overall quite positive. No, our friend Jim has not told us anything useful. No." Andy laughed. "We're kind of assuming he went from your couch to her bed. We know he was in it at least once before she went home. He has to be back here by the fourteenth. I know. You said what?" Another laugh; this one went on for quite a while and ended with giggles. "Oh lord. You are a good woman. No, he didn't mention that. We'll give him hell about it when we see him. Yeah, weekend before Thanksgiving for our show. It's tango again. Because we like tango. Because my hot honey can get me right off my feet. Mom! You have a dirty mind. We'll do bachata when he's your age. Oh, thanks Mom. Yes, I'll be the crypt-keeper by then. Counting down till we see you. Stay out of trouble. I love you too." A few more residual giggles reached Victor from the sunroom. "Did you get all that?"

"What did she say before you told her she's a good woman?"

"She said she told Jim to propose. Said, ask her to marry you. You know you want to. A woman likes to know."

"What did he say?"

"Turned five shades of red and fled the scene."

Victor laughed. "You're not going to be the crypt-keeper when you're eighty-eight."

"Oh, you don't think so? Imagine I never put on weight. Imagine I lose my hair off the top, and start doing a comb-over." Andy was leaning on the bathroom door frame now, watching Victor stretch. "Mom's father did that. It was not pretty."

"You can afford a good toupée." Andy laughed again. Victor finished what he was doing and went over there. "Hey baby. Still like me when I'm short?"

"You're not short. You're perfect. You're always perfect." Andy stood still, waiting for the kiss, enjoying the hell out of it. "Mmm. Did you think we'd start getting tired of this at some point?"

"I kind of did. I'm not, though. Not even close. Every time I see you, I want you. Want to kiss you, want to touch you. Want to put my mouth on you. Touch you all over. I always want to touch you." He was touching Andy as he spoke, getting his hands under the tee shirt, pushing it up. "This body, my God. Your mouth. The way you taste." Andy was backing him toward the bed. The tee shirt was off. Andy's hands were under the warm-ups. He started pushing them down as soon as Victor stopped moving. His mouth followed.

After a while, lying in each other's arms, Andy said, "And then there's this. I never had this. Never in my life wanted to cuddle."

"Me either. I was all, wham bam thank you ma'am." They both laughed. "Of course, the way I was, that makes sense. But I'm surprised about you. You're affectionate. You cuddle the girls all the time."

"Girls are different."

"Well, yeah." Victor's voice was dry.

"I mean there's no expectation with girls. They know my limitations. A guy wouldn't have known. If I cuddled with someone who was more involved than I was, that would be cruel. If I cuddled someone who didn't care, that would be masochistic."

284

"Well, I care. And I like it. If we could be skin to skin all the time, I'd be a happy man. Even happier," Victor amended, because he *was* happy. "Not even Alonzo?"

Andy lifted his head a moment, so he could make eye contact and check in. Victor's expression was untroubled. Andy put his head back down. "No, not even Al. Well, you know, we never lived together. Never had this kind of time. We both worked insane hours. After a date, we'd go straight to sleep, and then somebody would be gone before the other person woke up. That was the way it was. I might have missed it, once or twice. Might have thought, gee it would be nice to lie here in bed with him. But not enough to change my life for it."

"You changed a lot for me."

"I would have changed everything for you. You changed a hell of a lot for me."

"Yeah, I did. I'm glad I did." Victor was quiet for a moment. "Did you remember to invite Rowena to see us at Chrome?"

"Oh yes I did. He'll dig it the most."

The photo shoot for Red and Mary was in the evening, because Andy needed their neighbors' son Theo to play the Macduff child, and could only get him after school was out. He was mostly bored by the process and was happy to go back home when they finished. "That is the only minor involved in any of these photos," Andy remarked, after returning to the home studio from walking the boy next door. "Please congratulate me for completely avoiding profanity while he was here. Can you stay for dinner? We'd love to hear all about London. You were there for so long!"

"Well, Niall and Geoffrey found us a flat in their own neighborhood. By the time they flew off with Janis we knew everyone in it. Yes, we'd love to stay, wouldn't we darling?" Red seemed to agree. Andy had downloaded the camera while he was out with Theo. Now he started the backup, turned off his monitors, and they all headed for the main house. There was the usual chitchat while dinner got staged. Then Mary returned to the topic of London. "I spent so much time with my parents, it reminded me why I stayed away so long. Oh, you laugh. They can't be in the same bloody room. It was Mum one week and Dad the next, and each time all they mostly wanted to talk about was the other, and how vile they were. I'd have throttled both of them if Red hadn't been there."

Red was snickering. "She told me what they were like, and I didn't believe it."

"Because your parents actually like each other!" She shook her head impatiently. "Pair of knobs. So you're enjoying being gentlemen of leisure?"

"Well," Victor said with a glance at Andy, "that isn't entirely accurate. There's been this Shakespeare project, and two dances with the Cabaret. We're starting work next month on arrangements and choreography for a concert. I wrote a screenplay, with Jonathan and Loretta. And we bought the house next door."

Mary and Red were both staring at their hosts as if they'd shape-shifted. "You've done what?"

"We want a pool," Victor said, and started telling them how it happened.

Andy was still inclined to laugh about it later, when they were sitting in the sunroom, looking out at the nighttime city, with mugs of decaf in hand and their dog at their feet. "Those were two epic what-the-fuck faces."

"Red jumped through some hoops to get their house. You know he's been in there for going on twenty years."

"How long did it take him to get the place?"

"More than two years. The person they rented from liked having that income. Red had to get his finance person to do this thing pointing out the benefits of having the cash in hand. How they could invest it and generate almost the same income. Not a sophisticated seller."

"Kind of like our people next door." They'd heard that the former owners had finally decided to go with a condo after all. They were going to be out of their rental in less than a year. "If they'd thought it through a little better, we might have been able to get in there with only one year's rent tacked on."

"It's no big deal," Victor said, smiling. "It was better to get things worked out fast. Look how long it's taking to get the underground stuff done."

"Oh, 'how long.' It's been a month." The backyard next door was kind of a disaster area at the moment. The engineers had said 'do that stuff first.' Paige was reporting in regularly. "I can't believe the permits got issued so fast. And Paige lined up the work so fast. I thought the place would still be sitting there untouched, with its pants down like a wrinkly old exhibitionist." Victor snickered. Andy nudged him. "You're going to be popping some champagne when they pop that roof."

"You better believe it. When they said that was a go, I was like hallelujah. Even though it did mean losing the fireplace." Victor stretched, rolled his neck, winced. "I need to get another massage."

"I think you need to start having someone come here twice a week, till we get done with this routine.

You're doing great with those heels, but it puts different stresses on you."

Victor knew it was true. He'd tweaked his back a little the other day, and even though he hadn't mentioned it he knew Andy could tell. "Maybe you could set me up with that heating pad tonight."

"I can and I will." Andy leaned across the gap between the chairs. Victor met him halfway for a kiss. "There you go, wincing again. All my fault."

"No it isn't. And even if it were, I wouldn't care. I love you."

"I love you too. Go get washed up. I'll take Molly out, and then I'll give you some therapy."

November 2019

The first night of 'Spy Games' went off without a hitch. Andy and Victor were more than a minute into their performance before the audience clicked to who they were. They stayed in the green room for the remainder of the first act, watching the other dancers on the monitor, chatting quietly with those who remained in (or returned to) the green room. They didn't join the rest of the performers for the first-act curtain call. Instead, they listened to the reports from those people as they returned to change, and decided to hide out for the rest of the show. "Tomorrow night may be a little bit insane," Andy said after a few minutes, when they were alone. Victor snorted. "We may need to get here at, like, six o'clock. And fuck me, I'm *hungry*."

Rory heard that as she came in. "We're stretching intermission because everybody but everybody is Tweeting and Instagramming and Facebooking you fuckers. If you step out the stage door, you're going to be mobbed. Terry's sending a server back with some food for you, and some drinks.

Text your team and let them know you're still in one piece. They're probably seeing people go out for a smoke and catching some of the chatter."

"Thanks Rory." Victor was damned glad they had the security detail with their car tonight. "We can't actually text anybody because our phones are in the office with all our other shit. Could someone bring all that in here too?"

"Oh, you're ready to get out of those shoes? You both look phenomenal, by the way," she said. "I only didn't say so at dress rehearsal because I was trying to un-swallow my tongue." Both men laughed. "I mean, don't get me started on the costume, but this Inigo Montoya thing you're rocking, Victor, holy hell." Victor was cracking up. His hair hadn't been cut since they left the 'Countdown 3' set, and his mustache was a month old. "Yes, I'll take care of it. Tomás and Sam are watching the stage door, nobody'll get back here to mess with you." She went back out.

Victor decided to go ahead and take the shoes off. Andy was already out of his. Now he unsnapped the bottom of his dress, sighed with relief, and peeled off the fishnets. "Ow, holy shit," he said. "I think those things are permanently imprinted on my butt. You want to check for me?" The dance belt came off next. He scratched vigorously while Victor laughed. "How's your back, catnip."

"It's fine. All that therapy really set me up." He tugged his shirt out of his pants, unbuttoned it, wriggled around a little. "You went easy on me this week."

"Didn't want to break you. I can break you Tuesday."

"It's a date." The door opened again; it was the manager himself, with their gear, and followed by a pair of servers with food and beverages. "God, Terry, you're a lifesaver. Thanks so much. It's going to be nuts here tomorrow."

"Truer words. I already called some people for extra security. Y'all got some, right?"

"Yeah, we added an escort to our driver situation. Do you think we should get here early? We were thinking maybe so."

"Don't know if that would actually help. We'll make sure you get in and out safe." He gave them half a smile, his gold tooth flashing in his dark face, and went back out. The servers finished setting up their dinner, and followed him. Andy and Victor both got out of costume in the next two minutes, and into more comfortable clothes. They hung Andy's dress and cloak next to Victor's dance suit on the wardrobe rack, stashed their shoes and the gloves on the shelf above, and double-checked that a fresh shirt (for Victor) and fresh fishnets and dance belt (for Andy) were in their garment bag waiting for tomorrow. Then Andy slung his makeup case up on the shelf and they sat down to eat.

A few minutes later the P.A. clicked on, and they heard Rory's voice. "Good evening everyone. Thanks for joining us here at Chrome for the Underground Cabaret Dance Theater, presenting Mating Dance: Spy Games. Listen up. If you think you saw Victor Garcia and Andy Martin performing the Assassins' Tango in Act I, you were correct. If you are excited about it, so are we. Be advised that you'll get tossed out of here a lot earlier than they will, so please don't hang around trying to see them. Now settle down and get ready to enjoy Act II, with more great dancing from the Underground Cabaret. Five minutes to Act II. Thank you." The P.A. clicked off. The Act II performers started coming into the green room. There was a frenzy of costume and last-minute makeup. Andy and Victor tried to make themselves small. Nobody acted like they were in the way.

Then it was on with the show. They watched the performances again on the monitor, glad to be comfortable and fed and among friends. They'd all seen each other at dress rehearsal, where they'd had a chance to really talk. There had been considerable comment on Victor's footwear as well as on Andy's entire costume. "These folks did a great job not spoilering the whole thing," Victor said softly, as the closing performance was on stage. "Wow, did you see that lift? How did I miss that at dress? Holy fuck."

"That Anya." Andy was watching with enjoyment and respect. "She is fearless with Ricky. God I love that song. I love all these songs."

"Want to dance them all with me again?" Victor was smiling. Andy was humming along with k.d. lang on 'Surrender,' and only gave him a sidelong smile and a nod. After the performance was over, Anya and Ricky took their bows. Rory called the rest of the Act II performers up on stage for the curtain call. There was another flurry of activity in the green room as people changed clothes and collected gear. Finally everyone was gone except Victor, Andy, and Dmitri.

"Hey there," Andy said. "I would have said hi earlier but you were in the zone."

Dmitri nodded. "Is good. You will record the dance tomorrow?"

Andy nodded. "We told Jim how the intro's set up. Not sure where he's placing the camera. But whatever." He shrugged. They'd danced it through at home on video several times, though not in full costume. Somebody tonight had surely taken the routine on a phone as soon as they saw what was going on. In fact, now that he thought about it, Dana or Patrick might have. He knew they were both here, and both of them knew what was happening.

"You looked," Dmitri said, then paused. He touched Andy's shoulder lightly. "Most beautiful I have seen you dance. Victor, excellent. You are very brave. I would not." He seemed to shudder at the very idea.

Victor was charmed. "Thanks, Dmitri. That means a lot, coming from you. Is Patrick here tonight?"

Dmitri nodded. "I go now. You have security?"

Victor and Andy exchanged a glance; everybody seemed to be asking that. They wondered what it was like outside the club. "Yes. We won't head out without bodyguards," Andy said. "Say hi to the king for us." Dmitri almost smiled. He nodded again and went away.

They didn't want to hang around too long. The club was open for another hour or more, and whatever was happening outside would probably still be happening then. Might even be worse. After a little dithering, Andy opened a FaceTime call with Rory. She answered right away. "Hi cherubim. Are you guys still at Chrome?"

"Yes we are. I see you're still hiding in the green room."

"We're not sure what to do. We can ping our security guy to come and help make a path. Is that going to be enough?"

"Should be, especially if Terry helps. Outside looks like the fucking Oscars. There are news vans, paparazzi, and what looks like two busloads of tourist celebrity hounds. It's a mess. What do you want to do?"

"What do you think, catnip. Go on out and deal with it? If we've got Terry and Julio and our guy? We can feed the beast for five minutes, our car could be right there."

"That's fine. Rory, did you get that?"

"Got it. I'll ping the man in charge. Get your shit together." She disconnected. They texted their driver, assembled themselves, and went out to the stage door. It opened a minute later and Terry did a 'let's go' thing with his head. Sam and Tomás were there again, and with those three imposing men as well as their escort, they got upstairs without delay.

Outside, Julio and their driver were keeping a space clear in front of the door. There was a surge of reporters. Andy and Victor answered a few questions, declining to confirm or deny that they had performed at all, much less what they had done, or whether they would be back the following night. Somebody finally asked Victor about 'Countdown 3' and he said, "I'm told we should be seeing the rough cut in early January. I'm looking forward to it. Jonathan and Loretta and I had a great time making it."

"When will it be released?"

"As far as I know, the plan is for a May release. You'd want to confirm that with the studio."

"What are you doing till then?"

"Being married," he said with a smile. "Andy and I have never had a whole lot of time to just be married. So that's what we're doing. And thanks everybody for coming out, but we need to get home now." Their small phalanx of guards was still with them, so their path to the car was unimpeded. Once the doors were closed they looked at each other and both said, "Whew." Then Victor said, "I was not expecting that."

"You're a movie star, I keep telling you." Andy grinned at the snort from the front seat. "Also we did something tonight that's going to be considered scandalous in some quarters, so." He shrugged. "Hope it doesn't fuck you up with the 'Countdown' people."

"It's not like they don't know we're married. That we dance together. That you occasionally dance in drag."

Andy was snickering. "That's true. 'Mein Herr' went up a long time ago and they didn't call Raquel to say hey, you know what, we decided not to do that whole boat captain thing. Tell Mr. Martin to take his fishnets and fuck off." Definitely a laugh from the front seat. "Hey guys? Are we going to have you again tomorrow? Because you were great tonight. We really appreciate it."

"We can request the duty tomorrow, sir. Happy to."

"Awesome, thank you."

Chapter 21

After they got home, it was a quick trip outside with Molly, a fast shower, and then a long and much-needed sleep for both of them. They did next to nothing on Monday aside from eat, stretch, and walk through the routine. They answered texts, looked at emails, did not go looking for bootleg video of their performance, and got themselves ready to do it again.

This time there was a crowd at Chrome when they arrived. Julio and his squad met them at the car and walked them in. "It's sold out," Julio said. "Standing room only. We could stream it on the back wall and sell tickets if that wouldn't totally fuck Hollywood Boulevard."

Victor said, "It's fucked enough already. Jesus, it's loud in here!" And it was packed. It took what felt like forever to get to the green room. Now that the secret was out, they figured it would simpler all around to base themselves there. There were certainly plenty of people to watch out for Andy when he went to take his position at the bar. Victor stood out of the way, watching him apply his makeup. "If you had told me ten years ago that I would find it unspeakably hot to watch the love of my life put on false eyelashes, I would have said you were loco."

"I feel the same way," said Vicky, in the next seat at the counter. "And when she takes them off it's like, yeah baby, get naked." Andy laughed. "Oops, sorry. No sex talk while applying eyeliner. You're really good at that."

"Chorus boys have to do their own. It's been a long time, but I guess you never really forget." Andy checked the makeup, did a little work on his hair – slightly long, and carefully cut so he could replicate

Cyd Charisse's style – then stood up and went to his garment bag. "Okay everybody, avert your eyes unless you want to know everything about me." He dropped his pants. Victor was leaning on the wall, watching the whole process as he had the night before. Watching his handsome husband turn into a beautiful almost-woman. It was mesmerizing. "Better get your shoes on, catnip."

A minute later they heard Rory. "Five minute warning. Five minutes to Act I." They were both fully in costume. Checking each other, taking that opportunity for a last fond touch before they went out. "Two minutes. Beginners for Act I, please."

"That's our cue, sweetheart." Victor draped the cloak over Andy's shoulders. They went out into the wing. Terry and their own escort were there to take Andy over to the bar. "Thanks guys." Victor waited on stage behind the curtain. Listened to Rory make the announcement. The working light went off, and the curtain opened.

Same as the night before, the spotlight hit Andy, sitting on a bar stool with his legs crossed and his elbows resting on the bar top behind him. He opened up the cloak, revealing that sensational dress. Then, same as the night before, he straightened one long, long leg, pointing his foot at the ceiling before setting it down on the floor to begin slithering through the crowd. Victor hadn't registered who gave him a hand up to the low stage the previous night. Now he saw it was Terry and Sam. *Thanks guys*, he thought.

As soon as Andy was onstage, they began to prowl, circling like predators. Confronting each other, drawing embellishments on the floor with their feet. Quick, quick and slow. A tap, a flick, a spin. When he had Andy in hold, he said "I love you" almost soundlessly. Andy didn't break character, didn't quite smile, but spoke the same words. Then the fight was on.

They held their closing position for a few seconds. It was fairly dramatic. Victor was down on one knee with Andy's upper back across the other thigh. Andy's ankles were neatly crossed and his skirt had fallen away to show the knife strapped to his downstage thigh. His gloved hand wasn't on the knife, though, as it had been more than once during the routine. It was on Victor's neck, pulling him down for a kiss. After a moment they tuned in to the applause. Andy said, "God, I really want to plop my ass on this stage and sit here till you pull me up."

Victor said, "I feel like one shift of weight and I'm going to fall on *my* ass." They both giggled. "We need help."

"Oh screw it." Andy dropped his downstage hand to the floor and more-or-less sat down, folding his legs as elegantly as possible while extracting his upstage arm from around Victor's waist. "How's that." They were both still giggling.

Victor set a hand on Andy's shoulder and got to his feet, teetering only slightly. "Fuck, how did we do this last night?"

"I can't remember. Give me a hand." Andy was up on his feet and they were taking their bows. They were both cracking up when they got offstage.

"What the fuck was that?" Rory was looking at them like they were insane. "That wasn't how you ended it last night."

They both said, "It wasn't?"

"No! You did the split thing last night!"

"Oh damn! We did! No wonder we couldn't get out of it!" Andy was leaning on the panel, wheezing.

"Oh shit." Victor was laughing too hard to get more of a word out for a few seconds. "That was my fault. I took you down before you got your foot back. Jesus, we got lucky."

"They want you for another bow. Go take your bow. You complete lunatics." They went out, they bowed (still giggling), they returned to the wing. Rory brought the stage lights down so Sam and Mateo could get in position for their number.

As they headed to the green room, Victor was saying, "Were we late? Because I was like, there's the peak in the music coming, have to hit it, go down now."

"I'm going to have to see the video. Jesus Christ. That was a damn good catch, honey. I didn't even realize we did it wrong."

"Well, the way you had your legs, it looked so finished it didn't even occur to me they were supposed to be some other way. Your back okay?"

"My back is fine, how about yours."

"I'm good. Holy mother of shit." They both cracked up again. Everyone in the green room was looking at them the same way Rory had.

Paula Borodin held up her phone. "Somebody already posted your ending. That dude who won Dancing with the Stars a million times tweeted, I've done that drop with a dozen partners but never in spike-heeled platform boots, hashtag challenge accepted." Victor laughed all over again and told her to get out on stage.

They spent the rest of the show the same way as the night before, but this time there was the after-party. The downstairs lounge was a much more controlled environment. They were hanging out at the bar with Rowena when Julio sent down a message to say that a reporter they knew had asked if she could have a word. "I'm going to go up and talk to Sherry,"

Andy said. "She'll be disappointed that I'm out of costume."

"Explain to her about the dance belt, the fishnets and the crotch snap."

"Pop Quiz viewers should know how we suffer for our art." That was a semi-ironic reference to their dance fight on Tanith's movie. This routine had produced some bruises too, but only on the outside. "Be back in a few minutes, sweetheart."

"Hey."

Andy turned back. "What?"

"Kiss me."

Andy smiled. "Okay." They took their time over it. "God, I love you. Tell me you don't have any appointments tomorrow."

"My only appointment is with you. All day. I love you." One more quick kiss and then Andy was heading upstairs.

Sherry Martinez was actually inside. She had her little handheld camera on. "Mr. Martin, thanks for agreeing to speak with me."

It was a jolt, hearing that name. That name belonged to his father. Andy smiled professionally and said, "Sherry, this again? Call me Andy. Did you see the show?"

"Yes I did, I had my ticket a month ago. And I'm glad I did because I sure wouldn't have been able to get one if I'd waited till the last minute. That was a spectacular performance. How long have you and Mr. Garcia been working on it?"

"We started the choreography with Dmitri Vasko last April."

"Wow!"

"Well, Victor was going on location in May, I was joining him in June, and we weren't expecting to be back in town until August. We wanted to do this number as well as the one we did in September."

"I saw that too, but I didn't get a chance to speak with you. That music has been used here before, hasn't it?"

"Yes, about three and a half years ago for this brutal apache number. Ricky Castillo and Anya Ivanova. They performed tonight too."

"Those of us who are Underground Cabaret fans really love how so many performers stay with the company. I know I personally get very invested."

"Well, you may be interested to know that Vince Connor and Michelle Matsumoto are going up for the World Smooth Championship at the Ohio Star Ball next weekend. Some Cabaret fans may remember Vince made his performance debut here eight years ago."

"Oh my God, yes. Dance fans, I'll give you the title of that number in a second. Andy, when we spoke earlier this year you told me you wanted to make this a good dance year. Since then you've done your wonderful pas de deux with Zach Tyler, and now these two fantastic routines with Victor. What's next?"

"We're working on something," he said with a smile. "You'll be the first to know."

"Thanks so much, Andy. I'll let you go now. Tell Victor he's my hero for doing that in those shoes."

"Mine too! If anyone wants some of those, go to Molest Shoes, right down the road here in Hollywood. Ask for Rowena." Andy waved to the camera and went back downstairs.

Victor woke up slowly. The room was fairly bright; it had to be at least eight o'clock. Andy was speaking in a low voice, very close. Victor turned his head. Andy had Molly in his arms. "Who's a cuddly girl. Yes you're my very best Molly. Is it time to take you to the beach again? Let you get all filthy like a real dog?" He glanced over at Victor and smiled. "Hi catnip. I've already taken her out and made coffee."

"Your ability to not sleep constantly amazes me." Victor stretched. "Is it a day for the beach? If we go to the beach, we have a great excuse to not be online."

"That's very true." Andy accepted a kiss from his husband, then watched him go into the bathroom. "He has a cute little ass, doesn't he Molly."

"I heard that. Whoa, I didn't realize it was so late." When Victor returned with a cup of coffee, he picked up his phone from the nightstand. "Missed a call from John."

"Give him a call. We have the whole day to ourselves."

Victor leaned over for another kiss first. Drank some elixir of life, and then dialed. The receiving phone rang three times before John picked up. "Hey John, I saw that you called. Everything okay? Glad to hear it. Yeah, you know what, we're pretty much done for the year. Prep work now for that concert next spring, but otherwise all that's really firm is going over to Miami to see Eva. Leaving on the eighteenth." He listened for a minute. "This last thing? Well, I should probably warn you. It was a little bit out there." A snort. "Andy danced it in full drag. Yeah, a dress. Oh, he looked amazing. Well, you know I think he always does." A sidelong glance at his husband. "Uh-huh. High heels. Yeah that was a concern." He snickered. "Well, our solution was that I wore high heels too. Like, really high heels. Oh my God it was torture." He laughed out loud. "I got used to it. Oh *damn* it was fun being tall. At dress rehearsal everybody was like -" He made a confused Scooby Doo noise, then listened for another minute while Andy laughed into Molly's fur. "Next week? You mean Thanksgiving?" Victor made a what-the-fuck face at Andy. "With your kids? Okay, your other kids. Hang on." He muted the call, staring at Andy, who had instantly grasped what was going on. "T-day dinner. In Escondido, with the whole family. He wouldn't ask us if he thought it would be weird for us."

Andy knew that was true. He also knew this was big for Victor. "I'm game. Can we bring Molly?"

Victor un-muted the phone. "Hey John, I'm back. Could we bring our dog Molly? Yeah, you met her last time. Great. That's really nice. Thank you. Are you sure? Because we could bring something. Oh okay, pink champagne." He laughed. It sounded professional, if not quite forced. "Yeah, it goes great with turkey. Looking forward to it. We'll see you then. Bye." He disconnected, stared at the wall for a few seconds, then met Andy's gaze. "Twenty-five years later."

"What did you do those first two years?" Andy's voice was soft. Victor had come to California after getting out of the hospital. After the stabbing. When he left Mexico, his father had given him a place to live, in a finished apartment over the garage, formerly occupied by each of his half-siblings. John spent those first two Thanksgivings with his wife and their kids.

"I knew it was a thing for Americans. I didn't really feel like an American. Told myself I didn't mind. It was just another day, and there was a parade to watch, and football." Victor looked away again, rolled his shoulders, sighed. "Those guys really resented my existence at the beginning. His wife

302

knew all along, but they didn't. After I was eighteen I said look, I think it would be better all around if I wasn't right here. He asked me what I wanted to do. I asked him to stake me for a year in L.A. I'd already gotten some little things, local things. He apologized."

"For what?"

"For not telling them earlier, so they could get used to it. But you know I never blamed him."

"I know you didn't."

"He might be thinking, with Ronnie going this year, time to work it out. The other kids, well, you know. We haven't had a bad relationship, exactly, but we've never been close. Probably never will be. When he dies, though," Victor stopped, pinching the bridge of his nose.

"He wants to make sure you're cool before that happens. It's a good thought. A good thing to do. Come here, baby." Andy got a hand around Victor's arm and tugged. Victor lay down next to him and Molly, sharing that comforting hug. Molly licked his nose, then his face. They stayed there for a while without speaking.

Victor was fine by the time they left for the beach, and more than fine after an hour spent walking with Molly. He and Andy flopped down on the hotel's loungers. The breeze was cool, but they were comfortable in their wet-to-the-knees jeans and windbreakers. Andy pulled out his phone as Victor reclined and closed his eyes. "I'm going to check in with Dana. See what kind of buzz there is."

"Don't even want to know. Wake me when it's time to go inside."

"Okay, dinnertime then." Victor snickered. Andy patted his thigh and thought *this was a good idea.*

They did this a few times a year, and every time they did, it was great. They were at a hotel in Oxnard, one they'd been coming to for a long time. It wasn't in an obviously touristy spot, it was way out of the usual celebrity-hunting areas, and the hotel management pretended not to notice when people took their dogs out on the beach. It also had good security and a fondness for repeat customers. They might have hit an L.A. beach today, but after that phone call Andy had suggested Oxnard. And after that phone call, Victor had been easy to convince.

*Oh my God so many messages.* Andy had no intention of listening to voice mail. He worked his way through the texts, saving Dana's for last: *Hey big brother that shit was EPIC and you are breaking the internet again*

*Hey cutie. We aren't looking. Brought Molly to Oxnard for a little overnight escape*

*How sandy is she?*

*We're not even going to try to wash her, it's kind of chilly out here for a middle-aged lady. She's in the sun now. We'll let her get good and dry and then brush it all out*

*She'll be back in the water tomorrow anyway*

*Probably so*

*Glad you're taking a day. Wanted to ask if you had plans for T day, seems like everyone is going out of town*

Andy had gathered that, from chitchat at the dress rehearsal. *The B side are going to NY to see Vicky's family. We got an invitation to Escondido*

*Well that must have been unexpected*

*Very much so, but welcome.* An understatement, for both parts. Victor had always been kind of stoic about that situation, but after getting to know Andy's parents he'd let a few things slip. *What are you two doing?*

*We'll be at Dmitri & Patrick's with Kenji & Michelle. D asked me to check in with you*

*I'll tell him thanks for the invitation. Last year was great, you should have been there*

*Eh you know. A year in San Diego for Rory's parents, a year in Savannah for mine, a year for us*

*LOL We'll check in when we're back in town. I might convince the boy toy to stay two nights*

*Might as well. Have fun OXO*

*OXO.* Andy disconnected and glanced over at Victor, confirming that he was already asleep. Molly was too. Andy decided he might as well try for some of that himself.

Chapter 22

December 2019

"Jesus, it's as big as a house."

"Well, you're the one who wanted a bloody thirty by forty." Reggie helped heave the crated painting onto the luggage cart. Then he took a minute to recover, studying the people in tee shirts and shorts inside, then staring out the window of baggage claim at the clear blue sky in the distance. "Is it always like this? Is that some kind of special effect or is this, in fact, true?"

"I'm sorry to break it to you but yes." Andy was laughing under his breath. He'd checked the weather after getting Reggie's confirmation. When he'd boarded at Heathrow, London was thirty-eight degrees and raining. "Which one of those generic black bags is yours?"

"None." Reggie turned back to the carousel. "That one." His rolling bag was hard-sided and bright yellow. He had it off the conveyor a moment later.

"Right. Is that everything?"

"That's the lot. It was lovely of you to collect me personally."

"Well, you said it was your first time here, and this airport is a trial at the best of times. Come on, I'm parked right across the street."

"Street," Reggie muttered, looking at the multiple lanes. "God help me." They arrived at Andy's car unscathed, performed some serious contortions getting the crate into the cargo area, squeezed Reggie's bag in underneath it, and eventually made their way out of the airport. "It's appallingly vast."

"London isn't exactly a small town."

"Yes, but it's my town. And my bit of it is like a village. God's effing teeth, look at this traffic. Where is your masterpiece of a husband today?"

"He's up in the Valley at a meeting with our arranger. After that he has a meeting with our friend who directed last year's movie. And after *that*, he has a meeting at the studio lot."

"That's quite an agenda," Reggie said after a moment. "Thought you said you buggers were on vacation."

Andy snickered. "Well, those appointments could have been arranged for different days, but then he would have had to go to the Valley on more than one day, and he didn't want to."

"Can't say I blame him, if the roads are all like this. Bleeding Christ, what is *that*?"

"That is the 405 freeway, also known as the tenth circle of Hell."

"Fuck me!"

Andy laughed. His father had said that exact thing two years before. "I used to be the freeway master. Then I started working on the TV show, and before long they assigned me a driver. Boy did I get spoiled. We both did."

"Well, but that was for your safety, wasn't it?"

"It was, and a damned good thing. Since we got back from the movie tour we've been driving ourselves again, mostly."

"I don't drive at all," Reggie said. "Never had the need to, and a private car in London is more trouble than it's worth."

"So I've heard." Andy drove up through Baldwin Hills and eventually into Beverly Hills, where he made the turn onto Olympic.

Reggie had been looking around with interest all the way, with sounds of disbelief as they passed the oil field. Seeing the Metro construction around Wilshire and La Cienega, he said, "Is that meant to be an underground?"

"Yeah. It's taking so long. They should have let Walt Disney's people build monorails everywhere in the sixties. Los Angeles would be almost livable. Okay, that way is Museum Row, and we're almost home." Andy drove down the street in front of their house. "The triplex we bought last year, our place, and the latest place."

"I can see why you wanted to get your mitts on it."

"If the tenant situation looks stable after a couple of years, we might sell it to those people. Same deal with the triplex. This was all about controlling the outcome, not building a property empire." He told Reggie about the extended, blended family in the triplex, and about their friends who might be moving into the new old house, as he pulled around into the alley. He parked and said, "Let me tell Adrian we have this cargo situation, he'll give us a hand." Getting the crate out of the car was marginally less difficult than getting it in. Adrian didn't let Andy help carry it to the house. He and Reggie took it inside while Andy followed with Reggie's bag. "Thanks buddy. Take a load off for a few minutes, have a drink." Consuelo was looking interested. "This is a present for Victor, and this is our new friend Reggie Galant from England. Reggie, this is Consuelo Alvarez, who takes care of us."

"Lovely to meet you, señora. Oh, thank you, coffee's perfect." There were a few minutes of chitchat, then Adrian returned to his station outside. Reggie glanced at Andy. "Permanent situation?"

"We're hoping not. But after what happened last year, it's kind of in the 'utilities' category. So let's

308

unpack this thing, I'm dying to see it." That was quite a process, involving multiple tools, some gymnastics, and a lot of cursing from both men. Finally the crate was disassembled, the layers of bubble wrap were cut away, and there was only a layer of brown paper to get through. Reggie stood back with a 'help yourself' expression. Andy took out his pocket knife and carefully slit the paper, peeling it away from the frame. "Oh my fucking God. Reggie, goddamn. This is *great*. He is going to love it. Consuelo, look."

"Ay, Mr. Andy, how you get your leg so high?"

Reggie laughed. "Wouldn't I like to know!"

Andy was gazing at the painting. "You got his face just right. That expression. What you did with the lighting. Fucking sensational."

"The framers didn't know who you were. They said, were these models or did you make this one up? Can people even do that? Christ, I've pulled my groin just looking at it."

Andy cackled. "What did you tell them?"

"I told them, well *I* can't do that, but these blokes can. And they said, blimey, they're both men? Thought that was one of them ballet dancers." Andy laughed at the mostly put-on Cockney accent. Reggie was smiling. "I said, how long have you been framing my rubbish."

"This is not rubbish. This is in the top five best ways I've ever spent money. The only way it could be better is if it were twice as big."

Reggie was gratified. "Where do you want it?"

"Upstairs."

"Stand back, then. I can manage it myself now it's out of the bloody box." Andy followed Reggie and the painting upstairs. "Hell's bells, so this is how movie stars live."

"Wait till you see the bathroom. And the closet. Our neighbor designed those, she's basically a genius."

Reggie set the painting by the wall and gave himself a tour. "A turret in your closet? An effing turret. Christ save us." He crossed the room, ignoring Andy and his giggles, and went into the master bathroom. There was a prolonged silence. When he returned, he leaned against the bathroom door frame, pointed over his shoulder with his thumb, and said, "You'd never get me out of there."

Andy cracked up. "That's what our friend Patrick said. My King Lear."

"Your friend who designed it, she did the stairs, the coffee bar, all that?"

"I told you she's a genius. The sunroom was actually me. We had to have exit stairs," Andy explained. "It's code. You have to have a way to escape the building. But you don't want an exit door right there in the bathroom, right? So after Sharon showed us the princess closet and the palace bathroom I had to think, how can we not fuck that up, and having a private space to sit together seemed right."

Reggie nodded agreement. "I've never thought myself an envious chap. Clearly I simply hadn't seen anything I wanted before." He sighed. "Right then. Which wall?"

Victor knew Reggie was flying in that day. He'd apologized for having all those appointments lined up, but Andy told him not to worry about it, that he and Reggie would probably be looking over the Shakespeare shit for hours and Victor would have wanted to flee the scene anyway. Victor accepted this, because he had seen the gallery images selected

310

and processed so far (which was nearly all of them). Still, Andy had an air of sneaky glee about him. Considering Reggie's profession, Victor thought he could be excused for wondering what they were up to.

The meeting with Valerie was efficient. All she needed to do with any of the songs he and Andy had on their list was create arrangements in the correct range for their voices. Whatever instrumentation she thought was appropriate, they could contract the musicians later. Victor's lawyers were already working on clearing the music rights, for the performance and for a proposed album. Andy had given him carte blanche to clear anything else that came to mind; they probably wouldn't add anything to the concert set, but there was certainly room on a disc for a few more. Once Valerie knew what they were after, Victor headed off to his next meeting.

He'd blocked out more time for Tanith, because they hadn't spent any time one-on-one for a year, and had a lot of catching up to do. "What you and Vicky did on the screenplay was ace," she told him, once they moved on to business. "Really good. Solved all my problems."

"We were a little nervous about it," he said. "We had to start actually writing, and that's way different from tweaking a line or a bit of business here and there."

"No, it's good. Remember what we were talking about back in August? The art wants what it wants. I am more interested in getting a working story on-screen than in who wrote what. Also, frankly, I want this to be commercial. It's already got two big hurdles to jump."

Victor knew what she meant. "Forties setting and female-centric. We'll need to get the word out to all those people who are pissed about Agent Carter." Tanith laughed. "Hey, I know people. They're like, the best part of the whole Captain America story was the World War II thing, that shit's interesting."

"It is interesting. So all that new stuff with the post-war mob angle was really great, especially since it let you get some action scenes in there. All my action was either dancing in the club, or people getting quietly killed. Now, even though it is apparently set in San Francisco, it's more L.A. Confidential. It was getting too Agatha Christie."

"Eh," he said. "That's actually what Vicky said." Tanith gave him a dirty look. "She did! Sorry. Anyway, good. I figured you could still film all the great nightclub stuff, the dances and the songs, and cut them in the way you did those Tanguera scenes last year."

"You haven't done a historical piece before, have you? Aside from the play inside our thing last year."

"No I haven't. Andy's doing one next year. He's stoked." Tanith wasn't sure she knew about this; she made a 'tell me more' face, so Victor told her about the project. "It's that thing he was working on with Nick, back in August. He aced the audition, of course, so he'll be in Europe with me next summer."

"I'm glad he didn't hang up his spurs after all. He was like, never again, for quite a while there."

"Well." Victor looked away for a second, then back at her. "Our TV show was not fun for him, after the novelty wore off. And your movie, you know." He shrugged. "He learned a lot, and he always loves that. But learning he could do that was kind of a shock. Finding out he was capable of violence. And that he could bring it against me."

Tanith understood. "How is the whole aftermath thing for both of you these days?"

"We're both still seeing our counselor, but it's for maintenance now. We do a joint session once a month, and then each of us makes an appointment whenever we have something we want to dig into. A lot of times we'll talk something through with her, then go home and talk it over with each other right after. We've both had a few moments. Cranky, impatient, frustrated moments. Mean moments, sometimes. We're both learning to hear it, catch it, and deal with it right away. Having this time off together was the best possible thing we could have done."

"I always thought you were insane to go straight back into the show. You literally took no time off."

"It was easier for them to work the storyline, though. They didn't have to rush it. We got out of there with good feelings all around, instead of straight-up breaking our contracts. And best of all, they killed both our characters in a really no-doubt-about-it way. So nobody ever asks oh, are you going back to the show." Tanith snorted. Victor glanced at his watch. "Ah dammit. I've got to get over to the studio."

"What is it this time? Something about Countdown? Is that why the mustache?"

He laughed. "No, the hair situation is, well, it's me and Andy being goofballs. This is a new thing. Everybody knows I'm not taking any kind of movie project before we go to Europe, but there's always something. This time it's about a guest role that would be happening in May, for a streaming series that shoots here in town. It would only be a week of work. I asked Andy and he said sure. It's a good problem to have," he said, smiling. "Never thought I would be here."

"I never thought my little play would turn out to be such a talent farm, either. Get on out of here. When shit starts happening, I swear I'll put it on the shared calendar."

"You do that. Give my regards to Sid." Victor gave her a hug and a kiss, and headed out to the next thing. By the time he was on his way home, he'd gotten a text from Andy saying that dinner was underway and it would be only themselves and Reggie. Victor didn't even know for sure how long the guy was staying. He supposed it didn't really matter, unless they hated each other in person.

Andy and Reggie spent most of the afternoon reviewing photos for the Shakespeare shoot. Reggie didn't want to see only the gallery selections: he wanted to see everything. "These are really all friends of yours, are they?" He sat back, scrubbed a hand over his face, stifled a yawn. It had already been a long day.

"Either friends, or friends of friends. I've lived in L.A. a long time." Andy regarded Reggie for a moment, undecided about something.

"What?"

"Well, there was one more shoot. I haven't selected one for the show yet, much less done the processing. This could wait, though. You have time for a nap before dinner."

"If I close my eyes they won't be open again for nine hours. What've you got?"

Andy opened the last folder. "Margaret of Anjou." He glanced at Reggie, by this time expecting his guest to know exactly who that was.

Reggie leaned forward again, frowning a little. The person playing the role looked somewhat familiar. There was no obvious makeup. The costume was a sleeveless quilted tunic much like the ones Niall Phelps and Red Warner had worn for their Macbeth swordfight, over leggings and knee-high riding boots, with gloves. "What's the line?"

"'I am ready to put armour on.'"

"Well, so she appears to be." The expression was resolute. A long black braid was draped over her shoulder. The model was holding a blade; not a broadsword, but a swept-hilt rapier. In the pose Reggie liked best, she held it at an upward angle across her body, with the blade resting in the palm of her gloved left hand. "That's a real sword?"

"Borrowed it from Red. He loaned me a few things for this whole project. The model's five foot six, it was the biggest one that was safe to handle." Andy was watching Reggie, counting down till the penny dropped.

"Wait a bit. The boots! Is it Rowena?"

"His real name is Ronald Gallo. Rowena is his drag name."

Reggie looked delighted. "Oh go on, what's the rest of it."

"Rowena Canoe." Reggie laughed, as Andy expected. "I have a real problem with him, though."

"Why? Seems perfect for your collection."

"The problem is I want him to play all the fucking queens now." Andy shrugged. "He's a great model. We tried a bunch of different lines, you know Margaret's in four plays. He never bitched for a minute about all the costume changes. I might have to just do it someday, for a mini-show like I did for the Tempest photos. Obviously this is a straight reading of the line, it's only the fact that he's a he that makes it twisted."

"And even then it's only the way Shakespeare would have done it," Reggie said. "Well, of all things. Found yourself a queen at the boots shop."

"I wish we were all going to be in town for the Cabaret's December show. I told my friends there to hold a couple of tickets for Ro. But I know you can't stay that long."

"No." Reggie was regretting it for more than one reason. "Already promised me mum I'd be with her next week. Thanks for letting me have a look at everything."

"Still think it'll fly in London?"

Reggie gave him a look, answering indirectly. "What I like about what you've done," he said, "quite apart from the overall stupefying gorgeousness of your models, is it re-imagines the characters in a way that will send people straight back to the plays. They'll think, what else did I miss. It's brilliant."

"Thanks." Andy was pleased. That's what he and Victor thought, but they weren't English. He made a quick copy of the image Reggie had liked best, re-naming the file for future reference, then shut everything down. The dog was waiting at the top of the studio stairs. "And speaking of queens, Molly says it's time to go outside."

Victor and Reggie didn't hate each other. The Englishman had many things to say about Victor's hair situation. He complained at length about the cruelty of putting him in a guest room decorated with a photograph of a nearly-nude Andy. He told stories about his transition from starving artist to bourgeois pornographer. Dinner was so much fun that Victor didn't realize he hadn't been upstairs until they were winding up the after-dinner drinks (for everybody) and dessert (for Andy and Reggie) stage. By that time it was very late for the Englishman, and he was fading fast. "You should call it a night," Victor said. "You've had a long day."

Reggie said, "You have no idea. Well, of course you do. Your husband is exhausting."

"Hey. You're the one who wanted to look at *all* the pictures."

"It kills me to wait till next bloody summer to see them on a wall. Yes, all right. It's been a lovely evening, thank you so much for your hospitality. I shall now retire. Mr. Garcia, I believe Mr. Martin has something to show you upstairs."

Victor's eyebrows shot up. That was either unusually clumsy innuendo, or they really had been up to something. *What on earth.* He glanced at Andy; Andy looked excited; Victor remembered suddenly that Reggie was a painter. "You know, Mr. Galant, I believe he does have something to show me." After sending Reggie to the guest room and doing very minimal cleaning-up, they headed for the stairs.

Andy got there ahead of Victor, stood in front of him, and said, "This is your Christmas present. He hand-delivered. The suspense has been killing me."

"Are you going to let me go upstairs and see it?" Victor was smiling.

"Kiss me first." They didn't rush it. "Mmm. I love you."

"I love you too." Andy stood back, and let Victor go up. He followed two steps behind, so he was still on the top stair when Victor stopped moving. "Honey?"

Andy set his hands on Victor's hips as he stepped up. "Yes, sweetheart."

"How the fuck?"

"A still from the video. I sent him a few other things so he could get your beautiful face right. Do you like it?" He slid his arms around Victor's waist. Victor wrapped his own over the top.

"It's *amazing*. I love it." Victor turned his head a little, enough for Andy to kiss him again. "When?"

"I sent it that last day out in the Catskills. I was thinking about it for a while, but there was a reason I thought, I really need to do this now."

Victor thought he knew what that reason was. He looked at the painting some more, loving Andy so much he could hardly stand it. "It's such a strong shape."

"Yeah. You know what I thought when I was making up my mind?"

"What's that, baby."

"I was staring at that and I thought, you had me. We worked that shit out. It was kind of a mess for a minute, but you never let me fall."

"I never would." Victor turned around, put his hands on Andy's face, stroked his hands through his hair, and kissed him again. They held each other for a long time.

### THE END

*If you enjoyed NEVER ENOUGH, please consider leaving a positive rating or review. It really helps! Thanks for reading.*

Want more?
Andy & Victor's story begins with
**EXPOSURE**
They make that tango movie in
**THE GHOST OF CARLOS GARDEL**
And
Go on to new adventures in
**UNMASKED**

Discover this world of romance at
www.thelastories.com

\*\*\*\*\*

About the Author

Alexandra Caluen lives in a small purple house with her husband, a bottle of Laphroaig, a lot of books, and nine pairs of ballroom shoes. She works in patent law and has enough hair for three people.

*This book was inspired in part by Jon Arterton and James Mack. If you like the book, I recommend their album 'Legally Married ... and the sky didn't fall!'*

www.ingramcontent.com/pod-product-compliance
Lightning Source LLC
Chambersburg PA
CBHW030605180626
46816CB00005B/1679